Dublin Crossing

Romance and Adventure in the Viking Era

SANDY DENGLER

MOODY PRESS
CHICAGO

© 1993 by
SANDY DENGLER

ISBN: 0-8024-2293-4

1 3 5 7 9 10 8 6 4 2

Printed in the United States of America

Contents

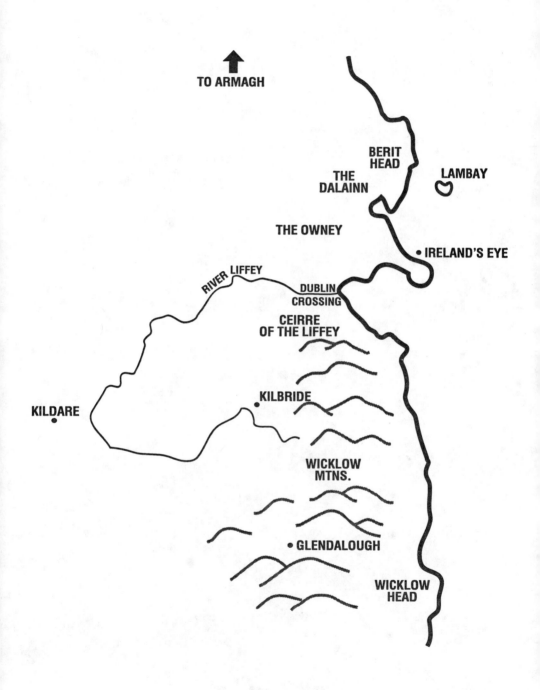

1

Dragons in Eden

Shawna of the Behr did not believe in dragons. Perhaps that is what led to her undoing.

Oh, she acknowledged that there might be dragons somewhere, but certainly none in her Ireland.

In fact, dragons possibly existed somewhere in Ireland, but most certainly not here on the island of Lambay, four miles off Ireland's coast. In all her twenty years—indeed, in all the centuries her family ruled here—no one had ever seen dragons.

A native child of remote Lambay, she was comfortably safe from dragons. She therefore greeted with some skepticism her nephew's "Dragons! Monsters!"

Skinny, ten-year-old Paul came hurtling down the slope behind the kitchen garden, his tousled blond hair damp from the mist.

"They breathe fire! Offshore!" He waved an arm wildly. "Come see, Aunt Shawna!" But he did not grab her hand and drag her away to look at his latest find, as he normally did. He ran off toward the house and barns to tell others.

This was most unusual, that Paul would not lead her to his discovery and then stand about basking in her response. She listened to his excited soprano shouts calling any who would come. She laid down her hoe and climbed the low stone wall that kept the pigs out of the garden. She stared out across the pasture, its stubble grass wet and cool beneath her bare feet.

Her black wool shift itched where her leather belt cinched it close. She should have worn cool linen on this fine day, but black hid dirt so much better. And gardening was dirty. She brushed her dark blonde hair back out of her eyes as the breeze tossed it ahead of her.

Forests once covered the island, her grandfather claimed. Now the trees were limited to a few aged oaks near the house and a wooded copse here and there. The land rolled gently, carpeted in close-cropped grass and studded with white stones, across a few low rises. It stopped abruptly at the sea.

On most of the island shores, the sea still warred with the land. No gentle slope, no beach to speak of, no caressing waves softened their clashes. At the feet of cliffs two men high, an occasional shelf of cobbles and a few black boulders took the brunt of the surf. There, in countless sorties, the sea chipped away at the island. The island could never win, not even one skirmish.

Here on the north shore, though, land and sea had achieved an armed truce. The land descended into the water gently enough that one might walk to the water's edge without plummeting, and the sea lapped endlessly at the stony beach without really changing anything, except during severe storms.

Shawna clambered up the final rise until she stood on the very brink of the northmost edge of her land. The sea was fairly quiet this morning. Apparently between battles, it gurgled and whooshed restlessly among the boulders below, but it did not crash. The truce would not last. The wind was picking up behind her, promising blustery weather before long, and higher seas.

She drew in air and tasted the peculiar, dank smell of the shore. Gulls mewed in the concealing mist. Below to her right, a little flock of dunlins prowled the stones, poking their beaks here and there. She listened to a linnet sing somewhere behind her.

Peace.

Shawna could not imagine living anywhere besides this tranquil bit of land within the ceaseless sea. Grandpapa claimed that when the angel guarding Paradise from Adam's return wearied of his task, he transported Eden to Lambay, thinking Adam would never find it. It wasn't quite what Scripture said, but it was easy to believe.

The mist was not thick enough to be called fog. It curtained but did not conceal. It turned the horizon into a soft continuum between sea and sky and tied together land and sea in a fragile bond. Where are your dragons, Paul?

And then she saw them.

In the hazy stripe 'twixt sea and sky, almost a mile offshore, two tiny vertical necks protruded. No, three. They were probably masts—some fishermen from the mainland.

The linnet ceased singing.

His voice a-babble to make up for the lost bird's song, Paul came running. His puny hand firmly gripped Brenna's.

Brenna's long dark hair looked almost as tousled as Paul's, its ringlets tumbling and tangling. (Shawna's fair hair hardly curled even in the dampest of weather.) Brenna was a bit more curvy than Shawna and, at eighteen, two years younger. Why would Shawna's little nephew consider Brenna a better witness to his dragons than Shawna?

Behind them, Paul's two brothers, Peadar and Padraic, stumbled and floundered up the slope. Peadar at seven was last as always. Padraic, twelve, would be a lot faster were he not so chubby. He would become the typical friar when he grew up, roly-poly and cheerful and given to the fun of life.

Huffing and puffing, Paul scrambled up the rise and stopped beside Shawna on this aerie at the edge of the world. "They used to be a lot closer. They breathe fire, Shawna! Really! They're really dragons! They used to be right in close here! I saw their eyes and everything!"

"They look like masts to me, Paul." Brenna's voice lilted as musically as the linnet's.

Shawna knew it was sinful to envy, so she did not envy the voluptuous, dark-haired Brenna. She did, however, feel a bit green with admiration.

"But I saw them!"

Shawna squinted in a futile attempt to enlarge the distant view. "Sure, Paul, and you've been warned about your lively imagination often enough. But if you say they be dragons, then dragons they be."

His father, Shawna's brother, insisted that Paul's imagination (lying, he called it) be brought under tight control. Shawna found it rather charming and encouraged it, when her brother wasn't around.

"This is not getting the blankets out on the line, and they'll take days to dry in this weather. If your dragons eat anyone, call me. We'll feed them Peadar and Padraic." Brenna turned to leave as her little cousins bellowed.

"Brenna?" Shawna shaded her eyes. "They appear to be moving this way. Too fast for fishing curraghs."

Brenna returned to Shawna's side to gaze out across the water. "No sails out."

"The breeze is against them. But see how swiftly they come."

"You see? I told you!" Paul bobbed up and down in place.

These dragons propelled themselves with banks of oars that dipped and rose in perfect coordination. It is one thing to get two oarsmen moving synchronously. It must really be something to keep dozens in perfect rhythm. True dragons' heads took shape upon what Shawna had first thought to be masts. One of the dragons turned aside slightly, moving apart from its companions, and Shawna glimpsed a bit of its flank. Prow and stern rose up into tall, proud, arching dragon head and tail. The belly splayed out wide above a graceful, narrow cutwater.

An uneasy feeling made her breastbone tickle. "Brenna? Remember the news Papa brought home last winter about Lindesfarne and Northumbria?"

"The raids there?"

"Might the raiders come here?"

"Of course not. Why? The priest says they were minions of Satan sent to punish erring mankind, and we aren't erring. Why would God punish us? Besides, they strike big, rich monasteries. We have only our little one."

"And two books."

Brenna wrinkled her nose. "You and Grandpapa think two books are so wonderful. I doubt many mainlanders do."

"The raiders weren't Irish. They were Northmen. Who knows but what they appreciate books?"

"Pagans?" Brenna tossed her dark locks and snorted.

Paul's dragons bore down, driving directly toward this northwest shore.

The wind tugged at Shawna's skirts and hair and flicked them forward. The few short wisps of hair around her face that always escaped her comb blew into her eyes. The breeze reversed in a little swirl and picked up harder. The wind with them now, the boats came swiftly.

She felt a chill, but it wasn't the misty air. "Brenna. Fetch the men. Warn them to bring arms."

Brenna's dark eyes studied Shawna's face a moment. She ran off down the wet, grassy slope.

What now? Perhaps Shawna was seriously misjudging these strangers. No doubt they were traders, turning aside here to Lambay seeking supplies or wool. But the ships . . . Not doves. Not even eagles. Dragons.

"Peadar. Paul. Padraic. Run home! Go!"

"Aunt Shawna, who are they?"

"Let's let the men find that out."

Already the dragons were close enough to shore that she could see beards on some of the men in the open craft. They were burly men, in conical helmets. Some wore shirts. Others went barechested.

And there were spears.

"Run!" Shawna turned and raced down the grassy slope. She had not gone a hundred feet before little Peadar cried out, terrified. "Paul! Keep going!" Shawna paused long enough to scoop Peadar up under her arm, like a sack of barley. Tubby Padraic trundled along as best he could.

Papa waddled almost as badly as Padraic, but then he was nearly as chunky. With sword and battle-ax he came running. He had not paused to grab his helmet, and Shawna prayed his haste would make no difference. Roaring up behind him, Shawna's three brothers like staghounds came racing, spoiling for the fight. Paul's father led the pack, tall and willowy, resplendent in breastmail and helmet. Did he sleep in his helmet? She ought to ask Peggy sometime. Trailing well behind, the field hands straggled up the slope. Lastly, Shawna's other cousins, Bren and Craigh of the Vale, came bumbling, much too obviously hanging back to avoid any unpleasant encounters. The only thing those two were any good at was getting the bungs out of ale kegs.

Shawna swung Peadar up onto the rock wall and scrambled over herself. Peadar leaped off and hit the ground running. From the corner of her eye she saw Padraic struggle over and tumble heavily into the onion bed.

She calculated mentally about how long it would take those sea-going vessels to find moorage near the north shore if they were up to no good. She had a few moments. Breathless now and not yet on her second wind, she ran out the east gate.

Like all farms, the rath of the Behr consisted of a dozen thatched stone buildings, some large and some quite small, ringed by a great curved wall. The wall would not stop marauders, but it did well at keeping livestock in their place.

She hastened now to the east paddock and swung her arms among the thirty cattle there, yelling. Startled, the heavy beasts lurched clumsily to their feet.

"Bo! Bo!" She ran back and forth behind the herd. Making it move at this time of day was like making a mud pie shift by poking with one toe. The stupid cows had no intention whatever of going home so soon. She pulled off her belt and flailed it like a whip. It was nowhere near a whip, but the cows heard the crack and failed to realize that.

Finally Spray took off at a trot toward the bier. Lily and Cockle followed. The others grumpily took off after their leaders. Now all Shawna had to do was keep up.

Everyone utterly winded, the cattle and Shawna arrived at the low stone bier about the same time. Shawna slipped and staggered in the manure-laced mud of the bieryard. Spray trotted right inside. Shawna threatened the stragglers a little and shoved tardy old Cloud through the door by her bony rump. She pulled the heavy oaken door shut and turned toward the house.

Did she have time to bring in the heifers from the south paddock? Perhaps she was being foolish about all this. Perhaps . . .

As surely as there are dragons, there are banshees. Now their unearthly screams echoed off the hill beyond the bier.

Roaring and howling, a dozen fair-haired, bearded giants came pouring down the rise north of the kitchen garden at a lumbering run. Where was Papa? And her brothers? These hideous beasts with swords and shields and battle-axes were running free, unchallenged.

Most of them aimed for the house, and Mum defenseless! Shawna could race to her mother's aid or she could hide. Her mind instructed her very sharply to run to the house to help Mum. Her arms hauled the oaken door open, and her legs carried her unbidden into the bier. She slammed the door behind her, closing out the light.

With all the cows milling nervously about inside, the air in the bier was very warm, very stuffy, very damp. It smelled strongly of urine and fresh manure. She stood in the darkness among her father's cattle and kept her bare feet close together, lest some careless cow tread upon them. Lowing and fidgeting, warm bodies pushed against her and shoved her this way and that. Bobbing horns poked her in the back, in the ribs. She did not dare drop to her knees to pray in this confusion of cloven feet. She prayed standing.

"Dear Father, my brothers! And my papa! And Mum. I hear those men screaming by the house. And oh, dear God, my little cousins! Deliver us! *Domine Jesu, libera nos!*"

She shifted between Latin and Erse without thinking, and between hope and despair. Oh, her papa! Her brothers!

The door shoved open, spilling light through the bier. Shawna tried to swallow her pounding heart, but it stuck in her throat. She moved quickly with little steps, her head low, keeping big brown Bell between herself and the door.

With her head tucked behind Bell's broad back, she could not see who was in the doorway, but a booming baritone voice called out to others in a strange, warbling language. He laughed. Others called, from the direction of the brewery.

Shawna heard crackling. Fire—in the roof thatch. *Domine Jesu, libera me!*

Someone—her mother?—screamed. Brenna cried out in the far distance; Shawna was sure of that voice. Brenna was shouting wildly, discordantly. Her voice grew fainter.

Shawna listened as here in the bier the alien laughed and scolded the cows. They milled more nervously. With slurping, plopping hoofbeats, a couple of cows galloped out into the bier-yard. No doubt that was Spray and Cockle, leading as always. Bell rotated in place, uncertain. And then she bolted out into the yard, leaving Shawna exposed.

But the raider had turned his back. Shawna watched him stride out through the muck into the light. He wore a tunic and tight-legged trousers and a heavy conical helmet. The brutes over by the brewery were calling to him.

She hurried to the darkest corner and curled into a tight little ball.

Surely the thatch was too mist-dampened to burn well. On the other hand it had not actually rained for several days. She listened to the crackle overhead grow into a roar, and she heard screaming and shouting—and that infernal laughter.

Domine . . . Domine . . .

Her poor father . . .

Four cows remained in the bier, moaning low, undecided whether to join their herdmates in the melee outside or huddle in darkness and safety. Smoke filled the bier now, obscuring the cows and even the doorway. A patch of the roof glowed red. Embers dropped into the damp mud. Then a whole section of the roof collapsed. Burning thatch dropped onto the cows. Frantic, they bellowed and leaped into senseless motion, slamming against the stone walls.

Shawna could smell their burning hair. Smoke made the whole bier so palpably black she could not even see the door, let alone the fire.

Desperate, Shawna worked her way along the wall toward where she knew the door to be. The bellowing, the fire, the shouting outside confused her. So much! Too much! More of the roof crashed down, but she could not see daylight for the smoke.

Choking and gasping, she literally stumbled upon the doorway, and through it. They would see her now. The fire had driven her into the open, and they would see her. A cow charged through the doorway and knocked Shawna down. It was poor, aged Cloud, her back afire.

Under cover of the thick smoke, Shawna ran for the hayrick beyond the bier, a few hundred feet to the west. They would discover her here eventually. They were swarming all over. She would find no real safety behind the rick either. The most she could hope for was respite, while she gathered her scattered thoughts and determined what to do. The smoke darkened the sky above and rained embers and burning flakes of thatch upon her.

She dived behind the rick—literally fell behind it. Six little arms immediately wrapped themselves around her, clinging tightly as an octopus. Three voices as one wailed in her ears. Peadar, Paul, and Padraic.

"What are you doing out here?"

Padraic sobbed. "They came to the house. They set fire to it. Mum grabbed up the battle-ax and told us run."

"Where is she now?" Instantly, Shawna wished she had not asked. She looked at the children's faces, and she knew.

She heard their violent sobbing.

And she knew.

* * *

Ulf Arildson. The Wolf. Proud name for a proud man from proud stock. Arild Thick Knee ruled as second to none in their Northland. And Wolf, though young yet, would rule someday as well. Unfortunately, "someday" hovered in his distant future, so veiled in clouds of doubt it might not be there at all. His brother, Reidar, the apple of Father's eye, would first have to be moved aside somehow, for he was Father's only choice for the headship. And Wolf would have to prove himself.

Not an easy task, for several reasons. One was his size. He was only of medium build, compared to the other twenty-year-olds in his village. His beard would be rich and full if he ever stopped shaving, and that was a manly trait. But he preferred shaving to trimming whiskers. And not the least of his impediments were his legs. The length of the right was three finger-widths greater than the length of the left. One does not command much respect galumphing along at a waddle.

Nor would he ever be able to prove he was better than his legs might seem, if this raid were any indication. While the lucky others leaped forth to battle, proving their mettle and having a roaring good time, Ulf had to sit here guarding the boats. While everyone else drew blood and garnered prizes, he proved he could stand up straight in a beached craft. He stood in the bow of the *Bounding Stag* and watched the fire and carnage go on without him.

"Ridiculous." He said it out loud. "Look at that, Skule! There's no male left to burn our boat. No resistance. The resistance is all lying on that hill, bled out like a herd of butchered hogs. And here we sit."

His slim, spry cousin draped himself casually across the gunwale near the bow. The boat, hauled high up on the rough cobbles, tilted a bit as Skule's weight shifted it. "Right now, blood of my blood, we are about exactly as close to the heat of battle as I care to get. We guard the boats and share the spoils and keep our swords clean. What more can you ask?"

"Action!"

"Just be glad the wind is blowing the other way, or you'd have your action. We'd be running hither and yon dousing fires aboard. Look at all the firebrands traveling on that smoke."

"Burning thatch. Remember when Gerta's hovel went up?" Wolf looked across to the other two vessels, beached to the east. Thole, in the next boat, didn't seem restless or frustrated, nor did Jargen in the far boat. Skule certainly wasn't. That just went to show they weren't leadership material.

Hegaard Broad Back and two companions from another boat—Wolf could not remember their names—came galumphing down the hill, singing. Their arms were filled with plunder. Hegaard Broad Back was the biggest, burliest, roughest fellow in Trondelag, Wolf's own father excepted, so those were brawny arms indeed. Envy leaped up and danced before Wolf's face.

One of the two men, the youngest, slipped on blood and sat down hard. He hopped back up and continued down to his boat, the far one.

Hegaard, still singing, dumped his armload at Thole's feet. "There's an iron pot there, Thole, to replace the one you lost overboard. Now we can have porridge again."

"*I* lost! You carry a memory even worse than you carry a tune, big man."

"What?" Skule taunted. "No women?"

"Be patient, tiny man." The croaking singer laughed. "If we find any truly ugly, scrawny women, we might save you one, or we might not, provided there are plenty of plump, pretty women to go around."

With a cheerful roar, Hegaard resumed his song and ran back up over the hill, hot on the trail of more pelf and plunder.

One had to admire his greed, if not his music.

2

Bounding Stag

Until this moment, Shawna of the Behr had prided herself on her ability to think clearly. No more. Her mind and heart were pudding now, her body buried beneath terrified little boys who clung and sobbed. Like the boys, she wanted to just curl up and weep, a sheep at slaughter awaiting her sure destruction. She could not. Their lives depended upon her.

She heard the familiar crackling, a growing noise. Embers from the farm buildings had ignited the hayrick. Fire above, the sea behind, and those brutes before them. Death from all directions. Her own face was wet from weeping, her nose clogged. Her thoughts cleared, by degrees, as the fire above their heads crackled louder and the drifting smoke dropped down over them. She must force the boys into action. Their lives depended upon themselves, just as much as upon her.

She gripped random gobs of boy clothes with her hands and shook her arms. "Enough for now! We must help each other. None of us will make it alone. I need you three. Will you help me?"

Padraic raised his head. "We're doomed, Aunt Shawna!"

"Hardly. Think how many stags survive the hunt because they refuse to give up. Padraic, where is your father's curragh?"

"West shore. Mum was gathering seaweed."

"We could escape by sea, but I don't know how. If we try to wait until dark, they'll find us first, and if we run now, they'll see us."

"Perhaps not." Paul had squirmed up to his knees and was peeking cautiously toward the buildings. "They raided the brewery, and I think there got stuck."

Shawna wrenched to her knees to look. The bier roof had collapsed completely. Horrendous billows of black smoke poured out of the stone shell. Partially obscured beyond the bier, the

20

brewery appeared to be the only building not afire. Dome-helmeted heathen were dragging out casks and tapping them with their battle-axes. Apparently these raiders knew something about ale. They broke into one after the other, sampling, laughing uproariously, doing whatever they chose.

Oh, my father! My brothers...

"We go now, while they're diverted!" Shawna scrambled to her feet and bodily removed Peadar from standing on her skirts. "Straight down the hill and then west to the cobble shore!"

"I've no cloak!" Padraic wailed.

"Nor will you have. We must flee." Shawna led the way, but very soon she had to scoop straggling Peadar into her arms. They ran until they were out of sight of the buildings, and still burning bits came flittering down out of the black sky.

The half mile to the west shore seemed like dozens. When they reached the concealment of the birch woodland beyond the westmost lea, Shawna could breathe a bit easier—when she could breathe at all. They slowed somewhat. Paul was spent and Padraic nearly so. Peadar snuffled, trying to be a man and having a terrible time of it.

The whole west end of the island lay awash in the most horrid stench—of broiling manure from the ruined bier, of death and fire and burning animals. The smoke pall covered nearly all of Lambay now and extended midway across the strait between the island and the mainland.

By the time they reached the cobble shore, Shawna simply could not suck in enough air to satisfy her aching, panting body. Her legs felt rubbery, her arms wooden. Sweat covered her, and she almost never sweated. She dumped Peadar unceremoniously in the grass and ran down across the cobbles to her brother's curragh. With Padraic's help she righted the little fishing shell and dragged it across the stones to water's edge.

"Aunt Shawna . . . " Paul hung back, frightened. "The wind is coming up proper now."

"We've no choice, lad. There is no safety here on the island, and nowhere to hide. Grab up the oars there. Hurry!"

She shoved the boat free of land and herded the boys into it. She clambered aboard and plopped down onto a center thwart.

21

"Padraic and Paul, you'll each take an oar. Peadar, move over to the middle—you're tipping it out of trim." She dropped her two oars into the locks and stroked deeply. The boat leaped away from Lambay, from death and horror, from those pagan murderers.

The windchop picked up immediately out in the strait, for the wind blew against the tidal current. The tiny curragh bucked. Peadar wrapped himself around Shawna's knees. Even at the tender age of seven, he knew their danger. He was of the Behr and, more so than most Erse, the Behr were of the sea.

Out here apart from land, Shawna could see more of the island, particularly the fields on the west side. Either from torches by choice or embers by chance, the barley fields had been set ablaze. Still more smoke, this latter a dense gray-brown, rose in an undulating line off the ripening barley. Fury was fast replacing fear in Shawna's heart. Utterly senseless it was, to destroy people and crops and animals! Theft, yes. Rapine if one must. But not mindless murder and destruction.

"Aunt Shawna! Over there!" Paul abandoned rowing long enough to point north.

A quarter mile to starboard, a curragh like theirs bobbed in the strait, headed for the mainland.

Padraic growled. "Bren and Craigh! Those worthless louts."

Paul resumed rowing. "That's what Papa always says. Why are they louts this time? Not for fleeing. We're running away too."

Shawna yelled above the wind and waves. "They should be moving down this way to stay out of sight of the north shore."

Padraic bobbed his head. "What if those raiders see their curragh and come to get them? They'll see us too!"

Shawna smiled briefly. Padraic would not only be a jolly friar but a clever one. True! The only way the raiders would spot this boat now was if they came to seize the other. "Let's trust that the raiders know better than to enter the strait with the wind and tide rising."

Like the Behr, the heathen were men of the sea. Sure and they could read her moods. That and that alone would save Shawna and the boys, once her cousins' boat cleared land's end.

* * *

22

Now why would the Behr be burning off their barley stubble already? The Dalainn barley was ripening, but it was nowhere near ready yet for harvest. A twinge of envy snagged Connleigh Dalainn's breastbone. The Behr, out there on their island, almost always kept themselves just a half step ahead of everyone else. Too, they kept themselves irritatingly aloof, disdaining the nurture of the privately sponsored Dalainn church or the security of the Dalainn militia and leadership.

Connleigh's father had little use for the Behr. Connleigh himself felt far less inclined to snub them. Several highly marriageable women were ripening out on that distant isle. He thought about the bounteous Brenna with her long dark curls, and the icy, self-assured Shawna. And that little Min would be quite a trick in a few years. And the girl-child with the long, flaxen hair out on the eastern periphery—he forgot her name.

Connleigh should have married two years ago. His mum often mentioned it. He was handsome, she avowed, with his blond hair and strong, craggy features. And his height! Women loved men who topped six feet. Connleigh didn't want to be attractive because of his appearance but because he loved learning.

The tentative curl of smoke Connleigh first saw far off to the east had rapidly thickened to a dark smudge. Something bigger than a barley field was burning out there. It couldn't be a raid. The Dalainn controlled all the war chiefs in the region—all except the Behr, and they would hardly attack themselves.

He swung aboard his gray mare and rode east, down across his cousin's meadows to Berit Head. He jogged her along the crest of the hill and out onto the head proper. Her hooves trip-trapped in rapid staccato across the bare rock.

Here along the shore the wind blew sharply, pushing a thick pall of smoke away from Lambay—much too much smoke for anything benign. Connleigh envied the Behr, 'twas true, but sure and he wouldn't want devastation that vast flung upon them.

* * *

Skule snapped erect. He pointed to the west. "Small boat pulling away from the island out there."

"I see it." Wolf watched it bob for a moment, calculating its speed and its distance from the mainland all shrouded in gray mist. He twisted toward his companions. "Thole! Jargen! Do you suppose an enemy will fall upon our boats?"

Thole laughed derisively.

Wolf pointed off land's end. "Someone is trying to make off with their valuables before allowing us to take our choice."

Jargen jumped over the side and came stumbling along the rocks. He leaped onto the gunwale beside Wolf—the *Bounding Stag* lurched crazily to its other flank—and looped an arm around their dragon's graceful neck. Perhaps he was not so content to stand about as Wolf had thought.

Thole climbed onto the other gunwale and twisted around to watch the tiny boat. "Think the four of us can handle it?"

Wolf eyed him. "You doubt?"

"Of course we can! The *Stag* is smallest anyway. Easy for four to ply." Jargen clapped his hands together. "We'll show the others a bit of booty of our own! Let them slay their unsuspecting rubes. We can be heroes!"

An oath burst out of the restless Thole. "Let's go!"

As one, the four heroes-to-be hopped down onto the cobbles and lifted mightily on the vessel's bow. With rasping and clunking, it slid backwards and floated clear.

Skule and Jargen were the two weakest rowers, and they seated themselves side by side aft of midships. Thole and Wolf settled afore of midships. Skule set his oar, Jargen stroked, and the vessel swung gracefully to the west. Wolf put his back to his oar and called cadence. He loved rowing. Here, it made no difference how long one leg was compared with the other. And what a magnificent crew these four made together! Look how they instantly knew the positions to take, how they quickly set the vessel into perfect motion.

As soon as the straked hull achieved glide, Wolf abandoned his oar and ran aft to take up the tiller. Waves and windchop rushed at the rocks not far off their port side, smashing noisy white foam against the shore, but the nearness of land did not concern him. The vessel draughted so shallow, and rode so lightly, she as much as skipped across the surface.

They passed land's end and swung to the south. Making way became more difficult as they fought the currents, but the wind was with them. *Bounding Stag* bounded, lifting and lunging forward against the chop.

"There's another, beyond this one," Wolf reported at the top of his lungs. "Like rats fleeing a burning barley crib. I think we can take two, don't you?" His companions laughed as they stroked.

Wolf whooped with joy. They bore down savagely upon the little punt, and he imagined what *Bounding Stag* must look like from the punt's point of view. Here came a wonderful work of art, a magnificent vessel born for the sea, looming ever taller, ever huger, bent upon cutting their insignificant boat in two.

"Thole," he called, "a hook!"

Thole shipped his oar and snatched up a grappling hook on a hundred feet of line. Buried in the sand or looped around a tree, the hook was used to keep a beached boat from sliding into the water. Now it would keep the little dinghy from floating away. Thole hurled it over the side.

Wolf threw a loop over the tiller to secure it and yanked out his ax. Sword in hand, Thole jumped off the gunwale and disappeared. *Stag* wobbled wildly for a moment. Time for action!

Not quite. By the time Wolf reached the other end of the vessel, Thole, down in the punt, had already put both its occupants to the sword. One callow young man, an expression of terror melting by degrees from his lifeless face, sprawled on his back across the bow thwart, arms and legs splayed wide. The widening pool of blood beneath him steamed in the dank air.

The other young man lay curled in the stern in a little ball, arms still tucked protectively around his head.

Thole sneered. "No challenge here. If we're going to be heroes, we'd better embellish our description of their resistance a little, you think?"

Laughing, Skule hopped down into the punt as Thole steadied it by gripping *Bounding Stag*'s gunwale. Together they tossed the booty, what little there was, up into *Stag*. The only truly costly items were a few gold collars very nicely wrought.

Gleefully, Thole held up an iron pot and described what Hegaard could do with his. They retrieved some excellent iron cook-

25

ware and a jewel box, cunningly worked in wood with silver inlay.

"What's this?" Skule picked up a thick block composed of thin sheets of some sort, tightly encased in leather-covered boards. It opened not like a box with a lid, but like a hinged door. Another like it lay on the bottom of the punt, soaking up blood.

"Any gold or jewels therein?" Thole looked at it skeptically.

Skule brushed through the sheets, whatever they were, and shook his head. He tossed it over the side and didn't bother at all with the other one lying at his feet.

"Now let's see what yon boatling has to offer." Wolf returned to his oar as Skule and then Thole scrambled aboard, the hook over his shoulder.

It didn't take them long to catch the second punt. One might say it offered no challenge at all, since the only adult in it was a nubile girl. She and three little boys were dragging valiantly at their oars. Their dogged determination touched Wolf, impressed him, gave him pause.

But business is business. Jargen had taken the tiller this time, a wiser arrangement, since Wolf was the stronger rower by far and the mounting wind was beginning to vex them.

Thole threw the hook over the side and had to toss it twice more. The girl kept heaving it back out of her little vessel. Angrily, Thole jumped down into the punt, holding his hook, and personally looped it under her bow thwart.

"The nerve of this wench!" he shouted.

"Put her to the sword, if she displeases you!" Wolf called.

"Not yet!" Skule shrieked. "Stop and think!"

"If we're going to be heroes," Jargen growled, "we'd better bring all four of these captives. Slaves are better than nothing, and we've precious little else to show for this romp in the waves."

Thole grabbed the girl by a wrist and yanked her against *Stag*'s gunwale hard enough that it stunned her. He shoved her upward, and Skule dragged her inboard. The children resisted, but not seriously. Seeing their girl protector subdued seemed to subdue them. The little one started sobbing.

Wolf realized suddenly that *Stag* was drifting, swinging wide. "We're going to broach! To the oars!"

Thole scrambled up over the gunwale. *Stag* rolled as he pulled himself aboard. The boat waddled back to an even keel. He shoved the girl and children up into the bow and settled beside Wolf.

Thole hauled on his oar. "We're going to have to come about into the wind. Jargen, take the tiller!"

Jargen shipped his oar and ran aft. "We're broadside!" he screamed, moments too late.

Stag wallowed mightily, throwing Wolf against the inboard gunwale. A heavy sea sloshed up over their starboard gunwale so high it swamped the furled sail amidships. It broke across the solid wooden fish in which the mast set. Thole pulled, and Wolf instinctively pushed. Their oar strokes together brought *Stag* around stern to the wind.

Jargen threw his weight into the tiller. "We can't come about here. We'll have to follow the sea down to the lee of the island."

Stag bounded and leaped and lurched. She flung her nose high, then dipped it deep. She creaked as she flexed, but Wolf wasn't worried. She had weathered far heavier seas than these.

Of course, that was with twenty-plus men on the oars, not three.

Jargen lashed the tiller in place and took up his oar. They struggled for control now, not for a destination. They must keep her from broaching, from drifting broadside of the heavy sea. Minutes passed, disguised as hours.

"The girl!" Wolf yelled. "She can row. She was driving that punt almost all by herself! We can use her!" He twisted around to grab the girl and pull her forward to the oar just ahead of him.

She and the boys were gone.

3

Northman

Once upon a time Shawna of the Behr rather liked the sea. Perhaps at another time she might like it again. But at this moment, she hated it. She bobbed in it helplessly, lifted and tossed by the waves, her eyes less than a handspan above the water. She could see nothing, she was so cold she could barely move, and she feared.

Oh, she feared! Not for herself—she could weather any trial. She would survive this one. She feared for her parents, for her little cousins, for the home and way of life that had been hers. For the poor cattle, caught in the fires. Dear, bony old Cloud.

The abbot in their little island monastery insisted that fear indicated weak faith. Like the one on Iona, the monastery on Lambay had been founded by none other than Colum Cille himself, so the abbot must know what he was talking about. Very well, her faith was weak—though secretly she could not believe that. She was strong in every other regard; sure and in that one as well.

Domine Jesu, aren't You tired of hearing me?

The moment the Northmen's backs were turned she had sent the boys over the side, one by one, with anything she could grab that would float enough to support them. She herself had jumped overboard with the lid wrenched from one of the storage chests the Northmen used as seats when they plied their oars.

The boys would float even better than she, for they did not weigh as much. And they could kick themselves to shore as well as she, for they were young and strong. But could they stay warm enough long enough to reach land? What if they washed back to Lambay? It was possible. But that dragon vessel and Shawna were all closer now to the mainland than to Lambay. Lord willing, the boys were too.

She wrapped her arms about the box lid, gripping, and began again to kick toward shore. The woodworking skill that had gone

28

into this simple box lid impressed her greatly. She kept her mind on the craftsmanship to keep it off her dreadful fear. And the cold . . . the cold . . .

* * *

Connleigh Dalainn stood tall enough that he had to duck to enter his mother's kitchen. "Bull-sized," Fairleigh the stable manager called him. For Connleigh, Fairleigh constantly grabbed the biggest horses he could find when he went buying and raiding. And still, when Connleigh stood beside his father, he always felt small. A boy on a pony beside Doyle Dalainn.

On this windy ridge overlooking the sea and Lambay, dark, burly Father sat his dun stallion and gazed off at the smoke. "Who was it fell upon Lindesfarne a year or two ago?"

"Northmen. Not Erse." Connleigh clamped his knees tight against his huge gray mare and rose to standing, so to speak, pretending a better view. It did not make him feel any bigger. "I'd say they're back, and they've struck the Behr."

"Then they've their hands full."

Not with all that smoke, Connleigh thought, but he kept it to himself. You didn't argue with Doyle Dalainn, not even if you were his firstborn. The Behr, if they still existed at all, were in deep, deep trouble. "Shall we launch boats to investigate?"

"Wind's too stiff. Take your troop up that way, and I'll lead mine down yon, and we'll patrol the shore. If we see something that warrants investigation, we'll go across when the wind dies tonight. Primarily, I'm interested in protecting our own shores right now."

With no further comment, Father called a heads-up and led off to the south. His force fell in behind him.

Connleigh sighed heavily. "Brian, take four or five to swing around behind the head and follow the shoreline this way. The rest of us will drop down through the gulch and move north."

Brian of Berit Head had been born and raised out there among those crags. Not only did he know every crease in the rocks, he also had a good eye for sizing up the opposition. Connleigh could trust him completely.

29

Connleigh watched the half of his force troop off northward across the ridge, the wind tossing their hair. This morning a peaceful mist had softened land and water. The mist was gone now, replaced by a brooding overcast and raw, cold wind. He spurred his mare down through the steep draw, letting her pick her own way, giving her enough rein that she could recover when she stumbled. Some parts of Erin were not meant to be easily traversed. Nor are some parts of life.

* * *

Once upon a time Ulf Arildson loved the sea. Perhaps at another time he would love it again. But at this moment, he hated it. He struggled, his head barely above water. Already he had tossed away his sword and helmet, lest they weigh him down like an anchor. Still he found it almost impossible to swim in this windchop.

The sea! He had grown up sailing her fjords, reaping her fish, admiring her flat, dancing surface as it reflected the glow of a lifetime of dawns and sunsets. Now she received his affection by turning upon him with a vengeance. She had crushed the *Bounding Stag* in her icy teeth and scattered his comrades, and now she was struggling to consume him too. And he was cold . . . so cold. . . .

* * *

What should she do? If one of the children should hug her now, he would think he was hugging a fish. She was so cold. Shawna curled up awhile and lay still on the rocks, clinging, sobbing.

Her father . . . her brothers . . . Mum . . . home and life . . . the poor cattle . . . everything. . .

She must find the boys. Paul and Padraic were smart enough to know they must run for the nearest settlement. They would bring help. But little Peadar was so frail, not yet tried by life. Oh, poor Peadar! She realized now that she should have kept him with her. She had failed him and thereby failed her brother. And Peggy. What would Peggy say when Peadar's body washed ashore? *Ah, Shawna, you have failed wretchedly!*

The smoke of Lambay did not billow so thickly now, and it had changed color to greenish gray. The pall still hung between the island and the mainland here, and Shawna could smell the devastation. It clung in her nose. Her eyes burned.

Sopping wet, the skirts of her wool dress grabbed at her legs, tripping and hobbling her. In desperation she hiked them above her knees and began climbing, up and away from the hateful sea.

She paused among the rocks, gulping air, and looked around. Down there . . . a tunic . . . wool dyed yellow with onion skins—that would be Padraic, curled up among the rocks at shoreline. *Praise God!* At least one made it ashore, no matter how cold he might be. Caution restrained haste as she clambered through the rocks and skidded down the gravelly washes, back to the odious sea.

Chubby Padraic, God's future friar, lay amid the seaweed. His legs still lolled in the surf. A swell rolled in and briefly lifted him and the seaweed together. It dissipated, and he settled again among the rocks. Shawna's heart quailed.

He was looking at God when she reached him, lying face up in the roiling surf. His eyes didn't sparkle anymore, or blink. He no longer minded that a strand of seaweed stretched across his face, tickling an open eye. His mouth hung loose. His arms and legs floated, flaccid.

Weeping anew, Shawna untangled Padraic from the clinging seaweed and dragged him above high tideline. She rested a moment and dragged him still higher, for if the storm mounted, so would the sea.

For all his clumsiness, Padraic was the biggest, the strongest, the last of the boys to feel the cold. If Padraic could not make it, neither could the others. Overwhelmed, she sat disconsolately in a clump of seagrass and stared at the smoke still rising to the east.

Numb in body and spirit, she lurched to her feet. She could not leave the boys' fates to guesswork and assumption. She must know. She would recover their bodies, and eventually she would have to face Peggy, either here or in heaven. She would have to confess that she had tossed Peggy's sons overboard from a perfectly good boat into a stormy sea to fend for themselves. Yes, even little Peadar.

31

And her justification? None. She walked a few steps, crawled across a protruding boulder, walked a few more steps, slipped on seagrass, and sat down abruptly. She regained her feet and continued on doggedly. No justification whatever. There was a fate worse than death, but the boys would not have faced it. They might go into slavery, but that was hardly the end of life. Patrick himself, the man who brought all Ireland to Christ, lived for years as a slave.

What could she have been thinking of? Whatever could she have been thinking of? The enormity of her folly, her utter stupidity, weighed heavier and heavier with every step.

Then she saw color down in the surf. It appeared a soft blue, but one cannot tell colors well in wet fabric. Paul had been wearing carded gray. The discovery galvanized her. She whipped herself to action as one would whip a pony in a cart, fighting her way down through the slippery tidal zone. *Paul!* Paul had reached land just beyond that outcrop! She sloshed down into slurping water. She scuffed her foot on something, or cut it—right now she didn't care—as she waded out around the rocks. She climbed back to a gravel spit on the lee side of the outcrop and stopped.

Her mind, so eager to find Paul, went blank. Mouth open, she stared at a strange young man in a bluish tunic, a broad leather belt, and dark trousers. He raised his head and stared back with crisp blue eyes that blinked.

This was a Northman. This was one of those raiders. This was one of the fiends who had pillaged her farm, torched her barley and her cattle. His ilk probably killed her brothers and her dear papa, all of whom would fight to the death protecting family and holdings. Were it not for this bloodthirsty pagan, her nephews would be peacefully and cheerfully pursuing mischief on the sanctuary of Lambay this very minute.

The memory of Padraic's sightless eyes momentarily blinded her. With an anguished wail she fell upon the Northman and commenced pounding on him with her cold, hard fists.

* * *

Connleigh Dalainn lived a hero's life. It was a pity that he was no hero. Oh, he had stature and strength of arm enough. But heroes possess the will and desire to be heroic, and that Connleigh did not have. He rode and fought in the shadow of his father, and he was content there. What would he do when the shadow passed and Connleigh faced the kings alone?

His father, lord of this local tuath, not only claimed the title *rui-ri*, king of the local chieftains, but also *ri ruirech*, lord over the whole province. Doyle Dalainn aspired to eventually assume the highest rank, *ard-ri*, high king at Tara. Connleigh knew it. Everyone knew it. But nobody actually said it aloud.

Tara. The kings really didn't hold sway there anymore. Tara was a title, a symbol, a glory that had been. But every ri-ruirech in Erin, nonetheless, dreamed of taking the title and the symbol. Tara was still the prize of prizes.

To wrest Tara from the ruling dynasty would require immense strength of arm. Doyle probably possessed it. Connleigh, next in the Dalainn dynasty should Doyle succeed, did not want to. Furthermore . . .

A ululating tenor voice shattered Connleigh's musings about the ramifications of heroism. Brian was calling from the rocks ahead. High above, in silhouette, one of Brian's minions stood on the point of Berit Head, waving his arms, indicating the route Connleigh should take.

Connleigh abandoned his bumble-footed gray mare to traverse the rocks afoot. It was not only safer but quicker. Behind him his stablemaster, Fairleigh, grabbed the mare's bridle. Connleigh fought his way through mussels and carragheen and weeds and slippery rocks, hating every step of it.

Amid the rocks at surfline, Brian of Berit Head stood purring like a house cat, murmuring soothing words, his strong arms wrapped about a sobbing, soaking wet girl. This powerful warrior with the graying hair was playing the tender uncle. The sight amused Connleigh. Nearby, Brian's fair-haired son, equally well built and powerful for his age, was unpinning his own woolen cloak. Gently the lad drew it around her shoulders and snugged it in.

Brian's men had firmly bound an equally soaked Northman, a lad barely mature, with a shock of brassy blond hair and the undefeated air of a man who owned the world. 'Twas the lad's face that was bloodied. His nose ran red, and a little blue mouse was swelling beneath his left eye.

Connleigh stood, literally, head and shoulders above this prideful postpubescent. He paused before the lad and watched those steely blue eyes a few moments. Boldly the steely blue eyes returned his stare.

"What's your name, and where are you from?" Connleigh waited, then repeated it. He drew his sword slowly and deliberately and said it again.

The lad's eyes followed Connleigh's fearlessly, even casually. Either he had no idea of the menace in a drawn blade or he boasted as much natural bravery as any Erse. The lad responded in a smooth and rolling tongue, but it sounded like neither a name nor a place.

Connleigh turned away to Brian. He recognized the girl. Shawna, the haughtiest and perhaps the smartest of the Behr.

Brian grinned. "We heard her cry out in the distance and came running. You would think we were arriving to save her from the brute, but quite the reverse was true."

Connleigh looked again at the captive Northman. "She, not you, visited that devastation upon his face?"

"Aye, and with an amazing energy for one who had just swum the strait. When I spoke her name she melted into my arms as you see here."

"And of course you said nothing else to invite this miserable burden of having to embrace a nubile girl."

Brian's son smirked. "He nearly thrust me into the ocean that he might be first at her side."

Shawna lifted her head and straightened. "I'm all right now." She heaved a heart-wrenching, shuddering sigh. Her luminous eyes turned to him. "So much. Connleigh, they destroyed so much."

Brian pulled the cloak more firmly around her.

Connleigh nodded. "Then there is naught but that I run him through. But I cannot skewer him bound. Loose the lad, hearties."

"No!" It fairly burst out of her, startling him. "Consider his value as a hostage and slave. That far exceeds the value of his death, even to me who has lost the most."

"You defend a Northman? Have you so soon forgotten the murder and pillage of Lindesfarne?"

Her eyes flashed with that stubborn strength that made the Behr a law unto themselves. "These are doubtless the very brutes who desecrated Lindesfarne. And now Lambay. Would it not be wiser to hold him as a hostage, should the pagans strike here?"

"Well spoken." Connleigh sheathed his sword. "We can skewer him any day, for sport. But once he's gone, he's gone." He pointed to Brian's son. "You, MacBrian. Take the lass to my mother to be dried out and warmed up and succored. Then arm some of the freemen from the south side to build a perimeter around the farmstead. You will defend my mother and sisters. Heaven alone knows what innocents these monsters next will fall upon."

Assigned a man's task, Brian's son swelled visibly with pride. Good. That pride would spur him to excel in an assignment that required no creative thought to speak of.

Connleigh waved an arm. "Patrol. Observe. If the fiends come ashore, blow the horn. I shall watch from the head." He looked again at the Northman. The fellow hadn't mellowed one iota. "Take him along. Treat any attempt to escape with the response it deserves."

Brian gave the prisoner a shove in the desired direction. The fellow tried with considerable success to negotiate the rocks with his arms bound.

What was peculiar about his going? Connleigh watched him cross a short, flat gravel pile at a waddling limp. And yet neither leg appeared injured.

He made his way back to his mare, mounted, and let her pick her way, scrambling, up to the open meadow. He rode out onto Berit Head and just sat there awhile, watching the chains of smoke still rising off Lambay. He would let his mare rest and recover her breath before he decided what next to do, if anything. Her flanks heaved. Her warmth and the soft aroma of her sweat floated up around his face.

Why did he insist on thinking about that Northman as a lad? The man was scarce two years younger than himself—probably not even that much. Shawna couldn't be but a year or so younger, and yet he called her lass. What was he at twenty-one? Some old man? He sometimes felt so.

His mother was pressing him to marry. Fate had just pried the aloof Shawna out of her island hideaway and deposited her in Connleigh's own household. Fate? Nay, God. This was probably God nudging him again. He really ought to marry sometime, and she was as good as any. In fact, he would not do better than this sensible, strong-willed beauty.

Very well, God. As You wish.

The winds were shifting again, and with them the smoke of Lambay. It drifted this way now. He could smell the stench.

He leaned forward, straining his eyes. On the very horizon where sea met sky, two tiny vessels raised sail.

They disappeared in the mist.

4

Wolf in Irons

There is a fate worse than death, and Brenna faced it. She really ought throw herself into the sea rather than submit to these butchering monsters, but she did not. And she could not explain why she did not.

She huddled in the bow of the raiding vessel, pressed against Peggy and a freeman's wife with her three children. An uncommon number of men were crowded aboard. The vessel leaped and dipped across the choppy sea, under sail. The oarsmen, more than a score of them, had long since shipped their oars as the sail went up. Dusk was falling, and Brenna had no idea where they were or where they were headed. She knew only that an offshore breeze was carrying them away from Lambay, away from the known world into the unknown.

She had hidden beneath a pile of loose thatching near the brewery, while these monsters overran the farm. She did not resist. She did not attempt to protect Grandmum or the children. She did not even try to flee. She did none of the heroic things Shawna would have done. What would she tell Shawna, should she ever see her cousin again?

And now here she cowered. The abbot would surely advise her to be seeking divine help. Fat lot the abbot knew about real life.

These men, exceptionally tall and fair haired, wore plain wool trousers and tunic shirts in the teeth of the cold, raw wind and seemed not to mind. A few wore cloaks draped over one shoulder. None hunched or seemed to feel the chill.

Two of them came strolling over to their coffle of slaves and looked down upon Brenna and the others, grinning. One of them, a blond-bearded fellow in a blue shirt, pointed to Brenna, talking in that rolling language. The other, in a brown shirt, laughed and nodded. He made a comment that sent Blueshirt into gales of laughter. Blueshirt called to someone behind him.

That someone strolled aft and stood beside them. From his manner, Brenna recognized him as the master of the vessel. He shook his head, indicating that Brenna ought not be the one, whatever the one was. He pointed to Peggy and seemed to ask something. Blueshirt nodded agreement.

The master reached down and gripped Brenna's wrist in an iron fist. He yanked her to her feet and dragged her stumbling to the huge and heavy wooden fish-shaped block in which the mast set. He stepped onto it and pulled Brenna up beside him. He made some sort of announcement to those aboard that seemed to involve Brenna, but she had no idea what. He asked something. The raiders mumbled a response.

The master gave Brenna a shove, and she felt herself fly forward off the block. Tough, bristling fellows grabbed her and dragged her back to the huddled group in the bow.

Now they were hauling Peggy up onto the block. From her corner of the bow, Brenna could barely see Peggy's head above the forest of legs and bodies. The announcement about Peggy was greeted with much alacrity. They seemed to either draw straws or elect someone. A general cheer went up. A huge, burly raider leaped onto the block beside his master. With a grin and a raised arm he acknowledged the cheers of his fellow brutes and hopped to the deck, dragging Peggy along with him.

As the freeman's wife was being pulled toward the block, Peggy screamed. She shrieked, "No! Help! No, please!" over and over. There was no way Brenna could help or even see for certain what was happening. With laughter and boisterous comment, the fellow's companions urged him on. All Brenna saw was backs and legs.

The screams abated to moans and begging and finally to sobbing. Poor Peggy! What was happening? By now the freeman's wife had been allotted. That was what they were doing. Parceling out the slaves. Eventually, Brenna sat alone in the bow, assigned to no one. Why not she? What set her apart?

Darkness closed down around the open, bounding vessel, and with it a cold rain. They tossed her a cover, a huge, dark, shaggy animal hide. Stiff from many rains, it could not be tucked in or snuggled beneath. It sheltered her from the wet, but cold air swirled up under it all night.

She cried herself to sleep.

* * *

The Wolf, Ulf Arildson, in irons. How degrading!

So why did he feel this warm, happy glow? It certainly wasn't his circumstance. He lay captive. He very nearly froze before his clothes dried. They had chained him in a pig sty. They fed him some stale bread. No ale. The chain around his waist weighed heavily. He lay in the utter darkness of a stinking little shed with his manacles rubbing open sores on his wrists, and he didn't feel the least despairing.

And while he pondered unponderables, he explored why he had let that blonde girl beat on him. He could so easily have struck back. Indeed, he should have. Instead, he did nothing but raise his arms in a feeble defense. He thought about the fury in her eyes, both when they brought her aboard the *Bounding Stag* and when she fell upon him on the shore. So like a Norse woman she was, expressing rage with direct action. And so tough and strong, to make it ashore in violent seas.

He heard horses' hooves approach, and lilting voices. The sty door creaked and swung open, spilling light into his eyes. He squinted, but he could see nothing in the sudden brilliance. Rough hands hauled him out into morning brightness. He gained his feet with difficulty and marveled at how very stiff and sore his whole body felt, every bit of it. His left eye refused to open fully.

A score of riders, all heavily armed, surrounded him. Even though he stood amid a random cluster of horses, he could tell instantly the leader of this band. A dark, burly, bearded Celt sat a splendid dun stallion two hands bigger than any horse on Norwegian soil. The man said nothing. He didn't have to.

At the man's side, on a little bay mare, the blonde girl sat watching Ulf with a steady, malevolent gaze. He admired the purity of her hatred. She alone carried no sword or shield.

The men who had hauled him out of the sty mounted and the whole band clattered off out the east gate, into the morning, drag-

39

ging him along by the six feet of lead on the chain around his waist. Two feet of lighter chain connected his manacles, but no chain tied manacles to waist. Were he chaining a slave he'd probably add that extra length.

In a way, this Celt farm was much like Wolf's own back home. But then, what else is a farm but a knot of buildings with pitched roofs, and walled paddocks for the livestock? The farms back home were not girt by a wall, though. Here, a circular outer wall described a ring of safety within which the main buildings clustered. Cattle and sheep dotted the treeless pastures for a mile all around. Wolf wasn't used to these low, rolling hills and the open grassland. He had already decided he preferred the steep mountains of home.

Wolf was the only one afoot. He ran as best he could, he dog-trotted, he fell a few times, he was dragged now and then by the chain around his waist. He would find no spark of kindness in these Celts. He expected none.

Darkness had fallen when they brought him into the farmyard yesterday. This was his first chance to see the track in daylight. He thought then that he had seen a most unusual building loom in the darkness. They passed it now. He'd been right. One would imagine from its appearance that its builders had simply stacked undressed or roughly dressed flat fieldstone to form its walls. The walls curved inward as they rose until they met at a keeled spine at the roofpeak. It appeared a bit more than twice as long as wide, more or less the proportions of a house one would live in. No one seemed to be living in it, though. An intriguing decoration sat in the stone house's front yard. Carved of stone, it consisted of a tall vertical column and a short crosspiece.

They passed it by without slowing and continued down the sloping, open meadows toward the sea. And as he stumped along, Wolf took a certain measure of pride in being able to keep up with these tall, rangy horses so well.

In his Northland village, he received little but ridicule. So he had told no one there about his ploys to build his strength—running straight up the steep slopes of the mountains behind town, picking up and throwing boulders, swimming out to Otter Island

and back. He planned that when the time came to prove himself, he would demonstrate a strength beyond that of any challenger.

But that was the plan then. This was now, his captivity, and not in the plan at all.

The path led down to a landing in a sheltered cove. The horsemen dismounted at the dock. The second in command, the tall fellow on the huge gray mare, the man who had overseen Wolf's capture, climbed into the stern of a little boat. It was a small, sailless fishing vessel of some sort, built of willow-wicker and covered with hide, about the size to accommodate four oarsmen. It lacked the graceful line of Norse boats. Wolf questioned its seaworthiness.

But then, who was Wolf to question? They were herding him into the boat. And now the girl climbed in and settled herself beside the man. Someone clunked an oar into a crudely chiseled oarlock beside Wolf. He took it up without thinking.

So he was expected to row. They were using their slave already. Should he resist or should he cooperate? What would resistance benefit? Nothing. Besides, he liked to row. A thrall sat down next to him and took up the corresponding oar. The boat waggled dangerously as others boarded, and the oarsman behind Wolf nudged them away from the dock. Beyond them, a second boat was loading with the leader and others.

As soon as they cleared and he had room, he dipped his oar deep and stroked mightily. The little boat lunged forward into the swells. It didn't take more than two or three strokes before he realized it was he setting the beat. To test his theory he slowed somewhat. The rhythm slowed. He quickened his pace. The pace quickened. Smugly, he set a pace certain to wear these Celtic toughies down to a nubbin.

For some reason, he knew not what, Wolf was being accursed by Odin thrice over. First, he was not allowed to die victoriously in battle. Second, he was not even allowed to see the battle, except for those initial moments, wild and vicious, as the island's defenders met the Norsemen. Half a dozen armed farmers, and one of them without a helmet, are no match for three boatloads of trained warriors. Third, he was being sent to view the aftermath.

They rowed out to the island silently, grimly. Except for the metered splash of the oars, and the loud *schplop* as the heavy swells slapped the bottoms of the clumsy little boats, only the wind spoke, and that softly. The wind caressed Wolf's cheek and churred quietly in his ear. It whispered, *I have been to the North-land, and all is well.*

And in reply, Wolf whispered, *Liar! You are southerly.*

They drove up against a cobble beach on the extreme western shore of the island. Wolf climbed out quickly, splashing to his knees in the water, to help draw the boat above tideline. His rowing companions were not nearly so winded and sweaty as he had hoped.

He followed meekly, like a bull on the end of a chain (which, all in all, he considered himself to be), as the blonde girl led the party up the slope and eastward. Wolf watched the trails of smoke in the sky ahead. The ruins still smoldered, and he dreaded this next hour.

They entered a sorry excuse for a birch forest, open and ragged, and emerged from the other side. They topped a rise, and the girl stopped in her tracks. Wolf walked forward far enough to see her face and instantly wished he had not.

Wagging her head, she murmured something in that lilting language. The tall young man placed an arm around her shoulders, but she seemed not to notice him, so intently did she gaze at the ruins.

Before him stretched a farm just like his captors'. Inside a broad, circular wall, all the fieldstone buildings save one were gutted, empty shells like offering bowls containing smoking thatch. Broken barrels littered the dooryard of the one shed left whole. When booty was brought back to the ships, no one had mentioned ale. A few stinking, bloated cattle and sheep lay about, some with burned backs. Ravens, hooded crows, and large birds that were neither—plus a rowdy flock of seagulls—feasted upon the remains. A thousand thousand flies droned.

The tall man spoke, and the girl responded by pointing north. He must have asked from whence the raiders came, for she was indicating where Wolf's ships had landed.

On the far hill to the east, a body of armed men appeared. For a fleeting second Wolf imagined that his companions had returned to rescue him, but no. They were obviously Celts like his captors, farmers from elsewhere on the island. They hesitated, as if fearing this party, then came ahead.

The two groups met in the middle, among the ruined buildings. On the surface they appeared to know each other comfortably and well. But Wolf got the distinct impression of two dogs circling about one bone, testing each other cautiously. Were these island Celts looters come to take what had been left? It appeared so. And if so, they would return with their bags empty. Wolf's comrades had left precious little, and nothing of real value.

A tug on the chain, and the tall man led Wolf north, up the rises between this farm and the sea. Most of the rest followed, but the girl remained behind.

The defenders' bodies lay as Wolf remembered them. Either birds or dogs had torn at them, and the eyes were pecked out.

The tall man dropped Wolf's chain and raised his hand to his forehead, to his belly, to each shoulder. Everyone else followed. One of the party, an older man with a poorly kept gray beard, began to chant in singsong, stooping over first this body and then that. Every so often he performed that same movement, strangely graceful, of touching head, belly, and shoulders.

Wolf looked off to the narrow shore at the foot of the cutbank and thought about the ships beached there so recently. Where was Skule? What happened to Jargen and Thole? Were they safe with the others? If they were able to reach the island here, they were.

He wheeled and raised his head, stretching, trying to hear—it sounded like *her!* One of the Celts cried out and pointed back toward the farm. Wolf hadn't been hearing things; this fellow detected it too. A woman's scream. As one, every man ran back up the hill toward the farm.

Wolf could easily slip away now. No one paid attention to him. No one held his chain. He heard that scream again, distinctly this time. He snatched up his chain, that it might not catch in the rocks, and ran with the others with his six feet of lead chain in his own hand. Utterly breathless, he crested the rise.

Halfway between the top of this hill and the farm, the girl was running toward them swift as a hind. A blackguard from the other party was catching up to her, reaching long, seizing her, dragging her to a halt. She fought him, flailing. And behind him came the others.

With war cries that rent the heavens, the two parties met on the hillside, and Wolf's heart leaped for joy. Odin was not cursing him after all! He was seeing battle, and it was battle against cowardly, ugly little people who would rob their fallen brethren. He too cried out, ferociously, eagerly.

This was nothing like practice fights and sparring matches. Directly in front of him, a swordsman thrust his blade into an enemy. The man fell so hard he dragged the sword down with him, pulling the swordsman forward to his knees. Wolf stopped and stood agape, and it was a count of five before he realized that stopping and gaping were not the things to do here. It also occurred to him that he had no way of knowing friend from foe in this melee, for all the Celts looked alike.

And now the tall man sagged against Wolf and dropped to his knees. He clutched at his side, gasping. Without thinking, Wolf grabbed the fellow to prevent him from falling. He reached for the man's sword, but the fellow gulped air and hauled himself back to his feet. With a yell, the Celt charged forward.

There went the girl, breaking away from the fight, running toward the boats so far away. And there went that same scoundrel after her. Wolf took off after them. Already winded, he feared his knees would buckle. The short leg, especially, felt weak. But the girl was winded too and not as swift as a hind anymore. The Celt caught her arm.

And Wolf reached the Celt. He had no weapon save the six feet of chain with which his captors led him. He wielded it, swinging it with all his strength. He caught the ruffian in the neck and sent the man sprawling. The fellow's grasp pulled the girl off her feet.

Wolf fell upon him, hooking the shorter chain between his manacles up under the fellow's throat, and shoved. The Celt grabbed Wolf's hair and pulled his head so far back he could feel his neck bones tick. Then the grip on his hair lost its strength. The fellow struck him in the face, but the blow lacked force. Wolf shoved. And shoved.

He heard men running this way. The Celt beneath him had gone limp. Still he shoved. The girl was shouting in Wolf's ear and pulling on his shirt. Her companions ran past them toward the boats.

Wolf leaped to his feet and gathered in his chain as he ran. He thought he had been out of breath. It surprised him, the strength and the wind he found when he didn't think he had any.

The landing party made the cobbles clatter as they reached the shore. The men of the other boat tumbled into it and put out. The girl had been running beside Wolf. Now she fell behind, crying, "Kon-lee! Kon-lee!"

She was trying to aid the tall man, holding him up, pulling him along. The fellow staggered, dropped to his knees, and regained his feet. Wolf gripped the man's arm and literally flung him into the little boat.

The girl scrambled aboard. Wolf tossed his lead chain into the bow and leaned on the stem, pushing the boat backwards out into the water. A wave rolled in and lifted it high. He literally fell into the bow end.

The wave receded and dropped them onto the stones, but by the time the next wave lifted them, Wolf had clambered up onto his thwart and locked his oar.

The girl was yammering something. She pointed wildly toward shore. Wolf glanced back. They were the last three to leave, this girl and the tall man and he! Comrades had fallen—the three thralls who had plied oars with him. He was the lone oarsman now.

The chain between his manacles stretched tight, and the open sores on his wrists burned like fire, but he could just so handle both oars. He planted one and stroked deep with the other. The little round-bottomed boat swung around in place. He set both oars well behind and put all his back into them. The boat practically lifted out of the water, and they were on their way toward the far shore.

Their attackers did not seem inclined to launch out in pursuit. Wolf watched them a few moments until they were obscured by the girl's shoulder.

As winded as he, she sucked in air in huge, shuddering sobs. Blood spattered her face and the front of her dress, but it did not seem to be hers. Tears had washed two bloodless lines down her cheeks.

Wolf had seen death come in many guises. He watched a cousin lose an arm when a mast broke and fell across its block. Of the six children his mother bore, only he and his brother Reidar remained. He had always assumed he knew all about grief. He looked at this girl's stricken face and saw there a whole new dimension. He didn't really know grief at all.

Then reality shattered his philosophical musings about loss. He was not accustomed to this artless little craft. A wave nearly tipped them when he lifted his oars at the wrong moment. The boat's strange round bottom skidded sideways on the heavy sea, tossed by every wave. Was it his imagination, or was the sea turning rougher, the wind harsher? Four men at the oars is strength; one man at the oars is folly.

The tall man, his face drained white, dragged himself to sitting, but that's all the farther he got.

The girl instantly flicked around to the thwart in front of Wolf. She, too, took up two oars. The girl was strong, for a girl. She added a little stability and a little movement.

Wolf was into his second wind now, and a good thing. It was Wolf, the stronger, who guided them. Glancing beneath his arm now and then, he aimed them toward the north of that jutting head. The way this foolishly made craft scudded about, the wind and waves would push them to a landing just south of it. They were nowhere near land when his second wind began to fade.

Frey directs these things. Odin watches over his warriors. Thor handles the heavens. Wolf called upon them and confidently awaited their gifts of strength and energy.

No gifts came.

The port gunwale rose high and dipped deep. A wave broke over it and sloshed across them. Wolf and the girl lost a stroke on the port side when the water dropped out from beneath their oars. Propelled only by the starboard oars, the boat turned abruptly. Wolf swung it back to course.

The tall man lost consciousness. His sagging weight tipped the round-bottomed craft a bit to starboard. Now Wolf must adjust his strokes, plying heavy on one side, or they would row in circles for the next ten years.

A lifetime or two later Wolf could hear the surf crash behind them. The girl paused and twisted in her seat. Her eyes went wide. In rushed phrases she gestured and pointed and babbled, trying to explain in a meaningless tongue exactly what Wolf ought to do. Frustrated she turned her back to him and attempted to turn the boat herself. He countered her strokes and tried to keep the erratic waves from breaking over their port gunwale.

Five hundred yards. He did not have to look. His ears told him where the rocks were.

Three hundred yards.

Wolf looked behind and picked his spot. For a moment he watched the water boil, identifying the rocks beneath the surface, watching the eddies.

A hundred yards. Fifty. He pushed on one oar to counter the girl's struggling attempts to guide them.

Wait.

This next wave . . .

Now!

He set an oar deep. The boat pivoted a half turn. An eddy caught it and sucked it around another half turn. The girl screamed. The back of the eddy picked their boat up and flung it landward. Wolf stroked once, strongly, and the bow wedged itself up between the two seaweed-clothed boulders he had chosen as their landfall. The next wave shoved it firmly, safely into the grasp of the rocky shore.

Utterly, utterly spent, he turned the oars loose and sagged forward, his elbows on his knees, his face in his trembling hands.

Blood. There lay the tall man, his whole shirt bright red with blood. The spatters across the girl's front. That total stranger dying on the point of the sword.

And the grief on the girl's face . . .

For a moment—for one fleeting moment—Wolf could not see any value whatever in a life of pillage and plunder.

5

MacBrian's Story

The old man could not possibly guess how ridiculous he looked or he wouldn't be doing this. There he went, Mahon of Armagh, running across the mud, his bare feet splacking, hard on the trail of a panic-stricken chicken. And there too went the chicken squawking, a Noble Hen of Kildare, flapping and flying remarkably well considering that the flight feathers of one wing had been clipped.

Mahon's scrawny arms and legs flailed. His big, round tummy bobbed. Most ridiculous of all, though, was the tonsure, and all men who had pledged monastic vows wore it. Why did the monks seem to think that looking different provided any advantage? Mahon's gray hair hung long in back, almost like an old woman's. The front half of his head was shaved, as are all such, so that he was bald from his ears forward. Compared to Mahon, the chicken looked absolutely elegant.

Ailan of the Two Dimples watched all this from, so to speak, afar. He was nearly twenty years old now and well past the age of foolishness. He didn't like looking undignified. He kept himself in the shadow beside the corner of the wooden chicken coop, knowing that sooner or later he would have to take part in the chase —and dreading it.

Curse the luck. The chicken was headed this way. Mahon yelled, so Ailan stepped out into the filtered sun. Ailan was taller than most young men his age, and women claimed he was more handsome than most too. Good looks and height help not at all when you're trying to catch a six-pound chicken. Ailan made a dart, a feint, a lunge, and a grab. He tumbled forward and plowed mud with his chin.

Mahon leaped over Ailan and continued the pursuit.

Disgusted, Ailan picked himself up and threw away his handful of tailfeathers. Mahon, the wise patriarch of the church in Ireland, didn't have the common sense to know you can't catch a healthy chicken in midmorning. You catch it on its roost after nightfall and bind its legs together with a thong. The next morning you collect it at leisure. None of this ramming about a muddy chicken yard.

From nowhere a net dropped over the chicken. The bishop of Kildare stepped out from behind the mud-and-wattle granary. So far as Ailan was concerned, she was the hardest, most obdurate woman he had ever known, and that included his virago of a mother. Also, as far as Ailan knew, she was the only female bishop in Christendom. The Abbess of Kildare was always a bishop, ever since the monastery's founder, Saint Brigid, received the orders of a bishop more than three hundred years ago. Traditions die hard.

She glared at Ailan as if it were his fault she had to step into the chase. She regarded Mahon much less harshly. "Next time, let's catch it the night before."

"Next time, let's have lamb. Sheep I can catch." Mahon chuckled, in a remarkably good humor for being mud-covered. He gripped the chicken as she retrieved her net, a simple fishing seine. The chicken purred low clucking noises from deep in its doomed throat. Mahon tucked it under his arm and walked off in search of his ax.

The abbess fell in beside Mahon. Her silver hair, peeking just so out from under the linen cloth on her head, fairly sparkled, even in the subdued light of the overcast. If she weren't so very stern, she would be a rather nice woman. Her build was certainly nothing to be ashamed of, or her smooth cheeks and honest face.

The two of them commenced a discussion of the dating of Easter. Again. The rest of Christendom had settled the issue a hundred years ago. Why could the Irish not let it lie? Ailan was tired of hearing about it.

Ailan faced a choice now. If he followed after Mahon he would end up plucking a chicken. Let the nuns in the kitchen shed dress the chicken. Ailan wandered aside, randomly on purpose, between two wicker-and-mud beehive huts. A few clochans, Ailan noticed, were built not of wood but of stone, cunningly laid tier upon tier. There was certainly plenty of stone about, and trees were coming into short supply round about here.

49

This was a double monastery, with both men and women in orders, the only such in Erin. Monks lived in these little beehive huts, as did monks everywhere. But where did the women live? He didn't know, but he could safely bet it wasn't anywhere near the men. Mahon watched Ailan as a cat watches a fieldmouse whenever a female came within a mile of him. You'd think women would rob a man of all his thoughts of God. Which, in Ailan's case, they often did.

The monastery crowned this gentle hill that extended just a wee bit higher than any of the gentle hills surrounding it. Most of the hills had long since been denuded down to open pasturage. Cattle and sheep grazed between thick hedgerows. Tracks traced brown lines everywhere across the land, the lanes through which the livestock were driven home to the safety of the monastery compound each night. To the east, in its flat plain, flowed the river Liffey.

Ailan could not see the river valley from here. Everywhere he looked he saw oak stumps, alder stumps, even rowan stumps. The oak stumps lasted so long, even in the wet. Sure and some of the buildings in the monastery were close to a century old, and their oaken timbers were still as strong as when they were first laid. Oak got no respect from Christians—not the way it did when druids held sway in the land.

He walked down beside a little brook lined with alders. They were now the only grown trees in the area, and fresh stumps told him that soon even they would be firewood. It seemed a pity, somehow, to use stately trees for warmth and cooking.

The brook itself was being used for laundry, another unnecessary pastime. The laundress was a round sort of girl with a rather rowdy and buxom plumpness about her. Her straw-blonde hair hung limply down behind her shoulders, tied back with a bit of yarn. She stood in water to her knees and did not seem to notice the cold.

Casually, in no hurry at all, she slapped a water-heavy woolen shirt against the rocks. She swished it about in the flowing stream, stood erect, and wrenched it in a tight twist. Her arms were amazingly muscular. Ailan liked her right away.

For a long moment she regarded him as he approached her. She didn't smile, but she looked bemused—just slightly short of actually looking interested. "You're not a monk."

"Not yet. I'm studying for it."

She nodded. "You didn't shave the front of your head like monks do. Going to be a pity when you do."

Her frankness startled him, not the least because he totally agreed with her. He liked his carefully groomed blond hair very much. To remove all his hair from the top forward would be to cut away the loveliest part of it. It pleased him immensely that this girl, a perfect stranger, saw his appearance essentially as he himself saw it.

She paid him no further mind. He now ranked neither more nor less interesting than laundry. He watched her labor for a few minutes longer and didn't know whether to speak to her again, let alone what to say. With a strange, empty little feeling in his heart, he turned and worked his way back up the hill to the abbey, through the oak stumps and roots.

He felt dissatisfied. The Christian faith was supposed to satisfy and reward one's devotion. He'd been following the observances (all of them—Mahon saw to that) for nearly a year now. He knew the litanies by heart, both in Latin and in the vernacular. But they echoed empty in his soul.

And yet Ailan's father obviously saw a spark of greatness, to send Ailan to Armagh at fifteen. Mahon maintained constant faith and trust in Ailan. Was it not Ailan that Mahon chose from among nearly fifty young pastoral assistants? Everyone back home in his neighborhood on the river Barrow oohed and aahed appreciatively at Ailan's good fortune. In fact, everyone praised his luck so highly that he himself had gotten caught up in the general celebration. A lad of God, soon to become a man of God, learning at the feet of the holiest man in Erin—who could discount that superb destiny? Of course, everyone who oohed and aahed and celebrated did not see Mahon chasing a chicken around the muddy yard of Kildare.

When everyone cheered Ailan's calling, no one bothered to mention the sheer slogging involved, the nearly constant travel between monasteries and raths, visiting ris and abbots, teaching the same lessons over and over to a people dull of hearing. His calling seemed to consist almost exclusively of ceaseless days on the road answering ceaseless questions and objections to essentially the same topics.

Sure and they did some blessing here and there. Mahon blessed everyone he came upon on the road and in the field. He and Ailan shared what they had and helped whomever they could—too much so at times, as far as Ailan was concerned. During services, Mahon preached not on doctrine but on service, over and over. Ailan was supposed to be learning from him. Instead he was being bored out of his mind. After you've explored the topic of service five hundred different ways, there's not much left to learn. Mahon, in the interest of reaching everybody else, seemed to be leaving his assistant behind to languish in boredom.

And his assistant detested it.

"Ah! There you are!" Mahon's exuberant bark jolted Ailan out of his musings. "Come along to the scriptorium. I've something exciting to show you!" From the door of the oratory, Mahon led out across the mud.

Ailan fell in behind. He could certainly use some excitement. He wondered if that blonde girl found laundry as unstimulating as he found life in general.

They entered a rectangular building with windows, one of the several at Kildare constructed of wattle. Mud daubed and sealed the thin willow-and-alder-withes basket—woven through heavy vertical posts. Inside, center posts helped support the heavy thatched roof.

What made this building different was the windows. There were two or three windows in every wall, despite that they're so hard to build into a wattle structure. They gave the place a bright, breezy, open feeling. In short, they let some of nature in for once.

Men and women labored together in this building, each at a different task. At one end they scraped the sheepskins for parchment. Ailan noticed that the lime vat in the corner was nearly full of hides soaking. One woman with a small quern sat on the floor grinding a red pigment. The color poured out from under her little grinding stone. Beside her, a companion stirred and stirred and stirred a tiny pot of red ink.

"Here!" Mahon wound among a dozen workers strewed across the floor, busy at their tasks. He headed for a monk seated beside a window. "Look," he whispered.

At a tilted writing desk, the monk worked on the last page of a signature, its parchment clamped tightly to the writing surface. Beside the monk, on another small table, lay the book he was copying from, opened to its last page. Surreptitiously, Ailan glanced at the text. The gospel of John.

Mahon moved in directly behind the monk and peered over the man's shoulder. If Ailan were that monk he would not like Mahon breathing down his neck like that, but this fellow apparently did not mind. In small, sharp letters he printed the final words.

"Exquisite! Now watch," murmured Mahon. His head moved slightly with the motion of the monk's writing strokes.

The copyist drew a single graceful swirl across the bottom of the page and spent several minutes carefully washing out his pen. He dipped it into a rich blue ink and made two more swirls. Again he washed it out.

This was certainly exquisite, all right. Exquisitely dull. Choosing colors with the care of a farmer choosing his horses' bloodlines, the monk built upon that simple set of swirls a complex and delicately interwoven border illumination.

"This is ours," Mahon whispered.

"Our what?"

"The book. Our book! We're taking it with us."

"It won't be ready for weeks."

The monk paused and straightened. He smiled. "Days at most. Improved light is half the reason for these windows. The other half is improved drying time."

Mahon continued, "We'll help with the pressing and binding. I'll take it along up to the Behr. I've not seen them in several years. It will be a gift well received. They're beautifully literate, the Behr, even the daughter."

"Where are the Behr?"

"Out on Lambay Island."

Oh, just fine! Not only did they face more traveling, threading their way through the dangerous and difficult country of the Owney and the Dalainn, they got to brave the perils of the sea as well.

Ailan could hardly wait.

* * *

Shawna, still of the Behr but no longer of Lambay, sat on a smooth rock at the brow of Berit Head and gazed across at her island in the mist offshore. She thought about the little church there, the monastery founded by Colmcille himself. Except for the post-and-wattle oratory, not much remained of it. The monk now lived on his own little rath apart from the church. The old burials, a people long before the Behr, lay on the western shore unnoticed now, for Shawna had been the only one to visit them and wonder about them. All gone.

All gone.

Why didn't Doyle Dalainn, if he was such a doughty hero with such a powerful retinue, help her go across to bury her family? After that first ill-starred encounter, when Wolf saved her from an unhappy marriage . . .

What is Wolf doing now? she wondered. He seemed to enjoy each task given him and pursued life as he pursued work— exuberantly.

Doyle had led a second, larger, contingent over. They buried the Behr in the soil of home, they claimed, and taught the people on the east side not to attack the Dalainn so thoughtlessly. Why didn't he at least let her go along?

Behind her she heard a horse coming along the faint track out onto the head. She twisted around to look. Clattering on the rocks, sloshing across the sloppy ground, Doyle Dalainn himself came riding alone. He rode up beside her and slid off his mare.

This was his new prized possession, this little bay mare. She was too short-legged for him, actually. He looked a wee bit ridiculous towering upon her with his long legs wrapped around her belly. But she was a flashy thing with a marvelously thick mane. When she moved, she snapped her legs high. It was probably her action and bright spirit that attracted his fancy.

Doyle gazed off toward Lambay a few moments, but islands in the mist apparently bored him rapidly. His voice poured rich and dark across her tangled nerves, smooth as oil. "My condolences." He dropped to a squat beside her shoulder. His little mare danced nervously behind him. "What do you think of the Norseman?"

Her head snapped around. Now why on earth did he ask that? "I haven't really been thinking about the Norseman."

"Your impressions?"

She shrugged. "He's very strong for his size. And smart. I'd say he's quick to think."

"My impression too." He waited a moment. Apparently silence bored him as quickly as did the island. "So what are you thinking about if not the Norseman?"

She glanced at him. Should she be brashly forthright or tactfully circumspect? She was too wearied, too sad, to be circumspect. "I shall sound ungrateful if I tell you."

"You're angry with me."

"Yes."

"For not taking you over to the island."

"Yes."

"I did what I thought would be easiest for you. I make no apologies."

Of course you offer no apologies. You never think you're wrong. But she kept that bit of brashness to herself.

He purred on. "I'd far rather bear your anger than my own. And I'd be furious with myself had I let you go. My foresight was validated. They did unspeakable things, especially to the women."

He stood up suddenly. "Here. The mare needs work. Take her out. Ride her hard."

Shawna's first impulse was to decline with a shy "Thank you, anyway." But she wanted to ride. She wanted to fly, to escape, to float free, and he had just offered. She lurched to her feet, feeling strangely stiff and tired, and gathered the mare's reins up into the mane.

She did not want this man, however solicitous, to touch her in any way. Quickly, before he could step forward to give her a hand up, she swung her leg up and over and squirmed astride.

"Thank you, Doyle. Thank you very much!" She drew her knees up against the mare's shoulders and reined her aside, down off the head, away from Lambay, away from sorrow.

Short and stocky though she was, the mare possessed a long stride, and she obviously loved to run. The moment they reached the solid track, Shawna let her out. The mare tossed her head, laid her ears back, and flew, joyously, enthusiastically. Shawna dropped forward and buried her face in the whipping mane. She let the coarse hair flail her face. They ran faster than wind, faster than arrows, faster than words. They followed the nearly straight track for two miles before Shawna finally sat erect and drew the mare down to a tight canter.

At the Owney Brook ford she turned the mare around. Headed homeward, the little horse wanted to run again. Shawna held her back, for there was much thinking to do and much time needed to do it.

What unspeakable acts, exactly, did those fiends commit? Shawna could imagine some of them, simply from having heard tales of Celtic raids. Men are not so different, be they Erse or Dane. But imagining is not knowing. How she longed to know! And now, with her parents and cousins and brothers buried, she would never know.

She could learn second-hand, though. Doyle obviously wasn't going to volunteer anything, so she would quiz the others of the burial party who went with him. She could piece together a fairly good picture from the eyewitness accounts.

The foamy, resinous sweat on the mare's shoulders and flanks had dried, gluing her coat into a dark crust, by the time they arrived back at the rath of the Dalainn. The little mare still possessed plenty of vim as they entered the south gate.

Over by the house, the young Norse slave was cutting firewood, and quite expertly too. He had removed his woolen tunic. He worked barechested. The muscles of his back and shoulders rippled every time his ax struck wood.

It surprised Shawna that they would allow him an ax. But he was tethered to the horse post by his six feet of chain, so the danger he posed was limited to how far he could accurately throw the ax. As happy as he looked as he split and chopped, he didn't seem in a mood to throw things.

He glanced toward her as she entered and stopped cold to stare. She felt her cheeks flush. Then they flushed worse, for she realized he wasn't watching her. He was admiring the horse. He shifted his look to her and flashed her the most charming grin. He warbled something in his strange tongue. It sounded complimentary.

On impulse she rode over to him and slid off.

He dropped to one knee and smoothed himself a broad writing surface in the dirt. He drew a crude outline of a horse. He said something like "Fross" and jabbed a finger at the mare. He scratched long marks down the neck of the picture. He drew another horse, more or less, and sketched an arching line above the neck. That, he indicated, was what his horse looked like.

She nodded. "A naturally roached mane. Stiff and erect. Some Irish horses are like that, though Doyle doesn't have any here at the moment. And ponies. Ponies often do."

Honestly, Shawna! He couldn't understand a single word of that! And yet, deep down, she wanted desperately for him to understand whatever she had to say. Quickly and cleverly, he had just gotten his point across to her, and he a barbaric pagan. Surely she ought to be as clever.

But then, his were the brutal monsters who did the unspeakable things. Poor Brenna. And Peggy. Peggy could not have escaped. And Mum. Why was she bothering to talk to this monster?

He stood erect, said something cheerful, and returned to woodsplitting.

She wandered off toward the stable, the mare in tow.

Fairleigh the stablemaster must have heard her coming. He stepped out from under the little storage shed where were kept the bridles and wooden saddles. She handed the mare's reins to him.

"Fairleigh? I am an adult."

"Verily."

"And as such, wise to the ways of the world—not that I have partaken of many of them."

Fairleigh eyed her suspiciously.

She must be direct now. "You were on that burial party to Lambay. You saw all. What exactly did the fiends do to their enemies? Especially Brenna and my Mum. And Peggy."

"Uh—er—unspeakable things, lady."

"Speak them, please."

"Uh—er—best not to ask." His eyes flittered everywhere except toward her. "A higher tongue than mine must speak them, lady."

"Doyle was by here, wasn't he? And he told you I would ask."

"Second sight, he has."

"A devious mind he has. And he instructed you not to talk about it."

"He's trying to spare you, lass."

Spare her! What was the big secret, that Doyle would warn his stable manager to silence? Who would not yet have been cautioned to tell the poor bereft girl nothing? "I've changed my mind. May I have the horse for a while yet, please?"

He looked puzzled, even say dark, but he handed the horse back.

She rode out to the north, keeping the mare at an easy jog, pacing her for a long ride. It was well past midday when she entered the farm of Brian of Berit Head. His was a small rath, circled by a high earthen wall that was topped with a pale fence. It would hardly keep out raiders but was high enough to protect the lambs from wolves. The ring wall was not much bigger than the round wooden house within it. To shelter his animals, Brian had roofed over part of the space between the earthen wall and the back of the house.

Doyle's rath had once been about this size, before he built the new stone wall that trebled his space. She remembered seeing some of the remains of the old earthworks over by his spring-house.

Just outside the gate, young MacBrian was doing exactly what Doyle's slave had been doing. Shawna pulled up beside him and slid off. Her knees and thighs were so trembly weak she could barely stand. She wasn't used to this long riding.

"Well, lady!" Beaming like the morning sun, MacBrian ceased his chopping. "I see Doyle Dalainn has a new mare."

58

"Why must men always see the horse first?" She smiled. "Has Doyle been by today?"

"No, lady. I've not seen him since—" he hesitated "—since our last trip out to Lambay."

"Ah. Then he must be somewhere else." She made as if to mount again, then turned back. "Perhaps you can tell me. You were there. It weighs on me painfully, not knowing the truth of what happened to Brenna and my mother and sister-in-law. Were they—you know—butchered? Or worse? Or . . ." She let her voice trail off.

He wagged his head. "Of Brenna—she's the dark-haired beauty, right?—I know not. I didn't see any such girl. I don't know your mother to see her, though my father did. An older woman was among those murdered. I suppose that would be she. That was the only woman we buried."

"How was she killed? Please tell me."

He waved the hand that did not hold his ax. "She was felled with a broad ax. One blow. They left her in the doorway of her house." He shook his head. "They didn't do anything really pagan. I mean—except kill her, of course, which is pagan. And they killed your old monk, which was very pagan, for sure. But I mean . . ." His inarticulation dissolved into a helpless shrug.

"Nothing really unspeakable, though."

"No. Nothing like that. I've seen worse desecrations in Erse raids."

"And you didn't see Brenna or Peggy. A pretty blonde woman a few years older than I."

He shook his head.

"My father and brothers. Were they beheaded?"

"No, lady. The pagans don't seem too interested in heads."

"What did they seem interested in?"

"Not cattle. You know my father is one of the best trackers on the coast, and myself am not too bad, either. When we arrived with that second party—after we buried—" the words seemed to come very hard for him "—anyway, there were no cattle in your paddocks, except for a few starving old family favorites. You know, cattle too scrawny and aged to keep except that you've grown fond of them.

"So my father and I tracked the fat cattle, to see where they had gone. They had been driven east."

"Not to the ships on the north shore, but to our precious neighbors."

"Aye. Doyle says we'll bring the Lambay cattle over to the mainland this fall. Sometime there's good weather for the crossing, after they've fattened over the summer. Swim them across, I suppose. And he wants to wait until Connleigh has healed up."

"The island doesn't support many cattle, what with sheep as well. We deliberately kept the numbers down so they'd stay strong and healthy. Sure and they'll make the swim in fine condition."

"Some nice animals there."

"Indeed. MacBrian, I appreciate your help. You've set my mind greatly at ease. As much as possible, I mean." She took her leave then, with further effusive thanks and God's blessings, and swung aboard the mare.

With the long summer evening, she had plenty of time to return, so she kept the mare to a walk, the better to ponder these things. Why did Doyle lie like that?

And where were Peggy and Brenna?

6

The Fox in the Henhouse

That fox had better know that three score years on this earth had not dimmed her eye or stayed her hand one bit. With confidence in her hand and murder in her eye, Ceirre of the Liffey hiked up her skirts, hefted her battle-ax, and crept around the corner of the chicken coop.

The fox pelts on my pallet keeping me warm at night came from chicken thieves just like you. Show your pointy nose, you little red devil.

So what if she was past sixty years? She'd lost count of exactly how far past, during an illness a few years ago. So what if she was tiny and wasted with age and a little hunched? The muscles that remained worked just fine, thank you.

Ceirre listened to her chickens mutter and squawk, disturbed on their roost but too sleepy to make much fuss. The door of the coop creaked as it scraped open.

Eh?

What fox opens the door?

Deftly, she rotated the ax a quarter turn. If it was a man, she'd strike with the flat. No sense killing a man over a chicken or two, though men killed each other for less. She saw movement.

"Hah!" She swung mightily. The flat of her blade connected with the fellow dead on. That didn't surprise her. She rarely missed. "Take that! Steal a poor old woman's chickens, will you?"

By the haze-filtered moonlight she saw the man go sprawling. Four of her chickens (and not her best ones either—the dolt had no eye for quality) fluttered in confusion out from under his arms. She raised her blade again, but she didn't need it. Barely conscious, the thief moaned discordantly and made a few random flaps with his hands.

"Paul! Fetch that thatching cord!" She rather looked forward to walloping this cheeky fool again, but he gave her no cause.

When little Paul arrived with the cord he still mumbled incoherently.

"Bind him well." She raised her voice. "Peadar? Bring light. Let's see what we have here." With her toe she helped Paul roll the fellow to his belly. The lad was strong for his age—ten or about. He bound the fellow's wrists so tightly Ceirre knew his hands would soon turn purple.

Tiny Peadar, a charming elf of a lad, came trundling out with a torch. Ceirre smiled. The boy was nearly back to full strength. For a brief moment she called up the fond memory of finding the frigid little child on the shore as she gathered seaweed, of how she had stripped off his sopping wet clothes right on the spot, of how she pressed his chilled body against her front, skin to skin, and wrapped him and her together in her woolen shawls. For half a day she held the child thus, until enough warmth returned that he could speak without slurring.

And Paul. Quick, willing, clever Paul. Paul she had found only a few minutes after discovering Peadar. Paul she placed hard by her little gorse fire and turned him every few minutes, like a roast on a spit, until he could drink honeyed goat's milk without choking. Everyone knows that when a body is very, very cold, that body risks death if you let it warm up one-side-toward-the-fire constantly.

The Lord God works in strange ways indeed. Rarely did she venture north of Dublin Crossing, but that day she had gone several miles beyond her usual range, across the Liffey and north along the coast into the lands of the Dalainn.

Peadar stared at the thief. Fear washed across his face. "Auntie Ceirre! It's one of them! One of the Northmen! He was aboard that ship. I saw him."

"It's true." Paul bobbed his head vigorously. "The dragon ship that breathed fire."

The thief's wits were returning—not that he had many to start with. He looked, wide-eyed, from face to face. He stared at the battle-ax waving above him.

Ceirre snorted. "Well, we can rest assured your companions are nowhere near, or you'd not be sneaking into my coop like this."

He replied, trembling, with something that sounded like "scuille."

She discerned then that much of his trembling was probably born of cold rather than fear. His shirt looked damp from the drizzle earlier this evening, and he had no warm cloak. Besides, he seemed extremely small and scrawny. Small people get cold easier. "Lead him into the house, lads."

Peadar and Paul tugged, and the man lurched to his feet. Inside the little stone cottage, the thief looked just as spare and wiry as had been her first impression. He was dirty, but not too dirty. His body smell was pretty well subdued—she had not detected man-smell in the chicken shed. He must wash fairly frequently.

She gauged the stubble on his face. If he were normally clean shaven, he probably had last shaved the same day she found the boys.

He flopped down cross-legged beside her fire unbidden and closed his eyes. For long minutes he drew in air, half a smile on his lips, savoring the warmth.

Ceirre plopped down on her stool, balanced her ax across her knees, and studied him. She looked at Paul. "And what did our Lord Jesus say about treating our enemies?"

Paul frowned. "To heap burning coals upon their heads. I don't think he's that cold, do you?"

"Nay, lad, Jesus said to do them good."

"I remember now. But Auntie Ceirre—" Paul grimaced "—I suppose we must. Sure and he is the enemy. But he's a murderer."

"The very best kind of enemy. You'd not want an enemy who's only half bad. You want a real one—all bad. Then the rewards are correspondingly greater, you see. You and Peadar feed him some of that lamb and barley stew in the pot, and we'll let him sleep near the fire tonight. Tomorrow we shall go a-traveling."

Peadar crawled up into her lap. "Where to? Back home to Lambay?"

"Up the road but a few miles, to the rath of Doyle Dalainn. I've no time to sit and mind a prisoner all day and all night. We'll give him over to the Dalainn and let them take the bother."

* * *

63

The Wolf as a beast of burden. Unthinkable! Ulf plodded patiently through the mud in an endless circle, turning the little grist mill behind the main house. His dark wool pants and blue tunic were getting pretty dirty. He'd have to figure how to do laundry one of these days. He still wore chains, but that was unnecessary. He had no plans to escape until Hegaard or some others brought a ship close enough to escape in. To live off the land, a fugitive on this foreign soil, did not appeal to him.

He had to give these Celts this much: they paid no mind to his one short leg. No teasing, no notice at all. For the first time in his life, Wolf felt normal and accepted.

The girl, seated nearby on a boulder, put aside her spindle and stood up. He stopped and leaned upon the heavy wooden bar as she emptied the barley meal from its iron pot at the bottom back into the top of the stone, to grind again. Why not have the finest barley meal, so long as it's not you who has to turn the stone?

He now knew her name was Sjana, or something of the sort. If he was going to be here awhile he ought to learn the tongue. Surely it couldn't be very extensive or complex. These were a simple people, farmers, and no doubt possessed a simple language. A few guttural phrases, and he'd be conversant with them. It would help matters a lot.

She returned to her seat, and he recommenced his endless walk around the ring, leaning into the bar. She began singing, a strange, haunting melody with words he could not fathom. He did discern this, though: the language in which she sang was not the language she spoke.

The Norse did not go much for music, as witness Hegaard's pitiful attempts, the way these Celts did. Ah, but telling a story—there his people of the Northland truly shone. These Celts probably wouldn't know a good story if you shouted it in their ear. Primitives. Unrefined.

He stopped again when she stood, and waited while she gathered the ground meal and poured new grain down the hole.

He reached out suddenly and caught a few grains. He rolled them between his fingers and watched her face. "Barley."

She said, "Barley," and spoke her word. He mimicked it. It didn't sound quite the same, but it was a start. A good start.

He pointed to the pot on the ground. "Barley meal." He mimed ripping off a piece of bread and chewing it. "Barleycake."

Her blue eyes danced. She repeated her words until he got them right. Well, nearly so.

"Ulf." He pressed his hands to his breast. "Ulf Arildson. Ulf."

"Ulf. Ulf. Shawna."

"Sjana."

"Shaw-na."

"Shh-yahna." Why did his tongue not lilt as hers did? These Celts' tongues performed gymnastics as they spoke.

The lesson went on.

"Millstones."

"Chain."

Laughing, "Mud."

The language lesson ended, and the grinding began again. He turned the words over and over in his mind, committing them to memory.

Then at the far side of the farm's ring-shaped wall, by the gate, a child called the girl's name.

Wolf looked up and gaped. *"Skule!"* It burst out of him before he realized it.

In through the gate, a doddering old woman with a battle-ax was driving Skule ahead of her on the end of a rope. From behind her skirts, two small boys came running. The girl leaped up, snatched her skirts out of the way of her legs and flew to the children. Wolf recognized them as the two boys in the little boat with her that day. Joyously the three wrapped themselves around each other in one massive, knotted hug.

Wolf left the millstone to its own devices and hurried over. "Skule! What of Thole and Jargen?"

"I don't know. I came ashore several leagues south of a rocky head. I was doing fine scavenging, until a band of warriors found me and subdued me. They left this hag to bring me here."

Much as he rejoiced to see his cousin, Wolf's eye and ear could not leave the girl. Her legs folded on the ground beneath her, she clutched the lads and kissed them and clutched some more. She was sobbing, for joy this time. He smiled. High time she found some joy in her life!

She moved forward onto her knees, raised her arms toward heaven and spoke not in the tongue to which his ear was becoming accustomed but in that language of song. Clearly she was offering extensive and exuberant thanks.

What was this? Did not her gods even speak her own tongue? But then, she seemed fluent in the gods' tongue, so it probably did not matter.

Her gods thoroughly thanked, she leaped up to embrace the crone. All babbled excitedly.

"What say?" Wolf asked. "Do you think Hegaard will be back for us soon?"

Skule snorted. "I don't think Hegaard will be back at all. We are expendable, my dear cousin. When has either of our fathers ever taken us seriously? A fool and a cripple."

"Wisely spoken, fool. Particularly when you factor in the loss of the ship. Besides, the only way Hegaard would know we survived and are here would be by exploring the area. And that he will not do. Strike and fly is his sole battle tactic. The only way we shall see home again will be to get there on our own."

Skule smiled grimly. "Not in the sorry skin boats of these people. Have you seen them?"

"Seen them? I've handled them. Extremely responsive. Maneuverable. Totally unseaworthy. They fill up with water at the slightest opportunity. I could make a better boat by hollowing out an apple."

Skule dipped his head eastward. "Now who is this?"

Wolf looked off toward the great, dark, burly man entering the east gate on his dun stallion. "The master of this farm and a jarl in the area. Your new owner."

"An ugly ring to it, that. When shall we break for freedom?"

"I don't know. You know what it's like out there. You've been foraging for some days. Can we make it through the winter?"

"Depends, I suppose, on just whose chicken coop we raid."

"I'm of a mind to remain until spring, unless our ships, or others, return and give us clear opportunity."

Until Skule arrived, Wolf had not considered the future much. He had glibly assumed his rescue and restoration, one way or another. This discussion redirected and crystallized his thinking. For the first time a hideous thought forced itself into his head:

Quite probably, he would never see home again.

* * *

Hegaard Broad Back did not become Jarl of East End only through inheritance or strength of arm but by means of his persuasive diplomacy. It was strictly through his careful tongue that he managed to unite the squabbling fishermen of the East End into a single jarldom under his hand. Without himself investing anything, he had diplomatically obtained the use of a ship.

The ship given him was not the ship they lost. That had been Arild Thick Knee's. And it was Arild's son and nephew lost with her. Hegaard could not balance those losses with booty, but he could ease their sting. More diplomacy.

He stood at the bow of the *Swift Lynx* and simply drank in the pleasure of the day. Already they had slipped past the familiar rocky point of Land's End, up into home fjord. A gentle southerly breeze shoved them forward. With the sail out, not only did their homecoming appear more impressive, it was a lot less work. Men shouldered each other along the gunwales, watching the mountains of home glide past.

The few hardwoods among the forests were turning color, splashes of yellow within the dark green. No snow yet softened the steep mountains to either side. The village had enjoyed a mild summer. Good. Good. Two ravens circled between ship and shore, dipping and gliding on the invisible breeze. Perfect day.

Squeezing in beside Hegaard, Jorn blew his trumpet. The hoot echoed off the mountains, giving the crags voice to welcome the homecoming heroes. Minutes later, a trumpet returned the call from ashore. Downwind of *Swift Lynx*, *Fierce-cutting Blade* sent out her own trumpet blast.

Jorn smiled. He didn't have to say how good it was to be home. His little round face behind the unruly gray beard, his stocky body, his vibrant energy all bespoke it. "Think Arild will like his present?"

Hegaard shrugged. "I've known Arild for years, and I still can't anticipate his tastes. I know better than to come home without the son unless I've some fancy prize, but whether he considers it fancy is always a gamble."

"Eclectic tastes, eh?"

Hegaard snorted. "The heart of a child who loves silly baubles and the head of the finest political organizer the North has ever seen. How do you gauge the preferences of a person so diverse?"

"Good taste in women," Jorn commented idly. His attention was held not by the conversation at hand but by the distant roofs of home.

"Always." And the roofs reached out to seize Hegaard as well.

7

Ritual and Union

Ailan of the Two Dimples didn't consider it strange in the least that he carried a skin of sea water and a skin of buttermilk with him in his travels. Mahon of Armagh, on the other hand, thought Ailan was mad, and said so. Probably that was because Mahon never watched Ailan take a bath.

Every few days, when Ailan bathed and washed his hair in some stream, he would pour buttermilk on his head and let it soak a few minutes. Then he would rinse that out and soak his hair thoroughly in seawater. He had heard of women in the ancient classical days bathing in buttermilk to make their white skin whiter, and he knew that seawater plus sunlight bleaches. That's how you make woven linen brighter. Ailan's hair was already the pale blond that you read about the Celts of olden times having. But those Celts of old bleached their hair even whiter, for beauty. Therefore, so did Ailan.

They journeyed now under a pearlescent overcast sky, Ailan and Mahon, headed north along the base of massive hills. To their right, the dark, unbroken forests poured down off the mountains and lapped nearly at the edge of the track itself. To their left, cattle grazed in broad, green clearings. They passed a herd of swine feeding in the distance, so there was surely a rath nearby. Swine made Ailan nervous. Vicious things. Would that pigs could be tamed and domesticated in the same way as cattle or sheep.

The track climbed toward the mountains a bit in order to skirt boggy land, but their feet slipped in soft mud anyway.

The mountains called to Ailan. Or was it the forests summoning his heart? Ailan knew Mahon loathed wildwood, because he said so more than once. Ailan loved it. He didn't mind the tangle of the forest edge, where brambles raked at your ankles and thickets of holly and hazel hindered your way. It was worth fighting through that to reach the forest depths, for the forest heart was where the true grandeur was found.

In the forest depths, the understory was limited to a few little green and sallow bushes. The giant trees blocked out much of the sunlight. Ailan had never been too fond of sun. It gave light with which to see, but the darkness gave peace in which to dream. Sure and dreaming was by far the better part of seeing.

The towering oaks with their knotted roots intrigued Ailan most. Some forked low, spreading their dark branches out head high. Others shot straight upward. Mistletoe crowded itself into the branches and crotches of the lucky ones. Soft, feathery rowan, spreading elm and somber yew, water-loving alder and birch— each spoke to Ailan in a different voice.

Mahon stopped in mid-stride. Fortunately, Ailan had long since learned not to follow too closely. The old abbot stood stock still, his head high. He turned northwest. "We shall go visit the Bevan." He left the track abruptly and headed off to the west, down into the boggy land.

Ailan shifted his load (and a heavy load it was, with their book, their baggage, and his buttermilk and seawater). He heaved a sigh and followed after, struggling across the heath. "Why not Glendalough? We'd not have to cross the river again."

"The word of God which just came to me did not say Glenda-lough."

Pity. Ailan enjoyed visiting Glendalough, tucked lovingly away in the folds of the wooded hills. Bevan's rath and its attendant church perched not only in the very middle of a vast expanse of treeless pastures but also on the wrong side of the Liffey. They had already crossed the river more than once on this trip. If Mahon received a call from on high to visit the Bevan, why didn't he get it before they crossed the river this last time? Now they had to go back.

Hours later they pushed through dense alder thickets to the river's edge.

"What do you think? Shall we swim it?" Mahon always said that at rivers' edges. He didn't seem to mind plunging into any stream.

"Not here. Too deep and swift." Ailan always replied that. He abhorred getting totally soaked. One froze for hours afterwards, even in the balmiest weather.

"Very well. Then let's seek a farmer with a boat." Mahon always said that too, though you could tell he would rather just swim it and be done.

"What's that?" Ailan tipped his head up to listen better.

"What's what?" Mahon's ears were getting as old as his wrinkled face.

"Merriment, it would seem. That way." Ailan pointed west to the far shore.

"Rarely is there merriment without food and ale. Let us investigate." Mahon might not be worth much at catching chickens, but he did use brilliant common sense when it came to already prepared food. His bulging belly attested to that.

Ailan struggled behind him along the water's edge and twice very nearly slid in.

Mahon stopped. "Now I hear them." The two travelers seemed to be directly across the river from distant laughter in full swing beyond a grove of hawthorn and alder. Mahon called out.

From beyond the river came an answering voice. A man stepped out to the edge carrying a bow and arrows. The Erse as a rule preferred spears and javelins.

"Mahon of Armagh."

The fellow across the way disappeared into the trees. Moments later, a big, burly man appeared. His voice boomed, "We're sending a horse over for you. Welcome to join us!"

"With pleasure, Doyle Dalainn." Mahon dropped his voice to normal pitch. "You've not met the Dalainn yet. Ri of ris. Powerful, powerful family. The eldest son is a clever scholar. I keep hoping he'll enter the ranks of the Lord, but he seems destined more to follow his father's warring ways. Not that there's any difficulty with that. It's just that the church could use a man with his talents."

A man on a sturdy little bay came riding out of the trees with a great dun horse in tow. He rode directly down into the water. The horses lunged and thrashed. Watching horses cross a heavy stream was always interesting.

The bay emerged onto the east shore here, dropped its head, and shook mightily. The fellow bobbed around in place on its back. Mahon greeted the rider as "Fairleigh."

Ailan handed his burden off to Fairleigh and gave Mahon a boost up onto the dun stallion. The two of them rode immediately down into the water.

Ailan watched them cross. They rode into the trees. Ailan waited. And waited. It finally dawned on him that when this Dalainn said he would send a horse across for Mahon, that's what he did and only what he did.

Why didn't Mahon request a horse for Ailan? Because Mahon did not hesitate to swim across rivers and never did grasp the fact that Ailan did. That was why. It would not occur to the odd little man. Resigned at last to his fate, Ailan waded out into the frigid water, following the sound of laughter and happy speech. He slogged into the camp drenched from tip to toe.

But what a camp it was! Two hogs roasted on a spit. The fire beneath them leaped and crackled as their fat dripped into it. Ailan saw the skins stretched between two trees. They were not wild boars. Someone had just donated two pigs to the ri of ris and probably didn't even know it.

A dozen warriors sat about, formidable-looking men. They sprawled in the moss at the bases of oaks or squatted cross-legged closer the fire. In anticipation of dinner they were tearing hunks off great loaves of barleycake and waving their drinking horns about as they talked.

"Here he is! What took you so long, lad?" His mouth full of bread, Mahon dragged Ailan over to the ri of ris and made the presentation.

Ailan paid the proper respects due a ri and backed away. He didn't feel comfortable here, the way Mahon obviously did. These men were not his kind.

And over by a gnarled oak he saw another who was not his kind. Ailan ripped himself off a chunk from Mahon's barleyloaf and walked over to the strange young man.

The fellow was chained to the oak as if he were a dangerous bull, but he was a slim youth and wiry, shorter than average. He didn't appear terribly dangerous. He wore a wool tunic and pants, but somehow they did not look Celtic. He was blond, but his features did not seem Celtic.

"Ailan of the Two Dimples."

The fellow glanced at one of the Dalainn retainers nearby, as if for a cue, and snarled like a dog at Ailan. His keeper tossed him a chunk of bread and told him to be quiet. With manacled hands he grabbed his bread. He backed away from Ailan and curled up comfortably at the base of the oak. Methodically he ripped his crust of bread apart and ate it.

Ailan looked to the keeper for explanation.

The fellow grimaced. "You heard of the hordes who pillaged Lindesfarne."

"I've heard of nothing else on our travels."

"This is one of them."

Ailan took a hard second look at the fiend. "From the tales, I pictured them eight feet high. This fellow would fit in a grain basket."

"He's the runt. The others are eight feet high."

This man chained to an oak was not in the least what Ailan had imagined. His snarl didn't even sound sincere. Ailan turned away and crossed to Mahon. He stopped cold. The old gentleman was gaping at Doyle Dalainn, and tears ran down his cheeks!

Mahon wagged his head. "All, Doyle?"

"The monk killed, the rath pillaged and torched, the cattle and sheep lying about with bloated bellies, their legs sticking straight out. The scene was beyond description. I don't know where they went once they left Lambay. I will, though, offer any amount that they'll be back, somewhere around here."

Mahon looked at Ailan with sad, hurting eyes. "This is distressing. So distressing. Lambay, where we were going to take the book. It's been sacked." He wiped his cheeks, paused staring at the fire a few moments, and crossed himself. "Ah well. The book will be a nice gift to Connleigh to speed his recovery. Connleigh is Doyle's eldest, injured in a skirmish."

Lambay. The island. Mahon was sad, and Ailan could understand that, but in a perverse way, Ailan felt happy. Now they didn't have to go there. He hated islands.

The cook declared the pigs ready. Doyle sent four men out into the woods, Ailan knew not where. Moments later, four other men came into the glade. They had changed the guard. Ailan kept forgetting this was a war party. Of course they would keep watches. No doubt the camp had known Ailan and Mahon were approaching on the far rivershore even before Ailan heard their voices.

The pork tasted superb. Was the luckless Northman allowed pork? Ailan twisted around to see. He was. And with exaggerated gestures he was talking to his keeper. Therefore, he knew Erse. Fascinating!

Ailan cut a chunk of pork off a pig's neck and stepped behind Mahon. Instead of sitting, he continued over to the Norse fiend. He sawed his meat in two and extended his arm, offering half to the Northman. "You may snarl if you wish, Northman, but I no longer believe you."

The fellow stared at him a moment, apparently translating, for his lips moved. He burst into a cackling laugh and took the chunk of meat.

Ailan sat down just beyond chain range. "I told you my name's Ailan. What's yours?"

"Skule. It means 'hide.' What means 'Ailan'?"

"'Handsome. Comely.' So why do you snarl? Is that a custom in your land?"

Skule chuckled. "I make—uh—dog noise, act bad—uh—and they—uh—give me more food." He spoke haltingly, choosing words with difficulty. He grinned. "They happy, I happy."

"Are you a Christian?"

"Christian!" Skule blurted something in a lilting alien tongue. The answer, obviously, was no.

And if he was not a Christian, that meant he was a disciple of Druidism in some degree or other. Suddenly, Ailan found himself inexplicably furious. And the more he thought about it, the more he realized his fury was directed not at the Norse fiend, or even this Dalainn party, but at all men who falsely called themselves people of Christ.

How many years had Christianity been around? Less than eight hundred altogether. Druidism enjoyed a history many centuries longer and richer. How did Mahon and all these others know that Christianity was the true faith? It certainly had not stood the test of time, as had Druidism. And now here they were treating like an animal a man of the old faith, the traditional faith, a man who had done nothing more than what the "Christian" Erse did to each other all the time—plunder and pillage.

If in the name of Christ the Celtic chieftains attacked each other, why did they condemn this fellow for the same thing? Because he was not doing it in the name of Christ, obviously.

"Ailan!" Mahon's voice interrupted his train of thought again, as it did so frequently. "Glinn here is sharpening tools and weapons. Fetch our ax, will you?"

The ax. Ailan lurched to his feet and walked over to their little pile of dunnage. He dug into the pack. The ax should be here with the iron rod they used as a spit when cooking on the track. It should be with the butcher knife.

It was not.

Reluctantly he crossed to Mahon, because he knew what was coming next. He announced, "Our ax lies in the track somewhere between here and Kildare."

Mahon wagged his head. "And a gift from the Abbot of Kells. I cherished that ax. When did you last see it?"

Ailan thought a moment. "You beheaded that chicken. Did you leave it in the block?"

"I didn't pack it. Did you?"

"I don't remember doing it. No."

"Wonderful!" Mahon brightened. "Then it's still at Kildare, and we are now on the west side of the river. I shall go on to Bevan's, and you shall go back to Kildare in quest of the ax. It's an easy day's trip. If it's not at Kildare, return the way we came, crossing the river and stopping at Seven Birches, just in case. Then meet me at Bevan's. If I'm not there I'll be waiting for you at Dublin Crossing."

And that was the end of it. Ailan had no recourse, no voice. He was chained just as surely as was Skule, but his chains were invisible. As assistant and disciple of Mahon, he did what he was told and learned what was put before him to learn.

And so it would always be, he mused as he lay awake that night. For nearly two years now he had followed Mahon faithfully, and he was as much a slave, a child, as he had always been. Two years, and no advancement. He thought of the men more powerful than he who aspired to the seat at Armagh. Not only was he powerless now, but he always would be. He had no resources with which to compete with such men. And as long as Mahon needed an assistant, which was forever, Ailan was bound to him.

How bleak is the future for a man of faith.

He left for Kildare at first light, but it was nearly midday before he arrived. The abbess, her bishop-ness, gave him Mahon's ax, fed him a dinner of lamb and stir-about, and sent him on his way with blessings.

Hollow blessings. Were Ailan actually blessed, he would not have had to come back all this way.

He walked down off the hill from Cill-Dara, the church of the oaks, among oak stumps and open leas. Disgusting, what Christians, so-called men of God, did to the land. How to heal the land? Return to the old ways, to the Druidism wherein trees were revered and nature respected. That was how.

Churchmen all over Christendom were claiming that the attacks of the Danes were a warning of God's wrath, a punishment. What if they were right, but it was not the Christian god? What if it were the old powers of Druidism, having given Christianity a chance and seen it fail miserably, warning Erin to return to her old ways? What if Christianity were strictly a temporary ascendancy, and the past was returning?

His thoughts were interrupted not by Mahon this time but by that girl, the laundress. He recognized her by the plump, round form and the rope of blonde, stringy hair braided down her back. She walked along the road in the same direction as he, a couple hundred yards ahead of him. He first saw her as he rounded a bend along a thorn hedge. She strolled the track with a bundle on her shoulder and all the time in the world, it appeared.

Ailan hastened his step and caught up with her. He fell in beside and matched his stride to hers. "Laundry done for the day?"

She looked him over. "You haven't shaved your hair off yet, I see."

"Nor shall I." Ailan's head was spinning. Nor would he! Until that response spilled out of him unbidden, he had not realized the conclusion of his thoughts. He must proceed carefully now.

"My name is Ailan of the Two Dimples."

"Two Dimples." She grinned at him. "And your father—he had but one dimple?"

Ailan felt his cheeks turn warm. "There were two of us born within a month of each other—myself and a cousin—and our fathers christened us both Ailan, each not knowing what the other did. Too, we were both towheads and looked much alike to the casual eye. So they kept us straight with details. I had two dimples. Ailan of the One Dimple, also known as Ailan Cowlick, was a farmer near Shannon cross. He died in a skirmish a couple years ago."

"Too bad, if he resembled you."

"What is your name?"

"Fiona. "

"No identifying epithet? Not even Two Dimples?"

She smirked. "Me mum never gave me one."

"Mmm. Tell me, Fiona. Are you a Christian?"

She hesitated in her walk and twisted to study him. "Now why would you ask that?"

"It's important. Extremely important. Speak your heart. The truth."

She shrugged casually. "According to the Abbess of Kildare, I'm not."

"Explain. Please."

"Not much to explain. Me mum sent me to the convent. But the abbess there didn't like me and made trouble for me. Then she sent me out, saying I had not the makings of a decent nun. Not that it matters to me one way or another, nor to me mum either, I suppose."

Her voice rolled on, cool and seemingly unconcerned, but Ailan was sure he could hear the hurt in it.

"Might you perchance be a priestess of Druidism?"

She looked at him and wrinkled her nose. "How so?"

"Do you like the wildwood, natural things? Brooks and streams, rocks and birds and wild things?"

"Well enough, mostly so long as I don't have to do laundry in them."

"You probably wonder why I'm asking you this." Actually, Ailan wondered himself, until he got his thoughts lined up. But the more he thought about it, the more he realized where power lay. Erin, vexed by the Northmen such as that Skule who were instruments of the druidic gods, would sooner or later see the cause of her ills. She would need a leader to bring her out of the eclipsing Christian cult and back to her roots. That leader, the new Patrick of Erin, would hold the power then. He must be a leader who understood the druidic beliefs, the Brehon law, the mood of the people.

Ailan didn't know much yet about Druidism. Under Mahon's tight hand, he had little opportunity to study anything other than Christian beliefs, though he'd picked up a few things here and there. He had a lot of catching up to do in that area. But he understood the essence of it. And the gods would surely honor his eagerness to learn by teaching him, through vision if nothing else.

Fiona didn't seem to wonder about his questions, because she didn't ask or press the point. She simply walked along as if he were not there. Yet he could feel her presence beside him, warm and plump, and she surely felt his nearness as well.

He must make it all sound delightful, as indeed it was. "Would you like to become a druid priestess?"

"What would I have to do?"

"Learn the ways. Participate in the rituals. It would all be very pleasant. There's a grace to it, a oneness with nature, that is absolutely exhilarating."

She shrugged. "Like what rituals?"

"Oh, dedicating sacred groves. They've been pretty much abandoned and would have to be found and restored. And calling on the gods to reclaim the land."

"I don't like building wattle and daub. When I try to weave withes, I keep getting hit with branch ends. And the mud is such a mess."

"No building at all."

"You sure?"

"Absolutely! Druidic worship takes place within nature, not in buildings of any sort. Buildings separate us from nature. There will be a focal point that draws the energy to you—a particular stone, a tree, whatever—in an opening within the forest."

"You do all this in the greenwood."

She obviously knew nothing about Druidism, but then few people did.

He couldn't hold that against her. "The goddess of each local area, you see, is the manifestation of the greater divinity, the over-all sacred being. So we go into each area and reestablish the local gods and goddesses. It will be exciting work."

"Just pray to them?"

"Prayer, yes. And doing ritual things, like forming a chain and dancing through the forest." Ailan licked his lips. "And ritual union, representing the unity of man with nature."

"Ritual union." She said it like she might say the word *robbery*, or *pillage*. "What's that? You mean, you and me?"

He nodded, suddenly feeling very shy and uncertain.

"So that's what you call it, huh? Ritual union." She smirked. "That's what got me on the outs with the abbess, was ritual union."

"It's a form of worship. The priestess embodies the spirit of the land, the goddess. She stands in the gods' stead, you see. She is Every God and Goddess. All that's Divine. And the priest represents all men. He is Every Man and Woman, seeking to be one with the earth. The union is a ceremonial thing, you know, and very effective. It's a physical representation of what mankind wants in his relationship with the earth and all that's in it."

She grunted. "I always receive gifts when I do a union."

Ailan had never encountered anything about gifts, but it seemed logical they'd be involved. "I have this ax. It's a fine ax, once owned by the Abbot of Kells and the Abbot of Armagh."

He handed it to her.

She looked it over as a farmer looks over a calf. She nodded. "All right. Where do you want your ritual union?"

The question stunned him. This was all happening too fast.

Yet it seemed so right. If he was going to absorb druidic power and wisdom he was going to have to get started with the rituals, and the sooner the better. To proceed, one must begin. No divine power would honor his hunger for wisdom if he didn't do his part.

They claimed that Kildare was the site of prior druidic activity—that it was a sacred grove for centuries before Brigid established her monastery there. So this whole area must be sacred. Any surviving grove or woodlot would work, surely. He remembered a wood of birch and alder less than a quarter mile ahead. The ground would be very mushy—alders always grow with their feet in water—but with the ax they could prepare some sort of raft of branches on the mud. That grove would do nicely.

He was about to tap into the strength of the earth itself, the power of storms and the sea, of wolves and wild boars, of love and hate. He was about to bring Erin from her abortive experiment with the Christian faith back into the true faith, the faith of her most distant ancestors. He was the new Patrick, the new leader, the new way, and the old way.

He had no idea of the specifics of a ceremony of this sort, a ritual union, and obviously Fiona was ignorant of anything druidic. They would just have to declare their good intentions and let the spirits lead. He would learn by doing.

Ailan of the Two Dimples was at last on his way to his true calling. He was about to become the new—and powerful—Patrick.

8

The Thing

Shawna decided as she watched Ceirre that she could learn something here. Ceirre did not stoop to rip flax from the ground. She didn't stand shaking the roots of each plant to get rid of the loose dirt. She simply tucked the stalks under her arms in passing and kept walking. They ripped out of the soil themselves as she moved beyond their height, and as the roots bounced along the ground they cleaned themselves.

For the system to work well, however, you needed to be short, with very strong arms and hands. The limbs of this aged woman could choke a cow. Shawna tried the Ceirre Method of Flax Harvesting a few minutes and went back to the old way.

The flax rustled behind her. She turned. Ulf was here. She frowned. He should be out fishing yet with Connleigh. The plan was that he would handle the boat, for Connleigh's wounds were slow to heal. She frowned harder. He had just adopted the Ceirre Method of Flax Harvesting, pulling up plants with the crook of his arm. And his cheery grin told her he, too, had just learned something new.

Still grinning, he snatched a plant out of the ground and raised it. He spoke its word.

"Flax." Shawna shaped the word slowly and clearly. He was not good at mimicking pronunciation, but heaven knew he tried.

He pointed to the plant and smoothed his hand across his wool shirt. He tugged at its hem.

Obviously he meant linen, not wool. They tossed a few more words back and forth. Shawna had to get him to repeat them.

In the loose dirt of a harvested row he smoothed out the soil and drew the outline of a boat. He looked at her.

"Curragh."

He repeated it a few times and gave her his word. He drew a longship in the soil, a fire-breathing dragon. He gave that a different word, something like "drakhar."

He said, "Curragh," a few more times as he returned to gathering flax. The man did gravitate toward boats.

Why did Muirgheal, Doyle Dalainn's wife, object at first when Shawna had asked to begin pulling flax? Muirgheal acted as if the plants were not ready yet. Surely she knew as well as anyone that if you let the spent flower heads go too long, the fiber became coarse and weak. This flax was more than ready. More than half the heads had yellowed.

A lot of things Muirgheal did, and did not do, irritated Shawna. The woman seemed so consumed by details, yet in the broad strokes of managing the farm she fell far short.

It was not Shawna's place to criticize. Shawna was a guest here, and not a permanent one. Let Muirgheal deal with life on her own terms. Shawna had problems of her own to think through.

Connleigh and three freemen were bringing the catch up. With Ulf and Ceirre pulling flax far faster than she could, Shawna was not needed. She hurried over to the path and fell in beside Connleigh. "Did you send the Northman ahead to help Ceirre and me?"

"So that's where he went. When he disappeared I wasn't at all sure this business of freeing our new slaves from their chains is a good idea."

"It is if he'll pull flax unbidden." She gestured toward Connleigh's netting bag. There had to be thirty pounds of fish there. "You did well."

"Better than well. Slevin and Keir are bringing the nets and two other bags of fish."

She walked beside him in silence, thinking of questions by the score and not daring to ask any of them. She did not want to appear to be unduly interested in the slave.

Was Ulf simply a good omen for the fishermen? She could not imagine so. He was pagan, an outlander. God would not thusly bless pagans. But then, the magi were pagans too, and look what He did with them.

Did Ulf have such a sure knowledge of the sea that he could see signs and minutiae and lead Connleigh to the fish? Irish fishermen read the sea, watching for disturbed surfaces where fish were feeding and reading the activities of seagulls. They knew to try one place over another. But Ulf seemed so much more attuned. She thought again of his skill in using the eddies to bring their curragh ashore. Of course, he was in that dragon ship that broke up—definite lack of sea sense there.

Or was it simply Connleigh's day to succeed well? Such days came on occasion, along with days when nothing entered the nets at all. One must never underestimate the effects of plain old luck.

They strolled into the compound at a leisurely gait. He moved slowly. Shawna shortened her stride to keep with him.

Connleigh dropped his net bag and flopped onto the tree-stump stool beside the door. He leaned back against the stone wall. "I guess I'm not as strong yet as I thought."

Shawna sat at his feet and drew her knees up so she could wrap her arms around them. What to say? She could think of nothing. Inanities did not seem in order, but one does not speak of profundities in a late afternoon. That is a thing to do before the fire on rainy nights.

Connleigh was studying her. "My father is thinking of adopting you and your nephews. Unless you plan to return to Lambay."

"No." She shook her head. "Not back to Lambay. I didn't tell you or your father about this. The man attempting to carry me off that day has wanted to marry me for two years now, but he couldn't make it through my brother gauntlet. The pagans provided him his chance."

And it was Ulf with his swinging chain who delivered me, but you failed to notice, and I didn't tell you that, either.

Connleigh smiled, bemused. "Your brother gauntlet?"

"You can't believe the barrels they made my suitors jump over, all of them. The Behr had that reputation anyway . . ." Her voice trailed off, strangled by the hurt. Yes, her three brothers were wild and boisterous, and yes, they often became a bit too possessive when it came to protecting their little sister. But it was their way of saying "love," and now they were gone. She had ranted at them so often for their brazen, boorish ways, but she never told them she loved them.

"Then I'm glad I never courted you. From the way you were struggling to escape, I take it the fellow was not your choice."

"A worse boor than my brothers."

"Have you considered marriage at all?"

"Only in a philosophical, abstract sort of way, I suppose." She twisted around to examine him more directly. Was he getting at what she thought he was getting at?

"That's true of me as well. The ideal wife, I think, would be smart, would love the Lord and love learning, and would appreciate the deeper meanings of the faith. I hadn't really found anyone. Until lately."

He was.

She watched his eyes, and he held hers. This may not be an invitation to marriage exactly, but it felt uncomfortably close to one. On the other hand, Shawna could do much worse than the son of the ri-ruirech, a man with power and an undisguised love of learning. He was one of the few men in the area who could both protect her well and nurture her interests.

She must proceed carefully, leaving all the doors open. "My life has been in turmoil, and I've not been able to think about much of anything. I believe it's time I started considering marriage less philosophically and more in its practical aspects. Don't you think?"

"And I shall also." He smiled. "I find it hard to think about practical things, sometimes. Now's the time, though." He cleared his throat. "So you will stay with the Dalainn?"

"We've nowhere to go and winter coming on."

Connleigh grunted. "You needn't make it sound quite so dreary and hopeless, eh?"

She looked up at him. He was still smiling, so he apparently wasn't taking it too wrongly. "I'm sorry."

"Don't be. I can imagine your world looks pretty dreary and hopeless just now."

She was going to return his smile, but she could not. Grief flooded her again, full force, and she bowed her head to her knees and wept.

* * *

What a glorious assemblage! Hegaard Broad Back loved a crowd, although he allowed that the next time he sailed, it would be a larger vessel with fewer men, and they'd land oftener. The

84

challenge of three boatloads of feisty men crammed into two longships—much too much of a crowd—was fading into memory now, and the spoils were here, to be displayed, distributed, and enjoyed.

And crowd it was, this meeting of the Thing, this last hurrah of gathering and trading before winter locked the Northland down. Freemen, farmers, craftsmen, and traders, with all the wives and children, gathered together in Arild's Great Meadow, drawn to the Thing. People of all sizes milled in the open sward, showing off their finery and trading gossip. Tent camps ringed the periphery, gray peaked teeth set closely together in the margins of the meadow. Dogs fought, children shrieked, nervous cattle lowed. It was altogether a splendid outing.

Here judgments were made, sentences meted, land transactions acknowledged, and disputes settled. Panels of freemen heard the cases that had accumulated since the last Thing—thefts, one murder, two accidental deaths with suspicious circumstances, and a couple of juicy adultery situations.

It was certainly not all work and no play. A lot of trading went on and some rip-rousing stallion fights. The leggy, graceful Irish horses Hegaard's crews had brought back proved worthless when it came to fighting, but their long, sleek lines drew a crowd anyway.

The Thing was entering its final hours, and among them would be Hegaard's finest hour. Arild convened the last assembly and turned it over to Hegaard.

Diplomacy. In sonorous, stilted phrases, Hegaard addressed the crowd. "More than once, my friends, has Arild Thick Knee told me, 'One can never be too rich or too lucky.' He tested luck to garner riches by building a longship and sending it forth to plunder."

Diplomacy. Hegaard failed to mention that Arild put his feckless, crippled son aboard her, to rid himself of the embarrassment and nuisance of the lad. Nor did he mention how very philosophically Arild took the news of Ulf's loss. Hegaard got the distinct impression that as far as the annals of Arild's ascendancy were concerned, a son lost during a raiding expedition sounded a lot better than a son gimping around town.

"Three ships voyaged fearlessly across open sea. They raised one landfall, then another, working their way to the lands of the Celts. But they did not strike Northumbria, the Faroes, the Hebrides, as others do. They turned southwesterly to raise a small island off an untouched coast. Lands that had never felt the savage hand of the North. Lands ripe with booty."

All gods and heroes, how he loved this! The throng was as quiet as he'd ever seen them. He recounted in gruesome detail that first raid, embellishing only when absolutely necessary. He merely hit the highlights of the subsequent raids on other coasts, lest he bore his audience.

He named Ulf, Thole, Skule, and Jargen, lost at sea. He named the seven lost in battle. Only seven, and all those skirmishes! All that plunder!

Diplomacy. Now for his pièce de résistance. He had already given the ships' owners, Arild and Thjorenson and the rest of the syndicate, their portion of the returns.

So they thought.

With the knowledge of the secondary commanders under him, he had withheld half of the booty until the Thing. Now, from his tents along the meadow's edge, his seconds in command brought forth more plunder, a wealth as great as that which they'd displayed when first they arrived. Even Arild's mouth dropped open.

Still more diplomacy. The gold and fine metalwork they presented not to the men but to their wives.

And last, Jorn brought out the dark-haired beauty and handed her off to Hegaard. Hegaard pulled her by the elbow to Arild's seat.

"The Celts are a funny, funny people." Hegaard rotated, addressing the crowd. "Would you believe that they're known to trade six slave girls for one cow." He pushed the girl to Arild's side. "Here you go, Arild Thick Knee. Five more of these, and perhaps you can buy a cow."

Hegaard basked in the waves of raucous laughter. But delicious as it was, the favor of the crowd did not concern him. The favor of the most powerful man in Trondelag did. Anxiously he watched his jarl's reaction out of the corner of his eye.

Arild was laughing as heartily as anyone. Indeed, the only person who failed to see the humor of it all was the dark-haired Celt. She tended to be a little pouty and stuffy anyway.

Arild's mirth subsided to a series of the deep, hearty chuckles that were his specialty. He studied his gift top to bottom. He grunted appreciatively.

"Unspoiled," Hegaard muttered. In a loud voice he boomed, "In gratitude for the opportunity you provided us, Jarl, a gift from your loyal warriors." Hegaard stepped back. His part was ended, and at an excellent point—at the crest of good will.

Applause, huzzahs, and general rioting indicated that the Thing was a bounding success. Trading and feasting would continue into the night, but on the morrow the participants would strike their tents and turn their sturdy little horses homeward.

Jorn sidled up to Hegaard and nodded toward Arild. "Beautiful coup, my friend. He couldn't like his gift better. Particularly to receive it publicly and unused."

"Let's hope this parlays into a vessel for a more extensive raid next spring."

Jorn nodded and paused. Then, "A bigger vessel. With fewer men. And we'll land oftener."

* * *

Time to go home. Ceirre gathered up her great bundle of line. Beside her in the shed, Ulf, the Dalainn's indefatigable slave, still worked away, scutching flax. He was working on last year's stored fiber, obviously. This year's crop, now retting in the pond, was not much greater than last year's flax stored here. If Ceirre was reading the signs rightly, the Dalainn had not even begun work on last year's stored crop until Shawna arrived.

But then, that was how Muirgheal was. She constantly did lots of things, yet got practically nothing done. If it weren't for Shawna, Muirgheal would probably have two years' worth of retted flax to process next year at this time.

This Ulf knew exactly how to break up the woody parts of the flax stems. He had obviously scutched flax a time or two. He beat it with the wooden blade against the scutching board with skill. Clearly, therefore, the Northmen wove linen even though this man's clothing was all wool. He did not have to be taught what to do.

And no one hackled like Shawna, except Ceirre herself. It was that final step, the combing of the fiber bundles, separating the long fibers, the line, from the short fibers, the tow, that made good linen. Shawna's finely hackled fiber would spin and weave into great linen.

Where was Shawna now? A couple hours ago the girl had stood awhile pondering a handful of tow and now she was off and about somewhere with a big wad of it.

Ceirre would have liked to bid the girl good-bye. She humped her load of line, the Dalainn's gift for helping with the flax harvest, and left the shed.

Ah! Here came Shawna.

"I'll be taking my leave now, child. God's blessing on you."

"Godspeed." The girl was a wonderful hugger. "Ceirre, are you sure you won't let me carry your burden home for you? Please?"

"When I'm too old to manage, I shall call upon you." Ceirre frowned at the white sewn pad in Shawna's hand. Gingerly she pinched it between two fingers. It was stuffed with tow, bulging nearly two inches thick. "What's that? A pillow for a leprechaun."

"No, Ceirre!" She laughed. "If you can spare another hour, come and watch." She stuck her head in the shed door. "Ulf?"

Instantly the young man appeared.

Speaking very slowly and distinctly, Shawna enunciated, "Come with me, please."

This looked too intriguing to ignore. Ceirre dropped her bundle of line and followed the two across ground made soggy by last night's rain. Winter would soon be hard upon them, though late this year, by the looks of things.

They trooped together to the smithy just inside the wall on the far west side. Glinn the smith presided over this end of the compound. He glared at life from behind a black beard, but his perpetual scowl masked a jolly, friendly nature. He was both saddler/leather-worker on this rath and the smith as well. His leather work was just as detailed and fine as his ironwork. An amazing man, to be so skilled.

Shawna handed Glinn her linen pad. "Is it deep enough?"

"Looks so." He nodded to Ulf. "Take off your boots."

Ulf stared at him, at Shawna. Frowning, he pointed to his foot. "Take off my boots?"

Shawna nodded.

"Take off my boots." His voice inflections amused Ceirre.

Resigned to whatever was, the young man sat down on the wet ground and pulled his boots off. The crippled foot looked every bit as normal as the good foot. That interested Ceirre. His limp, then, must come exclusively from the shortness of his left leg.

Shawna handed the boots to the saddler, and he whipped out a pair of new boots. They bent heads together, comparing the worn boots to the new pair. They did a lot of muttering and nodding.

The saddler shoved the thick pad down into a new boot and tossed the pair to the slave.

"Put them on," Shawna enunciated.

The slave held them. He studied them the way a child stares at the pen when first he learns to write.

Shawna explained to Ceirre, "I suggested just making him a boot with the sole much built up, but Glinn thought it would be too heavy. And too stiff. Glinn suggested building a regular boot big enough inside to accept a pad of some sort, and I thought of tow right away. You see how Glinn made the foot part of the one boot so much higher and roomier than normal, to accommodate it. Glinn is absolutely brilliant!"

Glinn glowed. "Sure and 'twas the lass's idea. Eh, look there!"

The slave lad was staring up at Shawna, transfixed, and then the murderous pagan's clear blue eyes turned wet. His mouth moved, chewing words, but none came out. Suddenly, even feverishly, he pulled those boots on—the oversized boot with the pad on his left foot—and stood up to face them. He stood proudly, evenly. The front part of the one boot was a couple of inches higher than its mate, to accommodate the pad, but if you weren't specifically looking at his feet, you probably wouldn't notice. Well, at least Shawna probably wouldn't notice.

Shawna jabbed Glinn's arm. "Look! His legs are the same size, essentially. His hips are level across when he stands!"

The lad took two steps and tipped drunkenly into the harness bench. He righted himself and tried again. He walked as a toddler walks, with tiny, halting steps.

He wagged his head, laughing, and burbled in that lilting language.

Glinn was laughing too. "Come on, lad. You're old enough to marry. High time you learned to walk, eh?" The two men stepped out into the compound, where Ulf had more room to lurch. Glinn coached, and Ulf commented, neither in a language the other knew.

Shawna started forward too, but Ceirre seized her arm. "I have a good nose, lass, that has not dulled with age. Indeed, time has made it all the sharper. It can smell trouble."

"Trouble?" If Shawna perceived what Ceirre was saying, she wasn't admitting it. "Ulf is now all the more valuable to the Dalainn. Hardly trouble."

"Life is meant to break your heart, but that doesn't mean you go out and invite the trouble in. I see his face when you come near him, and I see you come near him any chance you have. No, lass. Don't."

"I'm teaching him the language, and he's doing well. He understands it much better than he can manage it, but he's learning. He has to speak Gaelic sooner or later, if he remains with the Celts. And he will."

"'Tis far more than an exchange of words, and I prithee stay with your own kind. You know what God says. 'Do not be unevenly yoked to unbelievers.'" Ceirre raised a finger. "No argument. I've told you what I see and what I smell. Heed me." She patted the girl's shoulder. "Farewell, lass. I'm hieing myself homeward."

"Farewell."

Ceirre turned her back and hastened across the compound to the flax shed. Paul and Peadar were sweet, and her visit here profitable. A little work in the field with this year's crop and a bit of work in the shed with last year's, and she had earned enough line to keep her spinning and weaving into winter. But Ceirre was a woman of aloneness. She yearned to get back to her little cot, to the routine of chickens and firewood and rethatching the hen coop before the winter rains settled in in earnest. Enough of people!

She looked back as she left the Dalainn compound. In the broad, open avenue between the buildings, Ulf was practicing jumping up and down on one foot, and Shawna was watching from the saddler's shed. Suddenly Shawna raced forward to join the men, laughing. She demonstrated a simple jig. Glinn's booming "Haw haw!" floated across the compound as Ulf attempted with scant success to duplicate the demonstration.

Foolish girl. Foolish, foolish girl.

9

Swine

"Sorry you missed him," said Bevan of the Fat Mare. "He left this morning."

Bevan's house might be quite modest as size goes, but one couldn't fault its hospitality. Bevan was proud of that. Yesterday he had hosted no less a personage than Mahon of Armagh. And now, this pastoral assistant, Ailan, and a young lady of . . . well, he didn't really expect a young lady with the assistant. He wondered if Mahon knew about her.

They sat in Bevan's house, huddled before the fire. Midsummer though it was, a cold, dank rain had descended upon the area, thickening the sky and making the day chill. The pasture grass grew well in weather like this, but Bevan hated it all the same. He watched his wife turn the bream. The little fishes abounded in the quiet water of the slough behind his rath, and good thing. He was a poor man, with no sheep or cattle to spare when visitors came calling. Few people objected to bream with its mild and gentle flavor. Besides, fish made a nice change of diet.

"Dinner in just a few moments." Bevan continued. "Mahon said if his assistant showed up I was to send him on down to the ford. You know where that is."

Ailan nodded. His companion watched hungrily as the fishes turned on their spit. She moved in closer to the fire.

Out in the yard, a horse's hooves *splopped* to a halt by the door.

"Now who would that be?" Bevan crossed to the door and stepped outside.

A husky, blond young man, his sword flapping and flying at his side, nodded down to Bevan from his sturdy bay horse. "I bring you word from the ri-ruirech, Doyle Dalainn. He will be calling tomorrow. He's up at the Owney now, and he'll stop by here to talk to you on your way back to Dublin Crossing."

"I shall welcome him."

The young man grinned. "You've heard about the Northmen, I'm sure, the fiends that ravaged Lindesfarne."

"Who hasn't?"

"He has one with him. It'll be interesting."

A miserable thought struck Bevan. "How many in his retinue?"

"Sixteen."

"Sixteen." Bevan nodded. "A thousand welcomes to him. I look forward to seeing an actual fiend."

The lad hesitated a moment, wheeled his horse, and clattered out of the yard.

Bevan should have invited the young man in. He should have given the man a meal. But eight bream are barely enough for four persons, and adding a lusty youth to the group would have made more mouths than food.

Bevan stomped back inside.

"Is it still raining?" his wife asked.

Bevan had to step back outside to look. He was so exercised he hadn't noticed. He came in and settled by the fire. "Yes."

Young Ailan held his hands palm out toward the fire. "You look peeved. Or discouraged."

"The ri-ruirech appears here tomorrow with sixteen in his entourage."

His wife nearly dropped her carving knife. "How are we going to feed sixteen men? Doyle ate the boar the last time they were here. And if we kill the sow now we'll not have anything this winter."

Young Ailan wagged his head. "Too bad we don't live as the Erse used to."

"What do you mean?"

Bevan watched as his wife split two bream onto a bronze plate and graced them with a pat of butter. She added a ladle of peas and handed the plate to Ailan.

He crossed himself more or less automatically and then seemed to catch himself in the act, embarrassed. Strange.

Ailan watched his lady companion being served. "The old Brehon law, before Patrick. It required that a man traveling could request hospitality only from men of higher stature than himself. And even then there was a limit to things he could expect. Milk, cheese, and bread but not butter, meat, or ale, for instance. If the host wanted to supply them, of course, all well and good. But it wasn't expected."

"Now there's a law I like." Bevan accepted his own plate. A few more hospitality obligations like tomorrow's and they'd have scant peas to last the winter, either.

Ailan nodded. "The rich man cannot prey upon the poor man that way. It's sensible. In tune with human nature. Not like these days."

"You've been studying the old ways, I take it."

The youth bobbed his head. "As you know, I've been two years in the tutelage of Mahon, studying the Christian faith. In that time I've had many opportunities to compare it to prior ways. Doyle Dalainn—the ri—has a Northman with him, do you know that?"

"The young fellow said, yes."

"Punishment of God."

"So they say."

The intense young man momentarily abandoned his plate. His lady friend instantly reached over, speared a knifeblade of peas off it, and popped them in her mouth. "Let me tell you, Bevan, what I have found, based on my years of study."

* * *

When God spoke to Mahon, thunder rolled, sometimes. Other times, birds sang. Sometimes nothing happened at all. God was speaking now, but Mahon could not hear it. He felt a foreboding, a sadness, a darkness, but he could derive no voice, no specific message. He couldn't describe this oppression exactly or identify it clearly, but there was a weight upon him.

Perhaps something had happened to Ailan. Usually, inexplicable forebodings had to do with spiritual matters, but very rarely God would tell Mahon about some physical event. Ailan should have arrived here at the ford two days ago. What befell him?

Perhaps Mahon ought to backtrack and try to find Ailan. No, that wouldn't do. They would chase each other in circles if he started that. If something dreadful happened, Mahon would hear it at Armagh before he'd hear it on the road.

Doyle Dalainn was the power in this area. Mahon's best course of action would be to notify Doyle that Ailan was missing and let the ri investigate. Mahon would then return to Armagh and await word. Or Ailan. Whichever came first. Besides, he wanted to give this beautiful copy of John's gospel, the one that would have gone to the Behr, to Connleigh, and to talk to the lad. So he had to stop by the Dalainn anyway.

God have mercy on the souls of the Behr.

Mahon shifted to get rid of a hard lump under his shoulder-blade. He was lying on something discomforting—a stone, a tree root, a fallen branch. He stretched out anew on this grassy knoll above the ford. Blackbirds and thrushes busied themselves in the branches of the wood margin. Pipits waddled about in the grass of the riverbank. A falcon sketched casual circles across the open sky above the Liffey. The river was running high, because of all the rain these last two days. Its brown, rolling waters boiled across the shallows of the ford in wild, ceaseless patterns.

Why did Mahon not feel more at peace?

Grunting and snuffling, a herd of swine appeared out of the woodland on the far side of the river. They worked their way to the water's edge, groveling and exploring nose first. They squealed at each other and argued over goodies found. Swine don't get along together any better than do human beings. Mahon was heartily glad the pigs were over on the north side of the river. More than once he had been chased by swine.

The pigs spread out along the shore. One of them went mussel hunting. Mahon heard a hard shell crack now and then as the hog chomped down on a find. Mahon smiled. God gives to each of His creatures unique gifts, to swine no less than to people.

Mahon sat up. A traveler was approaching on the track across the river, coming down to the ford from the north. Mahon could not see details well at this distance, but the fellow looked to be a frail young man, hardly grown, and small for his age. He walked with a certain skittish nervousness. His stride and his body movements were jerky and quick. He carried a walkingstick and a bundle wrapped in a blanket and slung across his back.

Should Mahon yell to him? Too late. The young man had inadvertently wandered into the midst of the rooting hogs. Did he not hear them? But then, where would he go if he did? That stretch of track, from hill to rivershore, was devoid of trees.

Yes, he did hear them. He froze in place for a moment. His head twisted from side to side. The hogs turned their attention to him, their wiggling noses high. A couple of them, particularly the lead boar, took a few steps his way for a better sniff and view.

Mahon snatched up his big walking stick and ran toward the river's edge. "Into the water, lad!"

The traveler looked at Mahon. "I can't swim!"

Mahon plunged into the roiling river. "Come!"

The lad took two steps forward. The boar took three. And then the boar, its head low, shifted into a jiggling run. From the other side of the track a couple of the sows followed suit. Suddenly nearly the whole herd was converging upon the luckless fellow at a walk, at a trot.

The lad dropped his stick and burden. He raced to the river edge and plunged into the water. "Oh, dear God, help me!" he screamed.

Behind him the boar splashed down into the water.

The lad glanced back and struggled further out. He cried out again, panic-stricken.

Half swimming and half pushing himself along, Mahon worked his way across the ford. The river, nearly as high as it ever got, came almost to Mahon's armpits. The current came close to ripping him off his feet several times, for he carried his stick above his head, and that weakened his balance.

One of the sows ventured into water too deep. She squealed mightily as the freshet caught her and swept her downstream.

Mahon stretched out his walking stick, knob end first. "Grab on, lad!"

The young man hesitated only a moment. He leaned forward into the flood, stretching. He screamed as the water pulled him off his feet, but with a lunge and a grab his fingers wrapped around the knob.

Then Mahon was there. He snatched the traveler's icy hand just as the lad went under. The fellow bobbed back to the surface.

Mahon braced and hauled the lad in against himself.

The poor lad clung so desperately he nearly pulled Mahon off his feet. He sobbed with fear and babbled in excellent Latin with a Saxon accent, earnestly invoking God's help. "The swine—"

"They'll not venture into fast water beyond their bellies. You're safe out here. Come. Walk with me." Prudently, Mahon did not take his first step until the lad should loosen his hold.

The boy wagged his head and wailed. "I can't! It's too deep!"

"You can. I am with you. I won't let you drown. Come."

The young man kept protesting he could not, but he loosened enough to take a step. Gripping his hand tightly, Mahon led the way. He kept his stick on the downstream side and used it to brace against the current. A step at a time they crossed the ford, gripping each other as they went. The chilly water swirled brown around them.

Even when they reached shallows, the water knee high, the young man clung desperately. Suddenly he shook his grip loose from Mahon and ran forward, up out of the water onto the smooth south riverbank. He dropped to his knees and offered effusive thanks to God. He shifted instantly into a well articulated laudemus and then more thanksgiving. He could not be more than fifteen or sixteen. And whoever he was, he was monastery trained.

At length the young man ceased formal prayer and flopped around to sitting on the mud bank. He shuddered. "You are the Christ, sir."

"Hardly." Mahon flopped down beside him. "His servant, yes. Himself, not a bit."

"When you said 'I am with you.' And 'walk with me' . . . that was the word of God bidding me walk with Him. You saved me, sir. They would have rent me, or I would have drowned."

"Never confuse the ax with the woodsman who wields it. I am only the tool. But flattered, for all that."

On the far shore the pigs milled about, confused by the disappearance of one of their own, agitated and not quite knowing the reason why. The boar paced back and forth on the riverbank. Heaven help the next traveler southbound on the track there.

"I must get my bundle. It's very important." The young man pointed to the other side.

"The hogs were foraging when you entered among them. Once they get back to the business of foraging again, they'll move off. Then I will cross and bring it to you, since you seem not too enthusiastic about entering the water, and I don't mind it a bit."

"What if they decide to stay?"

"Then we shall retrieve your burden after darkness falls and they settle for the night. What's in it that you cherish it so?"

"Writing tools. I am a scribe, so to speak. A copyist."

"Wonderful! Here. I've something to show you." Mahon hopped up and returned to his own bundle. From the coarse-spun sack he pulled out the gospel. He brought it to the soggy young scribe by the waterside and handed it to him.

The lad knew a book when he saw it. He dragged his sopping tunic up above his lap, lest he get the book cover wet, and settled the book spine carefully on his legs. He opened it in the middle, then methodically closed and opened it every few pages on each side of the middle. "This volume is brand new."

"Less than a week old."

"And illuminated by a master. Look at that! The P in the *post haec erat dies festus Judaeorum* is a work of art. And this A in *Antes.*" He wagged his head appreciatively, instantly absorbed in the book and oblivious to the hogs on the far shore.

Mahon watched him intently. "In whose service are you now?"

"No one's, sir. I seek a position. Perhaps at Glendalough. I've heard their scriptorium is excellent." He looked up and grimaced. "I had no idea the river would be so deep."

"Kildare's is one of the largest. Or why not Armagh? You'd not have to cross the river to reach either of them."

The young man smiled. "I'm not skilled enough, sir. I've only been literate a few years. Armagh is for the finest. The best. Someday. . . ." A shadow crossed his face.

"Where did you serve before?"

"The little monastery of Septimus on the coast. Do you know where that is?"

"Initmately. Septimus and I traveled to Rome together once. I helped thatch the scriptorium. Why are you not there yet?"

"Septimus feels I'm not bright enough to pursue copying for a lifetime. He's right. In many ways I'm quite slow."

"As I recall, he didn't like my thatching, either." Mahon grunted and thought a moment. "Have you read Luke's gospel?"

"Actually, I just completed copying it, yes sir."

"The part about being invited to a marriage feast. Our Lord warns us not to take the seat of honor, lest someone more honorable show up and we get bumped to the bottom of the table."

The lad frowned. "Yes, sir." He had dark eyes, thoughtful eyes, deep set.

"Rather our Lord suggests we first sit down in a low place and let the master of the feast invite us to a more prominent seat. Then he is bestowing honor on us. Incidentally, what is your name, lad?"

The boy looked at him. "Declan of Ardmore."

"A descendant of the saint?"

The boy smiled bashfully. "You'd be surprised how many Declans live around Ardmore Monastery, sir, and none of us related." His eyes flicked momentarily to Mahon's shaved head. "You are in orders, of course."

"Mahon of Armagh." Mahon almost hated saying it. It sounded so boastful, somehow. "Anyway, just as the Lord instructed, you are graciously seeking a low position. Fine. But as a master of the feast, I am inviting you to a more elevated position. Come to Armagh with me, Declan. Join us there. We can use a young man of God like you. Even if he can't swim."

The lad muttered, "Mahon. Of . . ." He wagged his head. "Oh, sir, I couldn't! You don't understand. I'm too fearful. Septimus pointed that out. And I'm not quick to think, and my hand is not sure when I work. It wavers."

"The head and the hand do not concern me. The heart does. Your heart is for the work. Now Septimus is a sterling fellow and a powerful servant of God, even if his monastery is among the smallest in Erin. I've known him for thirty years, and I love him as a brother. But he tends to see only tangible results. I look for something more. Your faith and your love of books. That is what God needs. The head and hand will follow."

Declan studied him for the longest time. "There. You see, sir? I was right in the first place."

"What was that?"

"You are the Christ."

99

10

Muscle

A dark, massive menace was this bull, dozing on the shoulder of a copse. His jaw rotated mindlessly, his eyes drifted closed, his tail tip barely flicked as he reposed there, but he exuded power by his very presence.

A thousand pounds of muscle was this bull, untempered by patience or a sweet disposition. Here and there across the open slope below him, his harem lay about chewing their cud and flicking their ears against the summer flies. A grasshopper chirred, practically beneath the bull's chin.

Ailan crouched amid the holly and hazel that crowned the copse. He would have but one chance at this. If he made a noise, or if the breeze shifted, he'd have no chance at all. The bull must not hear or see or smell Ailan approaching him from the woods behind his back.

What would Ailan do if the bull leaped up? He would dive for that birch beside him, but everyone knows how swiftly a bull can reach his feet and charge. Slowly, smoothly, Ailan raised the ax, Fiona's ax, once Mahon's ax. He hesitated, in total awe of the great bull's latent power. He listened to the wet nose drag air in, push air out. The breathing echoed, hollow. Another step. Another.

The bull opened its eyes and grunted as Ailan popped out of the cover of the holly. The huge head swung toward Ailan, and he very nearly lost his nerve. The bull was pulling his hind feet under him as Ailan swung the ax. It glanced off a swaying horn and chopped into the top of the bull's neck just ahead of the withers. The bull bellowed and his rear end dropped back into the grass. Quickly Ailan swung again. He hit closer to the back of the bull's head this time, his original target. He chopped again.

His mighty roar faded as the bull rolled to his side. He jerked and spasmed about so violently that Ailan darted to the birch tree.

All over the hillside, cows lurched awkwardly to their feet, leaderless and uncertain. An old cow with a ragged horn tilted her nose high, no doubt smelling steamy blood. She cocked her tail up and trotted off down the hill. Her harem mates fell in behind her, their dewlaps swaying with each stride.

"Well, there's something, the likes I've never seen." Fiona stepped forward from behind the undergrowth. "I thought you were crazy, and I still do. But at least you did it."

"It's an important rite. Help me skin him."

"Sure and he's a chunk of meat."

Ailan jabbed his knife point into the base of the brisket and slit down the belly. "I read about this, but it was only a partial description. We're going to have to devise a few things as we go."

She sniggered. "Sometimes you read a little too much, I think. You've spent the most of the summer just going place to place, begging to read everybody's books."

"You've been taken good care of along the way."

"Plenty to eat—I'll give you that. They do feed you. Would they treat you so well if you weren't a disciple of that Mahon?"

Ailan stood erect. "I often wonder about that. Maybe at first it counted. But lately, it seems we've been received for ourselves. Did you notice? Here. Spread the back legs."

She grabbed a hock in each hand and pulled back. "You really going to wear the hide?"

"Of course. The hard part's done, killing the bull. As soon as we free up the hide here, we'll cut some meat and take it down to camp. You have to slay the bull, flay it, and eat it. Then, wrapped in its skin—that is, encompassed by its power—you gain the insights."

She let loose of a hock, or else it slipped from her grasp. The dead-weight leg folded up and slammed into Ailan's ear. Moments later he sliced his thumb going after the heart and liver. It took him half an hour, even with her help, to cut the warm, sticky hide off the bull.

Fiona wanted to take practically the whole back quarter. She agreed to a more modest portion when he handed her the knife and suggested she could carry what she cut. They took away the

101

heart and perhaps ten pounds of meat. The bull was hardly touched.

Their camp lay a mile and a half from the open lea where they had stalked the cattle. It nestled down in a pleasant little grove of elms on the edge of a bog. Ailan liked the location very much. They were sheltered, and yet wildness surrounded them. Nature in the raw enshrouded them. Stoats and badgers, thrushes and robins, heather and bog orchids were their companions as they more or less experimentally wove spells and recited law.

From a book here and a book there in this monastery and that one, Ailan was picking up a wide range of useful tidbits. Much of the old Brehon law had been committed to paper, and good thing. So few people in the world retained the lore in their memory, as the old practitioners did.

Ailan had never met a real druid with the full repertoire of rote law and illustrations, and more the pity. Think what he could learn! Three hundred fifty stories every bard memorized, each tale revealing its special precept, its unique portion of history. And the bards were the lowest order of druidic scholars. They studied twelve years. Druids of the highest order studied twenty or more.

Ailan cut their chunk of meat into slices and threaded them on wooden skewers to roast. He settled cross-legged by the fire to wait. He could not find in the literature anything about when to don the bull skin, so he slipped it over his shoulders now. Besides, he wanted it to take the shape of his shoulders as it dried and stiffened up. He was amazed at its immense weight.

He wished he had the iron skewer in Mahon's dunnage. It was as much Ailan's as Mahon's. He missed his buttermilk and seawater. But he did not want to come face to face with his former mentor. Perhaps someday. Not yet. Not yet.

At the beginning of his new quest, he had gone where Mahon had just been—to the Owney, to the Bevan, to others—for he knew that Mahon, having visited, would not return to them in the near future. Ailan wanted to sway those people, and indeed he had most successfully accomplished that, without Mahon's coming along and swaying them right back again. Ailan needed a power base of fellow believers. He rather admired his own persuasiveness.

He had not approached the ri of ris, Doyle Dalainn, so far. Sure and that would come, but Ailan didn't feel quite up to it yet. The man frightened him. Perhaps when Ailan was stronger . . .

Fiona screamed and leaped up as the brush behind them exploded. Ailan bolted to his feet and wheeled. An iron javelin point hung motionless, inches from his nose. Holding it were hands the size of plucked geese on arms like legs of mutton. Ailan's eyes flicked from the javelin to the hands to the face of the man beyond them, and he quailed.

"Well, well! A little man in a big hide." The uncouth giant on the other end of the javelin wagged his head. He grinned, displaying huge yellow teeth with a gap in the middle. His moustache drooped along both sides of his mouth, so long it trailed below his chin. And yet, he wasn't much older than Ailan. He stood as massive and ominous as that bull, and he held Ailan totally at his mercy.

Out of the corner of his eye Ailan counted four companions, all looking equally derelict. And if there were four there must be at least five, for one would remain concealed, on watch. Ailan knew that much, at least, about renegade bands.

He carefully arranged his face into a relaxed, even say bemused, expression. "You startled me. I am Ailan, a bard and druid of the old order." He dipped his head backward. "My companion there is a high priestess. Fiona. Please join us."

"Actually—" the fellow snickered "—we're thinking of disjointing you."

His companions chuckled merrily. One of them stepped in close beside Fiona and wrapped an arm around her shoulder.

Ailan forced a smile. "Always time for that. Sit. Make yourselves comfortable. I regret we have no ale to serve you." He turned around, half expecting that javelin between his shoulder blades any moment, and settled himself at the fire. His bull hide was getting stiff. He snugged it in closer.

Terrified, Fiona glanced from face to face. Cautiously, she sat down. The brigand settled in close beside her and resumed his hug.

Ailan was pleased with his persuasiveness? He must use every ounce of it now! "The meat roasting on our spit is consecrated to a special purpose. By means of it, and this hide, we shall endeavor to divine the future. You arrived at an auspicious time. May I ask what brought you?"

"Your tracks brought us. Next time you destroy my master's bull, don't cut quite so wide a swath escaping, eh?"

Ailan's spine tingled, cold as new snow. "If we were escaping, we would have covered our tracks, don't you think? And if we were raiding, sure and we would have taken more of the bull than this—to make the risk worthwhile if nothing else." He forced himself to look the giant in the eye. "And I daresay, good fellow, you may be in another man's employ, but no man is your master."

The giant roared, and his companions roared with him. It was a jolly sort of outburst that seemed to defuse some of the tension. He gave Ailan a clap on the back that nearly sent his teeth flying into the fire. "I like you, little man! Perhaps we won't disjoint you after all. What shall I tell the man who employs me when he discovers his bull lying heartless and naked on the lea?"

"Tell him the truth. That he has lost a bull in the short term and gained great wealth in the long term. The gods will enrich and bless him for providing this fine animal that we need. The provision is for a moment. The enrichment will last for years."

"A ready tongue you have. Now what's this about divining the future?"

"I slay the bull, establishing my primacy over it. I wear its skin and eat of its flesh, thereby putting it both outside me and inside me. As I thus partake of it, it conveys to me its power."

"If it had any power to divine the future, it would have known you were coming at it with an ax."

Ailan poked the fellow's tree-trunk arm. "You already possess the power of a bull. I do not."

Again the fellow roared.

Fiona seemed to be warming to her role. She chimed in with a somewhat distorted explanation of their rites and observances, and of Samhuinn coming up in a few short weeks. Ailan described how closely the old chaotic rituals of Samhuinn resemble the Eve of All Hallows in the Christian calendar, and how Christianity constantly took over the old festivals, thereby usurping the power of them.

The meat was ready then, so all partook of the luckless bull. Fiona explained ritual union as they ate. Afterwards, that fellow beside her decided to join the faith. They walked off into the woods, giggling. It bothered Ailan somewhat, how she seemed to approach her duties so much more enthusiastically with young men, reluctantly with older men, and hardly ever with Ailan anymore.

Beside Ailan the hulking giant belched as he wiped his hands on his shirt. "Terrible! Really terrible."

A companion grunted. "About what you'd expect of meat aged less than an hour. It hadn't even cooled out yet."

The giant leaned against a bigger-than-usual hazel and stretched his legs out. "So, lads. Here we are picking our employer's bull out of our teeth."

A man across the way scratched his armpit with a huge, hairy hand. "Don't like that fellow anyway. His bull is better than he, I aver, even fresh-killed."

"And smells better," a third chimed, and they laughed heartily.

The hulk waved a hand. "If he's going to be so blessed for donating his bull, sure and he doesn't need us. What has he lately given us, lads?" He turned to Ailan. "Why don't you join us, little man, and we'll go adventuring? You and the priestess. We could use a druid with us, to advise."

Ailan thought about that for less than a moment. "It would benefit the both of us, wouldn't it? But you're in the service of another."

"Him!" The brute spat into a heather shrub. "Last winter when he culled his cattle, he gave us a worthless old cow for wages and released us until spring. We've scant loyalty to a ri tuatha who turns his people loose for the winter."

Ailan bobbed his head. "Then let us join forces. We shall be your priestess and adviser, and you shall be our strength."

Yes! With this retinue, he could face any ri in Erin, even the Dalainn himself. Here was the power, the sheer muscle, he had been seeking to further his quest. This was perfect.

"Feeling any premonitions about the future yet?"

"That will come with ceremony, in the dark of the moon. What is your name, big man?"

"Garvan of the Turlock."
Garvan. Rough. Uncultured.
It figured.

* * *

Mahon of Armagh wished heartily that he were at Armagh. In theory, he was not tied to the things of this world. In practice he missed his comfortable, narrow bed of home. He missed the peace of routine, of saying matins and vespers and an occasional compline, of the steady march of the liturgical calendar, of days of placid study. He missed the jovial company of friends and fellow monks in the quiet darkness of approaching winter.

They would not reach Dublin Crossing tonight; too little daylight remained. Mahon glanced back at Declan. The lad slogged gamely along the track, not complaining but not quick either. Declan, weak of leg and courage, did not travel well. But he did his best. He always did his best, whatever the task. Mahon admired a heart like that, which never grew discouraged. Of late, Mahon felt a gnawing discouragement he could not place. It bothered him more than it ought to.

He would turn aside to Bevan of the Fat Mare. Bevan could provide a bit of porridge, a clean bed of straw. Tomorrow they would cross the ford. A gust of chill wind whipped up under his cloak.

By chance or providence, he met Bevan himself at Muirdach Cross, as the sun, cloud-shrouded, was slipping behind the western rise. His burden basket on his back, the grizzled old farmer stood in the cross and watched him approach. Normally, Bevan acted delighted whenever Mahon came by. This was not normal. The fellow watched him almost sullenly, with a guarded hangdog look about him.

Mahon nodded toward Declan behind him. "Our Lord's greetings to you, Bevan! My lad and I would like to rest with you tonight."

"Certainly, and welcome. Our home is always open to you." Bevan forced a smile, but actually all he did was spread his mouth enough to reveal his crooked teeth.

Declan came to a halt beside them. He looked utterly spent.

106

"My assistant, Declan of Ardmore. His gifts are as a copyist. Bevan, you should see the beauty of his work! It glows."

"Delighted." Bevan did not look in the least delighted. "I rather thought you were on your way back to Armagh when you left us."

"Oh, we were going to return to Armagh over two months ago. But I took Declan by Kildare to introduce him to Flora, and the long and short is we stayed there these last ten weeks. I taught a series on the psalms, and Declan made not one but two books. Flawless text, and even a bit of illumination. Study books, but beautiful. Psalms and Proverbs, and the Pentateuch. Very difficult book to copy, the Pentateuch."

Bevan grunted and led off toward home. He did not read. Therefore, books did not interest him. How Mahon abhorred that provincialism among these farmers. They could not see anything in the world past the weather and cattle and the lack of good yearling hogs in the area.

Mahon talked, and Bevan grunted. God's voice was speaking to Mahon in undertones, drowned out, he realized, by his own words. He shut up, then, and walked in silence awhile, until he knew he had the message right. "Bevan, you have separated yourself from God. Tell me why."

"Why do you say that?"

"Because it is true."

He scowled. "Of course you would know. He was your protégé. I realized the moment I saw you coming that you knew. Once you've come by in a summer, it's always a year or two before I see you again. Now here you are, a few weeks later. I should have hastened off and left you."

Mahon stopped in the road. "We walk no farther until this matter is settled satisfactorily. You are burdened with guilt, Bevan, guilt so heavy it covers you like a blanket. My spiritual eye this moment sees it like the hide of a great bull, draped over you and weighing you down. Go to your knees now, and confess your sins to almighty God."

Bevan glared at him defiantly.

Mahon glared right back, and he began to pray. He focused his strength—God's strength—as a well-cut ruby draws light to a point. He did not pray aloud. He did not pray in words at all. He knew Bevan's heart because God had told him. He knew the man's burden. And he knew the power at his disposal through prayer. He willed that power now with a will beyond words, rather than speaking a prayer of the mind.

Bevan's glare softened. His face tightened. Suddenly he dropped to his knees, raised his arms to God, and wailed. The basket he was carrying fell away, forgotten.

At Mahon's right elbow, Declan gasped. The lad appeared ready to bolt. If the lad ran, the lad ran. Mahon could not divide his attention or let his thoughts stray. This man, a child of God, was sorely oppressed. Bevan took priority now.

Bevan sat back on his heels. His back bowed as he covered his face with trembling hands and wept.

Mahon altered his will prayer from power for discipline to power for comfort and healing. Within himself, God seemed to speak clearly: "Release him." Only then did Mahon step in closer to lay hands upon the man's shoulder.

As God was speaking to Mahon, so also must He have been speaking to Bevan. Presently the farmer shuddered, still sobbing, and rested his head against Mahon's legs. With gnarled hands he gripped the tail of Mahon's coarsespun cloak. "Mahon." His voice cracked. "He sounded so wise. It sounded so right."

"Folly always does. Folly mimics the wisdom of God without actually providing it. Praise God for the few men who can discern between saving wisdom and dooming folly."

"Forgive me. Please forgive me."

"In the name of our Lord you are forgiven." He laid his hand on the tousled head. "And now, I believe I am about to learn why I have felt so spiritually oppressed all these weeks."

11

The Dogs of Owney

Dismal. That was the only way to describe this place. "Bleak" fit. So did "dreary." But "dismal" said the most.

Wolf trudged across sloppy lea, amid the naked, dripping branches of birches, through clammy winter rain. This Erin, this Misty Isle, did not enchant him in the least. He thought about the crystalline purity of true cold. Cleansing cold. Dark, encompassing cold. Honest cold, the way a winter ought to be. Not this half cold.

In his homeland, deep snow would be giving the sledges lots of glide. Men were hauling in firewood over the snow. Hunters were dragging deer and elk home by the antlers. Trappers were sliding across it on their wooden snowshoes garnering in splendid, rich pelts. Children on bone skates played games on crystal ice. And here, Wolf Arildson slogged through mud. His boots were soaked despite the soft tallow he so diligently worked into them. His corrective pad was soaked too. Tow is incredibly heavy and clammy when wet. Rain. Mud. In midwinter. Unthinkable.

As much as the drizzle turned colors into shades of gray, though, the green persisted. Plump cattle and sheep still grazed, their sparse pastures supplemented from the ricks of hay standing here and there in the fields. Wolf thought about his father's cattle, beasts so weakened by the rigors of the northern winter that they had to be helped out the bier door come spring. This was, one had to admit, a marvelous climate for livestock.

Daylight hours, even in the very depth of the year, extended a little longer here than they did back home. He watched the gray rain grow darker, darker, swallowing detail as night approached.

Like a graceful, undulating, pointy-nosed arrow, a stoat bounded across the track and disappeared among the birches. Wolf saw stoats every now and then, and otters frequently, but never weasels. Curious.

If only he had some traps, he could make a fine living as a furrier. Or with javelin or bow he could hunt red deer. And boars. How he missed the boar hunts of home.

He stopped. Beyond the whisper of rain and dripping, a man's voice sang. A lilting song it was, and cheerful. Wolf pressed forward, the stoat forgotten.

The track opened out into a vast meadow that spread up and over a great round hill to the west. It was on the edge of this meadow that Wolf was to gather a load of firewood and bring it in. He passed the fallen wood and continued down the track, lured by the sunshine in that song.

With a frightened yelp, the song ceased in mid verse.

Wolf broke into a run. Ahead he heard dogs snarl and bark. He entered the oak grove beyond the meadow, pausing only long enough to rip a limb off the first low tree he passed. The dog din was building rapidly.

He came upon them just past the great turn around the brow of the hill. The Owney's huge mastiffs! Wouldn't you know! More than once, this ranging pack of dogs had treed Wolf when they came upon him unsuspected. Now, irreligiously, they had run a monk up an oak sapling.

The sapling swung back and forth, back and forth, threatening to snap with every stroke. The chubby, balding little monk, wide-eyed and literally clinging for dear life, looked not the least spiritual. In a far heftier oak beyond him, a lad half grown, a mere stripling, perched on a limb.

"Cu!" Wolf swung his tree limb wide and hard. "Cu!" One dog went sprawling, and the others turned to meet him. Two slipped around to grab him from the back.

He was onto that ploy. He pivoted in a full circle with his leafy branch, sweeping them like broom dirt. He dived forward to snatch up the monk's fallen walking stick and wheeled again. With the stick he took out the blue brindled cur, the pack leader; he heard ribs break. He jabbed the gray brindle in the belly so hard the dog coughed blood.

"Cu!" Backing up against a broad oak bole to defend the rear, he flailed that marvelous walking stick, using its knobby burl end for power strikes, the pointed bottom end for stabbing.

Furious and frustrated, the dogs turned suddenly on the gray brindle, falling upon the only blood drawn thus far. The brindle found itself fighting for its life, and losing.

"Flee! Backward!" Wolf screamed in Erse.

The monk had no choice, for the sapling broke just then beneath his weight. Still wide-eyed, he scurried backward up the track toward the Dalainn, much as a crab scurries across a bar at low tide. The monk disappeared beyond the curve.

"I'll not move from here, where I am safe!" the stripling avowed.

"Suit your fancy. They'll probably leave by dark." Wolf gave the monk a few more moments and managed to beat another of the dogs senseless with the knobbed stick. Then he took to his heels, running backwards for the first hundred yards so as to remain faced toward the churning, fighting dogs. He wheeled and raced out of the grove, across the meadow.

It struck him, rather abstractly, that his tow pad, however wet and heavy it may be, aided his speed immensely. Back home he would run straight up mountain slopes, to build wind and strength. But he never ran this smoothly or this fast. He wished, almost, that Ireland had steep mountains like those of home, that he might try his new gait under more challenging conditions.

Shawna. Shawna of the Behr. He owed her so much.

The monk, totally winded and red-faced, had slowed to a walk—a very fast, rolling, shuffling walk. He had hitched up his cowled homespun robe as a woman hitches her skirts. He waddled ludicrously with his elbows straight out. Wolf caught up to him and slowed to match his pace.

"'Tis safe enough now," Wolf suggested in Erse. "We are nearly beyond their rath." He hoped rath was the correct word. He knew no other for territory or area.

The monk cast an excited eye over his shoulder. The hyperkinetic shuffle slowed to a normal walk. Wolf handed the man his walking stick, but he did not discard the tree branch yet.

Chubby men usually have smooth, filled faces. Not this wrinkled old man. He was chubby only in the middle. His arms, legs, and face were thin and crumpled by many years. "My gratitude, lad. You were sent of God. I am Mahon of Armagh."

He smiled back at the monk. "And I am Wolf, Ulf Arildson, a thrall of the Dalainn."

"Say it again."

Curse his faulty pronunciation! Would he never get this tricky Erse tongue right? Wolf repeated, enunciating (he hoped) better. "Can you understand me now?"

Mahon chuckled. "Oh, I understood you fine the first time. I'm trying to place the accent. I've slept under many a sky, and heard many a tongue, but yours is a new one."

"I'm from Trondelag."

"Where is Trondelag?"

"Norge. Far north."

Mahon stopped and turned to stare, as if Wolf's nose were attached nostril-side up. A smile softened the old man's face and shifted its many creases. "So. The hideous Northman." And his voice was swathed in gentle affection. "You cannot imagine, lad, the tales about you that are circulating on the continent. They say of the Danes that they are invincible."

"We are! Be it dogs or men."

Mahon chuckled. He had relaxed greatly. "I'll accept that!"

"But," Wolf added, "there are Danes and there are not Danes. I realize you Celts and Saxons call us all Danes, as if we were one. But we are Norse and Swedes as well as Danes."

"Danes. Norse—you are all one in the terror you create. They say you descend like all the minions of hell upon innocent and unsuspecting churches and farms."

"If they are so unsuspecting, why do they meet us with full battle dress?"

"They say that you seize the grails from the altars and with them drink the blood of the church's doomed defenders."

"How revolting! Who would want to do such a thing? It would taste terrible!"

"And your helmets have great horns upon them, like bulls' horns, with which you gore your defenseless victims."

Wolf laughed aloud. "Indeed! We love to stop in the midst of battle—" his mind sifted Celtic words a moment "—and expose the back of our necks to the enemy's ax while we stick horns in people. My good monk, there is no helmet in all the Northland with horns upon it. I'm sorry." He frowned a moment. This man could not be privy to the winter feasts. Still, "I take that back. Sometimes our jarls wear a—" again he needed a word that was not quite there "—a ceremonial helmet with a single horn. One horn. Very occasionally two. A victim or two may die laughing, but never from being gored."

"And do you deny the slaughter and rapine?"

"Of course I do not. Why be polite if you don't have to? As you say, we are invincible. The great Dalainn himself never makes nice unless he must."

The monk laughed uproariously and thrust his stick in the air. "True, true, true! You are wiser than many a Celt, fair Northman. And you do not deny you are pagans? Godless?"

"Godless? Hardly." He had learned *hardly* from Shawna. She used it often, and usually when he suggested something about her. "We've three major gods, the same as you. Frey, Odin, and Thor. And we pray to them as often as you pray to yours."

"The same as I? I have but one."

Wolf aped the religious gesture he saw so often, sweeping his hand from head to belly to shoulders. "In the name of the Father and of the Son and of the Holy Spirit. One, two, three."

"I see. What is falling out of the sky now?"

"Rain." The change of topic nearly unhorsed him.

"And what would be falling out of the sky in your homeland?"

"Snow."

"When you boil a pot, what does the water do?"

"It rises up as smoke. I mean steam." Was that the word? "Not smoke."

"Snow, rain, steam. They are all water, and nothing else is quite water. Not ale, not oil, not blood. Similarly—but not exactly the same—the analogy is inexact—God is God, and nothing else is God, but He manifests Himself as three forms."

"Yes, but the Son is supposed to have died but not the Father. How can they be one then?"

"Steam will burn you. Rain cannot. In the mountains of France in winter, small boys build snow forts, arm themselves with snowballs, and wage war. They cannot do that in summer. A water ball? Steam fights? Water in its different forms does very different things. It is still water, and nothing else."

Wolf perceived the lesson, sort of, but mostly he was beating back the tears. Ah, the snow forts! Ah, the battles! Ah, true winter, around which so many of the pleasures of his youth revolved. Lost forever.

"And you pray," the monk continued. "You pray up to your gods, and they send down blessings upon you."

"When it pleases them."

"My God doesn't do that."

It was Wolf's turn to stare. "Your god doesn't do that." He repeated it, assuming somehow that he had translated wrongly.

"He first reaches down to us and encompasses us as a father receives a child, as a hen receives her chicks—both scriptural allusions, I assure you—and prayer is our response to His reaching down. Not a question but an answer. A response to blessings already given. Prayer is not my reaching up, you see, but a result of my joy that He first loved me. I owe Him so infinitely much."

Wolf pondered this new thought, and the word "infinitely," which Shawna used now and then.

"And He is perfect." The monk cast him a sideways glance. "Can you say of your gods that they are perfect?"

"Well, I suppose, not exactly. Balder, perhaps. But he was not fully . . . no, I guess not exactly perfect."

"One is perfect, or one is not. There is no middle ground. Only a perfect God is worthy of full devotion, wouldn't you agree?"

"Well, I suppose . . ."

"Gods who are nothing more than magnified human beings may well instill terror, but not true worship."

"Well—uh—actually, that's what Shawna says too."

Mahon gaped. "Shawna of the Behr! She is alive?"

"Aye, and spending the winter with the Dalainn."

"Praise God! Praise His holy name!" And the monk lapsed into a flood of Latin, a language Wolf's ear found very confusing. The man crossed himself exuberantly. "The raid on Lambay is becoming known throughout the continent. And the story circulating is that the population of Lambay was wiped out completely. How I grieved! Who else of the Behr survived?"

114

"Two boys." Again Wolf had to pause while he foraged for the right word. "Nephews of Shawna. And everyone on the east side of the island. We struck only the western part. At least, I suppose so. My comrades may have returned to the east side later. The Dalainn thinks others of the Behr are alive but carried off as slaves."

"And what do you think? You know the Northmen."

Wolf shrugged. "I don't doubt there are Behrs in the North this moment. Slavery is a necessary part of life, in the North as much as here."

The monk nodded knowingly, and there was meaning there that Wolf could not read. "I look forward to visiting the Dalainn, that we might discuss this thing." He smiled grimly. "You Danes have posed us a pretty pickle."

"I suppose we could have come bearing gifts of flowers and linen." Wolf tossed the limb away and shot a sly glance toward the monk. "But 'twould not have been half so much fun."

* * *

Dismal. That was the only way to describe this place. Brenna opened the door of her hovel a crack to see outside. Look! The sun rose in the afternoon and set moments later. There had been a time, not many days ago, when the sun failed to fully appear at all. And the snow. Very, very rarely, mainland Ireland felt the kiss of snow, and only a few times on Lambay within Brenna's memory. Here in this forsaken land the snow did not kiss. It buried. Bitter, bitter cold pierced Brenna to the bone whenever she had to go out into it, and no amount of wool protected her from its ravages.

Dismal!

Where was Shawna now? Dead, likely. Brenna had constantly found her superior, goody-goody attitude irritating, but she certainly wouldn't want Miss Perfect dead. Possibly Shawna had got away. She was quick and clever.

What would Shawna say about this infernal weather? Something pious, probably. Piety irritated Brenna too.

Whatever had happened to Peggy, and to the freeman's wife and the children? Brenna often wondered, but she never knew.

She had not seen them since that hideous day when the ship's master gave her to Arild. And she would rather die than ask him. She closed the door and returned to her fire.

Idly, she picked up Arild's latest gift, a cunningly wrought comb. It was not made of bone, but it appeared too wide and flat to be deer antler. The plates from which the teeth had been cut were riveted to the handle so artfully that neither the smoothed bone nor the rivets snagged her hair. The carving on the handle intrigued her. A dragon wound, serpentine, through a leafy branch. It was the same delicate craftsmanship in miniature that adorned the wooden chest he gave her. She pushed more sticks into the waning fire.

The door thumped open, dragging in a blast of frigid air. The fire danced crazily, and Brenna jumped. Arild often barged in like that, and he never failed to startle her.

"I thought you were out hun—" Brenna sucked in breath and stared.

It was not Arild. This woman stood nearly as tall as Arild, though, with braids that reached her waist. She wore a scarf of exceedingly fine linen around her head and tied behind her neck, so she was married. Married women covered their heads. Like all the other women here, she wore over her gathered white shift a beautiful rectangle of fine cloth, covering her front from above her breasts to below her knees. This particular garment appeared in the flickering firelight to be a deep, rich green. The two huge silver brooches holding it in place at her shoulders badly needed polishing.

Despite the stabbing cold, the woman did not wear a cloak or shawl. She teetered slightly, off balance.

Brenna leaped to her feet, for the woman looked not the least friendly. Brenna circled far enough to put the fire between them.

The woman crossed her arms. "So this is where he keeps you."

"You are Arild's wife."

"And you are the wench who would steal his affection." She spat viciously.

"Not by choice, my lady!" Brenna used the Celtic term for lady, since she had no idea what title the jarl's wife carried. "Believe me! I would that he had never laid eyes on me—or hands."

Lies, lies, lies. Brenna knew how to survive, and stealing Arild Thick Knee's affections had been her first and foremost priority for survival. And now that she saw what Arild's wife looked like, her hopes rose dramatically. Brenna was far younger, far prettier, more delicate, more feminine than this husky woman. Her immediate concern, however, was survival this moment.

The woman moved to her right. Brenna moved to the right, keeping the fire between them.

"You curry his favor to better your position. Perhaps to supplant me, child-woman?"

Brenna wasn't at all sure of the language spoken, for Arild was teaching her only words he thought she ought to know, but she could clearly see its intent. And she could smell the ale on this woman's breath. "My lady, persuade him to stop coming to me, and you will not be happier than I."

Yes, I will supplant you. And your visit to me just made it easier, for now I know what you are like. Now I can counter your wiles point for point.

A word Brenna had never heard exploded out of the woman. The wife of the jarl snatched up Brenna's little stool, still another gift from Arild, and advanced upon her, gripping it by one leg. The oaken stool made a formidable weapon. Brenna knew, because she herself had used it once when she tried to drive Arild off.

Brenna feinted left then dived right. She grabbed the door and dragged it open enough so that she could squeeze outside. The cold leaped upon her instantly and sank through her clothes.

This was madness! She floundered in the snow outside the door, hiked her skirts, and commenced running in high, galumphing steps. Where? She had no idea. Arild was gone a-hunting; he could not protect her.

The woman's tracks would lead to her own hearth. Brenna would find no safety there. She must go in some direction other than the way pointed by those footsteps through the snow. She heard the woman panting and swearing behind her. She heard the *floof! floof!* of the woman's struggling strides.

A yellow light flashed on and off less than a quarter mile away. Someone had opened and closed the door of a house with a hearth. Brenna altered direction and ran toward it. She stumbled over a rail half submerged in the loose snow and fell. She scrambled to her feet and kept going. She screamed. She was gasping now, for the cold air did not satisfy her poor lungs. It merely set them afire.

The woman's *floof! floof! floof!* sounded closer.

Brenna screamed again.

The yellow light winked on and remained on. Brenna shouted as loudly as she could—not very loudly at all. Were Shawna running like this, Shawna would be praying, as if God visited this frozen hell. No. A compassionate God would not have ripped Brenna up from Lambay in the first place, let alone allowed her uncle and cousins to die so horribly. He certainly wielded no influence here. Anyone could see that. Brenna was on her own.

Only a few yards to go. The woman was breathing destruction on Brenna's heels. Three men stood in the lighted doorway of a great, longhouse, talking excitedly. No, "excited" was not the word. "Bemused" was. Behind Brenna the woman yelled something that sounded uncomplimentary. One of the men responded, laughing.

Brenna was lost! Of course these men would take the woman's side! She was the wife of the jarl, the ruler. And yet, Brenna had all manner of gifts to attest to the jarl's affections. Did that count for nothing?

"Save me!" she begged in her native Erse. Stumbling, she plunged past the men and practically fell through the door. She did not pause. She kept running, suddenly in blessed warmth, the length of the long, long house. She heard the woman's clumping footsteps right behind her.

She ran past the hearths positioned down the middle of the floor. The main light was now behind her, and she could see only dark shadows. There! Ahead, a scrawny young man was chopping up a cow-sized side of meat with an iron tool like a battle-ax. Brenna ran directly at him.

His mouth dropped open, and he stared at her. She slammed into him, snatched the ax from his hands, and wheeled to face her enemy.

The woman yanked a long, dagger-sized knife out of a chopping block. Again she spoke words Brenna did not know. The men, now standing by the fire, laughed heartily. They started this way cautiously.

Brenna hefted the heavy ax and gripped its worn wooden hilt with both hands. She probably would not win this fight, but that woman would be missing a few body parts before it was over. She would not pay for Arild's adultery with her own life and limb if she could help it.

The woman crouched and made an experimental stab toward Brenna. Brenna held the ax at ready, unflinching. Often enough she had watched Shawna's brothers at their battle games. She had sparred with some of them. She would not be quite the helpless victim this woman assumed. But dare she kill or maim the woman? Would that advance her cause—survival—or destroy it when Arild returned?

One of the men cried out, "Lenveig!" as the woman lunged forward with a shriek. Brenna swung her ax as the woman stabbed wildly with the knife. Steamy-hot blood hit Brenna's cheek, and she had no idea whether it was hers or the woman's. It didn't matter. In this gloom she could not see to fight effectively.

The woman wrenched the ax from Brenna's hands.

No, she didn't. It was one of the men. And another was disarming the woman, cooing soothing words in her ear. The man said her name several times more. Lenveig.

The woman melted against her captor sobbing. She babbled about Arild's fickle ways. Brenna recognized *fickle*. Arild used the word on her frequently.

The blood was Brenna's. Lenveig had sliced her arm where it met the shoulder. Brenna felt suddenly giddy. Her own captor, a fellow altogether too cheerful, led her to the hearth.

"Sit," he said.

She sat hard by the glowing fire, suddenly too shaky to stand.

"Delightful!" He grinned. Delightful was a word Arild used a lot also. "Nothing brightens a boring winter day more than two jealous women at each other's throats. Arild is going to be pleased as punch when we tell him about this."

"Is he back yet?" Arild was Brenna's safety. She must reach him.

119

"Tomorrow perhaps, or the next day. Every winter, Arild holds a feast." The man casually, nonchalantly dragged Brenna's sleeve down off her shoulder to examine and bind her injury.

"He mentioned something about it, yes." Brenna looked over toward Lenveig. The woman was surrounded now by other women, all consoling her, agreeing what a heartless lout that Arild was.

"The fun part is the hunt, of course, and his wild game is always the best. He never leaves the fun part to his subordinates. Who knows. Maybe he'll invite you."

Brenna growled in her halting Norse, "He'd better. He owes me more than even that would repay."

A woman, presumably this man's wife, was helping him now, wrapping linen tightly around Brenna's arm. Her fingertips began to tingle.

The fellow bubbled on, so cheerful he was obnoxious. "Arild seems to like you, so we dare not let Lenveig have her way. You can stay here in the longhouse until he returns. We'll let Arild decide your fate, eh?"

A cluster of sympathetic people led Lenveig toward the far door. They purred and exhorted in their undulant language.

The snow, the cold, the alien land with its steep peaks and deep, somber fjords, the foreign tongue—all things alien heaped themselves upon Brenna's heart and weighed it down. She was alone, so utterly alone.

There was no God here. There was no friend. Jesus preferred the people of warm climes and sunny skies. Indeed, all the years of chiding she received from monks and Shawna convinced her that Jesus did not prefer her at all. And now she was cast out on her own. She must forge herself a brand new life here.

And she knew she would never see home again.

12

Brenna

Connleigh would be glad when winter ended—he always was—but he didn't really look forward to summer either. Twice now, that he knew of, the Northmen raided in early summertime. Connleigh had the distinct foreboding that the Norse raids were not something that would go away soon.

Mahon said the oak grove beyond the meadow. Connleigh rode his gray mare across the last few yards of the meadow and pulled his lance out from beneath his knee. He rode down among the trees.

The Norse slave had beaten off a pack of dogs with far less than a lance. Of course, Mahon said the slave had wisely chosen an elder branch. Everyone knows that if you strike an animal with an elder branch, the animal will cease growing. Quite probably the elder branch conferred other dark, arcane powers as well.

"My lord?" A squeaky voice in an oak tree ahead as much as told Connleigh he had arrived.

"Mahon said you were comfortably ensconced on your oak limb. The pack has left, I see."

Not all the pack. Three dogs lay dead, one of them obviously ripped by its companions. Ah, wait. This third dog still lived. It whined and squirmed as Connleigh rode near. Connleigh reached forward in the saddle and drove his lance through it. He could not let even a base cur suffer so.

"Do you think 'tis safe?" the lad asked.

"No matter. Drop down off your perch there and ride behind me. You need not touch earth at all."

"Thank you, my lord."

Connleigh swung his mare's rump around under the oak limb. The lad handed down a large coarse-spun sack.

Connleigh hefted it. "Feels like a book."

"It is indeed, sir." Carefully, reluctantly, the apprentice twisted and squirmed, aligning himself just so, and slid off the branch. He dropped onto the mare's rump and instantly seized great handfuls of Connleigh's shirt. He was not a horseman. "My master, Mahon, was bringing it to the Behr. When he heard they are destroyed, he thought to continue on with it to Armagh."

No use waiting for dogs that probably would not return. Connleigh turned the nervous mare toward home. She did not like carrying double. "How did Mahon hear the Behr are destroyed?"

"Why, the ri ruirech himself, lord. Doyle Dalainn. He has one of the heathen beasts captive, you know. He displayed the fiend when we were down at Kildare, and he promised that many more like the fellow would come, and all larger than he. The ri claims that the captive is the runt of the litter."

"Yes. I hear the Dalainn has been mustering troops around the countryside, for defense. Tell me about the book, lad."

"'Tis the gospel of Saint John, lord. Complete and illuminated. A lovely work."

"I can't wait to read it." And suddenly, the murky day turned clear. Day? Connleigh's whole life. Of course! Of course!

He did not want to engage in political machinations. He did not want to become ri in his father's footsteps. He wanted to travel around with a monk such as Mahon, carrying books and reading them, writing them, illuminating them, studying them. This lad had the best of all worlds and probably did not even know or appreciate his wonderful position. Study. Serenity. The life of the church.

Why had Connleigh not considered this years ago? His father, that's why. Doyle Dalainn assumed Connleigh would follow in his footsteps, and Connleigh had blindly accepted that assumption. Until now.

Not until this moment had he realized that his life need not be what his father envisioned. Let one of Connleigh's brothers slip into the cloak of leadership. Or pick the next ri from among his many cousins. Connleigh would pursue his own dream.

But then, how does one explain a dream to Doyle Dalainn?

* * *

"Ah, your elderberry wine!" Mahon of Armagh sipped again and wiped his mouth on a sleeve. "Doyle, you're an artist."

"With certain things one can be a bit slipshod and get by. Other things require perfection, wines among them." The dark, hulking lord leaned forward to refill Mahon's flagon.

They sat as close to the hearth as crackling, leaping embers would permit. Doyle's house was one of the largest in this part of Ireland, befitting so extensive a rath, but it sat close and huddled by continental standards. Across the sea they built vast halls, as for instance on the romanesque model. Here in Ireland, houses were lines of small rooms stuck together in a row, with thick, thick stone walls and deep, deep thatch on the roofs. In these low cottages pasted against the soggy soil, a small fire of wood or peat sufficed to keep the place evenly warm year round. Mahon could not imagine keeping an Italian villa warm in an Irish winter.

Close by the hearth, Doyle's Muirgheal picked ineffectually at a knot in a bit of sewing thread. Mahon could hardly call himself a seamstress, though he was not above making himself a new smock if the old one fell apart, but even he could stitch a garment faster than she was doing it.

On the other hand, there stood Shawna in a corner across the way. Casually she would let her spindle fall, forcing the twist in the fine line she was spinning. As the spindle tapped the stone floor she would instantly be winding in her length of new thread, ready for another pass. Now there was a capable girl. Intelligent too. Increasingly, the church—particularly those snooty lords of the church in Rome—frowned upon marriage in the brotherhoods, and Mahon was too old for her anyway. But it was tempting.

Mahon stretched his legs out, to get his cold feet a bit closer to the fire. "Slipshod. Yes, I agree. Some things can slide by, others require exactness." He skewered Doyle with his gaze. "And honesty. Above all, honesty."

"Honesty. Of course, that." The Dalainn's eyes narrowed, and he sat forward, his elbows on his knees. Was he anticipating Mahon's diatribe? Quite probably.

"One of the most important functions of the church in society," Mahon began, "is to act as conscience to the king. I, and others, serve that function for the kings at Tara, and I am constrained to serve that function for you, for you are nearly as powerful as they."

Doyle smirked. " 'Nearly?' "

"Nearly. You do not have the strength of tradition behind you, and they do. And you do not yet enjoy the favor of the southern kings."

"That may change."

"I don't doubt it. Which is why, I assume, you trot that little Northman around like a prize heifer on display. A scare tactic to muster their armies to your side."

"My motives are pure."

"Nothing about you is pure." Mahon glanced hastily at Muirgheal. "Save of course for the purity of your marital bed."

"The Northmen will not go away, Mahon. You know that. They've found a chicken easy to pluck. Their strike-and-flee tactics make them virtually invincible. To protect Erin, we must change that. Mahon, they strike monasteries! You of all people should be welcoming my efforts."

"Of course they strike monasteries. Were they to sail into the Mediterranean, they would attack Rome, or Ostia, for that is where the wealth is concentrated. Farms would not be worth their while there. Were this the land of the Franks, they would sail up the river and raid Paris. But Erin is nothing but farms. Raths. In all the land we have no city, no town, or anything similar. Not even Tara comes close to the cities of other lands. So they go for the monasteries, which offer the only concentrations of the wealth they prize."

"Then you agree that defense requires special tactics on our part. Right now, their raids last at most a few hours. By the time a fighting force would hear of the raid and come running, they'd be gone. I purpose to place a small defensive force at every monastery on the coast, at least in summer. They strike, we counterstrike instantly. A few such pitched battles, and they will go find other chickens easier to pluck."

"And to that end, you've been, shall we say, embellishing the descriptions of their ravages."

"Embellishing?" Doyle twisted his mouth into a "what nonsense" sort of sneer.

"The raids are horrible enough that you need not exaggerate. And so, as conscience to the king, I ask myself: Since the mighty Dalainn is, speaking quite frankly, not above lying to sway others, might he be garnering military support not for the noble purpose of protecting the coast against Norse incursions but to further a dream of primacy? Of one Erin united under the Dalainn."

"Now who is exaggerating?"

"You of all men are closest to that goal already. Your only rivals in this region, the Behr, are gone. The rulers sitting in Tara now are from the kingdom in the north. The next will come, by tradition, from the southern kingdoms, the very ris you are courting. Your ambition frightens me, Doyle Dalainn."

"Then you frighten much too easily, Mahon, my conscience."

Mahon glanced over at Shawna.

She had not missed a beat with her drop spindle.

Nor, he could tell, had she missed a single word.

* * *

Brenna had always assumed she was accustomed to boisterous celebrations. After all, no one was wilder or more boisterous than Shawna's brothers, her cousins. But when it came to feasting, these Norse could match the Behr any day.

She sat in a dark corner of Arild's great hall watching the goings-on with a detached bemusement. The detachment was rather forced upon her by the fact that she was nowhere near comfortable yet with the language of these pagans. The bemusement came naturally, as she watched rowdy men and exuberant women yell and laugh and eat and drink and quarrel.

This hall, its high-peaked roof supported by great columns (never had Brenna imagined that tree trunks could grow so large), seemed bigger and taller than any building in Erin. It stretched at least one hundred fifty feet, end to end. The pall of smoke from the fires more or less kept to itself up in the gloom, which was probably why the hall was built so tall.

Roasted joints of beef and pork, all manner of game, a wonderful array of breads, peas, and kale—the table rivaled any in Erin. And quite a table it was. Along one side of the longhouse, sleeping platforms held the woolen blankets and furs to keep one warm and secret, for everyone save the jarl slept on these plat-forms in full view of everyone else. Only the jarl had his own bed compartment. Fires crackled bright in the three hearths in the center of the hall. And lining the other wall, that long, long table stretched, with sitting benches behind it and a flutter of slaves before it serving the celebrants.

Brenna missed Erin sorely. But what would her future have been had not the Northmen struck? She would almost certainly have had to leave the island. The only marriage prospects on Lambay were those two boys on the east side, and no one in her right mind could stomach those oafs. So she would not have been able to stay home with kith and kin anyway.

True, winter was miserable here, but they enjoyed nice summers. In fact, Arild commented on them. And look at the virile young men gathered around this table. What prospects! Brenna thought she was pretty enough and young enough to surely snare one of them, if not the jarl himself.

That must be Reidar at the jarl's side. She had heard of Reidar, Arild's only surviving son. Some of the women called him spoiled, and others said he was merely a pawn of his father. Right now, he seemed to sit in the next-most-honored seat with an easy, casual grace, born to rule. What would Reidar be like as a husband? Second choice. Arild was the one to win. He ruled the North.

Brenna, quite obviously, sat at the lowest station possible in this feast, but it was an important step forward that Arild allowed her to come at all. Even more than his gifts, this gesture proved his affection. He sat now between two ornately carved house pillars, with Lenveig at his side. He seemed so far away. For now.

Lenveig appeared already in her cups. Her head lolled a little as she tipped aside to speak to this nearby woman or that one. What a disgusting woman. One would think it would be an easy matter to turn Arild's heart away from Lenveig the Sot. Brenna could hear her piercing laugh clear down here—and her belches.

A minstrel of some sort was singing the praises of Hegaard Broad Back. Brenna thought no one was listening, but every now and then the celebrants would cheer something he said and wave their sloshing flagons.

The more she watched, the more like Celts these people acted. Arild had warned her when he told her where to sit, "If a fight breaks out, slip out the door immediately."

A fight? Back home, Celtic feasts awash in merriment could turn instantly into vicious bloodbaths, particularly when the ale flowed copiously. Apparently it was the same here. Men with swords at their sides could erupt for little or no reason.

And then Lenveig shrieked, and the great hall fell virtually silent. Over and over, Lenveig was screaming, "You let her in!" and she was pointing right at Brenna!

Arild wrapped his arm around her and purred something too quiet to discern. Mumbling and chuckling up and down the hall drove the sudden silence away. Lenveig leaped up, fell over her seat, scrambled drunkenly to her feet, and stormed out.

Arild wagged his head and shrugged mightily. All the men and most of the women laughed and resumed the feasting.

This was quite a predicament. What ought Brenna do? She probably should absent herself and return to her slave's hovel beyond the main house. On the other hand, it pleased her immensely that, in a way, she had just prevailed. She still sat at the feast, and Lenveig did not. She would revel in this tiny victory. She would show Arild that she wanted to be here, she deserved to be here, that she was far superior to Lenveig in this matter. His own wife had disdained his feast. She thought about all that a minute and decided that, yes, definitely, she would resume eating. She dragged the nearby joint of boar closer, to cut herself a chunk.

The thrall beside her yelped.

Brenna twisted on her bench, and looked eye to eye into the face of the enraged Lenveig. She only peripherally noticed the raised knife. Without thinking, Brenna swung the joint of meat at Arild's wife. Lenveig staggered backward.

Brenna leaped onto the table, her only way out, and started running directly down the middle of the long table amid the food and revelers.

"My lord!" Brenna heard Lenveig's heavy feet right behind her. Men roared as tankards flew. "My lord, save me!" She dropped to her knees before Arild, clasped her hands together and looked him straight in the eye. "Save me, my lord!"

But Arild was already rising to his feet. In a bellow that told all present who ruled, he roared, "Hold!"

And the whole world held its breath.

Lenveig stopped beside Brenna, that huge blade in her hand, and glared at Arild.

Arild pointed to the knife. "Put it aside." He paused. "And not in her."

The silent hall erupted in laughter. A happy titter began and swelled, and Brenna realized the men here were making side bets galore.

Lenveig hesitated the longest moment before she dropped the knife and stood defiantly before him on the table, arms akimbo.

Arild looked from woman to woman and sighed heavily. He sat down again. "Brenna."

"My lord."

"Stand up. Don't grovel."

Brenna leaped to her feet.

"The slave called Peggy. The woman Hegaard gave to Junken. You know her?"

"She is wife of my cousin, lord."

"You are both of the same religion?"

"Yes, lord. Christians."

"Christians. Junken says she calls upon her God day and night. He says she is a model slave in every way, claiming that her God calls those in slavery to remain willingly in slavery. Do you not call upon your God in this extremity?"

Brenna took a shuddering breath. How, in her halting Norse, could she explain that she—and Peggy, for that matter—was too far from God's scrutiny and power to call upon Him? How could she explain that she refuted His very existence, that a sovereign God should allow these fiends of destruction such a happy life while her kin rotted in their graves and Lambay lay a-smoldering?

She stammered, "Do you see churches about, my lord?"

Arild burst out laughing. "A quick wit!"

Praise! He had just praised her in Lenveig's presence. Her heart jumped. Already he was choosing her!

Arild turned to his irate wife. "When I returned from the hunt and learned of your first attack on this innocent child—you remember, Lenveig?—you said it was either she or you. In fury you gave me an ultimatum."

"I remember. I say it yet."

"Lenveig, most men enjoy a slave or two on the side. It's accepted. You know that. Why—?"

Her voice rose, amazingly steady for a woman so tanked with ale. Perhaps fury has a sobering effect. "You are not most men, my jarl. You are jarl above all jarls in Trondelag, and you are mine by right. I will not share you."

"Then you leave me no choice. I must kill one of you." Arild drew his blade so swiftly and smoothly it seemed to leap into his hand.

Brenna's heart quailed. "My lord . . ." Her voice faltered. All she could see was that hideous iron blade hovering between her and the man who owned her.

And then her heart changed its mind. Should Lenveig die this day, it would be by the hand of Arild, not Brenna. And think of the doors that would open, the ways through the wildwood it would cut wide into highways.

The silence hung so heavy down the hall, you could hear breathing.

Arild spoke loudly. "Brenna. When first I claimed you, you declared you would never willingly submit to my lordship. And you have not. You fight me even yet. Tonight is the first time you have ever called me lord. Does this mean you've changed your mind?"

"Spare me, lord, and I will become whatever consort you wish, I promise."

"Anything I wish? No more resistance?"

She hoped she translated resistance correctly. "Yes, lord!"

"Lenveig, my own, will you not rescind this silly ultimatum, made in haste and fury? Do not seal your doom, beloved."

Brenna glanced over at the woman beside her. Lenveig's craggy face broke into a cold sweat, but her voice remained steady. "What I have spoken is spoken."

Brenna's heart sang. The woman had just sealed her own doom. Brenna would survive, would supplant her. In fact, with Lenveig gone, Brenna wouldn't even be guilty of the sin of adultery, assuming that such a sin existed. If there was no God powerful enough to save, there might well be no God powerful enough to punish.

Arild grimaced and bobbed his head. He raised his voice still further, addressing the hall. "Now here, my friends, a choice. I was going to say a difficult choice, but the more I mull it, the easier it becomes. A nubile girl of childbearing age who can provide me with sons to replace those lost. Who knows? She may already be carrying my child. Or a woman past her prime, sagging into an old hag. A cranky one at that."

Nervous laughter.

"She's not been pregnant for fifteen years, though I've given her every opportunity."

Exuberant laughter.

Lenveig stood rock steady. In a way, Brenna could feel the woman vibrate with tension. And the tension was leaving Brenna. In but a few more moments, Brenna would be well on her way to becoming queen of the North.

"But—" Arild's voice dropped a bit "—Lenveig cares enough about our union that she's ready to kill for it, or die. She does not come sniveling to me with appeals for mercy. She handles her own affairs. Most of all—" he paused for dramatic effect "—she holds her word good in the face of death."

But wait! This was not the way it was supposed to go. Where was God's hand to spare her now? She didn't really yearn for sinful things. She only wanted to survive, perhaps to rule. What was happening?

Arild's commanding voice boomed. "Be it known, my friends and cohorts, that I value a person's word above all else, even above sons and beauty."

The huge iron blade flicked toward Brenna. *It keeps coming.* She could not believe he would choose the blowsy Lenveig over her. *This is wrong—unfair!* It did not hurt nearly as much as she would have guessed. But she could not breathe, or move, or think. Her legs and arms melted, her mouth ceased framing words.

The face of Arild Thick Knee before her was blotted out by a bath of white light—was it the gates of heaven opening? Was it true? Even as her body collapsed, her heart steadfastly refused to beg entry into those white-light gates, and it refused to say the name of Jesus.

13

Puppy Love

Gwynna Fat Feet's last surviving baby might have drowned if the rain had not ceased when it did. Everyone agreed on that. Everyone disagreed on whether the world would have been a better place if it had. Gwynna Fat Feet was not the best of hunting dogs. She could not follow game with a map, smell any odor more delicate than a polecat, course animals larger than squirrels. On even the easiest of hunts, she tagged along behind the pack and barked a lot. And now, here she was with her first litter, curled up in a den of her own making under the north wall of a fieldstone shed that was about to collapse upon her.

"So she refuses to come out, eh? She can't even whelp a litter right." The great Dalainn stooped without kneeling in the soggy moss and peered under the wall into the den. "Try to save the shed," Doyle advised. "Just rock her in where she is."

"Bury her alive?" Connleigh shook his head. "She'd panic and dig out two other walls escaping. You forget how destructive she is." He shrugged and smiled gamely. "I've work to do, or I'd attend to this little puzzle sooner."

"A few javelin thrusts under there and then the rock work," advised Brian of Berit Head. He favored javelins over lances for just about everything, including some jobs requiring a knife.

Snorted Shawna of the Behr, "Men. Honestly."

Shawna planned her solution to the problem of Gwynna as she wandered out across the rain-soaked compound. She paused to watch a skein of geese nattering their way across the sky. They were headed not north but east, toward Lambay. What would they find there? Fallen, neglected grain? Scorched earth just now greening? In a way, Shawna yearned to return, to fly to Lambay as these geese were doing. But it was not the same there now. No. She had best turn her back on that former Eden, that tragic visitation of dragons.

Wolf and Skule were rebuilding the plow down by the south gate, as Shawna recalled. She wandered around the bier and down that way. The rain began again, a fine drizzle. Shawna drew her wool shawl up over her hair.

There they were, out on the lea south of the gate, literally turned upside down working on the plow. She had to smile at these young lords of the North. She walked out holding her skirt hem high.

"Well, gentlemen!" She dropped the lid on the tool chest and sat there. The cold wetness made her toes ache, even in her leather boots.

"Well, lady!" Grinning, Wolf rolled to his feet. He was mud end to end, and rainwater dripped from his blond beard.

Skule squirmed and got caught momentarily in a compromising position as he tried to wriggle out from under. He popped up to standing. He was muddier than Wolf, and wetter. And neither young man seemed even to notice that he ought to be cold.

"Did it ever occur to you," she suggested, "that you could turn the plow upside down and thereby work on it standing up?"

"We tried that." Wolf wiggled a finger toward the tool chest, so she stood up. From it he drew a towel. He dried his face and hands and tossed the towel to Skule. "It's too heavy. Sags out of plumb, and the bolt holes won't line up."

She sat again and reflected a moment on his marvelous grasp of the language. His accent was still thick as porridge, but he had the vocabulary. She hesitated and then switched tongues to his Norse. From the beginning they had traded idioms, his word and hers, her phrase and his. She did not in the least have the easy skill with Norse that he did with Erse, and she admired his quickness. So why did he consistently refuse to even try to learn Latin? He obviously was capable. What a strangely inconsistent man.

"How good are you," she asked, "at saving dogs?"

"Better at killing them." The slave grinned knowingly. "What strange little task has the Dalainn put you to this time?"

"Why did you say it that way?"

"Because whenever it's something out of the ordinary, requiring a clever or unusual solution, he shrugs it off onto you."

"He never asks me to do these strange little tasks, as you call them."

"He need not. All he need do is point them out. You undertake the solution on your own. And he knows it. He's a manipulator like my father is, using different methods with different people to get what he wants. One man he orders. Another he cajoles. You, he simply shows the problem to."

"Your father is a ri? A king?"

Wolf looked at Skule. "We were talking about that, Skule and I. We think that probably the titles are pretty much the same. Ri and jarl. Some ris bigger than others, some jarls more powerful than others." He shrugged.

Skule dived into the conversation. "And Arild Thick Knee—my uncle, you see—is the biggest!"

She looked at Wolf's face. Skule might bask in reflected glory, but Wolf didn't seem to care. Which told Shawna that Skule's father did not possess in the least the stature of Arild Thick Knee.

"An hour. Less." Wolf waved toward the plow.

She nodded. The boys went back to work on the task assigned them, and she mulled the approach they would make to the Gwynna problem. But her mind kept slipping back to Wolf. She watched his grace and his easy way with tools. She watched the way he naturally took command. Skule was following his lead. It was always like that, not just between these two but between Wolf and others he worked with. Yet he never tried to domineer or control others. He just sort of stepped into the role of foreman, and everyone else stepped in behind him. He might be a slave, but he would never ever be enslaved.

Shawna, of course, ended up helping. She forced a rivet down a series of holes while Skule and Wolf jiggled the various plow parts to line up the holes. She held things. She helped dry the tools off afterward. She explained the problem of Gwynna Fat Feet as they strode up the lea with the tool chest slung between them. The silly dog refused to leave her den, and it was about to fall in upon her.

They joked about worthless dogs. Wolf, obviously, held all dogs in utter contempt, and by name he was related to them!

134

Shawna expected him to be of the school that said, "Rock her in." Surely, he'd recommend use of a javelin. But no. Instead, he gathered kindling as he said, "Let's cook some bacon."

Skule brought fire from the house. Shawna, all happy smiles because that was her plan also, exactly, donated a few rashers of bacon from the meat safe. They sat before their fledgling fire and held the bacon out over the flames on a stick. The grease dripped and crackled and flared up. Its rich aroma filled Shawna's nostrils.

She watched the burning rowan and wagged her head. "Rowan."

"What?" Wolf tucked a few more sticks of rowan into the fire.

"Patrick converted Ireland over three hundred years ago. And yet, it still seems strange to me to burn wood that once was considered sacred. I know it's not, but old beliefs die hard."

"Sacred. The Christians once considered this wood sacred?"

"No, the Druids. The Celts were Druid before Patrick."

"I thought Mahon said the old sacred groves were oaks."

"In England. Here it was rowan."

"So what is sacred to the Christians?"

"Jesus."

"That's all?"

She smiled. "What more do you need?"

"What kind of wood was the cross made of?"

"No one knows, I think. It's not in Scripture. It's not important."

"He was a carpenter. He'd know."

"True. I doubt it was important to Him either, though. I don't think, were I hanging from that cross, that little details would be consuming my attention."

"But they did."

She looked at him. "What do you mean?"

"Remember the story Connleigh told that evening in the cattle camp when we were trimming hooves? Jesus said to His disciple, 'Behold your mother,' and to His mother, 'Behold your son.'"

"John. Probably Jesus' best friend. Jesus was giving the care of His aged mother over to John."

"That was a detail. If I were hanging on a cross, I wouldn't think of that. Not then."

"Nor would I, probably." Shawna pondered this slave's grasp of stories. He heard the passage once. Not only did he have it memorized, he was obviously meditating on it. The Irish used to be like that. Centuries ago their Brehons memorized, literally, years' worth of information—laws, tales and myths, precedents, property transactions. But the Irish learned writing, and their Brehons' collective memory faded. Now, if it wasn't written down, it did not exist.

If writing came to the Norse, would they lose their ability to instantly absorb details into memory?

And what did that passage about Saint John say to this slave? How could she present the gospel in a fresh light to him?

Then her thoughts were brushed aside, for Gwynna, the hound who would not leave her lair, appeared and wedged herself in among them, her tail wagging. Wolf wrapped an arm around her and scratched her brisket as he fed her bits of bacon. Shawna wrapped around her in the other direction. Skule left the camaraderie of the fire, tiptoeing off into the gathering dusk of the rainy late afternoon. By the time the ditzy Gwynna caught on, Skule had taken her puppy somewhere and tossed half a dozen rocks into her former den.

"Victory!" Shawna's smile faded. "Where did you put the pup, Skule?"

Skule tied a bit of cord around the dog's neck. "Under that stump outside the wall on the northeast. I'll take her over there."

Wolf laughed aloud. "The one Connleigh wants us to dig out? Brilliant, my foolish cousin! With any luck, she'll do half the work for us making herself a new den."

Skule shrugged and grinned. "She's got to be good for something, aye?" Alternately tugging and crabbing, he dragged Gwynna off to the northeast.

And they called Skule foolish? Wolf called him the brilliant fool. Shawna reflected that she and Wolf were not all that much brighter than the brilliantly foolish cousin, for here they sat in the drizzling rain, as their little fire sizzled and died of terminal wetness.

The day was far enough gone now that Shawna had to look at Wolf's face more or less from memory. Despite the feeble light of the embers, his features were dissolving in the gloom of night. They sat elbow to elbow, knee to knee, as rain soaked them top and bottom, inside and out.

He showed no sign of leaving.

She felt not in the least like leaving. If ever there was a time to bring up religion, this was it. "It's not for the love of the puppy that I undertook this problem. But the decency of it. It seems wrong to kill them for no cause save motherhood."

"I got a look at the pup. A color only a mother could love."

She smiled. "You've come a long way with the language."

"I've the best of teachers."

"What do you plan to do with your life?"

"I had no idea a slave made decisions of that sort."

"You'll earn your freedom, if it's not given to you outright. You know it. I know it. Do you know what Saint Patrick did?"

"Ran a crozier through some king's foot. Mahon told me the story."

"I don't mean that. Patrick was born in England, you know. And was captured and lived some years as a slave here in Erin. When he gained his freedom he returned to England, took holy orders, and returned here as apostle to the lost of Erin."

"I know that." Wolf sounded impatient, as if this were not a topic of his preference.

Shawna twisted around to face him in the gloaming. "Don't you see? He was so successful in bringing the gospel to the Erse because he had absorbed the culture. He wasn't an outsider coming in. He knew how to deal with the local chiefs, and what the power structure was, and what the local customs were. You are learning all that right now."

He was eyeing her suspiciously. "And?"

"And that makes you the perfect man to be the Saint Ulf of Norway."

"Was your saint a Christian?"

"Of course. He—"

"I have no plans to be. I should think that would be the first step, and I'm not taking it. Other than that, it's a splendid little notion."

"Ulf, you cannot fight destiny. I was reading in Isaiah, about two-thirds the way through the book. 'The coastlands wait for your teaching.' Coastlands. Didn't you say nearly all Norway is coastlands? That's your country, Ulf, your people."

He was looking at her incredulously. "It doesn't really say that!"

"It does indeed. I'll show it to you then, not that the writing means much if you don't read. But it's there. You can't fight destiny, Ulf."

"Destiny. We all have our destiny." He hesitated. "Do you?"

"Everyone does."

"What is yours?"

"I don't know yet. It's not something tattooed on your nose when you're born, you know. Sometimes it unfolds slowly."

What was going on in that lively Norse mind? She watched the few embers left and let what she had been saying settle in. She had impressed him in some way, she was pretty sure. She knew not how.

"The word in the slave quarters," Wolf said, "is that you and the boys will become of the Dalainn. Adoption. They seem to think it's an honor."

So he was changing the subject. She allowed that. "It is. What it really is, is a political expediency. A ploy."

"What is not, ever?"

She snorted. "Isn't that the truth of life?"

"With the Dalainn it seems to be. And my father. I grew up with political expediency. What is adoption among the Erse?"

"An old, old custom, in place centuries before Saint Patrick. A wealthy mentor takes in a boy—sometimes a girl—as his own child, with all the rights and privileges of his blood family. But the child does not lose his original parents or heritage in the process."

"It gives him a double prestige. Power."

"Exactly. Adoption into the Dalainn will be wonderful for the boys. They keep all their rights and privileges as survivors of the Behr, and they'll carry all the political strength of the Dalainn. Conceivably, either of them could rule Erin someday, or enter the priesthood with privilege, or build their own monastery. Anything they choose."

He pondered this for a long stretch of minutes. Shawna wondered idly what had become of Skule. Probably the bright young fool was curling up in a warm, dry bed.

With exaggerated casualness he said, "That's the boys. What about you?"

"I think I will decline."

"And enter the Dalainn instead by marrying Connleigh."

Her head snapped around to him. "Whatever makes you think that?"

"Just repeating the gossip. I understand many of Erin's young men never marry."

"True. Warring takes its toll, and—"

"The Norsemen haven't cut that wide a swath."

"Oh, wars with the Norse are the least of it. The petty infighting between minor chiefs. It goes on forever, and it takes so many young men. So does the priesthood, for the church in Rome is claiming now that priests and monks ought not marry. How they think the church will perpetuate itself is beyond me. Not that we here in Erin pay all that much attention to Rome. Also, a lot travel to the continent seeking their fortunes and never return."

He nodded. "Which confirms their gossip. The house girls think Muirgheal is anxious for you to marry Connleigh, not only so that he'll settle down but to take you out of circulation, you might say."

Shawna snorted. "To give her own two dull daughters a better chance at a shrunken marriage pool. I wouldn't doubt the gossip a moment." She laughed. "So Muirgheal considers me a rival to her daughters. That explains a lot. Why she resists all my suggestions around the farm, why she's always shoving me at Connleigh."

"It's not all her. You and Connleigh enjoy the same things—studying books especially. You can read, they say."

"I was the only woman on Lambay who could read. We had two books there. I've no idea what became of them. I hope they found their way to the monastery there. I'm surprised you don't read. You're so quick with everything else."

"Among the Norse there is no book, no reading. Runes—inscriptions—but not the kind of books these people talk about. No writings that convey deep thought. So you and Connleigh can marry and have lots of children who read."

She arched around to study his face, to see past that wet beard and nervous sort of look into the mind of this man. "And why not? Connleigh is an excellent choice. He enjoys the same rank and privilege here in Erin that you would were you home in your Northland. And I'm sure you consider yourself a fine catch indeed for any young lady."

She had been altogether too snide in that last comment. She bit her tongue, wishing the words had not been spoken.

And he took her hasty words exactly as they had come out. With equal shortness, he replied, "I do, lady. But I've had my fill unto death of political expediency. When I marry it shall be for love. My father can have his alliances and manipulations. There are things more important than that in life."

Here was her moment to make amends, to get back in his sympathy. "I agree about political expediency. But women must concern themselves with other things. Protection, for example. It's a dangerous world we live in."

"You really think Connleigh would protect you?"

"He's powerful. But he's thinking about the priesthood. If he becomes a monk, he ought not marry. Most of all, though, I do not think I love him. I will have my choice, and it will have nothing to do with other people's expectations."

He was studying her again, but she felt the attention rather than observed it. "I shall have my choice too."

In the total darkness of true night, all detail disappeared. She must depend now on her ear, on interpreting the inflections in his voice. "You can't. You're a slave. A slave has no choice."

"Can a slave be chosen?"

"Yes."

"That's one way."

She smiled in the darkness. Indeed it was. There was more than one way for a clever slave to exercise choice. They sat in the wet silence for long, long minutes.

She thought fleetingly of what was appropriate for a young woman to say and what was not. She justified her thoughts with the blanket reasoning that this outlander had no idea of what was proper and improper in Erse culture. It made no difference, really, whether he heard proper or improper comments.

So she asked, "Do Northmen kiss?"

"Kiss." His thoughtful, even say puzzled, inflection as he repeated the word suggested to her right there that he hadn't the slightest notion what she was talking about.

Now what?

She licked her lips. "It's a gesture of affection. Love. The apostle Paul said to greet each other with a holy kiss."

"Oh." His interest flagged right there. Religion always did that, any time she brought it up.

"It has other purposes—not just sacred. Profane also. You kiss babies to show them you love them. And a man and woman express affection for each other with a kiss. I think it goes back to Roman times. I know the custom is at least eight hundred years old."

"Oh." His interest quickened instantly. Just the way he said "Oh" could convey so much. He poked their dying fire with a stick, spreading the last little embers. One by one, the feeble red dots winked out. The feckless fire had offered no real light at all. Now, with it gone, the stars hidden, the moon obliterated, total darkness closed down around them.

Feeling suddenly very nervous, Shawna raced forward. "It's a custom you ought to acquaint yourself with, if you're going to be Erse. Don't you think?"

"Always best when in Rome to do as the Romans do. That's one of Mahon's favorite phrases. I don't think much of your Erse monks, but Mahon is exceptional."

"And wise. He's so wise. He cannot tell you where he left his sandals an hour ago, but he can recite Isaiah page after page. And then discourse on it for three days." She did not want to talk about Mahon now. "I mean, you're pretty much here for good, don't you think?"

He was pressing closer to her now than he used to. He purred, "I have more tying me here now than ties me to the Northland."

"Slavery aside, of course."

"Slavery aside, of course. I miss the North, and true winter, and the mountains and all that. But here . . ." He stopped.

She wanted to hear more. She wasn't sure what she wanted to hear. Her life certainly needed no further complications, but she wished so much he hadn't stopped.

She took a deep breath. "Anyway. About kisses. You should look into them if you plan to do as the Romans do."

"Do slaves kiss?"

"Why, yes. I'm sure they must."

"Ah. Then perhaps I've observed one. The house girl and the stable boy. A joining of lips normally accompanied by an embrace?"

"That's it." It sounded so dull. She almost giggled aloud.

"And there's got to be a Latin word for it if it's a Roman custom."

Osculare, I believe." Even that sounded dull. Let's osculate, my beloved. Hardly.

"Mmm," mumbled his voice thoughtfully in the blackness. His hands grasped her shoulders and turned her toward his voice. "In fact, I've observed several related activities. Now I am confused. Is it this?" He ran his fingers down her arm, took her hand in his, and kissed it the way Doyle Dalainn greeted women of stature. His lips across the back of her hand felt remarkably dry and warm. "Or this?" He touched his lips to her forehead. Where had he seen that? "Or this?"

And that latter this was that.

He kissed awkwardly, a man who had until this moment seen the gesture only from afar. But Shawna was not much less awkward. Her brothers had successfully shielded her from any number of chances to practice the craft. And the few swains she actually kissed in her youth (so far away those days on Lambay seemed now) were not much more experienced. Her brother had sat down with her one winter's night and explained all the theory of it, but of course none of the actual practice. Her brother had just been entering his I-Know-It-All-Now early male adulthood.

She didn't remember a thing of what he said, for this present reality surpassed any theory however grandiose. Wolf drew her in against himself, tighter, tighter. Her wool shawl slipped off the back of her head.

The awkwardness passed quickly.

He lifted away. "A Northman," he murmured, "would take his woman now, to prove his love to her."

"The Christian waits until marriage."

"So Mahon said. I'm not a Christian." His mouth found hers again and pressed his point home.

She wrenched away. "I am. No. I'll not betray my Lord's trust. No. Words as you wish. But not actions."

"Then words they must be. I love you." He spoke it in Erse. He repeated it in Norse.

And in either language, they sounded equally exhilarating.

14

Heroes

The door of the main house flew open. Happiness poked at Wolf's heart with a cheery finger and made it flitter. It was she. She must have snatched her shawl on the way to the door, for she was three strides into the early morning rain before she swung it out and around to cover her shoulders. She was magnificently angry. Wolf expected steam to rise where the rain hit her scowling brow.

From the seed shed door he watched her march out across the Dalainn compound.

Happiness quit pestering Wolf's heart and tiptoed away, for behind her came the tall, insipid Connleigh, cloakless and pleading. She wheeled upon him and threw up both hands, a "Stop!" gesture. He stopped. What that woman needed more than anything else was a real man who would ignore such gestures and have his way with her. Slaves are not real men, or Wolf would gladly carry her off in a moment.

Whatever she normally saw in the listless Connleigh was hidden from her at the moment. "It's despicable!" she stormed.

He purred something to mollify her. She would not be mollified. And then the gutless book reader simply stood there looking lost and watched her stomp away from him.

Right toward Wolf.

He must play these next few minutes carefully if this simple Norse slave would win favor. He waited until she saw him. She slowed her stride, then continued this way, past the bier, past the seed shed, past Wolf, toward the east gate.

He fell in beside her. "Well, lady! You look absolutely enraged, and I could not be more delighted."

She paused and stared at him. The glare softened ever so slightly.

"You are irate with Connleigh, and I am of the humble view that he is not the man for you. Therefore—" he added hastily, jabbing a finger skyward, for her frown was fast returning "—I applaud your good taste in ire."

"You would do well, slave, to seek out the occasion of my ire."

"It pertains to me?"

"Probably. Certainly it pertains to Skule. The Dalainn are trotting him around the country again, organizing the militia along the coast." She huffed out the gate and left it standing open.

Wolf swung it to behind him. "They did that all last autumn. Why does it enrage you now?"

"He goes in chains." Her voice dripped disgust.

"They did that too, last autumn."

"It's uncalled for! You and he have more than proven yourselves. You've assimilated splendidly." She glanced at Wolf. "That means, you and Skule have fit in very comfortably to the Celtic way and language."

"I would guess the chains are strictly for show."

"Of course, it's all show! And when Doyle and Connleigh bring every ri in the southwest here, to wine them and dine them, you'll find yourself in shackles as well, don't think you won't. Don't you care?"

"Of course I care." He dropped his voice. "What delights me is that you care. Not just for a heathen slave, but for justice and fair play."

"Mine is a just God. He calls me to serve justice. We talked about that."

"Doyle Dalainn espouses the same God, and Doyle's crooked as a hound's hind leg. No. You delight me. Your God does not."

She lost the fury in her face. "And that, Wolf, is the only barrier between us—I mean, between . . ."

"A barrier erected in the months since you defined for me what a kiss is."

"No, it's always been there. It just wasn't as obvious until then."

"All the same, you've been keeping away from me."

"Intentionally. I must think."

"Pity. I can't think of a greater waste of time, by and large."

"You go out on a raiding expedition thoughtlessly?"

"Plenty of planning. Almost no thinking. If you thought about it, it wouldn't seem worth the danger. Or the excitement."

She paused, so he paused. She gazed out across the barley field sown less than a month ago. It was well up now, a billowing, rippling, undulant spread of brilliant green. "There is a passage in Saint Matthew, called the Beatitudes. It's a speech Jesus gave a gathering of listeners. He said, 'Blessed are the peacemakers.' Not the warriors. The peacemakers."

Wolf wasn't quite sure where this was going.

She turned to face him. "Wolf? Would you give up raiding if I asked you to?"

He pondered not the question itself but its heavy ramifications. He must not permit his eager desire to please her, his need to look better than the ri's blond son, stampede him into the wrong answer. Whatever he said this moment he would have to live with forever.

And so he hedged his bet. "I would try, lady." Somehow feeling very pleased with his answer, he repeated it. "Sure and I would try!"

* * *

Hegaard Broad Back stood with both feet balanced precariously on the small deck behind his ship's lean stem. He wrapped a stubby arm around the dragon neck and listened to nothing.

They hung in the midst of nothing, tasting nothing, seeing nothing but the dense fog enshrouding them. Never had Hegaard or his secondary officers ever drifted in a fog this dense for so long. No sound of surf to indicate land. No sea birds.

No horn from the other vessels. Seven of them had sailed south from Trondelag. Now three had drifted so far off, lost in this fog, that Hegaard dismissed them. They must go a-raiding on their own. If they were still within earshot of the horn they would have responded. They would have rowed back. The remaining four tossed lines out, vessel to vessel, to keep them together lest more drift away.

The fog closed in so tightly they could not make out north from south now for three days. An even, pearlescent gray, the sky divulged not a crumb of information. They would gladly row, if they only had some indication which direction.

They slept at sea, stretched out among the sea chests they used for seats. They whiled away the days at sea. But you cannot risk fire aboard by cooking at sea, so they ate cold biscuit and raw fish. Hegaard for one was heartily sick of it. He wanted porridge and roast meat. He wanted his feet on solid ground.

To Hegaard's right, in the next vessel over, Jorn of East End climbed up onto his foredeck and leaned against his ship's stem. "With our numbers reduced, we probably ought to amend our plans. Your recommendations?" Sound travels easily in fog. Jorn hardly had to raise his voice.

"That island last year. No sense going back there again. It wasn't that rich to start with, and we cleaned her out well."

"I agree. What do the Celts see in their blasted cows, anyway?"

Hegaard grimaced. Up and down the Irish coast, they hit the same thing over and over. They were looking for booty of their own preference, and the crazy Celts were trying to protect their verminous cows and books. "And the mainland there is probably waiting for us. We should strike farther south, where we're still just a rumor."

Jorn nodded. "That river. What did the slave call it? The Liffey. Beyond there, maybe. Beyond that chain of mountains on its south shore. Wicklow? Besides, that will leave that area and north of it to the others, if they ever find their way to Erin."

That sounded good. Hegaard ran a few alternatives through his head and came almost immediately back to that one. "Sail straight south to the Liffey and start working well below that area." He snorted. "The minute we find out where south is hiding."

* * *

Ceirre of the Liffey wagged her gray head at the political machinations that men thought passed for wisdom. Did Doyle realize how silly he looked with his single scrawny slave in tow? And why didn't he take the other, if he was out to impress the ris to the south? The other, the quick one, would be so much more effective than the little chicken thief. Doyle always had reasons for what he did and did not do. It puzzled Ceirre greatly why he did not exploit his best Northman.

Ceirre was getting too old to travel so far afield. Here she went to the Dalainn, when so many other raths lay closer to her tiny domain. She had to cross the Liffey at Dublin Crossing, then walk all day to reach the Dalainn. If it were not for Shawna and the boys, she'd stay home, as she preferred.

What was this? All along the road leading to their rath, the Dalainn were finishing planting. Nearly a month early, it was; three weeks, at least. Look at the velvet barley, doing so fine already. And their broadbeans. Slave children with banners of red wool were keeping the jackdaws and ravens away from the newly sprouted peas. Occasionally the little finches learned to pull sprouts to eat what was left of the germinated seed, but somehow finches were so much easier to forgive than were the prideful ravens.

Where were her boys? She did not see them out in the fields here to the south, so she continued in the gate. She dropped her burden by the door of the main house and rapped. No response. From her bundle she drew two small linen rolls and wandered out the east gate.

With whining, cranky *peeents,* a loose flock of lapwings lifted off the meadow north of the wall in flapping, erratic disarray. Their dark green backs flashed a bit of iridescence in the almost-full sun. Pipits prowled the meadow, and a lark. Ah, spring.

There in the distance at one fell stroke, everyone she wanted most to see was working. Or playing. Sure and they seemed to be laughing a lot to be working. And yet there are few jobs more strenuous than plowing.

They were using one of Doyle's black teams. Peadar sat on the far horse, and Paul rode the near one. Paul handled the reins for both horses, and Wolf worked the plow. Behind him, her skirts tucked high to keep them clean, Shawna led three slaves in raking and hoeing the furrows down to smooth soil, ready to receive the seed. They stacked stones in a neat, dense windrow down a furrow. Every three or four furrows was another of those lines of stones. Why not remove them completely from the field? There was almost certainly a good reason. Shawna did nothing without a sensible reason. Except choose men.

When Doyle or Muirgheal directed planting, they were until July getting their wheat in. Ceirre stood at the side of the field and warmed herself in the gentle irony. While Doyle busied himself fortifying Erin against the Norse, Shawna, forced to the mainland by Norse incursions and accompanied by this quick young Northman, was revolutionizing Doyle's farming methods. The Dalainn were notoriously slow to plant and harvest.

Obviously this was the Behr's timetable, not the Dalainn's, to have so much of the year's crop in already and sprouted. It's an ill wind that doesn't blow at least a little good.

Peadar spotted her first, slid from the horse in motion, and came running. His soprano "Auntie Ceirre!" pretty much halted the whole plowing process. Paul and Shawna raced each other across the plowed land. Even Wolf came jogging over. The field slaves saw their chance and quickly spread themselves out, flaccid, in the unplowed grass. Steam rising from their backs, the black horses stood abandoned, and grateful. They shook themselves, rattling their harness, and ventured a few nibbles of the fallow grass around them.

The Northman did not hug her, but then, he had no reason to. He watched from apart, with a certain curious bemusement.

"This is for you, Peadar." Ceirre distributed her little rolls of linen. "And Paul, this is for you." She looked sharply at Shawna. "The smell of trouble I told you about last fall lingers even heavier in the air this spring."

And Shawna held Ceirre's eye just as sharply. "Fortunately, I choose to ignore it."

"Obviously."

Paul had unrolled his gift, a new linen shirt. He squirmed out of his old one instantly and tried it on.

"Perfect fit!" Ceirre purred. "But you know? I made it intentionally too large, thinking you would grow into it. You've grown so fine over winter, Paul of the Behr! And you, Peadar! Let's see how yours fits."

Peadar, too, had grown, and everyone praised him in his new shirt. He glowed like a peat fire.

Effusively, Paul thanked her. And then, shyly, he boasted, "I am of the Dalainn now, Auntie Ceirre."

So. The adoption prospect was now fact.

"The horses need rest. Come." Ceirre walked over to the only tree in half a mile, a wind-twisted little white gum on a rocky copse. She settled down under it, glad for the rest. Shawna sat at her feet and drew her own legs in under her skirts. The boys clambered into her lap. Apart, observing, obviously missing nothing, the Norse slave sat down on a rock a few feet away.

"Once upon a time," Ceirre began, "there lived a hero with an island kingdom. His people under him feared no ris from elsewhere, for who wants to govern a kingdom you must row out to?

"One day this young hero was out plowing—sure and you should see how he plowed! Furrows as straight as arrows, and his little horse, far from working up a sweat, had to trot to stay ahead of him, so powerfully did he thrust his plow forward."

Paul giggled. "Our horses are sweating, Wolf."

"And I am but a humble Norseman, not a young hero of the Celts." The Northman was smiling. "Obviously, Celts and Norse are not cut of the same bolt of cloth."

"Obviously." Ceirre continued. "As he worked, plowing, he saw a flock of thrushes flush out of the grass on the hill beyond him. From the behavior of the birds he knew instantly that danger came that way. He cut his horse loose and drove it off. Then he seized his plowshare out of the ground, for it was his only weapon. With a mighty war cry and a great salmon leap, he ran forward!"

The boys sat rapt, all eyes and ears. They had not heard the story before. Ceirre glanced briefly at Shawna. She knew the tale, for tears streamed down her cheeks.

"Our hero's instincts were good. Here came a raiding party, people from a tuath on the mainland, intent on plunder. The hero roared straight over the hill and fell upon that very surprised raiding party approaching from the other side. With the broad wooden blade of his plowshare he deflected their javelins, and with its sharp edge he beheaded their leader. The raiders fell back in disarray.

"The loosed horse had returned to the rath, alerting others. The hero's brothers came instantly and arrived barely in time to take part in the battle, for it was all over quickly. The raiders trampled each other returning to their boat. Swimming with the strength of a salmon, our hero followed the boat out and dumped it over, drowning all but one of its crew, who swam ashore to tell the world of the hero's exploits.

"Never again did raiders approach that island kingdom, when the power and glory of its brothers became known. The raiders came to steal, and instead, the hero and his brothers gathered in all the raiders' fine weapons and gold collars. Sure and you should have seen the cunningly wrought sword he took from the leader's corpse. The gold wire filigree in the hardwood handle, the carving on the stub end, the swirls and the woven knots incised on the tempered blade."

"My father had a sword like that!" Paul twisted around in her lap to face her more squarely. "The gold was beaten into the handle and into the haft too."

"Your father, Paul, is that hero."

The boys gaped. Shawna lurched to her feet and hurried off. Her shoulders heaved as she left. The Northman very nearly leaped up to follow her. He fought himself to a standstill and settled back on his rock to listen.

Ceirre pressed her point home. "You are the sons of a great hero. Someday you will be heroes in your own right. Never ever forget your heritage among the Behr, lads. 'Tis a proud family, the finest family in Erin, and rife with honor and heroes."

"Tell us more about our father!" Peadar snuggled in closer. "And what is a salmon leap?"

"Nothing for an old woman to fling herself about demonstrating. We'll let the Dalainn show you. They fancy themselves heroes." She wiggled a finger at Wolf. "This old crone has disrupted spring plowing long enough. You can handle it without the boys' help, can you not?"

"I shall try to make do." The scraggly Northman hopped to his feet. He again gazed off toward Shawna. Then he left her to her memories and strode away to the horses, calling the slaves in behind him.

"Norsemen have their heroes too," Paul offered, "and some very strange gods. Wolf tells us about them. Thor, and Balder, and Loki. But his stories have sad endings most of the time. They're dark stories."

"'Tis a dark culture from whence he comes. You are wise beyond your years, Paul of the Behr. To judge a people, listen to their stories. You'll learn all you need know about them."

The Northman had taken up the reins and recommenced plowing. Shawna walked disconsolately across the field and picked up her hoe. She fell in behind him, her face still somber in grief revisited. The slaves knew better than to dawdle now, though they certainly could not be called lively. Rocks clicked, and the horse snorted, and hoes and the plowshare whispered. The world was marching in step again.

Ceirre would see to her trading with Muirgheal later. She would give the Dalainn her extra eggs and ask to borrow one of the horses as soon as the plowing was completed. With it she would bring in firewood for sale. Her summer rounds were beginning again.

But not now. All that could wait. She had a more important task now, to inculcate in these small boys some of the richness of their heritage. "Now let me tell you about a hero who fell into the duck pond."

And she proceeded with another well-known story about Paul's father.

* * *

Pouting hardly becomes a warrior. Connleigh pouted like a small child denied a treat, and he didn't care who knew it. He rode in lordly isolation, his father just ahead. Behind him, their fighting force strung out along the track. The shackled slave barely kept up among them. They wound down now out of the mountains to the south, toward the Liffey and Dublin Crossing. The few scattered raths among these wooded hills gave way to extensive holdings of farms clustered fairly close together.

Much as he was enjoying (in its own way) this grumpy aloneness, it was coming to an abrupt end. Doyle Dalainn reined in his stud, dropping back until his horse matched strides with Connleigh's.

Father studied son. Son studied the track ahead. "Enough, Connleigh. You never have understood the way power works, have you?"

"I understand more than you think. I suspect many of the clans we've been visiting with that misbegotten pagan devil back there understand as well. And the clans that do not see through you are too dull to be good company, let alone good soldiers."

"I'm saving Erin from the outlanders."

"You're trying to gather Erin under your banner and your hand, whether they wish to be gathered or not."

"You saw the Behr. And still you discount the menace these pagans pose."

Desperately Connleigh fought the urge to keep his mouth shut. He would never be his own man so long as he let Doyle Dalainn enjoy the last word, the final thought, the closing phrase. "Those Norse marauders were surely renegades, driven out of their own country and forced to plunder other shores in order to live. They were shadows in the night, a scourge of God to be used for divine discipline and then discarded. No threat."

"Lindesfarne. Northumbria. Lambay. We're next, lad."

Connleigh glanced back at the Norse slave strolling lackadaisically among the horses. He seemed accustomed to his fetters. Whatever was it that set Shawna off so hotly when Connleigh first mentioned this trip? He did not understand women in general, and the women closest him—his mother and sisters, the grieving Shawna—he fathomed least of all.

On the other hand, he didn't understand his father all that well either. He could understand Doyle's present snit. The great one sat astride his latest favorite, an absolutely huge, feather-legged sorrel mare, scowling as dark as his mount. His journey had not gone well.

Yes, Connleigh could understand that just fine. He broke the silence. "This is a poor time to second-guess what might have been. But had you brought the other Northman, do you suppose the southern tuaths would have been easier persuaded to your plan?"

"If I thought it would help, he would be here."

Feeling seven or eight inches tall, Connleigh tried again. "Explain to me why he is not here."

"Too dangerous. In any skirmish or problem, the slave is first to die. I'm saving him."

Saving him. For what? Connleigh really ought to ask, but he didn't like getting cut down. Skirmish? Who would dare attack Doyle Dalainn and his retinue of warriors?

Connleigh changed the subject. "My brothers aren't here, either."

"When they're older."

"They've been sparring all spring, practicing with lance and ax. You'll be pleased with their progress."

"And you have been neglecting all but archery. Or did you think I didn't notice?"

"You miss nothing. We both know that. I find marksmanship relaxing and pleasant."

"Work with lance and ax is more to the point." He smirked at his pun. "Hand to hand is where you live or die." He cast a sidewise glance. "You do not intend to just shoot arrows from afar, I trust. You plan to lead forth from the front line?"

"I plan to travel to Rome."

It was out. For the first time, the issue was raised. Nothing would be settled here today. Connleigh knew that. But the opening parries and feints could now proceed. He looked again at Doyle.

The dark man sat staring straight ahead. Connleigh had not made his journey any brighter. Indeed, he should have raised the subject months ago. It was only with heroic effort he was able to mention it now.

Now that the winter winds were past and summer southerlies offered some small modicum of safety, he ought begin his travels soon. His father's first response would be, "Why not to Armagh?"

Doyle spoke with rage thinly masked. "Why not Armagh? There's nothing in Rome for the Erse."

"Even Mahon keeps contact with Rome. It's the place you begin, the place Patrick began." Connleigh pondered but a moment the point most likely to impress his father. "The Dalainn can surely make use of contact and patronage with Rome."

The Dalainn rode in sullen silence.

Connleigh absolutely hated this lull before the storm.

15

Free Flight

Of all the world's feeble, doddering, unpopular crones, Ceirre was most blessed by God. Shawna gave her all she could because Shawna appeared to like her so, and because that was how Shawna was. Giving. Ceirre seemed to fill a hungry place in Shawna's life, and she wondered what the relationship between Shawna and her mum had been. Close, no doubt.

Muirgheal lavished gifts upon Ceirre because Muirgheal would have given her the farm itself to send her on her way. She was an intrusion in Muirgheal's life. And she cared not a whit.

Glinn, the smith-and-cobbler, had given her presents also. That one she could not figure out.

She walked with purpose down the slippery, muddy track. Very shortly this track would turn to dust. Even after all those months of winter and spring rains the road dried out quickly, instantly the weather cleared.

The head of the big black farm horse bobbed beside her ear. On its back it carried enough thatch to cover most of her cottage roof where a leak had developed in the winter, and enough cord to tie it. Behind Ceirre, and under her protest, walked Shawna with a great bundle of newly hackled line. It was nice of Shawna to give it to her, but one reason she made shirts for the boys was that she herself was not in need of garments this year.

Up ahead, the Northman led the party. He carried a load half the size of the horse's and just as heavy—a bundle containing fresh lamb, salted pork, and dried peas from last year's crop. Glinn the smith himself carried his gifts ("Would I give these to an old woman and then expect her to tote them home? What kind of a man do you think I am?"). He carried the heaviest load of all: an ax, two pothooks, a new pair of boots, and a bright iron pot.

Wolf paused and raised his head. "Horseman coming. Rapidly."

Ceirre knew from long experience whether horsemen pay much mind to traveling crones. She hastened to the side, dragging the horse out of the track. The load of thatch stuck out so far on both sides that the horseman might well slam into it and knock it askew.

Here came the hostler, Fairleigh, astride that new sorrel mare that had taken Doyle's fancy of late. At full gallop, Fairleigh came clattering. He hauled to a stop beside Glinn. The mud from his mare's flying hooves spattered Ceirre. Churl!

"Northmen!" the churl cried. "Flee! Northmen!"

Fairleigh saw Glinn, saw the man instantly shed his burden. He saw Shawna, probably noticed Ceirre. He quite obviously did not notice the Northman.

The Norse slave leaped instantly forward and seized the sorrel's bridle. As Ceirre watched amazed, he hooked his leg in the mare's near foreleg, and with a twist and a lunge he pulled the horse over on her side. She slammed, writhing, to the ground. What a splendid move! Ceirre had never seen anything remotely like that before.

His fist whipped out and knocked Glinn backwards into Shawna. The smith doubled over, his sword only half drawn from its sheath. That sort of thing Ceirre had seen many a time. The Northman's foot lashed out (was that the good leg or the bad leg? Ceirre had forgotten which was which) and caught the floundering Fairleigh in the stomach.

The sorrel squirmed wildly, flailing. When she lurched to her feet, Ulf was in her saddle. Fairleigh yelled, and Glinn flopped about on the ground like a beached salmon. His knees high on her shoulders, the Northman brought the frantic, dancing mare under control and swung her around. He reined the mare aside to avoid Ceirre, which is more than Fairleigh had done.

Fairleigh snatched for the bridle much too late to expect to grab it.

Glinn sat in the mud looking confused.

Shawna, both hands pressed to her mouth, was sobbing.

* * *

Ailan stepped into the glade and spread his hands wide.

"Can't you feel it? The energy! This for certain is one of the old sacred grounds."

He pivoted to face Innis of the Lower Lake. "Think of it! A grove held sacred for thousands of years—and right on your forest land. What a fortunate man you are. I'll bet this area is productive for you."

The stocky little farmer behind him scratched his beard. "Now you mention it, when I turn my hogs out into here they fatten quickly. I attributed it to all the acorns. You think it's sacred, eh?" Innis shook his head. "But not to the Christian faith."

Fiona wandered over to a stump and perched on it. She looked disinterested, but then she usually looked disinterested.

Ailan nodded. "I have learned that the Christians usurped power from the old ways every chance possible. For example, most of the churches of Christ are built in places where Druidism was once practiced. Think of all the saints from three hundred years ago who sound suspiciously like gods and goddesses that lived here before Patrick. Why, even Brigid had a Celtic predecessor, a druidic goddess named Brigid."

Innis stood open-mouthed.

Ailan pressed his point. "How many miracles do you see performed nowadays? Does it not strike you as odd that although men have been studying the Word of the Lord here for centuries, and ought to be three hundred times more spiritual than the men of old, they can't produce miracles like the old saints could?"

"Yourself is courting blasphemy, you know."

"Or speaking truth. Think about it. What do your eyes and heart tell you? Is God to be found in little wooden churches or in this greenwood?"

Innis mused. He hooked his thumbs in his belt and gazed up into the whispering oaks. "I always have rather fancied this glade."

"We were talking early about the unity of man with the earth and how important that is for a farmer. For anyone. We all are of the earth. You are aware, aren't you, that there are ceremonies which can invoke that unity?"

"You mean like the monk blessing the animals in spring?"

"More than that. Man himself, united with the earth that nurtures him."

This was Fiona's cue. She was supposed to step up to Innis and explain ritual union to him. But she was idly picking at her cuticles, her face empty. It sometimes appeared that she didn't take this great mission in life the least bit seriously.

A woman's voice called from afar off. Ailan grimaced. Getting a farmer to observe the rite of ritual union with Fiona usually swayed him to the old ways when nothing else would. But no chance of that now, for here came the wife crashing and running through the wildwood.

"Here!" Innis called. He headed back the overgrown track toward his rath.

Ailan grabbed Fiona's elbow and yanked her into motion. He jogged off into the woods, following the farmer.

Innis's tubby little wife came wheezing to a halt as he joined her. "Northmen! At the crossing! The ri sent a rider this way for help! Here is your sword. Go quickly! Godspeed!"

"No!" Ailan grabbed Innis's arm. "I must speak boldly. And quickly. Your whole life you have been observing the rules and the faith, have you not?"

"As best I can."

"You've confessed your sins as they occur and cleansed your heart."

"I try."

"Then what is God punishing you for, dear Innis?"

The man stared at him.

"The Northmen raided Lindesfarne, one of the finest and most devout of holy places, sure and devoid of sin there if anywhere. Why? To punish what?"

The man nodded slowly.

Ailan kept talking. "The ri is trying to stay punishment by force of arms. You know and I know that can never work. To avoid punishment, avoid the transgression. Even Jesus blessed the peacemakers, though no man in Erin pays attention to Him."

Innis's eyes narrowed. "You are saying, to defeat the Northmen we must return to the old ways."

"Does might of arm do the job?"

Innis looked at the sword in his hand. "Meself be no hero, heaven knows. I've not killed a man in all me days, nor have I the taste to do so. But I can add me weight to the defeat of the Danes in this way."

His wife stood wide-eyed. "Why do ye stand here blathering? The ri wants men now!"

Innis nodded. "The ri wants men to step in front of Danish battleaxes. I want peace and safety." He lowered his sword and turned to Ailan. "What shall we do to heal the land?"

* * *

The sorrel was almost too much horse for a man who had grown up with the sturdy, pedestrian little North horses. Ulf kept his knees high and locked against her shoulders, his heels dug deep into her sides. Still her stride, so long and powerful, nearly unhorsed him at every bend in the track.

He rode at full gallop across the broad, open pastures, down toward a dark little network of glens to the south. The Northmen would be hard against the sea, though, so he knew in a general way where he must go.

He drew the mare in as the track approached broad bluffs. The breath roared in her wide nostrils. Her flanks heaved mightily. The resinous sweat on her shoulders provided his legs a good purchase.

He could hear the surf wash against the rocks far below. Where would Northmen come ashore? He turned the mare aside to a rocky headland, the better to scan the sea far and wide. The fresh breeze in his face would be easy to row in, brisk enough to sail in. Perfect weather for a raid.

The mare's breathing quieted enough that he could pick up other sounds. Gulls mewing. A corncrake's raspy voice. A pipit's thin *tseep* down by the sloshing water. Smallish, gray, crowlike birds with their *chaka-chaka-chack.* He wished he could read the land better here, to know when the local birds were excited by intruders, or deer were absent when they ought to be present.

A small flock of those crowlike birds rose off the cliffside far to the south. He turned the mare that way and drove her down

160

through the rocks into better footing. This Erin was paved with as many pesky boulders as the Northland, but they were mossier. He regained the trail a quarter mile to the south as it looped out and skirted the bluffs above the sea.

In the distance he saw the Dalainn party approach. The ri-ruirech on his dun stallion led the pack, with the party strung out in bits and clumps behind him, disordered. Struggling along among them came Skule in his chains. They were hastening—was it a retreat? Wolf could not imagine the head man backing out of a fight. He didn't seem the sort.

As Wolf watched, Doyle Dalainn drew his horse in and let half his pack pass him. The horse looked spent and did not seem to resist the slow-down at all. Now Doyle was haranguing the fellow who dragged Skule along.

There! Just beyond that far point, moving out into the open water—three longships! They were raising sail to capture the land breeze. And they were too far away to hail.

* * *

Connleigh smarted inside and out. Out, he had borne a terrific wallop in their surprise skirmish with those Norsemen. Inside, he strongly suspected his father, ri-ruirech, lord of this part of Erin, to be a coward.

It had all happened so suddenly. Probably the surprise would not have been so great were the Dalainn traveling properly, with weapons easily at hand. But the Dalainn were coming up out of Dublin Crossing, carrying burdens and weapons above their heads to keep them dry as they waded through the thigh-high water. When a dozen Northmen came upon them, both sides seemed equally startled, equally afraid.

The Norse were clearly just as amazed to come upon the armed Dalainn party as the Dalainn party had been to discover invaders. Doyle Dalainn, dragging that poor Northman about in chains for so long, suddenly faced the real thing, and at a most inappropriate time.

Connleigh was absolutely certain the Dalainn could have handled these raiders had they seized the moment of surprise more quickly. The raiders had actually turned tail, until one of

161

their number rallied them and they turned again to fight. A head-on attack then would have routed them. Seven foot soldiers and three mounted men—the numbers were about twenty raiders to ten Celts—not bad odds at all and practically guaranteeing a Celtic victory.

But the Dalainn fled. They yanked their screaming, begging slave off his feet and dragged him with them. They summarily and hastily left the field of battle. Connleigh was not by nature a militaristic person, but this disgusted him.

And most disgusting of all, by default Connleigh was leading the retreat. Doyle had dropped back to goad the stragglers. Fairleigh had ridden away on Doyle's new sorrel mare to muster help. That left Connleigh at the head of the party looking most cowardly of all.

What was this? Fairleigh was returning, alone, and much too quickly to have raised the alarm in the nearby tuaths.

A hundred yards back, Doyle swore under his breath, a vice Mahon and his minions had never been able to shake out of him. "Other raiders lie in wait ahead of us!" he shouted. "See, here comes Fairleigh with the warning!"

Something was wrong, and it wasn't just raiders. Here came Doyle's mare, all right, but never before had Fairleigh ever ridden her with his knees so high on her withers, his head tucked so low. Connleigh watched her come, mildly confused, and she was nearly upon them before he realized. . .

As he reached for his sword he caught himself most uncharacteristically swearing under his breath.

* * *

Wolf might well be put to death for this. A slave dare not turn upon his masters. This was probably his last act as a living man. Still, entering Valhalla a hero was far preferable to enslavement. He urged the mare forward at a hard gallop, straight toward the Dalainn's fleeing party. He hunched low in the horse's flying mane, hoping they would not notice until the last moment that he was not their hostler.

Connleigh was the first to realize, and that rather surprised Wolf. He would not have guessed the Reader Man was so observant. The gangling rider was slow to pull his sword, though. Was it the Reader Man's poor reflexes or his distaste for killing? No matter. It worked to Wolf's advantage.

Wolf aimed the mare straight down the track. At the last moment, startling the mare as well as Connleigh, he reined her sharply aside against the Reader Man's big gray mare. The sorrel's shoulder caught Connleigh's knee. As she scraped his leg off his horse, Wolf reached out. As the mare slammed past Connleigh's horse, Wolf's fist connected with Connleigh's neck and completed the unhorsing.

The mare had lost her momentum in the collision. It gave the freeman named Brian enough opportunity to grab her bridle. Brian was in too close to the mare's neck for Wolf to reach him with a kicking foot. With his one rein remaining, Wolf turned her toward the freeman. It worked—she ran the man over, stumbling as her legs tangled in the fellow. Terrified, she regained her feet and lurched forward. Brian had let go.

The only man effectively standing between Wolf and freedom now was not standing. He was charging his huge dun stallion straight at the sorrel mare. He brandished his sword high. This was a man leagues beyond Wolf in fighting skill. Wolf could not hope to win a hand-to-hand with the great Dalainn himself.

But he would die a hero. Another of the party tried to grab his mare's bridle, and Wolf discouraged him by planting a toe forcefully in his ear. With the exultant cry of a doomed warrior, Wolf drove the mare forward, pounded his heels in her ribs, shot her like an arrow toward the great man and his great horse.

He heard Skule's chains clanging and whistling, heard Skule's war cry just as loud and as ringing as his own. The lumbering horses met at an angle, but not shoulder to shoulder. Wolf's mare nearly bellied right up over the top of Doyle Dalainn's big stud.

Dalainn wore a surprised look on his face. He screamed and swung his sword, but he had lost his aim and his position. His sword thrust whistled past Wolf's ear. The blade thunked into the cantle of his saddle behind him.

Without really thinking, Wolf grabbed the sword arm at the wrist and twisted violently. He was dragging Doyle toward him.

He tried to rein his mare free of this horrible smash-up. He realized then that Skule had flung his chain-lead at the dun stallion's legs and broken his charge, for the horse was still staggering, flailing, trying to regain his footing.

Wolf grabbed the sword at its haft and wrenched. Doyle's hand let go as his horse lost its balance and fell.

Wolf was armed now! But the others of this party had fallen back. Some lay flattened, and Skule—bloodied, muddy Skule—was gathering in his chain to swing it again.

Wolf hooked his right arm, sword and all, against the mare's neck, for leverage, and reached out with his left. Skule grabbed his arm with both hands and lunged. The cousins had done this a hundred times in fun. One would gallop by and scoop up the other onto the back of the running horse. But Norse ponies are half this size, and neither lad wore heavy chains in play.

As he caught Wolf's arm, Skule made a nearly clean vault onto the back of the mare. He was much too heavy, though, to complete the full leap. He hung against her side, flapping, squirming, trying to haul himself up straight. Wolf did not wait for him. He dug in his heels and drove the mare forward down the track, away from the Dalainn and toward the point where he had seen the longships. The mare kicked up her heels a few times, protesting the double riders, then settled to the track, stretched her neck out, and ran.

Skule just about pulled Wolf's tunic off. Panting, he jerked himself up onto the mare's back and yelled triumphantly, "We made it!"

Wolf shouted against the wind in his face. "Not yet! The ships are too far out. There's no way to reach them. I doubt they can see us. We're no closer home than we were an hour ago."

"Behind us!" Skule shrieked.

The dun stallion was on its feet, and the Dalainn hard behind them. Much belatedly came Connleigh on the gray mare in pursuit. The sorrel had just run for miles, and now she carried two grown men, not to mention all the chain and manacles. She could not possibly outrun those two great horses.

Wolf reined her aside to the east, up along the grassy bluffs. Out there, so near and yet so far, the three longships were setting their sails. Wolf yelled to them. He screamed. Skule's ululating howl could have called down stars.

The Dalainn were nearly upon them now and breathing fire and fury.

Wolf dragged the mare's head aside sharply to the east. Without thinking, she turned. The bluff fell away from beneath her clattering feet, and for a few very brief moments they hung suspended in the sky, like soaring ravens and cruising ospreys, in utter whistling silence. Wolf pushed away from the horse and fell free. He dared not hit the water when and where she did.

Wolf knew that within the minute he would die. Sure and he had carried Skule to his death as well. Ah, but in this last delicious moment of life, as the sky opened and the water below called, he was blessed by Odin twice over.

He had stolen the sword of their tormentor.

And he was tasting the thrilling freedom of flight.

16

Refuges

Shawna of the Behr sat in the hearth corner of the Dalainn, curled up like an old woman, her head against the stones of the wall, and she did not care.

About anything.

Muirgheal fluttered around the room, busier than ever and accomplishing absolutely nothing. She would spin a few moments, then go do something else, which meant that when she next picked up her spinning she had to sort the line again. She trimmed a leg of lamb for dinner, but she did not swing its spit anywhere near enough the fire for it to roast properly.

And today Shawna felt in no mood to save the feckless woman from her own inanity.

She was not in a mood for anything. She felt dead but not at repose, numb but not unfeeling, tired but not weary. She could not lift her head, and her eyes burned from all the weeping. The weeping was ended now, but the lethargy still pressed her down.

Connleigh emerged from somewhere in the back end of the house. He carried with him a large, billowy bundle and a smaller, angular one. He stood in the middle of the room and looked at Shawna. "Are you sure? Please."

She shook her head. They'd discussed this so much over the last three days that they no longer needed words for it. No, she would not come with him to Rome, married or unmarried, chaperoned or unchaperoned. No.

"Mum?" Connleigh embraced his harried mother, and she fell to weeping loudly on his neck. She begged again, reciting the full litany of arguments she had been using these last three days. Connleigh was the only one who really cared about her. She didn't know what she would do if Connleigh left. She would die early, and it was Connleigh who was sending her to her grave. He didn't want that on his conscience, did he?

Apparently he did. Eventually he pushed away from her. She clung to him, without the least shred of dignity, as he forced his way out the door. Shawna listened to her keening wail and felt strangely unmoved.

She followed by ear as Muirgheal trailed Connleigh to the east gate. Muirgheal did not venture beyond the wall. The keening died away.

Shawna could not sit in a huddled little wad forever. She could not always live among the Dalainn. Perhaps she could spend the summer with Ceirre. For all her brusque, no-nonsense ways, Ceirre was most infinitely wise. Heaven knew the old woman could use an extra pair of hands around the place, to rethatch that corner of her roof and prepare for winter.

But Ceirre, unmitigatingly cheerful, talked. Wisdom or no, Shawna did not care to listen. Besides, Ceirre would not fail a thousand times to say, "See? I told you so." Already she must have said a hundred times, "You cannot tame a wild animal. He was bound to leave, given half the chance."

And there was Mahon.

Muirgheal's silhouette blocked the sunlight in the doorway. Obviously, the grief-stricken woman had just identified the source of all her woes. She pointed finger and arm at Shawna. "You! Get out! You're the one who talked him into this, you serpent! Out!"

Shawna pushed herself to sitting. Let the woman rant and rave. Shawna didn't even care about that anymore. She was on her feet when the doorway was blocked completely by the Dalainn himself.

Doyle nodded toward Shawna and motioned to a stool by the table. "Sit. I wish to talk to you."

Muirgheal wailed a silly sort of protest about this evil girl, and Doyle sent her to the back of the house. Like an errant child she obeyed. Her distant moaning sounded as though it was coming from Connleigh's little room at the far end.

Too weary to look alert, Shawna flopped onto the stool and propped an elbow on the table. "What can I do for you, my lord?"

Doyle settled onto the stool across from her and leaned forward, both arms on the table. "You and Connleigh talked together freely and openly on many an occasion. I've seen no romantic interest between you, but you seemed to share a close friendship."

"You are a good observer."

"How long has he had this fool notion, do you know?"

Shawna looked evenly at the dark man. "I will translate fool notion into plan to travel to Rome. I don't know when the idea became clear, but he's been restless for years. He is not the man you are, Doyle, which is not to say he is less. Only different. His family ties are strong enough, rest assured, that he will profit the Dalainn whatever road he travels."

Doyle smirked. "You are the one with the gift for diplomacy, telling me what you know I want to hear."

"Diplomacy involves duplicity. I spoke truth only."

Doyle studied her a moment. "Do you believe him when he said I should have remained to fight?"

That would be in reference to the skirmish three days ago. Now what? "I've no idea. I was not there."

"Those boats carry thirty or more men each. I saw at least three in the cove. That's a minimum of ninety to ten. Even Celts don't do well at those odds."

"You need not justify a military decision to me."

"I want you to know I have some idea of the strength of our enemy." He studied her a few moments, so she held his eye. From the back of the house the keening started up again, then subsided.

Doyle shifted slightly on his stool. He was not a man to sit well or long, unless it was a horse. "You did an excellent job teaching the slave Ulf Erse. Skule could get along, but Ulf was fluent. Terrible pronunciation—it was hard to understand him at times—but he conveyed the thought clearly, whatever it was."

Was it the mention of Wolf that set her on her guard or this man's smooth speech? She felt suddenly wary. "He's quick."

"Very." Doyle licked his lips. "Skule served adequately as the demonstration, the proof positive that such people exist and that they threaten the church. Their greatest destruction is to the church. And of course, Irish women and children."

Hardly, Doyle. It is the warlords and the constantly bickering tribes and clans who pose the real threat to women and children if not the church, you chief among them, and it's been that way for centuries. These Norse are only the latest danger. But she held her peace.

"But the Wolf. His loss is costly."

Not to mention embarrassing, to carry your sword and favorite horse away.

Doyle pressed onward. "I needed him for those occasions when communication between the raiders and the Erse were necessary."

"As when you captured slaves, to extract from them the raiders' plans. Something like that."

"Precisely. However, you and the Wolf traded languages, so to speak. Is that correct?"

"I don't do nearly as well with Norse as he does with Erse."

"Better than anyone else in Erin at the moment. I need you. I wish to retain you as a paid translator, for the occasion when we seize more Northmen."

"Muirgheal would be displeased."

He smirked and said nothing. So much for Muirgheal's needs and preferences.

And then an awful truth began to wedge itself into Shawna's weary heart. She worked Doyle's offer this way and that, his statements in every possible light, and it came out always the same.

She found herself with a new vitality she could not have mustered five minutes ago. She sat erect. "You were going to use Wolf to obtain military intelligence?"

"Right."

"No, Doyle. You were keeping him tucked safely out of harm's way, keeping him nowhere near where raiders might be seen. It was only by fickle chance that Glinn sent him with Ceirre and the rest of us. You had not told Glinn you wanted the slave sequestered. Which means you didn't tell anyone. Not even Connleigh. He likely would have mentioned it to me."

"I don't disclose any more than I need, as a general rule. Sure and Connleigh has complained about that a time or two."

"Why not mention it if you wanted the slave kept tucked away? Because someone would ask why. Why would that simple little thing not stand the light of scrutiny?"

"You're blowing it out of proportion."

"No. No, Doyle, this is different. You see, you know and I know that you couldn't trust any bit of information you got from Wolf. Either your captives would lie, or Wolf would lie in the translation. He and your captives could speak freely in their native tongue, concoct any story they wished, and you'd be none the wiser. Not for a moment could you trust Wolf. Therefore, you were holding him back for another purpose."

"Are you impugning my word?"

Shawna must tread carefully. "I'm suggesting your word is incomplete, Doyle Dalainn. You have additional motives, other objectives. You want to negotiate. That's it, isn't it!" She watched Doyle's face. She had hit it squarely. "You're not as successful as you wish in uniting the southern clans, so you want to negotiate with the Northmen. To buy them off?" The enormity of this conversation practically raised her out of her seat. "Or as mercenaries to support your own grand designs? That's why you wanted Wolf! A broker to enlist the services of Norse mercenaries!"

She yanked herself to her feet so violently the stool went spinning. "The home of the Behr lies in ruins and her finest in the grave, and you want to enter into a power ploy, hand and glove with our murderers! Doyle Dalainn, you are a monster!"

She ran from the house and out the east gate because that gate was closest. Doyle called behind her. She kept running out around the east side and north up through the barley fields. She trampled the new growth and didn't care. She ran onward, clear out to Berit Head.

Only when she reached the edge of the world, the brow of Berit Head, did she pause to catch her breath. Gulping air and sobbing, she stood on the breast of the head and let the wind pull at her hair.

Offshore in the mist hovered Lambay, sullen and gray. A world away. A world gone.

She would rest here awhile and marshal her thoughts. They flew about in such disarray now. This headland awash in mist and wind was a refuge to her. A respite. She sat down heavily on the smooth gray rock of Berit Head and let the Lord in heaven cover her with His hand, because she had no other shelter now. She heard the sea whisper to her from below and listened to the ravens offer their hoarse consolations as they dipped and glided in the air currents off the head. More so than other Erse, the Behr were of the sea.

So why did the sea claim everything Shawna held dear?

* * *

It was a quiet little cluster of those stone beehive-shaped buildings so common in Erin. It perched on a ragged islet hard beside the Irish coast. Why did men so often establish these monasteries in such unusual places? As a refuge from the cares of the world? Whatever, this particular refuge clung to an island hardly larger than the buildings. The sea lapped against stark rocks, with only a tiny cobbled beachhead on the south shore.

There was a familiarity, too, to the black smoke boiling out of the building with the cross on its gable. Two monks lay in the rocks at the base of the northshore cliff, listlessly rising and falling with the surging surf.

Wolf watched from the *Straight Arrow* offshore while his fellow seamen of Trondelag yelled and laughed and jeered each other as they swarmed across the islet. Of the three vessels in this raiding party, only one had room to haul up on the tiny beach, and by the luck of the lots' cast, it was not his.

Luck. Wolf suffered not a little confusion here, deciding what to attribute to luck and what to attribute to the fickle intercession of the gods (Norse and Erse both). Shawna would be quick to tell Wolf that her God was watching out for him. She would painstakingly explain the theories about angels again.

He could not imagine her God doing anything nice for him after he and his crew did such despicable things to churches and monasteries. Why should the God of the Erse bother? No, he would send up an offering to Odin, Thor, and Frey, were he to thank anyone at all. But he wasn't sure they had much to do with it either.

The horse had a lot to do with it. She had gone galloping straight off that cliff without hesitating. Too bad the creature drowned. She must have been injured in the leap somehow, for by

171

the time the crew of the *Straight Arrow* pulled Wolf on board and he could look about, she had sunk beneath the waves.

His and Skule's voices aided the cause. Olaf claimed he heard the boys above the snap of the sails filling and the creaks of the oarlocks. Of course, the Northmen saw the boys' wild ride along the breast of the cliff and watched them dive into the sea, so perhaps the gods ought be thanked for clear weather. In mist and fog, all would have been lost.

But the Northmen heard, and saw, and turned back for them. They rescued Wolf still carrying the sword. It hung at his side now, idle in the attack against this little nest of monastics. And they rescued Skule, chains and all. They had offered to throw the chains overboard. Wolf could not explain why he wanted to save them, but he did. They were good iron, if nothing else.

The skinless patches where Skule had been dragged, and his possibly broken arm (no one could decide, so they determined to treat it as if it were, just in case) were healing well. By the time they raised Land's End off the mountains of home, Skule would be whole again. Wolf was whole now. From certain death to vivid life.

Someone, if not the gods, ought to be thanked. Wolf felt indeed so very thankful.

Not the least of his gratitude was rooted in the pleasant summer he was enjoying. His capture had ended his career as a corsair very early on their first raid. He had no idea this raiding business was so casual and easygoing. Between strikes, the party would haul up on a remote shore or island and lounge about in camp for a week or so.

Occasionally they met resistance, as when some rui-ri came thundering to the rescue of his tuath with a few pickup troops. They always squashed the ri, not just with superior numbers but with superior skills and tactics. Those flurries of armed defense, though, would result in injuries, and camp was a good place to bind wounds and provide rest. They would sort and distribute their slaves and booty. They would slaughter the cattle and sheep taken and roast the tenderest.

The jarl in command would set up his dismantled bed inside his personal tent and assume all the comforts of home. With access to fire ashore they could sharpen and repair tools and blades, and eat well. Very well. Erin was such a rich land, full and overflowing with good things. The ale, grain, and livestock appropriated during raids they supplemented with wild vegetables, berries, and fish. Wolf smiled at the thought. These wolves of the sea, the scourge of the North, these bloodthirsty murderers picked berries as little children do, eating more than they saved and returning with purple lips.

Beside him, Skule pointed laughing toward the islet. He was watching a raider in close pursuit of a monk. The monk scrambled over the rocks out onto a tiny headwall. The bearded Northman—it looked like Olaf of Hedves from here—clambered after him, roaring.

The monk crept out upon a tiny pinnacle among the rocks, as far as he could go, taking refuge in precariousness, and thrust a crucifix toward the Northman at arm's length. With it he sketched the sign of the cross between himself and his enemy. Even from here beyond the surf, Wolf could discern the monk's rapid, frantic Latin.

Olaf Hedves, apparently unwilling to risk life and limb on the slippery boulders, wedged himself among the rocks and took a wild swinging swipe with his sword. The crucifix—and the hand—fell away. The startled monk lost his precarious perch and dropped out of sight among the craggy rocks.

Skule cackled with delight.

A year ago Wolf would have cackled. In fact, just about a year ago he had urged Thole to run Shawna through with his sword. Now he considered himself lucky to avoid throwing up over the gunwale.

He thought about Shawna and what she had lost. He thought about these monks, weaponless, and what they were losing. The losses were infinitely greater than any gains the Norse might make. His countrymen's destructive greed and bloodlust angered and shamed him, but a year ago he would have taken part with pride.

What in the name of Odin had that stubborn, smart, gentle, Christian girl done to him?

17

Dublin Crossing

Home.

Well, not quite, not yet.

But close. Close enough that tears filled Wolf's eyes as he espied Land's End in the cloudy distance. He brushed them away angrily. He was a warrior. He was returning a hero, more or less.

Loons and murres bobbed on the gray swells of the open sea, their pointy beaks tilted upward, as the three longships passed. The gulls as always found the ships and came circling, mewing. Lovely sound.

Geter of the Far North, master of this vessel, stepped in beside Wolf. "You know these waters."

"Intimately. I've fished them since my earliest youth."

"Take the tiller."

"With pleasure. Do you want to beach her? Do you wish to make camp?"

Geter shook his head. "We're close enough home that we prefer not to spend the time it takes to enter your fjord. We ought to press north. The weather is turning."

Wolf nodded. "So it seems. In fact, from the heavy snow I see extending down to the shore, I'd guess the winter has already closed in. Early this year. I hope you didn't tarry so long on Erin's south coast that you'll have trouble getting home now."

"The season's late, but we'll make it."

Wolf headed for the tiller. "I'll bring you around the seal rocks and in next to a cobble beach on Land's End. Skule and I will walk up the northside track and be home in two days."

Wolf and Skule spent an hour at least taking their leave of their shipmates. Wolf was exactly one sword richer than when he left his homeland nearly a year and a half ago. And what a magnificent piece of ironwork it was! Doyle Dalainn had lavished much work and expense on his weapon, for it represented not just power but prestige. Gold and silver inlay swirled in intricate designs up and down the black iron. Sure and it was very fine iron, damascened, tempered long and carefully. It held an edge keen enough to shave with, were Wolf of a mind to shave. He was not.

Wolf and Skule had each received a small, small portion of this ship's pelf. Skule accepted readily, but Wolf did not really consider it his.

And Skule had his chains.

Wolf brought the *Arrow* within a few feet of the shore. With a final wave and halloo, he gave the tiller back to Geter. He and Skule leaped overboard into the shallow surf of home. It was snowing.

Holding their possessions above their heads they waded, stumbling, up out of the water. A foot of snow filled the fisherman's track down here at Land's End, so they began their walk home below high tide line, where the rocks and cobbles remained bare. They made pretty good time, until the incoming tide drove them up into the snow.

Their wet boots and trousers froze stiff and rubbed raw spots on their cold skin. Skule threw aside the leather bag containing his chains. Wolf retrieved it. He threw aside his leather bag of plunder from the *Arrow*, and Skule hastily retrieved it. Thus burdened by each other's cast-offs, they trudged up the track.

Darkness came early because of the thick, heavy snowfall. Neither said aloud, "We dare not stop or we'll freeze." Neither admitted, "I can't see the track anymore." They were, after all, heroes of a sort. Heroes rise above such inconveniences. Instead they stumbled silently through darkness, tripped over fallen trees, slogged blindly through the deepening snow.

But when Wolf walked into a tree so hard his nose bled, he knew they were in trouble.

* * *

Connleigh Dalainn walked along the quiet shore of the River Liffey, a few scant yards from where the Dalainn had so unceremoniously fled the Norse. It seemed so long ago, and it was only a few days.

He had never appreciated the power of his name and station until now. In the realm of his father's influence, he enjoyed the prestige of eldest son of the ri-ruirech. Across the Liffey, beyond his father's frontier, he was just another Gael.

He ought to call at the hut of Ceirre. Originally he had thought of staying there. But the day was too young to stop yet—over an hour of sunlight remained—and he could travel another five miles at least. So he would not stop at Ceirre's, lest she talk him out of his desire to see Rome. Indeed, he was nearly talking himself out of it. Even as he told his aching heart that this would be the adventure of a lifetime and that now was the time to embark upon it, his aching heart was demanding his instant return to his home hearth and to his mother.

He arrived almost without thinking at Dublin Crossing. On his father's travels with the slave in tow, they had visited a minor ri-rui south of the Liffey on the coast. That ri sailed to Wales frequently, and Connleigh could surely obtain passage from him. Once he reached Wales, Connleigh could loop around the south Welsh coast into England or perhaps even find passage directly to the continent. Continuing south and east, however blindly, was bound to get him there.

He stepped into the cold, cold water. He hated cold and being constantly wet. He shifted his bundles to his head—the book in particular must stay dry—and began wading across the smooth rocks of Dublin Crossing, in frigid pursuit of his destiny.

When he obtained passage east across the sea he would try to send home a letter for Shawna to read to his mum. He would reiterate his love and affection. He would assure her he would return one day, after he had studied at the feet of the finest men of the faith. He would explain how much all this meant to him.

Sure and it was a good thing, for Mum's sake, that Shawna could read.

* * *

Wooden claws—naked tree branches—reached out and dragged her light shawl off her head. Brush tangled her ankles and brought her to her knees. She was cold.

She should have swallowed her pride and returned to the Dalainn. She should not have simply walked away from her silent communion with God on Berit Head to amble southward along this track. She should at least have grabbed her heavy winter-weight shawl before she left. Now she was paying for her folly.

Shawna and "folly" were synonymous lately. In fact, she had been making ridiculously poor decisions throughout this last year. The only good choice she made since the Norse dragons first raised Lambay was to resist that churl from the east side.

And Wolf was the one who had saved her from him.

Wolf. What a horrible decision that had been, to have anything to do with the slave at all. By teaching him Erse she had played right to the Dalainn's sickening duplicity. The more she thought about Erse and Norse teamed together against other Irishmen, the hotter she burned.

Wolf. He as much promised that he would remain with her. They were becoming so close—comfortable with each other, and affectionate. And then, at the first opportunity—the very first opportunity. . . .

Fury teamed up with sorrow to fill her eyes with hot tears. Again.

This unfamiliar southbound track wound in leisurely fashion around hills, through wooded vales and creases, out across scarred flatrock. She had by-passed the Owney rath. She feared their dogs. Now she was not certain exactly where she was. This was not the track she normally took to Ceirre's. She saw nothing resembling a cottage, let alone a farm, and no livestock along here.

It was too late to return today to the Dalainn; she had walked too far. She thought about Connleigh, off on his personal quest. He saw an end, a purpose in his travel. She did not. She had no idea where she was going or what she ought do next.

She knew what she would not do. She would not return to the Dalainn. With Connleigh gone, she could think of no reason to go back there anyway. The boys would do fine, with Ceirre to drop by now and then to remind them of their heritage and destiny. She might send them a letter by and by. And Doyle's duplicity—no, she would not darken that door again.

Undisturbed leaves carpeted the path. This track was not used frequently. It wound down through dense thickets and opened out into river bottom. Networks of stone walls laced through open leas again. She had returned to civilization.

In the distance, the Liffey ran its undulant way through green meadows. She paused to get her bearings and angled south. She had to crawl over wall after wall to reach the river. She stepped out onto its bank less than a quarter mile above Dublin Crossing. Darkness had nearly beaten her to the river, and the sun was gone.

She hastened down to the ford and paused. If she crossed the river now she was leaving everything behind—her heritage with the Behr, her friends, the only people who cared . . . except Ceirre.

She stepped into the cold water and hiked her skirts. The next step. Another.

Dear Ceirre. Shawna would stay there the night because it was the only place she could go. On the morrow she would travel forth, regardless what Ceirre advised. The cold water boiled around her thighs.

Go where? She did not know. She pulled her skirts higher and still they got wet. The river was running high and cold with the early rains.

She was a person of thoughtfulness and order. She abhorred this aimlessness.

* * *

"There! Aren't you glad I saved your chains?" Wolf followed the six-foot-long lead chain back to where Skule had fallen. The sky, the forest, the snow itself were all black, black on black. It had been Wolf's idea to link the two of them together with the chain, and good thing. Above the wind and blowing snow he had not heard Skule go down.

Skule sat in loose snow, wagging his head. "I'm knackered. Continue on, cousin. I shall follow shortly."

"Get up!"

"No."

"Then you'll cause me to freeze, for I'll not leave you behind. You wouldn't want to be responsible for my death, and that not in battle."

"If you sit here and freeze, that is your concern, not mine. No one is asking you to. Go on."

Wolf sat down heavily beside him. To tell the truth, he too felt like simply going to sleep. His cold body ached all over. He thought of Shawna, warm and comfortable in the cottage of the Dalainn, and he wondered why he had ever thought to leave.

He would not have remained a slave there much longer. Either he could have arranged to earn his freedom or could have obtained it by marrying Shawna—let her emancipate him. All sorts of ways would have worked. He was disgusted with himself for taking flight.

Ah, but what a magnificent flight it was. What a tale he would have to tell when he reached his own hearth again.

His mind slipped back to that final wild ride along the edge of the sea, and the plunge down off the bluff. Even the long, frantic minutes struggling in the water, helping Skule swim with that anchor chain around his waist, took on a warm glow. And he would never forget the heady exultation of rescue, as comrades eagerly babbling Norse gripped him in their strong hands and dragged him up the rough planks of the *Straight Arrow*. And the smoke. . . .

Smoke. Wolf opened his eyes. He jabbed Skule's arm. "Smoke!"

"Wha—?"

"The wind has shifted. I smell smoke. There is habitation nearby. Get up! Get up!"

Wolf lurched to his knees and tugged on Skule's arm in the darkness. He dragged his cousin bodily to his feet and felt like wrapping the chain around the simpleton's neck. Fie on Skule! If Skule had not stayed down, they would not have gotten so stiff. Wolf would still be walking and all the closer the source of the smoky smell. He led his cousin by the chain, practically dragging him through the darkness.

Skule slurred, "I shmell id now."

"Uphill this way." Wolf inhaled deeply and changed course.

Ahead through the trees, a tiny orange light winked in and out as they moved. It was nothing more than a chink in a cottage wall, but it bespoke fire. And warmth. Wolf fell twice getting there. He was literally dragging Skule by the chain when he at last stumbled to the door.

He pounded upon it.

Skule muttered, "I don' believe d-this," over and over.

The door creaked open. Wonderful light poured out and splashed on Wolf's frozen face. The warmth from inside stung his cheeks.

A wizened old man dragged his door open farther. He studied the two a moment in silence.

Wolf knew he ought say something, but no words came to his lips. In fact, his lips were now so stiff they couldn't handle words anyway.

The old man reached past him, took the chain out of his frozen hand and hauled Skule inside. He dropped Wolf's scrawny little cousin directly by the fire. Wolf started to step forward, but he wasn't quick enough. He, too, was pulled roughly over to the fire, and with amazing strength.

He allowed himself to be set on the floor, allowed his ice-stiff cloak to be removed, allowed his frozen boots to be taken off. The old man peeled his trousers off him, and only then did Wolf realize that Skule had already been stripped and wrapped in blankets. Where had these last minutes gone?

Time passed not as a flowing river, a continuum, but as little chunks like a child's building blocks, stacked upon one another. He sat, disengaged, as things happened or failed to happen around him. He slept now and then, he was pretty sure. The old man poked him occasionally.

Wolf knew this old fellow, but he could not place the name or circumstance. He began to shiver violently, and poor Skule was bouncing, he shook so.

The old man prepared some sort of hot brew, with herbs and who knew what else. It looked like the bilge beneath the deck of a longship. He instructed Wolf and Skule to drink.

They drank.

The old man finally sat down by the fire beside the boys. "So. You are Arildson. I forget—Ulf?"

Wolf nodded and forced down another swallow of bilge. "And I know I know you, but my mind is misty."

"Halvor of Land's End, though I no longer live at Land's End, obviously."

"Halvor. Of course. One of the heroes, the mighty men of old." Wolf frowned at Skule, at the old fellow. "I apologize for this, but I rather assumed you had died long ago. You are a legend, Halvor. I grew up listening to the tales of your exploits as jarl and fighter. You sent the expeditions out to the south islands. You led some of them."

The old man smiled. "You've a fine memory, or my name is more than I deserve. I led settlers down to the south islands, yes. I planned for a while to live there. The Shetlands. My wife and two of my children are buried there. But I decided to return here to the mountains."

"Just where do you live, exactly?" Skule tentatively sipped at his tankard of bilge.

Halvor chuckled. "Aha. I thought you two were lost. You are about two miles inland, back that little drainage that opens out into the clam flats near Osprey Rocks."

Wolf wagged his aching head. "I had no idea anyone lived back here."

Skule grunted. "I had no idea anyone would wander back here. That's what comes of letting the Wolf lead the way."

"Easy to do in darkness, to end up in the drainage," said Halvor charitably. He smiled at Wolf. "So you are coming home to your father's roof to attend your brother's wedding. Good. Good."

"My bro—Reidar's getting married?"

In a fit of coughing, Skule spit bilge into the fire. "What's her name? It isn't Astrid, is it?"

The old man cocked his head. "Then I bear tidings. Interesting, the timing—that you would appear now, and not knowing. Yes, I do believe it is Astrid, the daughter of a jarl named Sten, to the north a ways."

Skule cackled. "They deserve each other."

"She's a spoiled, self-centered virago." Wolf was still frowning. "I thought Reidar couldn't stand her. He must have told me that a dozen times. Just shows what love will do to a man."

Shawna burst upon his thoughts again for the thousandth thousandth time. She was just as strong and self-assured as Astrid of Sten, and totally opposite in nature. Totally.

"Or political necessity. More broth?" The old man pointed to the bowl of bilge.

"No. No, thank you, I'm not quite done with this yet." Wolf swirled his tankard a bit, hoping that would improve the flavor somehow. "When is the happy union?"

"Is tomorrow new moon?"

Wolf had to think a moment. It had been several days since they last saw a moon, the weather had been so thick. Exactly how many days? Skule and he nodded simultaneously.

"Then tomorrow night."

"Good! Splendid!" Wolf forced down some more bilge. "We can be on the track—the right track this time—and make it back in good time. If we're two miles from the Osprey Rocks, there should be no problem."

Halvor smiled a that's-what-you-think smile, but he said nothing.

The next day, falling snow filled the air so thickly that Wolf could not see trees fifty yards away. It piled up against the north wall of the little log house until the drift covered the peaked roof. Wolf would have borrowed the old man's snowshoes and tried to reach home, but Skule adamantly refused to leave the fire. Halvor counseled strongly against travel.

It was too late anyway. If the wedding was set for new moon, Reidar was happily bound for his honeymoon retreat by now, making love day and night to his selfish little shrew. Wolf pouted.

Skule and Halvor babbled about the far-flung raids of the last few years. They discussed the progress of the Danes down in Northumbria and the recent Swedish incursions into the far east. Wolf sulked.

The storm abated somewhat the next day, but travel was still out of the question. Wolf and Skule spent the brief daylight hours digging out the roof, lest the snow crush the ancient cabin.

That evening Wolf removed the pad in his boot and carefully picked the stitches out. Halvor had no clean tow, so Wolf spread the stinking, wet tow across the floor and thoroughly dried it. He liked to change the padding every couple of months. That hadn't happened for quite a while. He stuffed the dried, aired tow back inside and stitched it up again.

The longer he sat in this dark and suffocating little cabin, the worse his anger burned. With whom was he angry? The gods.

Over and over, Shawna recited a passage of her Scripture saying, "Ask and you shall receive." Over and over she stressed how her benign God delighted in helping out people. She added that apparently His largess extended to those beyond the faith. She then talked on and on about Samaritans and Balaam and Magi and a host of other tribes Wolf had never heard about. She as much as promised that her God would help Wolf too.

Well, He hadn't. Here sat Wolf penned up in a tiny cage, trapped by no less a personage than the God Himself, it would seem, and the God was helping not at all. Wolf wanted more than anything in the world to attend Reidar's wedding feast. Nothing would be finer than to steal a little of the Perfect Son's thunder, and on the Perfect Son's most auspicious day. If coming back from the dead didn't steal it, what could?

Wolf planned, he dreamed, he fantasized about striding up to Reidar (without limping!) to congratulate him on the biggest mistake of his life—marrying Astrid Sten. The open mouths of his village friends, the gasps and chuckles of his father's companions . . . what a homecoming it would have been.

Late in the afternoon of the third day, well after the sun made its momentary appearance and fled, the snow ceased. Wolf dug his way out the front door into the crystal clarity of a fine evening. Clouds in great blobs still moved around up there, but stars winked alive in between them. The storm was broken. It would snap cold now as it cleared.

And, in and out behind the scattered clouds, the first-quarter moon sailed high.

A cloak draped casually over his shoulders, the old man stepped out into the crunchy snow beside Wolf. "There is no substitute for this land. That's why I could not stay in the southern islands."

"It is beautiful." And penetrating. Wolf thought again of the mild wet summers that passed as winter in Erin. The cold did not pierce there as it did here. On that misty isle where true winter never came, cattle grazed in peace this moment. Here the grass and moss were buried eight feet below the nearest cow.

"Let us travel with first light tomorrow."

Wolf looked at the old man. "Us? You would go along?"

Halvor shrugged. "For the last day or two you've been casting the vilest of aspersions upon the God of the Irish. I understand Junken Trygveson has an Irish slave, and she's very wise about her God. I want to learn more about it."

"If He's effectual at all, His influence is limited to Erin. He certainly doesn't lift a finger up here."

"So you keep saying. I don't understand why attending Reidar's wedding became so important to you."

Wolf watched the stars appear and disappear. "Our whole lives, Reidar was the son who could do no wrong, and I was the embarrassment. All errors were mine, all victories his. 'Why can't you be more like Reidar?' It would have been so satisfying, the timing. To show up then, at that great moment in his life."

"It sounds selfish. Petty."

Wolf smiled. "It is."

"Interesting." The old man watched the moon scud out from behind a cloud. "You condemn selfishness in Reidar's bride, yet boast it in yourself."

"I have earned mine, wise one, a hundred times over."

"Does the God of the Irish reward selfishness?"

Wolf thought a moment. "Actually, as I understand it, He's more for humility." Wolf tried to remember what Shawna had quoted from her Scriptures. Something on the order of "Take the lowest seat at the feast, and let the master invite you to a higher one. Better that than taking the highest seat and being humiliated when he sends you to the back of the room." Something like that.

"That may be why the storm held you here, don't you think?"

Wolf stared at Halvor in the darkness, for the moon had hidden herself again. "Surely not!"

But the seed was planted.

The cold drove Wolf back inside shortly. He hunkered down beside the fire to watch morosely the little flames lick at their latest log.

What if the long arm of Shawna's God extended clear up here into Trondelag? What if that God listened to Shawna's prayers and manipulated Wolf in ways that she requested? Wolf would be pestered forever by the influences of a God he did not know and did not care to know. Saint Ulf of the Coastlands indeed.

Halvor accepted the possibility. Before he retired he explained that that was precisely why he wanted to talk to Junken's woman. Just how powerful was this God of the Irish?

Wolf curled up in his bearskins that night angrier than ever, and not a little confused.

18

Feast

Flup.
Flup.
Flup.

Step on step, foot before foot, Wolf punched snowshoe prints into the fresh snow. Behind him, Skule stomped down the powder snow that slid instantly into the long boards' tracks. Third in line, old Halvor walked in the boys' footsteps. Even so, he could barely manage. Were he to walk alone he would never make it. This new snowfall was too deep, too soft, too exhausting for such an old man. He constantly surprised Wolf, though, with his ability to get a thing done.

It impressed Wolf, too, that the frail old man seemed comfortable in a wool cloak draped loosely. Skule hunkered, all hunched, in his bearskin, looking miserable. Wolf was wrapped in a doubled wool cloak with a cowl hood, and he felt just as miserably cold as Skule looked. The bag of chains slammed against his thigh with every step, and he was sore tempted to fling it aside.

To their right, the fjord shimmered in the afternoon sun. The clouds had cleared completely, leaving the sky awash in pearlescent blue. Everywhere, crisp white snow softened the landscape and blinded the eye. It clung to the dark firs in great blobs. It capped the craggy rocks. Wolf drew a deep breath of the bitter-cold air. It cut his lungs like knives and frosted his beard and moustache with hoar. Ah, home! Real cold. True winter.

Yet, for some terrible reason, this cold that he had grown up in also made him uncomfortable. Somehow a single winter in that ugly, wet clime of Erin had ruined him. No matter. Sure, and he'd become accustomed to his native cold again shortly.

He stopped dead to laugh at himself. Listen to him! He was thinking in Celtic! He certainly had been warped by those pagans. He had a lot of unwarping to do.

Wolf raised his head. What did he hear in the track around the bend ahead? The cowl pulled down so close around his ears dulled his hearing.

But Wolf's ear had warned him rightly. Here came a pony sledge slogging down the track. Good! They could walk henceforth in the snow packed down by the sledge. Going would be much easier from here into the village.

The sledge driver drew his little horse to a halt. The creature shook its head, and the stiff, erect mane wagged. It startled Wolf that this horse looked so stubby and short. He was comparing it to the Irish horses without thinking.

"Halvor!" The sledge driver leaped off the sledge runners into the snow to clap his mittened hands against Halvor's shoulders. "You've come to the feast after all!"

"Gang, you're looking fit! Marriage obviously agrees with you." Halvor's hands shook a bit as he greeted Gang. Perhaps the old man was colder than he pretended. "But if the feast you mention is that of Reidar's wedding, are we not four days too late?"

"Storm put it off a week. The whole affair is fraught with politics, you can imagine, and Arild . . ."

Wolf's heart thumped. His ears listened to Gang describe how certain prominent jarls were delayed, but his heart was listening to the gentle words of Shawna. *Prayer is your conversation with God. You praise Him, yes. And you make requests, yes. But most of all you trust Him to provide what is best for you, and then you thank Him for His provision.*

Wolf had asked Shawna's God to help him attend the wedding and then pouted like a spoiled child when her God did not speed him to his party. It never occurred to him that her God might simply postpone the party for his benefit. But the one solution was just as practical as the other.

It dawned on Wolf that Gang was treating him and Skule as if they were strangers—not only did Gang offer no greeting, he offered no hint of recognition. With the cowl, and Skule's bearskin up around his ears, and their long beards. . . .

Gang urged his pony forward eventually, and the three travelers slogged on up the track. Did Skule revel in this crisp, dry air of home as much as Wolf did? One would never know. Skule never discussed such things. Probably he could not frame his feelings in words. There were a lot of things Skule could not frame in words.

Skule sniggered. "You're legs are so alike, Gang failed to recognize you."

"Think that was it?"

"What else? Actually, you look as weird as ever, but you're now a balanced weird."

"Do you realize, Skule, that Shawna's God is a person?"

"We already went through all that at Halvor's. I'm tired of the subject."

"No! Look. He acted in a very personal way for me, but not to sin and glory. More as a favor. You recall Shawna's story in which Jesus deliberately delayed until He knew Lazarus was good and dead. Timing. The God is a master of timing."

Skule snorted.

Wolf pressed on, for thoughts were filling his head like apples being thrown into a barrel, and overflowing. "You remember what Shawna talked about that time we were treading out wheat? That her God delivers us from our slavery to sin?"

"I for one am not a slave of sin." Skule smirked. "I prefer to think of myself as being in voluntary service."

Only when Halvor asked, "What is sin?" did Wolf remember there was no good word for it in Norse.

"Evil. Wrongdoing. Wrong thinking. Moral error." Wolf sifted through his memories for other definitions, for he had asked the same thing of Shawna. "You offend the God, and common decency, and He forgives by paying for it."

"Paying with . . ."

"Blood. His own Son's blood."

"A heavy price."

"So Shawna says." Paying in blood was a concept most familiar to Northmen. They made blood common currency when anger or greed flared. But to pay for someone else's sins—that seemed a bit much to ask even of a god.

And yet, this God had just granted Wolf's request, not in payment for Wolf's devotion or gifts but—well—simply as a favor. A thing done for a friend.

Was Wolf then this God's friend? Shawna certainly was. In the midst of tribulation He over and over gave her solace when she asked it. But she served Him faithfully. Wolf had heaped sin upon sin of late, offense upon offense against the God of the Irish.

Very well. In silent prayer to a God he did not know, he asked that his sins be dissolved as Shawna had described. He even ended his prayer with a sign of the cross—a very tiny sign, done discreetly, that Skule would not notice.

Now he would sit back, so to speak, and see where this led.

From the rear Halvor called, "Does the God of the Irish ever do special things? Unusual things, to prove His power?"

"Aye, every now and then, according to all I've talked to. Miracles, they call them."

"Miracles!" Skule hooted. "Then let Him lend us wings, as He did that Stephen, to whisk us home instead of subjecting us to this forced march."

"Suffering builds character," Wolf teased.

"I would rather have less character than comfort."

"You do," purred Halvor quietly.

They arrived in the village Wolf knew best just as dusk was starting to rob the houses of detail and turn the rock walls into featureless black lines. He could smell the goats as they passed Old Ingrid's. He sniffed the smoke in the air. Going on two years later, the Jungvoldsons still burned green alder. When would they ever learn to cut wood ahead?

Skule squared his shoulders as they approached Arild's great house. "Won't they be surprised to see us! Delighted, maybe and maybe not. But surprised for sure."

Wolf grabbed his elbow. "Hold, cousin!"

Skule turned and frowned. "Another of your bold ideas?"

"One of the boldest. Let us sit in the foreigners' seats."

"The for—" Skule looked at first as if he would refuse, but then his face softened. "None of the women there will know me, will they?"

"No remembrance of the Fool at all."

"Then I shall. Strictly as a favor to you."

Wolf clapped his arm and struck nothing but bear fur.

The warden tonight was young Borg. Wolf smiled to himself. Poetic justice that Borg, once a half-hearted swain of Astrid's, should be relegated to doorkeeper on this occasion. Borg glanced at the hilt of Wolf's sword. His eyes met Wolf's and flicked back to the sword.

Wolf drew a foot of it from the scabbard, enough to show the graving on the blade. "Celtic."

"Striking!"

Wolf slid the blade to rest and walked through the door, limping not at all. Borg showed absolutely no hint of recognition.

From clear, bitter cold they stepped into steamy, smoky warmth. The great hall was well above freezing already, and as the revelry picked up tonight it would grow warmer still. Wolf paused momentarily to look at the chair he would have taken were he, a son of Arild, to make his identity known. He settled then beside Skule at this end of the hall where sat guests from neighboring towns who carried no special rank.

Smoke and the essence of burning fat filled the top half of the long hall. At the far end, made distant by space as well as station, Father and Mum sat between the house pillars. Father was already well oiled with ale. Mum gossiped with her friends at her side. She appeared in her cups, which was not unusual, but tonight she seemed somewhat more thickly shingled than usual. Astrid, the bride, sat beyond Mum, as if she were an afterthought to this whole affair.

Halvor, predictably, was ushered instantly to a seat of honor. From his position at the table, Hegaard Broad Back appeared to be second in command now under Arild himself.

No one bothered to greet Wolf and Skule. Wolf began to feel an outsider in his own village. He took his place at the far corner of the table, where torches did not reach well. In near darkness he dropped the cowl and loosened his cloak, and no one noticed. He would have to find his own food and drink. No one served him. No youngsters eager to curry favor would cut him a chunk of boar meat. He would have to cut his own. He had not until then realized how highborn were the sons of Arild Thick Knee. How privileged.

Shawna of the Behr had been born privileged, but she worked as hard as any slave. She knew the skills of women and spun flax with the best. She handled horses and cattle as well as any man. Her God, she said, was born privileged also and took on the cloak of mortality so that He could make His sacrifice. In a small way Wolf, born privileged, was taking on the cloak of the commoner, but not for sacrifice.

For revenge.

Reidar arrived late at his own party and took his seat of honor beside his father. He had not changed in the year and a half. He was neither more nor less haughty.

The familiar ritual began. His father invoked blessings, and Wolf could not help comparing the bombastic invocation with the quiet, fervent prayers of his Celtic captors, Latin aside.

Father welcomed the guests—those of station personally, and Wolf's dark corner generically. He gave Halvor a special greeting, and the old man smiled. If Arild only knew that Halvor had been playing host to his lost son for four days. . . . Secrets are sweet.

They named and toasted the departed. "Skule Johaldson . . . Ulf Arildson . . ."

Skule jabbed Wolf's arm. "How often do we have the pleasure of toasting our own demise, eh, cousin?"

"I notice that no one seems terribly broken up about their loss." Wolf was surprised that he felt so detached here. He listened for familiar names in a curiously remote way. At one time he had been an intimate part of this village and this clan. Gone one short year and a half. It seemed a lifetime. He felt different now, familiar with every nuance of his father's speech and with nearly all the faces, yet apart.

He felt as much a part of the green and mossy hills of Erin as the snow-clad crags of Norway. Norway had not changed one dot, nor had the clan of Arild. Here it all was, as always. Wolf had changed. Profoundly.

And that bothered him. Throughout his exile he had dreamed of this moment. On his walk up the track from Land's End he had savored this frozen land so much. And now, as he sat under his own roof, off on the periphery of festivity, he realized he yearned for misty Erin. He listened to the fluid Norse of his childhood flowing all around him. Sitting there he suddenly realized he missed the lilting trills and gutturals of Shawna's Celtic.

And Shawna. She constantly invaded his thoughts. What would she think of these customs? What would she say to this and that? He was done with that phase of his life. Why did it keep intruding? Were these constant thoughts of her more machinations by her God?

The formalities trickled to an end. The aroma of roast beef, a new smell, mingled with the pungent smells of wood smoke and human bodies. The cooks came out carrying piles of loaves of wheat bread. There came Aunt Eike and Auntie Jorun among them! Some things never change. Wolf grinned. The haunting aroma of the fresh-baked bread, the favorite aroma of his youth, made his heart sing. Village lads hauled out the roast pigs.

Wolf thought about the Celtic custom of giving the privilege of the first cut to him who earned it best, the greatest hero. Who in this array of men would have earned the honor?

He thought of Shawna's smoky eyes and her lovely hands as she sliced her little chunk of beef in her quiet, happy hut. How Wolf preferred that simple elegance to this chaotic noise! In her own way, Shawna with her strange foods was every bit as good a cook as Aunties Eike and Jorun.

He drew his Celtic sword and lopped a chunk from the beef. He handed it to the stranger on his left and cut another for himself. Skule sawed off a chunk of pork. And the bread! He savored the bread of his childhood, sweet and fresh. And the smoked salmon. . . .

He ate his fill, but he did not gorge. Not tonight. He had things to say and things to do tonight. He waited.

The toasts began anew. Laughter. Good-natured joking. The funny tales. Camaraderie that could turn ugly at any moment. It never ceased to amaze Wolf how these jovial men could laugh and celebrate one moment and be at each others' throats the next, whether some slight be real or fancied.

Shawna was right. The gods of the Norse were not heroic. They were simply much magnified mortals. They had their foibles and sins just as mankind did. They were prone to senseless, explosive violence just like mere men—from laughter to fury in a single stroke. Just like the clan of Arild and his guests.

Arild rose to his feet. Here came more political oratory. But then that's what this feast was all about, really; the wedding was secondary. "At this propitious moment, my greatest joy is to gather my loved ones about me. Alas, in spirit only are my four stillborn children present." He paused, with a melancholy sigh. "And my son lost, Ulf. He had his short points."

No one seemed to know whether the tenor of the moment permitted laughter, and Wolf, as an outlander, dare not lead the giggling. Besides, he trusted a better moment would come. After much hesitation, a nervous titter prevailed.

Arild droned on. "But he was Arildson, the son of the Thick Knee, all the same. I shall mourn him to my grave."

Now!

Wolf leaped up and scrambled onto the tabletop. "Mourn no more, my father! Your son has returned!" He addressed his father as he whipped his cloak off, but he made certain his voice could be heard throughout the hall.

His mother yelped and gawked, her hand clapped over her mouth. She shoved her tankard away. She started to stand up and fell back onto her stool—indeed, she nearly fell off her chair completely.

Beside Wolf, Skule jumped up onto the table and did a turn in place, his arms raised triumphantly. How the little cousin basked!

Hegaard roared, with a happy grin too wide to fit through a bier door. "You survived the loss of *Bounding Stag!* And you, Skule! Reidar! Do you not greet your long-lost brother?"

For a long, long moment Reidar hesitated, with a muddled look on his face. Wolf loved it! There sat Lord Perfect in a total quandary. With inner glee Wolf watched the mix of emotions play across Reidar's face. Reidar never was one for keeping his thoughts to himself. Here was his lovely party, spoiled by the little kid. And yet, a lost brother had returned. He, the shining star of this sky, of the whole Arild clan, was being momentarily outshone by a lesser light. Never had Wolf upstaged the man before. Never. This tasted so—so sweet! Thank You, God of the Irish!

What could the bridegroom do? Everyone was watching. Magnanimously, Reidar too leaped upon the table. With the cold confidence of a man at the top, he strode the length of the long table, kicking over tankards along the way.

Wolf opened his arms, and Reidar accepted the embrace.

Reidar mumbled in his ear, "You've changed."

"And you have not." Wolf pushed back and strode the way Reidar had come (without limping!), up the long table to his father. "My mother, Lenveig of Wald." He knelt and grabbed her hands. He kissed her knuckles as the Celts did. She sat open-mouthed, staring.

"My father, I greet you and bow to your lordship." Still on bended knee, he bowed his head before his father. If that didn't grease the old man's wheels, nothing would.

The jarl gathered his wits a thousand times more quickly than Mum or Reidar could. He stomped onto the table, no doubt to remain taller than his son.

Never before, not once, had Wolf ever hugged his father. Now the old man opened his arms, and Wolf stepped inside them. He clasped the man now, with all his strength and took a certain perverse pleasure in his father's startled grunt. His sack thunked against the old man's hip. He smelled again the unguent his father used in his beard to make it shine, and the pleasure of family washed over him. Family. For far too long he had neglected the pleasure of family.

"My joy is complete!" Arild wheeled and resumed his place of leadership between the pillars. He flopped back on his chair. "A year and a half, nearly! You must have a rousing tale to tell!" It occurred to Wolf, still up on the table, that symbolically—indeed, not so symbolically at all—he now stood closer to his father than his brother did.

Would he hop down now and give place to his brother? Do fish climb trees?

He extended his arm. "With joy I salute my brother, the pride of Arild, who is about to embark on the greatest error of his life—marriage."

General laughter and foot-stomping made the hall vibrate.

Reidar addressed the hall in a slow circle, orating sonorously the way his father so often did. "And I salute my brother, praising the gods for his return, even though he clearly cannot recognize a good deal when it sits right in front of his face. Error? Not at all! For I have the best of deals, marriage to a beautiful woman from a powerful family."

Reidar gestured grandly in Astrid's general direction. "There, my friends and compatriots, you see the loveliest maid in Tronde-lag. Her loving touch; her affection so freely given; her—ah—" he put just the right twist on his inflection "—most personal gifts bestowed in private. Lucky is the man who enjoys a lifetime of such giving."

Astrid flushed red as she yelled down the long hall for her fiance to shut up.

Huzzahs and laughter rang.

"Always the lucky one, my brother." Wolf loosened the cord on the bag at his belt. "Over the last year and a half, Skule and I have not embraced fair damsels, alas. We lived in servitude among the Celts, and these were our only embrace." He held aloft the great handful of chain and let it drop. He would have preferred that the chain ring and clatter on the table, but half its length landed on a quarter of roasted mutton and didn't make much noise.

He glanced down the hall at Skule. Skule was watching him, and Wolf could read on his cousin's face the thought that surged to the top of his own heart: for the first time in his life, he and Skule were being held in respect by their own people.

Reidar again addressed the hall loudly enough that his voice echoed in the rafters. "My brother has shed his chains, and I rejoice! Soon now I shall take up my own chains, and I rejoice in that also. The chains of matrimony."

"There are other chains, chains of bondage you cannot see." It surprised Wolf that found himself speaking thus, for when he opened his mouth he had no intention at all of saying it. "The Celts call them the chains of sin. Of evil. From them I am now released. I have escaped slavery both physically and spiritually. I of all men rejoice most deeply."

Why did he say that? What possessed him? More machinations by Shawna's God? Skule and Halvor both watched him oddly. No one else seemed interested in the vanquishment of sin.

"Fine. Fine." An impatient edge surfaced in Reidar's voice. "And now, my brother, gather up your chains there. Get them off the mutton, if you would, and join us at a place of honor. Let the feasting resume."

"Reidar, Reidar! You are not master of this feast, but the guest of honor." Wolf turned to his father. "Is this not your feast, my father, rather than his, and your place to invite me?"

Arild Thick Knee played many roles, not all of them savory, and Lord of All was one of his biggest. He nodded expansively. "And I do invite you! Skule and you together. But first, tell us your tale, Ulf Arildson, that our poet here can begin assembling an appropriate song for you."

Reidar obviously had been lying when he said he rejoiced. Not a shred of joy did he evince now. He turned to face Wolf squarely and came halfway up the table. "Would it not be better, Father, to call a feast specifically to welcome back our beloved brother? Let the poets and cooks do their work, and invite these guests to another banquet, say, in a month or two. We can hear him then."

Arild, bless his obtuse heart, failed to catch the hint. "Nonsense! I want to hear his story now!"

Reidar took another few steps forward. "You did this a-purpose, didn't you, Ulf! You've long envied me." A light dawned on his face. "And I don't doubt you've hungered after Astrid as well."

"Hunger after Astrid? After all those mean things you said about her? Of course not. I'm not stupid. Why, I remember the first time you met her, you said no bigger pig rooted in the forest."

Astrid and Mum together bellowed above the raucous din of laughter. Apparently Mum liked Astrid. The two women did indeed share much in common.

From the far end of the table, Skule cackled. "And when you described her tongue as sharp enough to cut granite, Reidar, you sounded so sincere!"

Astrid was on her feet screeching.

"Spoiler! You've always been the spoiler!" Fury twisted Reidar's face. "This is my feast! You'll not spoil it!" He wheeled suddenly and yanked his sword. As the company whooped and hollered he flailed it toward Skule.

Laughing wildly, swift as a stoat, the unarmed cousin leaped off the table and tucked himself behind a bench.

Reidar swung around, his blade high, toward Ulf. "Go!"

"The master of this feast invited me."

"Go! You seek only to embarrass me!"

"I needn't bother. You're doing well enough at that by yourself."

Wolf well knew that the happiest of such parties can turn sour in the wink of an eye, but he never expected his little coup to go so far. He didn't want this escalation.

Reidar strode forward. Wolf pulled his own sword—the inlaid, damascened sword of Doyle Dalainn—and Reidar stopped short. A general rumble of approval arose from this gathering of men who know their edges.

Arild stood up. "I have always believed brothers should work things out on their own. Any man who interferes dies by my hand."

No, Wolf didn't want this at all. Reidar was bigger and sturdier. He was probably stronger. He most certainly had been sparring and practicing at least two years longer than Wolf. And Astrid's dubious qualities aside, it was, after all, the man's wedding feast.

On the other hand, Wolf enjoyed one valuable advantage; he had not yet touched the ale, and Reidar had.

He braced, without hesitating or backing away, and raised that powerful sword. "No, Reidar. Not on your wedding. To kill or be killed either one would prove bad luck to the marriage."

"Ah, yes. The silver tongue. And you've polished it. You've always had a gift for words. Always able to talk your way out of the mischief you did." Reidar grasped his own weapon two-handed and advanced. The ale had not affected his steadiness in the least.

"I talked you out of a few holes, too, as I remember."

"And into a few others. You owe me at least one blow for that business concerning the fire in the wheat bin."

Wolf wrapped both hands tightly around his hilt. "That wasn't my fault. Besides, the dog survived."

"And bit me, you swine!"

Reidar feinted.

Wolf ducked aside and jumped the roasted mutton. He balanced lightly, watching, hoping and wishing that this would all come to a quiet end.

Reidar kicked a bowl of cabbage, but one of the women grabbed it before it was spilt. Several men prudently lifted their tankards aside.

Wolf must stop thinking. He could not afford to consider his response to any move Reidar made. He must react much more quickly than thinking permitted. He must move instinctively, whenever Reidar did.

Reidar's move came before Wolf expected it. The furious bridegroom brought his sword whistling down even as he closed the gap between them. Wolf swung his up before he thought about it. The blades clanged. Just barely did Wolf's response turn Reidar's strike aside.

Quick as a lizard on a rock, Reidar swung his blade around for a stroke upward from below. The tip of Wolf's blade clipped through Reidar's sleeve on its way down to parry the stroke. The blades clanged again, and Wolf felt the hilts lock.

Still gripping two-handed, he hauled upward, twisting his body away from his brother as he moved, until the back of his head was level with Reidar's nose. Wolf snapped his head backward. It clunked into Reidar's face. Wolf kept twisting, kept his sword hilt locked in Reidar's.

Reidar's arm came snaking up over Wolf's shoulder as the bridegroom tried desperately to hang onto his sword. Wolf arched forward until his head was nearly level with his knees. Reidar's full weight lay across his back.

And now Reidar was lifted off his feet. Wolf lurched forward and jerked back. The sudden moves tipped Reidar off Wolf's back. The bridegroom landed heavily on his side and in the process released his sword. Lightning fast he squirmed around to his feet and snatched the pile of chain off the mutton. His nose was bleeding profusely.

Wolf knew better than to consider that chain too lightly. With it Skule had brought down Doyle Dalainn's great stallion. Swung well, it could pull the sword right out of Wolf's hands or yank his feet from under him.

Reidar leaped backward to gain some swinging room. Wolf pressed forward. Reidar swung the only loop of the heavy chain that he could free up quickly, about four feet of it. With one arm Wolf was already snatching up the mutton roast. He thrust it at the chain. The chain wrapped around the roast and his arm. Its end whipped harmlessly against the mutton.

Wolf rotated a full circle in place, winding the chain. It brought Reidar in flat against him. Wolf swung the weighted mutton against Reidar's ribs and with the hilt of his sword caught Reidar squarely in the face. The bridegroom staggered back.

Wolf pressed the advantage, striking again with his sword hilt. Reidar let go of the chain as he went down.

Wolf stepped on Reidar's neck before the man could gather his wits. It took Wolf a second to disentangle his arm from the mutton roast and the loop of chain. He cast them aside.

"I felt bad because I brought no wedding gift, Reidar. Now, thanks to this unfortunate misunderstanding, I have one. I give you the ultimate wedding present: your life. And gladly. I came home meaning you no harm."

He stepped back and looked at Astrid. "You, woman, are too accustomed to acting the shrew—to having your own desires. I beg you, change your ways, for this is a man worth changing for. I've known him my whole life, and there is no finer man in Trondelag, myself and my father included. So be gracious to him, and gentle, and giving. May all blessings be yours, and his."

Gracious. Gentle. Giving.

Shawna.

19

Kildare

A well-thatched roof, they claim, will last three hundred years. Tell that to the mice tunneling through the rotten thatch on Ceirre's chicken shed. Shawna straddled the ridgepole, clawing at the black, stinking, slimy thatch, and pitied herself over the miserable turn her life had taken.

She meant to spend just the one night under Ceirre's roof. A month later here she was yet. She had finished thatching the cottage roof and was now commencing an even messier task. She uncovered two nests of pinky mice and a lizard so far. Heaven knew but that creatures as big as badgers lurked in here somewhere.

It was growing too dark to see well. She would have to quit before much longer.

Something squirmed beneath her fingers. She screamed and nearly fell off the ridgepole.

"What is it?" Ceirre came running out of her newly thatched cottage.

"Enough! I'm done with this!" Shawna scooted her way along the pole to the stone gable. She didn't bother climbing down. She jumped. "Your chickens will just have to make do with a hole in their roof."

"We'll throw a blanket over the top for tonight and recommence in the morning." Ceirre hustled inside, no doubt for the blanket.

What should she do? Shawna desperately wanted to go on. And yet, she couldn't just traipse off and leave this old woman with half a chicken-shed roof. On the other hand, already the woman was talking about their next project, mending the sagging gate down by the bier. The problem, of course, was that the gate really did need repair.

Ceirre brought out a threadbare woolen blanket, and together they managed to toss it up over the ridgepole. The chickens snugged in for the night, Shawna followed Ceirre dejectedly into the cottage.

She ate her chicken broth and barleycake because Ceirre placed it in front of her. Ceirre cooked well. Why wasn't Shawna more interested in food?

Ceirre put aside the bowls and took up her spindle. As a cat settles in before a mousehole did Ceirre settle in before Shawna, watching. Watching. Finally she declared, "You're sick."

Shawna looked at her. "With what?" There was only one spindle in the house, so Shawna assigned herself the task of winding the thread Ceirre spun.

"Love."

"Hardly!"

"And not Connleigh, either."

Why did she subject herself to this? She would leave on the morrow, chicken shed or no. Now, above all times, she did not need the old woman's constant meddling.

Ceirre continued, as if Shawna had asked her to. "You are afraid of your own passion, child."

"Nonsense. And 'passion' is hardly the word, anyway."

"It is exactly the word. Are you afraid you'll be considered less a woman if you let your passion wave like a banner?" The crone paused in her spinning. "No! I see. You're afraid you'll be considered less a scholar."

Shawna raised a hand. "Please. Let's not."

Smugly, the old woman pressed on. "You study Scripture. What does the Scripture talk about?"

"God. Jesus." Shawna frowned. Ceirre knew that.

"What does much of Scripture talk about?"

"Ceirre, you do not read. How do you know?"

"Passion! And not just our Savior's passion, as He suffered at the cross. Israel married Leah. Why did he marry Rachel too?"

"He loved her. He was hoodwinked by—"

"Passion! Amnon and Tamar, and Absalom. Remember how the story tells how Amnon lusted after Tamar? And after he forced her, it says he hated her with a greater passion than when he loved her."

"Yes, but . . ."

"David and Bathsheba! David was the greatest of God's heroes. And he loved and hated with the greatest passion. Jesus loves mankind with the most intense passion of all, to suffer and die for us, and most of us not caring a whit for His sacrifice. He sweat blood. He drove out the money changers. Passion completes us, child; it does not diminish us."

"Yes, but . . ."

"And you burn with passion for the Northman."

"Ceirre, stop it!"

"Deny it."

"Of course I'll deny it. I don't—" And she stopped. Had her sails any wind at all, it was gone now. Her arguments hung slack. Wolf.

Ceirre bobbed her head triumphantly. "And what are you going to do about it?"

"I don't know. Nothing. Connleigh saw his countrymen pull him aboard their vessel. So he's surely home again, far beyond my reach. And he'll not return. You know that."

"That's his side of the fence. I didn't ask about his part. I asked, what are you going to do about it?"

Shawna sighed heavily and put the winder down. "Very well, old woman, what am I going to do about it? You're aching to tell me, aren't you?"

"Other than to tell you not to hide passion, for it is the best part of any man or woman, I do not know. But you must consider it. You cannot simply drift along here, however pleasant our time together has been."

"Pleasant!" Constant preaching and philosophizing. Slimy, rotten thatch. Vermin and ugly creatures. Hard toil and meager rations. Slopping in the mud of Ceirre's bier to milk a cow that was not Shawna's. An obstreperous old cow at that.

"Indeed, and I've loved your visit. But you are young. You must not hide your life here with an old woman. You must go out and make your way. Marry. Make your mark in the world for God."

"Saint Brigid herself renounced her passion."

"No, lass. She renounced marriage. Her passion burned strong for God. There is more than just erotic passion, though heaven knows you've a heavy enough dose of that."

"Oh, honestly, Ceirre."

"Whose face would you look upon this moment, above all others, if your wishes be granted?"

The appropriate answer, Shawna knew, was Jesus.

The actual, honest answer was Wolf.

Ceirre was not about to get an honest answer, and she did not wait for one. Her voice softened. "Unrequited love fades, with time. This is why, I am sure, God loves us first and best, so that our own love not go unrequited."

Shawna smiled. "Probably why Saint Paul wrote, 'Do not neglect your coming together.'"

"There! You see? You've much to offer. Now. What would you like to do with your life? Marry Connleigh?"

Shawna thought about that—not about the whether, but about the why. Connleigh was an excellent choice, of high standing and therefore great power, and as intellectually oriented as she. And yet . . . and yet. The reason she had no desire to marry was passion. She hated to tell Ceirre that the old crone was right, but it was passion after all. She felt no warm desire for Connleigh at all. Friend, yes. Beyond that, nothing.

"Kildare." Ceirre took up her spindle again, so Shawna took up the winder. "You and Saint Brigid are soul mates, Shawna, in many ways. Go to the place she founded—Cill Dara—and see what you find."

Kildare. Shawna was an island girl. She had spent her whole life on Lambay, save for a few trading ventures to the mainland east coast with her father. Kildare was a myth, a legend, a name hung behind the mists of time just as were saints Brigid and Patrick. Shawna could not possibly presume to travel there.

The old woman paused as she let the spindle drop. "Yes. You ought go to Kildare. Right after we rehang that gate by the bier."

* * *

Spring in Trondelag. Nothing in the world compares. Wolf was certain of that. He measured this bold and gladsome spring against the casual change of seasons in Erin, and in this regard, at least, Erin lacked greatly. But then, after a half-hearted winter such as the Misty Isle's, one could expect no more than a half-hearted spring.

The willow and oak leaves, gathered as fodder, had long since been consumed. The villagers had fed the last of the hay to their emaciated cattle. Now in spring, gently they ushered the feeble beasts out to the sheltered coves and meadows where the snow was first to melt, where the first tender grass sprang. Within a month, as the snowline retreated up the mountains, the freemen would drive the fattening cattle to the high meadows for summer grazing.

Wolf planted his stool against a house post, leaned back, and stretched his legs out under the table, sated. Wolf was not a big enthusiast of vegetables, by and large, but he did love spring greens. The sons of their new house thrall cleared the remains of dinner away. They were almost the same age as Peadar and Paul.

And there was plenty to clear. Arild had called together the syndicate of jarls and farmers who financed the ships. Fifteen men gathered around Arild's table here, Wolf and Reidar among them. Hegaard, Jorn, Junken—all these men were familiar faces. Wolf grew up playing with some of them—or with their sons. It rather surprised Wolf that Skule had been invited also. Neither Skule nor his father had any wealth or supplies to invest in an expedition.

Beside Wolf, Arild waved a massive paw toward the smoke hole in the thatch above the hearth. "Look at that. Still light outside. Ah, I love spring."

"I was just thinking the same thing. You know—" Wolf drained his tankard and leaned forward far enough to set it on the table "—in Erin they have an interesting expedient. During the autumn—up here it would be before the snow—you plow the fields you've marked for early spring planting. Here come the first warm breezes of spring, and although the ground is still too wet to plow, you can put in the early crops. The soil is tilled. Ready. Apparently the Dalainn never thought of it, and the Behr did it all the time. Perhaps it would work in the Northland too."

Arild nodded. "We could try it."

"And when we plowed, Shawna would stack the stones in a furrow down alongside the rows."

Reidar wrinkled his nose. "Leave the stones in the garden?"

"Right next to the planting. She claimed that stones warm up faster than dirt does, and they make the whole plot warmer. Make the vegetables grow faster."

"Never heard of such a thing."

"Can't fault her results."

Arild chuckled. "One of the benefits of travel. New ideas. Speaking of which . . ." He reached forward and rapped his knuckle against his tankard. The serving lad hurried to his side and refilled it. "Are we agreed we send out a party this year as usual?"

They certainly were. These independent-minded jarls rarely agreed upon much, but they reached instant consensus on the prospect of garnering great wealth at little risk.

Arild swilled a gulp from his tankard. "And I want Ulf to lead it."

Wolf's heart thumped. "Why me?"

Jarl Thjorenson boomed, "Good idea! Of course, you! You've been there. Not only do you speak the language, you know the lay of the land and where the good things are."

Wolf shook his head. "Actually, I don't know the country nearly as well as Skule here. The Dalainn dragged him all over Erin. Literally, at times. He knows every place and what you'll find there. He's been in the homes of all the ris. I had to stay home and plow. Or send Hegaard. He's done splendidly so far."

Hegaard leaned forward, elbows on the table. "The only coasts I know are the areas I've already plundered. I don't really know enough about the place to pick the best targets. There may not be any unspoiled yet."

Junken looked at Wolf. "I agree. Use these two for their knowledge of the land, and let Hegaard handle the battle plans." His eye turned to Skule. "Are any of the coastlands down there still unspoiled?"

Wolf's mind raced. He should have been expecting this. The fact that his father considered him an oaf when he was growing up had blinded him to the notion that Arild might call upon him for any real task. He thought briefly about leading a pack of invincible raiders against Shawna, or her relatives, or her friends. No.

He glanced at Skule. The foolish cousin, so wise in so many ways, was looking at him intently. The rest of the group were looking at Skule.

"Unspoiled coasts." Skule studied the smoke hole overhead a moment, and then looked from face to face. "Not many. Of course, you can hit a place more than once. I don't know how long it takes them to recover—to replace stolen objects. Every few years, I'd guess. The real wealth, though, is in the interior.

"Erin is shaped something like a bowl. Mountains around the edge and lowlands in the middle. A lot of wealthy churches and monasteries in the middle."

"Yes, but how do you get to the middle in a ship, though?" Hegaard frowned.

"They took me to this one place, Clonmacnoise. It's been a center for hundreds of years. Monastery, church. Gold everything—candlesticks, chandeliers, dishes. And a large river runs nearby. I mean a very large, flat river. Navigable clear to the sea, I believe."

"Where's the mouth?"

"West side somewhere. That's the area you want, around that way." He looked right at Wolf. "I'd forget the east coast. That's pretty well picked over by now."

Wolf could barely swallow his grin. Skule knew. Skule understood. The wise little fool understood clearly.

"No." Hegaard shook his head. "I don't want to spend the summer exploring rivers hoping to find one that goes to Clawn-wherever."

"Then go on up the Liffey. You know the Liffey. Get into the interior that way."

"Skip the coast and row inland."

"Right." Skule bobbed his head. "For instance, just a few miles from the Liffey—easy striking distance—is another ripe plum. An important monastery, started by a woman. I forget her name. They call it Kildare."

* * *

206

"Hic est discipulus ille, qui testimonium perhibet de his, et scripsit haec; et scimus, quia verum est testimonium ejus. Sunt autem et alia multa, quae fecit Jesus; quae si scribantur per singula, nec ipsum arbitror mundum capere posse eos, qui scribendi sunt, libros."

Solemnly, Connleigh closed his book.

He counted seventeen men and boys crowded together around him in the little church. Some wore cowled robes, others the common dress of farmers. All claimed to be either men of God or trainees. All spoke Latin with some degree of success, and that was good, because Connleigh could not begin to understand their Saxon garble. And no one here knew a word of Gaelic.

Silence. Should he speak? Should he wait? For lack of a better idea, he sat on his stool and waited.

From the back, a lovely tenor voice began in Latin a liturgy Connleigh had never heard. The man did not say it; he sang it, in a melody new to Connleigh, like nothing the Irish church ever used. Other voices picked it up and even sang parts of it antiphonally, so it must be in common use locally.

And Connleigh's heart swelled with joy. This was true, pure worship! This was glorious! He could not keep silence. Above the liturgy being sung, he raised his own voice in prayer, spoken prayer, a paean of thanks and rejoicing to his God.

These men who could not speak Connleigh's language, who did not know the rites of Connleigh's home church, who tilled alien soil and claimed alien ancestors, were one with him, soul mates in the most intimate sense. No one else in the world, except the Picts in the north and the Welsh behind him, spoke anything close to his native tongue. Connleigh had assumed from the moment he left the east gate of his father's rath that he would encounter difficulties on his travels, particularly with language. He had never guessed that he would find this joy and oneness on foreign shores.

About half an hour later the service apparently closed. With a hearty "Thanks be to God" in unison, the men stood and began to mill about.

An older fellow in a cowled robe seized Connleigh's hand. In Latin he crowed, "Praise God! I've not heard the gospel of John for years! You must stay with us a few days and expound upon it. We'll try to get some of the people over from Watley Cross."

"I am not a teacher. I'm traveling to Rome to become a student."

"How many times have you read John's gospel lately?"

"Over and over."

"Then you can expound upon it. Spare us a few days, and we will send you on your way with God's blessings."

What could he say? Twice now he had, in essence, read his book before a church in exchange for lodging and victuals. It certainly would not hamper his trip to stay here a few days. He would ask for an offering of food to take along and then travel eastward across England until his food ran out.

He wanted so much to somehow tell Shawna about this experience. She would understand. She would appreciate it much more so than his own father or mother ever would. She sought this same sort of experience herself.

Why did she refuse to come with him? They were perfect for each other. Saint Brigid, founder of Cill Dara—Kildare—refused to marry even though a number of appropriate suitors, men who understood her, asked her hand. Would Shawna go the same route?

Connleigh suddenly felt a sad communion with those thwarted suitors of three hundred years ago. Women. Honestly. Whatever did the faith do to them?

20

Greed

Men and boys together, laughing and jesting, lent a hand. Wolf stood off to the side. With all those eager hands to open up the boat shed, they didn't need him. Against the hillside behind Arild Thick Knee's house, Arild's longship had spent the winter in peaceful slumber. The narrow end of her thatched stone shed had been closed up with a stack of logs.

Now the crew, already well oiled with beer, unstacked the logs and cast them aside. Enough sunlight entered the shed that Wolf could just so see the ship's proud head in the musty gloom. A happy, somewhat drunken cheer went up.

Arild himself tossed the first log down in front of his ship unaided. He might be getting on in years, but you couldn't say his strength and vigor had abated at all. Junken and Jorn laid the second log down. A dozen men disappeared into the darkness of the shed. The dragon head waggled.

Here she came, hesitantly at first, rolling on the logs that had been her bed all winter. Her cutwater whumped up over Arild's log and onto the second. By now another dozen logs had been laid crosswise to her path. She rolled forth, clunking and creaking, with a score of men shoving her along. As the stern moved out into the light, the men started bringing the logs from behind and laying them ahead of her, an endless band of rollers to carry her down to water's edge.

She crossed the dirt street beside Old Ingrid's hovel and rolled on down the hill, foot by foot. There was a magnificence to her, surpassed only by her magnificence under sail.

Everyone in town watched her awakening. Women laughed and talked loudly and gossiped as they stood about. The children ran and argued and climbed up on the rock walls to get a better view.

One woman did not laugh or gossip. She stood apart, down by the butcher's house, and her hands were clamped over her mouth. Wolf watched her a few minutes. Her chest heaved. She was sobbing.

And he realized who she was.

He walked down to her. He'd not met her before, for Junken had kept her sequestered on his farm until now. He was struck by her beauty. Her hair was a bit darker than Shawna's, her eyes set not quite so deeply. But she had those finely chiseled Celtic features Wolf loved so much in Shawna.

He stepped in beside her and spoke in Erse. "You are of the Behr."

She wheeled and gasped. Her cheeks were wet, her eyelashes crystalline with tears, her nose clogged up. "How do—oh. You are the man named Ulf, who escaped from the Celts."

"And you are Junken's woman, taken in that raid on Lambay." He was surprised that his Erse, with which he had once been so comfortable, did not come freely. He had to struggle with it.

Her eyes went wide. "Can you tell me any news of survivors? I saw my husband and father-in-law dead on the hillside. I know I'm a widow. But what about my sons? The others? Can you tell me? I pray thee!"

"Peadar and Paul are safe, adopted by Doyle Dalainn. Shawna is living with the Dalainn, and there's some possibility she might marry Connleigh. They have much in common."

And his heart burned.

"Padraic?"

"Who?" Wolf knew Padraic was the third boy, but he wasn't about to volunteer anything.

"Then he must be dead. But Peadar and Paul. Safe. And Shawna. Praise God! Praise His holy name!" She seized Wolf's hand. Before he could snatch it back she kissed it and got it wet with her tears. "Thank you, good man."

He retrieved his hand, embarrassed. "You're weeping because you know the ship is going to sail south to Erin."

She nodded. "I know what's coming, because I've seen it."

What could he say? Against his better judgment he was about to take part in this expedition. He didn't want this beautiful woman to know that, at least not while he stood beside her. So instead, he asked, "How has life been here for you?"

She tried to look at him, but her eyes flicked away. "Fine. Well."

"Tell me your heart." He smiled. "It's safe. No other ears here can discern Erse."

She looked at the rolling ship, the sky, the ground—anything but him. "I am ashamed."

"Junken owns you, and there is no wedlock."

"That, yes. I was surprised to learn, though, that he is not married—was not married when he received me."

"His wife died of pneumonia the year before."

"Pneumonia. No one told me how. Mm." She paused a moment, and Wolf thought the conversation might be ended. Then she continued. "He's a good man. A very good man. You Northmen keep yourselves and your homes very clean. Junken is that way—neat and clean, and orderly. I like that. And he's gentle. I wasn't expecting that at all. And kind. I didn't expect that either, because you're pagans, without the good influences of the living faith. And he treats me very well."

"That can't be why you're ashamed."

"I'm ashamed of myself. Ashamed that I like this life better than my life on Lambay. Junken gives me little gifts now and then. Just little things. But . . ." She licked her lips. "The boys' father never once gave me a present. And Junken is a . . . a better lover."

She forced herself to look at Wolf. "I'm ashamed because I should be detesting my life as a slave and praying to my God to release me, and instead I'm enjoying it. I would not have guessed, until I came here, that I could be so greedy."

How much like Shawna this woman was! Wolf could hear Shawna saying the same sort of thing, voicing the same doubts and self-loathing.

Wolf considered for long moments what to say, and nothing wise or profound came to mind. "I learned during my time with the Dalainn that your husband was a great hero. Your sons are very, very proud of him. Hegaard gave you to Junken because Junken is a good man who acquitted himself well—a hero in his own right and popular with his shipmates—and he had lost his wife. You've lost a great deal, but you've gained a little too. I wouldn't call it greed."

"I suppose I should be calling it the grace of God."

"Grace. Ceirre and Shawna use that word a lot."

"Ceirre of the Liffey?" The woman smiled. "Dear old Ceirre. Grace means receiving more blessing than you deserve."

"Ah." All sorts of things Shawna had said came clear.

The ship had nearly reached the water. Wolf nodded toward it. "I must go."

"God bless you richly. Thank you."

God bless you. Why should He? On the track north from Land's End, six months ago at least, Wolf had asked that very God to take his sins. Since then, Wolf had not done a thing about the God, nor had the God done a thing to him that he could see. Essentially, each had forgotten about the other.

He strode down to the shore.

"Junken?" Wolf raised an arm. "Talk to you a moment?"

Red with sweat and anticipation, Junken turned his back on the festivities and joined Wolf. He grinned. "It's going to be another glorious summer. I can't wait."

Wolf grinned too, just to be sociable. He could wait. "I just talked to your slave. What's her name?"

"Peggy." Junken frowned suspiciously. "Why were you talking to her?"

"My Gaelic's getting rusty. She was good to practice on. She asked me about her family, the people on that island. I told her what I know. Her sister-in-law and two of her sons survived the raid. That seemed to please her. She praised her God."

"She does that a lot, yes." He looked Wolf in the eye. "So what do you think of her?"

"She's a splendid woman, and I think you've captured her heart. Congratulations."

"Really? She said that?"

"Not in so many words, but you can tell. She likes you very much. Maybe even loves you."

212

"Mm." Junken nodded more or less to himself. He smiled slightly.

"Know what you could do for her, more than anything else?"

"What?"

"While I was in Erin I learned a little about that God of hers, about what's right and what's not right. What she thinks displeases Him. If you really want to make her happy, marry her."

"Why? I own her."

"I know. To you and me, that's fine. Not to her God."

"That's crazy. Marry a slave?"

"It happens all the time."

"Not to me, it doesn't." Junken snorted, but he was smiling. "I'll think about it. I'll talk to her. She is a good woman. Never a moment's trouble."

Wolf nodded. "You going with Hegaard and me?"

"Unless I get a better offer from the *Fierce Cutting Blade*. Their percentages tend to be as good as Arild's or a little better."

"Grab it while you can."

"You said it." Junken wandered off to stand around the longship with everyone else, doing nothing, just standing about. She had come to a casual halt. She reclined now with grace and dignity on the beach. She would be checked for light leaks first, and then floated to caulk any water leaks. She would be loaded with provisions. Within days she would be pushed off, to go adventuring and despoiling in the land of Shawna and Peggy.

Here came Wolf's father up from the water's edge. The man glowed like an aurora. He spied Wolf and came on over.

He turned to survey his ship from this distance. "A beauty, isn't she?"

"And she acts as beautiful as she looks."

"She does, she does. And a beautiful crew. First class fighting men, you and Skule to show the way, Hegaard, Halvor, Jorn, Junken, and the others."

"Halvor! You've talked the legendary Halvor into going raiding?"

"Not yet. I was hoping you could help there. You enjoy a close rapport with the old man. More so than I."

"Why do you need Halvor?"

"Why do we need anyone? Another sword, another skilled fighter."

It had to be more than that. Wolf let it go by. Pressing the wily old man would avail nothing. Arild disclosed only what he wanted to disclose.

"In fact—" Arild added it almost as an afterthought "—I'm considering going myself."

"Really! All this talk about Erin has whetted your appetite for glory and plunder."

"Glory. Worthy foes, the Celts, if that sword of yours be any indication."

"They certainly try to be." Wolf thought but a moment about Shawna, and about Peggy's sorrow. He recalled the discussions between Skule and Halvor during that storm. "You heard the Danes are moving into Northumbria."

"That's the rumor."

"And the Swedes are exploring east—finding some rich towns indeed."

"So I hear."

"Erin is one misty little isle. Limited pickings, with so many of us descending upon her. Wouldn't we reap a better return heading east as the Swedes are doing?"

Arild thought a moment, staring at his ship without seeing her. "We know what's in Erin. Anything in the east is guesswork. We know we can best the Gaels in combat. We don't know that about the east." He clapped Wolf on the back and spoke without the least hint of sincerity. "'Twas a very good idea, though, all in all." And he trundled off to stand around staring at his ship with his mates.

A better idea than you know. Wolf grimaced. So much for that. On the other hand, Arild valued Hegaard's counsel. Wolf sought out Hegaard.

The Broad Back was up on the deck of *Swift Lynx,* pointing out to his crew of carpenters the things that needed improvement or repair.

Wolf fell in beside him and dogged his heels until he paused.

Hegaard smiled. "As eager to go as I am?"

"Always up for adventure. Which reminds me. I was wondering if we might not have even better success sailing southeast, as the Swedes are doing. The mainland of the northern tribes."

Hegaard studied him a moment and hope tiptoed into Wolf's heart.

Hegaard burst into a wide grin. "Ah, yes. Skule warned me that you're in love."

"Skule's big mouth is going to get him a battle-ax between his ears."

"What is winter like in Erin?"

"Warm and wet."

"Cattle graze all year?"

"Very nearly so. Hay supplement."

"That's what Skule says. He and Arild and I sat around one afternoon talking about Erin. What it's like there. Your father was fascinated. I think he wants to see it for himself."

And Wolf had not been not invited to that discussion. Wolf grunted. The jarl of jarls wishes to see a foreign land he's never been to; therefore, men, women, and children die. Some trade-off.

How in the world could Peggy and Shawna and Ceirre and that strange, wry Mahon and all the others cling to their God when He permitted such nonsense? Couldn't they see He was ineffectual? In nearly the same breath, Peggy said, "Praise His holy name!" and, "I know what is coming, because I have seen it." Two statements diametrically opposed, if you looked at it sensibly and logically. What was the draw of this God who promised to scrub away sin?

And just wait until his hands reached the throat of that Skule!

* * *

Beaming, the monk handed Connleigh a little drawstring bag. "Go in God's grace, Connleigh of Erin. Godspeed!"

Connleigh proffered his thanks in florid Latin, for he had no grasp whatever of the language of these Saxons around Londinium. Indeed, it wasn't called Londinium now, its Latin name, but London Town. And so, with waves and smiles and mutual promises of prayers and blessings, Connleigh turned his back on his new friends and walked east.

215

The little purse jingled. Here was something else Connleigh must become accustomed to. Coins. There were no coins in all Erin. Trade consisted of whatever it was you wanted traded. Value was measured in cattle. No need for coins.

He had read about them, though, in Scripture. Jesus instructed Peter to go fish for his tax money, and the fish Peter caught held a coin in its mouth. Sure and you couldn't do that with a cow. "Render unto Caesar." Until Connleigh entered the land of the Saxons the phrase meant nothing. Coins no longer carried Caesar's image, but the mere act of holding one in his hand became a beautiful object lesson. Two lessons. For Connleigh perceived as he never had before that although a passage of Scripture may not fit into your range of experience, it still carried the full weight of meaning.

He yearned to expand his range of experience to cover everything Scripture talked about. Everything. And he was on the right road to do just that, the road to Rome.

Was it greedy to want it all? Shawna's faith was no less deep than his and she spent her life on a little island. These monks he just left had never traveled to London, and that just down the road, so to speak. Was Connleigh seeking too much?

He opened his drawstring bag far enough to shove his fingers in. He removed a coin at random and examined it. A copper. No doubt all the coins in the bag were copper. He thought about Jesus' story of the widow's mite. These people freely gave him their own mites, to see him on his greedy quest. And all he did in return was read to them.

He tucked the bag away, but he held back the coin in his hand, a warm copper link between him and the Jesus who preached so much about money.

Up ahead, a woman sat on a low rock wall beside the road. Connleigh hesitated in mid-step, at first thinking it was Ceirre. It was not, though for build and carriage the two old women looked much alike. Connleigh smiled at his silly error of recognition. But on second thought, no, it wasn't so silly. Of all the people Connleigh knew, except perhaps Mahon, Ceirre would be the one to turn up here a world away from home. Ceirre was like that.

As he approached her, the ancient woman looked less and less like Ceirre. Ceirre bustled. This woman sat flaccid. This woman lacked the healthy glow that Ceirre still possessed. This woman's shoulders hunched even more than Ceirre's, and no joy softened the hardness of her face.

Connleigh paused before the woman and smiled. "God bless you," he said in Latin.

No response. No smile. She obviously did not speak Latin. He handed her his copper coin, giving the widow his mite.

Her brows knit; her mouth dropped open. She babbled something effusive in her native tongue and crossed herself.

The sign of union in Christ. Grinning, Connleigh crossed himself, bowed to her, and continued on.

Here in this alien land, he was at home.

21

Deceit

Gulls and kittiwakes rode the churning air between Lambay Island and Berit Head. Vagrant winds blew this way and that as jackdaws circling the bluff argued over nothing at all. Amid all this, Mahon squatted on a low, flat rock and pondered the little island in the distance.

He called to mind the bits and snips of information that had come his way from time to time. They were like a broken pot. Reassemble the broken sherds in just the right way and you could determine the shape of what the pot had been whole.

The phantom shape that emerged from his sherds troubled him. In fact, it troubled him so greatly that he stood up, letting the wind riffle his hair a few minutes. Then he wound his way down to the sandy shore, where three of Doyle Dalainn's boats lay beached upside down. The two curraghs were too big and clumsy for one man to handle easily. Mahon chose instead a little round coracle.

Mahon had grown up paddling coracles about. He knew all their whims and eccentricities. He launched off the sand into the gently slapping surf. He sculled for a minute until he reached water deep enough to row. Then he set out for Lambay.

A couple hundred yards offshore he glanced up on the head. Someone stood on its brow watching him. For size and build it was probably either Brian or the MacBrian. The man turned and ran off toward the Dalainn rath.

The hide cover had dried terribly on this boat, and all the seams leaked. Like all coracles, the tiny, round, skin craft had a mind of its own. Fortunate indeed that Mahon knew that mind. Mostly by superior strength of mind, he rowed the boat to the west shore of the island and pulled up onto the cobble beach.

An ancient burial ground lay in this area. He found it after fifteen minutes of idle wandering. The weeds and grass had grown high, obscuring the flat stones that marked the graves of saints long gone. The graveyard was undisturbed. No one recently had been interred here.

He took to the boat again and rowed around south, in the lee of the island, seeking the Behrs' wharf. There it was, though the sea had ripped half of it apart. Mahon ran the boat aground and stepped out. He would follow this track up to the rath. He wanted to see what—

Howling and snapping, a pack of seven dogs came running down the hill toward him. Far more rapidly than he had landed, he launched out again, poling furiously in the shallow water.

The curs stopped at water's edge, barking. There are joyous dog barks and warning dog barks. These were desperate dog barks. The dogs were the thinnest Mahon had ever seen. Their flanks caved in. Their ragged coats were so thin he could see the knobs strung out along their spines. Mahon could count every rib in the pack from out here.

The lead cur plunged into the surf and struggled toward him. Mahon backed further, but the surf kept shoving him landward. Here came the dog resolutely, snorting, swimming, struggling, its nose barely at waterline. Three others leaped in and came swimming as the remaining three barked encouragement from shore.

Terrified, Mahon swung at the closest with an oar. He knocked it beneath the water. It surfaced and kept coming. If they tipped his boat, or he did, he was dead. They'd tear him apart in minutes, so hungry were they.

He lost his composure completely and flailed wildly. He was his own worst enemy, and he knew it. Terror drove him frantic. He whacked another. It sank and did not rise.

Mahon sat back quickly and drew a powerful stroke. The coracle jumped and bobbed and danced forward on the rippling surf. He stroked again, long and slow. You could not row this little boat as you would a curragh. You must be firm and smooth and cautious.

The three remaining dogs pursued for a few yards, then started back toward shore. With a weak, plaintive howl, one of the three simply stopped swimming and sank. The other two struggled into shallow water and stumbled up onto the beach. They were too tired to shake themselves. They flopped on the sand, their tongues hanging.

The three dry dogs followed him, clambering over rocks and through the sand, barking and threatening. These dogs were going to curtail his investigation severely. He wanted to get ashore and test his horrible theories. He could not, with the threat of death these curs posed.

He rowed back, around the western end of the island and toward the north shore.

Near the ancient graveyard, the ragged dogs gave up the chase. They flopped on their bellies on the cobble beach, utterly exhausted. Poor starved beasts.

Mahon rowed on in blessed silence. Somewhere along this north shore the dragon boats of Wolf the Dane had landed. Cautiously, Mahon ran the coracle aground and got out.

What a sorrowful sight. Mahon crossed himself. The burial crew had not carried the Behr to hallowed ground for interment, as Mahon would have expected them to. They had simply buried them where they fell. The dogs had dug open three of the graves. Bones lay scattered all over in the dense, high grass—large bones, men's bones.

When Doyle's burial party arrived here, Connleigh was still too weak to travel. If he had come on the burial detail, would he have permitted this? The question went begging, for Doyle was here. He knew better; he had built a monastery and financed a school of monks on his own property. He of all men should have done the job correctly.

Timidly, ever listening for dogs, Mahon ventured up the hill. The Behr died here. He couldn't shake the thought. At length he looked down upon the rath of the Behr. The earthen wall was already falling into disrepair. Dogs had dug into it here and there. Black burned thatch lined the empty shells of the house and outbuildings. Bones of cattle and sheep lay everywhere. The paddocks and leas, all weeds and tall grass, had not been grazed in a long time.

The dogs must have lived sumptuously during the first months after the raid, with all the animal carcasses to feed upon. Then the meat would have rotted too much for even a dog to stomach, if indeed anything was left. There were probably originally far more than seven dogs.

Mahon returned to the coracle and rowed around to the east end. Here was where his questions would be answered, his puzzle solved.

The remains of a small rath perched on a low rise above the sea. It had not been burned. Seabirds squawked and circled. The kittiwakes and gulls were nesting here. Again, people had been buried where they fell. The dogs had dug up a dozen bodies, and they did not have to dig far. Shallow graves. Essentially ineffectual burials. Children had died—some of the scattered bones were saddeningly small. None of these bones appeared to be those of livestock.

More than a dozen graves had been opened. There couldn't have been many more than a dozen people altogether on this side of the island. They had been summarily slaughtered. From the number of graves, Mahon surmised no prisoners, no slaves—or very few.

Sorrowful, Mahon climbed into his coracle and began the long haul back to the mainland. The mindless rowing gave him ample time to think. The dogs barked from shore as he passed the west end, but they made no move toward him.

Doyle had said there were no survivors and laid the island's depopulation, all of it, at the feet of the Danes. Wolf said he didn't think his people raided the east side at all, though they might have returned without his knowledge. Connleigh mentioned he saw the Danes' ships sailing off to the south quite soon after the raid. Apparently, they did not return to strike again.

The very nature of the raid on the east side differed from the work of the Danes. There had been no fire. No animal bones. Danes apparently cared nothing for cattle and either slaughtered them or took along a few to eat. Danes seized slaves; witness their attempt to carry off Shawna and the boys. And they did not seem to kill children.

The only armed hostiles to visit this island, so far as Mahon knew, were the Danes—and the Dalainn burial party. The Danes were accounted for. But the Dalainn party—they had been driven into the sea once by these people from the east side and no doubt smarted for revenge. But they would not blithely slaughter valuable cattle. They would not take slaves from their own backyard, slaves who knew what happened and could speak.

The enormity of it stunned Mahon and mangled his thoughts. Raiding and cattle theft were an honored way of life among the Erse, even in the face of three hundred years of Christianity. But the wholesale slaughter of a whole clan, children included, constituted nothing less than outrage.

Doyle's outrage and Ailan's perfidy. *Ah, Doyle. Ah, Ailan.* They weighed so very, very heavy upon his heart.

He was about halfway across the channel now. He glanced behind, gauging his distance—and glanced again. By the Dalainn wharf in the far distance, two men lurked behind the bushes just upshore of the curraghs. Mahon could barely make them out, but make them out he did. And "lurk" was the only way to describe their furtive attempts to avoid being seen.

Might robbers fall upon a humble monk bound for Armagh? Not if Mahon had any say. He called upon God for some immediate guidance and rowed as he waited. He received none. In the face of divine silence he must act on his own. He let his course drift south somewhat. It was difficult—the coracle tended north, following the wind and changing tide.

He worked his way far enough south of the head that the curve of the shore would screen the coracle from view of the wharf. The moment he reached that point, he abandoned his oars and, standing, carefully rolled out of the boat.

Icy cold water pierced instantly to his skin. It filled his ears and nose. He twisted himself around, took a bearing off the head, and began to swim south, fighting the wind and current all the way. Fortunately, he had also grown up swimming. It was, besides prayer and study, the thing he did best. He never feared to leap into a stream in freshet, though he admitted to discomfort, especially in the spring. In essence he was swimming upstream now.

He reached shore well south of the head and the Dalainn wharf. He slogged through soft mud and sand and up onto the grassy slope. One of the two dangers—the sea—now lay behind him. God had provided him the strength and the means of escape.

Even if He didn't guide Mahon directly, He was responsible for his success so far.

Had the two at the wharf figured out what had happened yet? They surely had seen the coracle by now and almost certainly realized it was empty. Mahon prayed confusion upon them and the misconception that an old man would not fight tides and winds—that an old man would drift to the north as he attempted to swim ashore. He headed off southwest at a rapid walk.

When he reached a safe haven—and that was not any place this side of the ford in the realm of the Dalainn—he would send a messenger to fetch Declan. He would plan his strategy from thence.

Were the men lying in wait for Mahon? He would probably never know for certain. He carried no weapons with which to challenge them and no protection against them. He dared not move close enough to learn their identities or mission.

There were times he wished he were a warrior.

It was disgusting. Conal, Garvan's best warrior, knocked Daray backwards into the creek. Daray snatched up a boulder the size of a sheep's head and flung it at Conal—not towards his head but at his tender parts. His aim was absolutely true, and Daray came roaring up out of the creekbed and kicked Conal a couple times while he was down.

As all this mayhem ensued, Fiona sat idly by on a weathered stump and picked at her cuticles, not the least interested, apparently, that they were fighting over her. This was such a perversion of what had started out as a well-intentioned attempt to unite ritually with the nurturing earth!

Ailan did not try to hide his contempt.

Fiona had gained considerable weight over the winter. Was it the fat of idleness or the burgeoning of impending motherhood? Nothing in the writings about priestesses mentioned anything significant about pregnancy.

Ailan had not considered that possibility until just now. There was no way he could control that sort of thing. In fact, everything here had slipped past his control. Garvan and his minions asked their druid's advice, and then did as they pleased. They never listened to Ailan. They did not care to improve themselves through learning. They either paid him no attention when he attempted to instruct them by stories and precepts, or made silly wisecracks and rude remarks.

By their winter of extensive raiding and mindless destruction, they were now essentially outlaws in the land. Had they listened at all to Ailan, they could not only have been respected, law-abiding leaders but also could have established themselves—and him—as the cutting edge of the new faith, the return to the old ways.

He could not control them. He could not control Fiona anymore either. She listened to them, not him. Obviously he had reached a dead end here. He was not going to draw anyone into the faith so long as he associated with these brigands. He watched Fiona, giggling, disappear into the forest with Daray.

Deceitful things, women. Deceitful, too, were the gods who held before him the false promise of success. On the other hand, perhaps he had simply misread their signs. Whatever the case, he must take a new track in his quest.

He would simply leave camp, Ailan decided, and walk away into the woods to the east, out toward the brushwood track across the bog. He didn't like following brush-paved roads, but he'd do it. Brushwood trackways—small hazel branches laid longwise to form roads for miles across the wetlands—were usually waterlogged, always slippery, difficult to walk on, and they undulated with every low spot and hummock in the bog. However treacherous the footing, though, following the rickety trackways was infinitely better than struggling a hundred extra miles up and around the bogland.

He would return to the east, whence he began, and start over. This time he would choose his personnel far more carefully.

Once gone he would not return to this camp. He could travel light, with only the clothes he wore. He and Mahon used to do that, before the Abbot of Kells gave Mahon that ax and they began to accumulate dunnage.

Ailan stood up and stretched. Over by the fire, Garvan was intently sharpening a new sword he had stolen, testing its edge after every few strokes across the stone.

Farewell, infidels. Farewell, Fiona.

Casually, he strolled across the camp and into the woods eastward, the first steps in his renewed quest. No one paid him any mind.

He did pause long enough, however, to pluck up the ax.

22

Beginnings

Once upon a time, a beautiful girl child was born of a king and his slave-consort. Fair of face and fair of nature, she grew up blessed by God in every way. Any number of love-struck suitors pursued her, and the king himself urged her to marry well. She felt called of God, however, to bind herself not to a man but to the church only. Ah, the furor that raised! Distracted, she prayed God to disfigure her in some way to discourage the swains. In answer to that prayer, an eye burst within her head. Her beauty thus marred, she went on in peace to gather a school of devoted scholars, men and women both, at Cill Dara, the Church of the Oaks. Kildare. Her name was Brigid.

Patrick and Brigid, the twin columns on which all Erin rested.

Shawna of the Behr, the girl who grew up on an island remote from the mainstream of the faith, stood gazing upon a place she had never dreamed she would ever see. Kildare.

Far behind her the Wicklows brooded, misty gray. Before her, groves and woodlots splashed across the undulant valley, somewhat more trees than had either Lambay or the Dalainn. Feathery pines studded the light green of oaks and elms, birch and hazel. Ragged lines of pale alder traced the stream courses across the valleys. Brown cattle and white sheep dotted the great green leas here as they did back home.

In the middle distance, not nearly as imposing as one would expect from its legendary status, sat the simple wooden church and monastery of Kildare.

Shawna stood on the crest of a small rise and blotted up the scene before her awhile. This could conceivably be her home from now on. Or she might not stay here long at all. What a curious feeling this was, to have no home, no hearth to sit beside, no place to be.

More curious still was to render herself totally dependent upon the prioress of the abbey at Kildare, to be accepted or refused as the woman wished. Shawna had never before been dependent upon someone else in this way, much less a total stranger. It chafed.

Ceirre claimed that Shawna shared a spiritual sisterhood with the Brigid of three hundred years ago. Hmph. Shawna absolutely, definitely did not want to lose an eye, no matter how many swains came swarming. Brigid's reputation as a saint rested heavily on her charitable works and a list of miracles two books long. Shawna had never performed a miracle, unless it was teaching Gaelic to that ungrateful Northman. On the other hand, she loved doing charity. She loved study, and the real Brigid, the woman behind all the veils of rhetoric and myth, loved study also. Perhaps there was a spiritual kinship there.

How could Ceirre be so wise, when books are the font of wisdom, the Holy Spirit being the source, and Ceirre could not read?

Uncertainly, even say fearfully, Shawna started forward, down off the rise and toward those simple buildings.

* * *

London Town. What a strange, squalid, magnificent accumulation of people! The first thing Connleigh noticed as he approached the city was the stench. He was accustomed to the farm smell of manure, and the privy out by the wall of every rath. But London was permeated with the stink—a thousand raths all crowded into the space of two or three.

The buildings amazed him. Some were of wood, some of wattle. Almost none were built of stone. They squeezed together shoulder to shoulder like a hundred cows in one small paddock. People churned about in the alleys between buildings—dirty children, groveling old men, prideful merchants, haggling women, shouting, laughing, cursing, calling out wares, jeering, scolding, singing their way. How in heaven's name could anyone voluntarily live in these noisy, stinking, degrading circumstances?

No one spoke Latin. He tried his universal cross-cultural communication, the sign of the cross, and nobody returned it.

Several, though, pointed up one alley or down another. Obediently, he turned where they indicated. He would have missed the church completely had he not noticed the cross attached to its gable. It was a great box of a building, larger than almost any building in Erin. He stepped inside the cool darkness and used the only Saxon word he knew. "Hello?"

When the Saxons displaced the Celts in this country, art suffered. Connleigh might even venture that it died. He looked at the rudely drawn pictures on the walls of the musty sanctuary and thought of the intricate carvings and delicate brushwork adorning even the simplest of churches back home.

A rather harried looking little monk appeared in a far doorway beyond the altar. He asked a question, and Connleigh regretted using his hello. He switched to Latin. "I am Connleigh Dalainn of Erin, traveling to Rome."

The monk smiled. "Excellent. Excellent. Godspeed." Good. He spoke Latin.

Connleigh smiled. The little monk's smile persisted. Connleigh continued to smile. So did the monk.

With the smile pasted on front and frustration building up behind, Connleigh explained. "I have with me a gospel of John. I would be very pleased to read for the assembled brethren."

The monk considered this a moment. "Ah. If you are seeking patronage, go down to Canterbury. They handle all that sort of thing. We are a very poor church, as you see, and not really prepared for scholars. They are the see, the center of the faith. They'll help you." The smile.

"Canterbury. You are not prepared for scholars." Connleigh perceived that his smile had faded, and he couldn't see it coming back in the near future.

"That is correct."

"How do I get there?"

"I'll take you to the crossing myself and show you the road."

"Thank you."

Canterbury.

Because these men of the faith were not prepared for scholars.

* * *

Her deck was crammed with barrels and crates of provisions—grain and dried peas and salted meat. Fresh water. Tools and weapons, and more tools and weapons to replace those broken. The personal chest of each man, placed as his seat at the oar. Bearskins and woolen blankets for sleeping. Pots and caldrons. The jarl's tent and collapsed bed frame. Rope and chain for captured horses, cattle, and slaves.

Thirty-four men crowded the stern of the *Swift Lynx,* caught up amid the wild and heady hoopla of setting sail. Everyone within walking distance of the launch stood on the narrow little beach to see them off. Women waved scarves and shouted blessings. The children of those men leaving huddled close in their mothers' skirts. The children of the townsmen ran and played and climbed the walls.

Stalwart beside his sternpost stood Arild Thick Knee—at his right, his Reidar; at his left, his Ulf; and at Ulf's left, Halvor. From ashore, slightly tipsy, Lenveig watched her men depart. Beside her, Astrid stood in sullen silence, her belly bulging out beneath her shift.

Wolf scanned the crowd twice over, but he did not see Junken's woman. Their deck tilted slightly. The incoming tide was starting to float the ship.

"Oars!" cried Hegaard, and twenty oarsmen took their place. The human part of her load having shifted forward, *Swift Lynx* lifted free of the beach mud. Jorn called cadence. Three strokes brought her to glide. As she slid out into deep water, her sail crew began the difficult work of hoisting her four-hundred-pound mast to raise sail. Three days hence, at full moon, they would join two others in the Vik, the sea passage to the south of Norge, to form a swift and terrible fleet.

Arild wandered back to join Hegaard. Reidar wandered off who knew where. Wolf belonged to neither the oars nor the sail. He felt at loose ends.

But then, Halvor had no duties at the moment either. The old man twisted and craned, watching the sail spar swing out. "How long to Erin?"

"Ten days to Man, weather permitting. Another three or four

to the Liffey, depending." He turned to Halvor and leaned a shoulder against the sternpost. "Tell me something."

"If I can."

"Why did you let me talk you into coming? I know better than to think it's my gift of speech."

"Your brother calls you the silver tongue."

"My brother calls Astrid the perfect wife."

Halvor chuckled. The old man tipped forward and leaned both elbows on the curving gunwale. For a long, silent while, he watched the village roofs grow smaller in the distance.

Wolf settled in beside him.

Halvor's voice grew misty. "Once upon a time, when I was young like you, I thought I would spend my life adventuring. Performing heroic deeds. When I lost my family, adventuring lost its charm." He smiled. "But then you boys appeared on my doorstep."

"You mean we said something to persuade you then?"

"In a way. While you sat in a corner pouting about your God, Skule and I talked about the great wave of Northmen suddenly going forth throughout the world. There's never been anything like it. It's an exciting time. A heady time. I thought about my quiet life in the mountains, and the old days. And I thought about Arild's offer."

Halvor turned to face Wolf more squarely. "I have decided I was right in my youth after all. While I still have the wind and limb to do it, I want to go back to adventuring."

"And perform heroic deeds?"

"If they present themselves. But I am content to leave heroism to you youngsters. I want to see new places. Taste new climes. Burn brighter at this last than I have burned in many a year."

Wolf considered all this awhile. "I'm glad you gave up adventuring."

"Oh?"

"Skule and I would have died, had you not sought out the quiet life."

And what would Shawna say to all this? *You see? My Lord works in mysterious ways, but He works.*

Shawna! There she was again, intruding on his thoughts, his heart, his life. And yet, this couldn't all be coincidence.

Could it?

Wolf lurched erect and gripped the old man's hand and arm. "Welcome back, Halvor, to the grand adventure!"

* * *

Shawna laced her fingers together to keep them from shaking. She perched on a stool in the middle of a bare room. Across from her sat a crotchety middle-aged woman with an apparently permanent scowl and a suspicious tone in her voice. This was the woman Shawna dreaded most in the whole world, the woman with the power to approve or refuse Shawna's petition.

"We will speak henceforth in Latin," Mother Flora announced. She did not look the least bit flowery, and Shawna found herself wondering, inanely, how women of the faith came by names such as that. She waited.

Mother Flora's iron eyes bored into her. "What are you escaping?"

Shawna paused in mid thought. She was sure she understood the question correctly. "I am not escaping anything."

"Invariably women such as yourself come here to escape a responsibility of some sort. An unhappy marriage? Relatives who need help? Slavery?"

"None of those." Shawna told her story, from the first sighting of dragons in Eden to her adventures on the ridgepole of Ceirre's chicken shed.

Mother Flora listened in silence and sat in silence as she finished. Should Shawna say more? There was nothing more to be said until the next question came.

The woman shifted back to Gaelic. "Your Latin is nearly flawless. I have two more questions, and then a request. The first: What do you plan to do here? 'Study' is too vague and ill-defined a word."

"Meditate upon the Scriptures, and copy them. Also . . ." Shawna hesitated. Should she mention this? "My grandfather on Lambay would talk about the Brehons of old. The law-givers. He said they spent twelve years or more in preparation, memorizing

231

law and lore. Those who were Christians memorized the law of Scripture as well. All of it. Then they would be called upon as arbitrators in legal disputes, and as advisers, and as augurs. I would like to commit their oral law and traditions to the written word, lest it be lost forever. It is something I could do to my grandfather's memory."

Mother Flora nodded. "My second question: Are you satisfied that the last known survivors of the Behr, your two nephews, will be raised in the nurture and admonition of our Lord?"

That question, too, puzzled her. "Doyle Dalainn has shown his faith by building a monastery and church under his aegis. Quite a nice one, in fact."

The woman's face twisted as if she had just bitten into a spoiled onion. "Every ri tuaithe in Erin has built a monastery. There are hundreds such monasteries. The land costs almost nothing, and the ri buys his way into heaven thereby. You will be provided room, fire, and food tonight. I ask that your meditation as you lay you down be this last question of mine. What do you know of the character of the boys' adoptive father? Will they learn to love the Lord?" She stood up brusquely. "Come with me, please."

Shawna followed numbly. She had never been inside a place quite this big before, with a roof this high. They passed down a dark, narrow corridor and out into a room of windows. Between the windows on all the walls, each on its own wooden shelf, lay books. There must be two dozen books here! Shawna stopped and sucked in air. A score and more of precious books!

If the woman noticed, she gave no sign. She marched directly to a particular book and lifted it off its shelf. She brought it to a copying table and opened it. "Read for me, please."

Shawna perched on the stool and drew the book down a few inches for a better view. She scanned the title page, uncertain whether she ought begin there or with text.

Collectio Canonum Hibernensis. "A Collection of Erse Law." Her eyes dropped to the descriptive paragraph. She translated from Latin to Gaelic as she went. "Includes scriptural quotes and quotes from the early church fathers. Next paragraph: Laws dealing with theft, inheritance, and sanctuary for all on holy ground."

She looked at Mother Flora. "So what I proposed to do has already been done. The laws of the Brehons have been put into writing."

"And the oral tradition is already dead, for all practical purposes. Not quite a hundred years ago, scholars and lawyers assembled the Senchas Mar. Law tracts. And other works, such as Crith Gablach, codify social structure. You are a few hundred years too late."

Shawna returned to the book, her thoughts all a-jumble, and turned the page.

Mother Flora laid her hand on the page. "I am satisfied." She studied Shawna's face, so Shawna held her eye. "I perceive that you read and comprehend without error or hesitation. By your past you have revealed your future. You have prepared yourself for a scholar's life. And quite well, I may add.

"We of Kildare exist to glorify God, and to perpetuate the memory and intent of our founder. Brigid was a scholar. You are welcome here."

"I am accepted?"

"You must agree to submit yourself to the discipline of the order, and you've much to learn yet. With those two requisites, yes. We accept you with gratitude to our Lord."

Shawna's eyes began to burn, and she didn't care. Even as they filled with tears, she was burbling her joyous thanks.

Yes, Ceirre, you were right as always. There are passions other than erotic ones. And watching a dream take form before your eyes is one of the brightest of them.

* * *

"Is it true Erin has no towns?" Across from Connleigh, the bishop himself, head of the see at Canterbury, sliced himself another morsel of the roast pig.

Connleigh cut himself a bit of the duckling, just to try it. "It is. Raths—that is, farms—are closer together in some places than in others. At the mouth of the Liffey, for example, there is quite a cluster of them. But there are no towns such as you have here." He shrugged. "We don't need them. We like our independence."

"But what about your artists and craftsmen? They must have towns where people come to buy their wares."

"Each rath has its own."

"There can't be that many men gifted in the skilled arts."

"There are. Every Gael is an artist, Your Holiness, and every farm has its craftsman."

"Remarkable." The bishop wiggled a finger toward Connleigh's sword. "You're a warrior."

"So my father says."

"Do you think you can submit to the discipline of the church? The Irish have a reputation for falling short in that area."

Connleigh smiled. "From Patrick on. Yes. We're a practical people, Your Holiness. We deal with the world as it is, not what some authority a thousand miles away thinks it is. True, we bend the rules of Rome and work somewhat outside her policies, but that is because our local customs." Connleigh waved a hand, trying to find the right word in Latin. "The mindset of our people demands adjustments."

And a thought came to mind that he would sketch out now and mull over later. "Consider, Your Holiness, that the church in Erin has never been persecuted as it has elsewhere. Rome herself leveled terrible persecutions on the Christians, for centuries. Because Patrick knew the Gaelic mindset he could work within the culture to supplant Druidism without provoking persecution. We do not have the history of pain and suffering that you do. So our approach to the faith is different, and we don't necessarily consider pre-Christian customs and beliefs a threat or danger."

"Then why are you seeking Rome?"

"What?"

"If the authorities in Rome do not understand your Gaelic people, should not Gaels be serving in Erin?"

"I wish to go to Rome to study."

"Is Erin not called the land of saints and scholars?"

"I've also heard it called the land of saints and sinners. Much closer the mark."

"Scholarship in Erin is the best in the Christian world. You are going in the wrong direction, my friend, if you seek study and enlightenment."

Connleigh pondered that a moment. This was a man who knew whereof he spoke. "You've been there. What is Rome like?"

The bishop set his tankard down. "You've been through London Town. Picture that five times larger with six times as many people. The Subura, in central Rome just north of the ruins of Trajan's forum, has for centuries been what you'd call the soiled district. Crowded, sin and debauchery, crime. Worse than anything in London Town. Some other areas are quite nice, though. To your picture add a few great buildings of dressed stone. Most of the abandoned marble buildings have been torn apart and their building stone used elsewhere, but you can still catch a gleam of what the city once was." The bishop rocked back in his seat and leaned against the wall.

"Then there are the ruins." The bishop's voice drifted with his memories. "Wonderful ruins of massive buildings and a great coliseum—a huge oval—toward the south end of town. Huge! And the old city baths. No longer used, of course. The city wall is in ruins, but you can see its grandeur and some of its gates. And picture great marble tombs all along the roads leading out of the city. They are stained and damaged now, in sad disrepair. People's sheep and goats keep the weeds trimmed around them, but time has not been very good to them."

"But the church. What of the church there?"

"The church there." The bishop grunted. "They are consumed by worries about who is following the rules and how well. They are the watchdogs of our faith, guarding against heresy. They spend days arguing over some trivial point. They produce few if any new thoughts, but they defend the old ones jealously. All head knowledge. Nothing practical." He pointed again at Connleigh's sword. "You are probably safe from bandits; you appear formidable with that fine blade at your side. But you are ill dressed for Rome, my friend."

23

Reversals

Bringing Arild Thick Knee along on his own expedition was a mistake.

Bringing Reidar Arildson along on his father's expedition was a mistake.

Putting both of them in the same ship was the worst mistake of all.

"You ought not let two boys play in the same mud puddle," Halvor philosophized, "if both are spoiled rotten."

Arild and Reidar did not actually argue about whose mud it was and who got to play in it. Arild fumed, and Reidar sulked. Arild barked commands, and Reidar half-heartedly obeyed or, more often, put on a pretense of obeying. Hegaard the diplomat knew when to back off and keep his mouth shut.

During the tedium of open sailing, as they worked their way south from landfall to landfall to landfall, Arild could order people around to his heart's content. After all, he owned the ship. No one argued that. But should an emergency arise, when knowledge of sea and ship meant the difference between safety and disaster, Arild would be just another seaman, and not a very good one at that. Hegaard, diplomacy or no, would immediately become her absolute master.

Arild knew it. Perhaps that's what put him on edge, Wolf mused—the prospect of losing control at any moment. And Reidar? Reidar was like a second tail on a horse—of absolutely no use to anyone. That feeling of uselessness could annoy a saint.

Reidar was no saint.

Shawna.

She was.

Saints. People of faith in the Erse God. Saint Ulf of the Coastlands.

Bah!

Saint Ulf was assigned an oar when their next leg took them directly into the wind. Hegaard furled the sail, and Wolf guessed it was more a chance to give his bored and restless crew something to do than a navigational decision. Hegaard assigned Reidar the oar behind Ulf's. Good. Let the listless man-boy work out some of his frustrations.

Not that Reidar was very good at it. More than once, Wolf would lean forward, planting his oar behind him, and it would clunk into Reidar's. A couple of times, Wolf heard Reidar's oar strike that of the man behind him. Any other oarsman would have been dressed down by now in terms to make a public woman blush, but Hegaard was a diplomat.

Unlike most, Wolf enjoyed this respite of rowing. "Sure a lot better than just lolling around, isn't it, Reidar?" he called over his shoulder.

"Rowing is for thralls and convicts."

"Since you're not a thrall, what did the Thing convict you of? Too much love making?" Wolf giggled. "No worry, brother. You can rest for the next three months at least."

Reidar cast a most unkind aspersion upon Wolf's cleanliness and ancestry. He must have forgotten they shared the ancestry.

For a few minutes, Wolf watched Halvor, three oars ahead. The old man plied in perfect rhythm, pulling his weight with an easy grace, a seaman with more years at the oar than Wolf was old. Amazing fellow.

Another thought struck Wolf. "Reidar? Why isn't Junken here? I was sure he was among those scheduled to come. Father said so."

"Shut up."

"No. I'm serious. Where is he? Get a better offer from the *Fierce Cutting Blade?*"

"As a matter of fact he did. Don't tell me you didn't hear. At the last minute he said he was staying behind to get married. I don't know who he thinks is going to believe it, but that's what he said."

Wolf grinned. In fact he cackled aloud. Peggy! Happy Peggy! Her God would be pleased, and that would bring her joy.

And that, for some curious reason, delighted Wolf immensely. Her God would be pleased. No, surely the delight came from Peggy's happiness. Yes. That must be it. He chuckled again.

"Shut up! It's not funny!" Reidar kicked Wolf in the back. "I know what you're thinking! Just shut up!"

The fury in Reidar's invective sobered Wolf instantly. Now what was going on in the brat's mind? "Reidar, you don't have the faintest idea what I'm thinking."

"Everybody on this ship thinks the same thing, and I'm sick of it! So don't you start!"

"You're full of flax fertilizer if you think anyone here cares about what you think they think."

Reidar slammed his boot into Wolf's back hard enough to shove Wolf off his seat. The oar blade dipped into the water. As the ship glided forward, the oar shaft swung back and caught Wolf in the throat. For an eternal moment Wolf could not breathe, strangled by the oarshaft. The moving ship dragged the oar outboard, freeing Wolf's neck. Then the oar slipped out of its port and into the sea.

Hegaard yelled something frantic.

Wolf sat on the deck, his tailbone aching mightily, his breath slow to return. He tried to speak; no voice came. The only thing mounting faster than his pain was his fury. He would not let this pass. His sword lay flat on the deck, stowed against his sea chest, but he would not use it.

He swung around to his knees, grasping his aching throat. From the corner of his eye he saw Reidar smirking. Wolf lunged from kneeling, without bothering to gather himself. His shoulder slammed into Reidar's belly just above his belt buckle—the best place for knocking a man's wind out of him. Wolf's legs kept pumping, driving him and Reidar into Borg, the oarsman behind.

Reidar's knee caught Wolf wrong and sapped some of his strength. Reidar got a lucky punch into Wolf's ribs even as Wolf slugged Reidar's face.

The whole boat came instantly alive with laughing and cheering and heckling, and Wolf was too·enraged to care. He was also too pummeled to fight well. Perhaps he should have pulled his sword after all. They rolled off Borg's oar and onto the deck, locked in a struggling lump. Reidar's arms were wrapped about Wolf's chest in a bear hug. Reidar squeezed down, harder and harder. Wolf quit breathing altogether, and not by choice.

Wolf doubled into a tight little knot, his knees against his head. Reidar's arms, overstretched, relaxed a bit. Wolf snapped open suddenly and caught Reidar's chin with the top of his head. The arms relaxed. Wolf rolled aside, kicked Reidar with a loud *thwack* that set off another blizzard of cheering, and grabbed the nearest thing not tied down—an iron pot.

He swung it, and it clanged against the side of Reidar's face. The fight, for all practical purposes, had ended. Wolf fell upon Reidar, rolled the man away from him, and pressed his neck to the deck. He twisted Reidar's free arm up behind him.

Sucking in air through a throat that still objected mightily, Wolf hauled himself to his feet. He dragged Reidar to his knees.

"Hegaard, we need the stern. Alone." His voice croaked, barely understandable.

"I need the stern to retrieve that oar."

"Retrieve it from the bow." Wolf was not in command of this vessel by any stretch of the imagination. So he added a hasty "Please."

Hegaard grimaced. "If it'll settle you two down, go." He took a position by the fish.

As Wolf shoved Reidar toward the stern, Hegaard flung orders to this bank of oars and to that, turning the ship, bringing it back to the oar afloat somewhere out there.

Wolf slammed Reidar against the stern post and pressed close, that they might talk in undertones. "What's going on?" he muttered. "Why the big burst?"

"You know why." Reidar sounded as if he couldn't talk any better than Wolf could.

"I don't know why. What has you so prickly?" He waited a moment and gave Reidar's arm a jerk. "Say."

"You know. Junken."

"What about Junken?"

Reidar twisted around to look Wolf in the face.

Wolf held his eye and tried not to appear hostile.

"Are you really that stupid, little brother?"

"I'm really that stupid. Explain it to me. What did I say wrong that you turned loose on me?"

"Junken waited until the last minute, after he knew I was leaving, and then begged off and stayed ashore."

"So?"

"So he can cuckold me. Why else?"

"Astrid?! Reidar, she's six months pregnant and big enough to plug a boat-shed door. You really think Junken would be interested in her when he has his Peggy?"

"The excuse about marrying . . ."

"Is valid. It has to do with Peggy's God."

"Yeah, yeah, the big expert on all things Celtic."

"On the Celtic God? You better believe it. I got it stuffed down my throat the whole time I was there." Wolf sensed the sag in his brother's body. He released his own hold, but he stayed aside, lest the man erupt again.

Reidar snorted. "You get the luck. You always get all the luck. Our father did you a favor. You sure weren't going to earn your way into Valhalla stumping around the village on half a leg. He gave you the chance to earn glory in battle. Instead you come back a hero without ever lifting a finger. You could have any girl in the village. In fact, I'm not so sure Astrid didn't open her window for you. Or at least want to."

Wolf himself was sagging. He knew even as he spoke that he wasn't going to change his brother's mind about a single thing. Not the jealousy, not the envy, not the irrational fear. Not anything. Why did he bother with this talk? "Why did you come, if you're worried about Astrid's fidelity?"

Reidar twisted around to meet Wolf eye to eye. "Because I am going to be the next jarl of jarls. Not you. And with your constant luck, you could supplant me somehow. If you came on this voyage with our father and I didn't, you might talk him into naming you. I don't know how. But it's not going to happen."

"To rule, you have to prove yourself in battle, so you're coming along this summer to do it." Against unsuspecting monks and nuns in a simple Irish church at Kildare, and then on to other unsuspecting prey. "Not a thing I could say will change your feelings or thoughts. I won't try. But hear this. You must have figured out by now that I'm under protection of the gods. Don't you ever attack me again, from behind or from any other direction, or you'll find out what the word 'supplant' means."

Wolf rolled aside and leaned against the gunwale, disgusted with the whole affair. He watched them retrieve the lost oar and thread it back through its oarport. Then he took his place again to row, but not at his seat. Taking his sword with him, he moved to the chest behind his prior seat. He did not want Reidar behind him.

With nowhere else to go, Reidar sat down ahead of him and took the wet oar.

The rudder man leaned into his blade. Hegaard himself called cadence to bring the great ship back to glide. They were on their way again, moving faster now to catch up to the other ships before nightfall.

Wolf glanced back at Arild Thick Knee. The brooding father stood leaning against his dragon's slender neck, and scowling.

* * *

A perfect dawn, this. Shawna watched the pale pink sky turn pearl gray. It would not be sunny today exactly, but not cloudy either. Hazy. She walked out into the herb garden behind the priory. Dozens of varieties of plants grew profusely here, each in its tiny squared bed. Berry and fruit trees hung over the garden wall at the far end. Dill and camomile were the only large shrubby plants she recognized against the wicker fence on the west side. She sat down on a little bench against the wall in a far corner.

It was so peaceful here. Her soul yearned for peace, real peace. She didn't get peace with the Dalainn, not when she felt so constantly the need to help Muirgheal. She certainly didn't feel this kind of peace at Ceirre's. The old woman nattered endlessly. She realized as she sat here that this was one of the things she missed most about her dear lost Lambay. The peace.

She watched a pair of wagtails fly about, busying themselves with a nest in the elderberry by the kitchen door. Their long tails bobbing endlessly, they hopped onto the wicker fence, flitted among the herb beds, poked about for bugs and other vermin in the rock wall. They seemed so cheerful in their business.

And cheer was the last of Shawna's feelings.

This place was perfect for her. The peace. The books. The beauty. This place delighted her beyond her wildest expectations. But.

But.

Unable to sit (as a meditator and contemplator, she was a complete failure; how she envied the sisters here, with their quiet ways), she walked back to the gate in the wicker fence. It sagged mightily, just as Ceirre's had. But, being built of wicker, it would be a lot easier to rehang than Ceirre's had been.

All Shawna really needed was some cord—linen would do— and a pole. She noticed a small shed beyond some nut trees along the far wall. She pulled the crude door open. The shed was literally crammed with gardening tools in various states of age and condition. Some looked old enough to have been used by Brigid herself. From the single low rafter hung a bundle of twine in short lengths. From the size of the pieces, Shawna guessed they were used to tie pea vines to stakes. As orderly and well organized as this place seemed to be, they probably staked their broadbeans too.

A well tended garden said much about a place. She took five pieces of the cord.

The pole she found among other poles and posts in a pile beyond the garden wall. She had quite a choice of lengths.

Why was she doing this unbidden? She was nervous. Upset. True. She could not sit still. But there seemed to be other reasons, down deep, and they would not reveal themselves.

She lifted the sagging end of the gate, measuring by eye the angle of the corrective pole. She had to let the gate down again as she tied the pole to one corner of the gate so that it angled down to the opposite corner. Now she would have to hold the gate up in its new position and tie the other end of the pole, all at the same time. Perhaps if she propped the gate on a rock. . . .

The gate shifted, creaking, out of its sag. Shawna clapped her hand over her mouth. Mother Flora, silent as a flower opening, had stepped in beside Shawna. Patiently she held the gate at its preferred shape.

Flustered, Shawna lashed the pole down at the bottom corner and then in the middle, lacing the cord as tightly as its length permitted. She tied the remaining two strings where she thought they might support best.

Mother Flora let go. The gate shifted only very slightly. She pushed it out, pulled it in. No longer did it drag on the ground. She did not smile, but as she dropped the latch loop over the corner piece to secure it, she seemed to add a triumphant little fillip.

Mother Flora served in the capacity of a true bishop, actually, as leader of this original church of Brigid, but she did not seem to like the term of address *Your Holiness.* Shawna did not much like to call her *Mother,* her preferred honorific. So Shawna, as much as she was able, called her nothing at all. Should she bow? Kneel? Smile? What should she say now? She had not the faintest idea.

Mother Flora walked off, winding between the rosemary and the sage, so Shawna followed.

"Please sit." Mother Flora gestured toward the bench.

Shawna sat, much relieved by the little expected of her.

Mother Flora sat down. "What is the fruit of your meditations last night?"

"About whether the boys would be raised in the nurture of the Lord?" Her heart ached, and she very nearly melted down to tears on the spot. "I've listened to Doyle Dalainn, his conversation with others and with me. I distrust his motives and the depth of his faith."

"You feel his spiritual leadership is lacking?"

"His elder son has said more than once that he—Connleigh, that is—developed an intense interest in things spiritual with no guidance at all from his father or mother. None of the other children shows any interest in spiritual matters."

"In what direction do you feel led?"

"To return to the boys."

Mother Flora sat nodding. She folded her hands and contemplated nothing at all a few minutes; or perhaps she, too, was watching the wagtails go about their housekeeping. "You would leave this behind now that you've tasted it?"

"For my nephews. Yes." The tears overflowed and ran down Shawna's cheeks despite her bravest efforts to suppress them. Her nose clogged up instantly. And yet . . . "Strange. I've just watched my dream shatter. But now we've said this—brought it to the open, if you will—I feel a certain peace about it. As much as it hurts, it seems right."

"I am very pleased you said that. We made it a matter of communal prayer last night—and fasting. All of us. There are eighteen of us altogether, as you may know, now that Berta passed away."

"Thank you. For the prayers, I mean. I appreciate it. I feel so at home here."

Mother Flora almost—almost—smiled. "We've never had children in the community here before. But then, Erin has never been ravaged by Northmen before. We came to accord, following prayer, that you should join us and bring the boys here to be raised. Do you think the Dalainn would find that a problem?"

Shawna tried to close her mouth, but she couldn't right away. Her heart thumped and leaped for joy. She took a deep breath. She must think. "I believe the reason Doyle adopted them in the first place was to show a good face to the ris beneath him. The face of a generous man of charity, to take in his rivals and raise them as his own. Were they to be turned over to a renowned monastery, and there is no greater name than Kildare, I believe he would consider it another evidence of his status. He'd be freed of their responsibility, and under the best of circumstances."

"We rather thought that ourselves. We've met the man. Go. Bring them. And join us."

Shawna must phrase her words of thanksgiving exactly right. She must render immediately her praise to God for orchestrating this wonderful turn of events. She must appear intelligent and mature before this stern judge of women.

But her heart and body failed her. The weeping came unchecked. Though not for sorrow but for joy, it was weeping all the same. She melted forward, her face in her hands.

And the strong, unyielding arms of the quasi-bishop wrapped around her and held her close.

* * *

The setting sun, swimming so low near the horizon, burned his eyes. His decision burned his heart far worse.

244

Connleigh would have to swallow a lot of pride. His stomach ached already at the thought. Sure and he had planned someday to return to his Erin, but not this day. Not so soon. He would have to endure his father's caustic jibes. The student has come stumbling home without ever doing any studying? Pity. Smirk. Smirk.

He would have to face Shawna and admit that his dream had shriveled up and turned black. That was almost worse than facing the Dalainn. Shawna loved learning and had such faith in him. He had let her down dreadfully.

He would probably have a great deal more difficulty resisting his father's plans for his life by coming home like this. He wanted to be able to come home on his own terms, prepared to accept a bishopric, or to head up a monastery. Something like that. This was not what he wanted at all.

And yet, it was the right thing. What had turned him? The bishop's ugly description of Rome? Spare him the prospect of living in such a dismal place! The bishop's attitude toward the Holy See? It was probably fairly accurate. The bishop's strong opinion that a Gael should serve in Erin? That too.

Very well. Connleigh would travel to Armagh. In fact, he might go directly to Armagh and bypass home altogether. No. That would do no good in any lasting sense.

Perhaps Shawna would go with him to Armagh. She might not want to journey to Rome, the frontier of the cosmos, but she just might travel to Armagh. She would do well there. She fit in well with scholarly types.

It was interesting, when you thought about it, that God seemed to be prospering Connleigh's westward journey so much more so than He had the easterly one. Things just seemed to be going better, his walk faster, his way easier, the weather more cooperative.

At the first little church where he had read on his journey east, now his last stop before reaching the coast, he called to tell them his decision. He left the gospel of John with them. They appreciated the Word so and had no book of their own. He felt that a great burden had been lifted and indeed it had—a good twenty pounds.

God's providence held fast. When he arrived on the coast of Wales approximately across from Rosslare, a fishing vessel was just ready to put out. With the last of his coins, Connleigh purchased passage to the Irish shore, and gladly.

In Erin, coins are not needed.

24

Confusion

She rehearsed, yet again, what she would say to Doyle Dalainn once the greetings and apologies had been made. She had better have her words firmly lined up, for she was only minutes from his gate now. In her journey of four days, she had gotten lost only once, trying to avoid the Owney with their huge dogs.

Over and over she praised her God. To raise the boys at Kildare—what an overwhelming blessing! Here was an answer to prayers she had not even thought to make. Leave it to her God to respond to petitions she had not given Him. This obviously was what it meant in Romans when the apostle Paul described the intercession of the Holy Spirit.

As she walked the familiar final slope toward the Dalainn east gate, the sun was just touching the horizon. Well, she assumed so. A light drizzle had commenced, and the overcast prevented any clear view of where the sun might be exactly.

Shawna entered the gate. Great watchdog that she was, Gwynna Fat Feet came bounding up, with an enthusiasm unbesmirched by the mere fact that she was a simpleton, and greeted Shawna with licks and barking. Shawna brushed the watchdog aside with some difficulty and rapped at the door of the house.

It was Muirgheal who answered the door. She stared at Shawna aghast, let out a little moan, and dropped the wooden bowl she was carrying. It spilled barleymeal in all directions as it rolled on the floor.

By the hearth, Doyle Dalainn sat erect. "Well, well," said he in a voice dripping with sarcasm. "Look who we have here."

The whole family was home tonight, which rather surprised Shawna. Usually, most of the family were off other places this time of year, tending livestock and crops. The brothers and sisters lolled about in this center room, apparently awaiting supper.

Peadar and Paul leaped to their feet instantly and came squealing. Joyously, Shawna knelt with open arms to receive them.

"Get away from her!" Doyle's roar shook the walls.

The boys stopped cold, terrified.

Shawna stared. She took a deep breath and stood up. She expected his displeasure and certainly his sarcasm. She had refused his offer as translator for the Northmen. She had run off without so much as a by-your-leave. But she saw fury in his eyes. "My lord, I wish to apolo—"

On his feet, Doyle strode toward her like a charging bull, and she realized how this man's sheer bulk and stature might be sufficient unto itself to cow his enemies into submission. She held her ground and tried not to let her trepidation show.

"My lord Dalainn . . ."

"You flaunt your immorality for all the world to see. You make the Dalainn a laughingstock. You ruin forever the reputation of the Dalainn and the Behr as well. And now you have the gall to return here." He planted himself squarely in front of her. "To top it off, you have the temerity to soil two innocent boys with your filthy hands. You never cease to amaze me."

"Soil. Temer—" Her thoughts were darting all about like a warren of rabbits dug out, and with about as much purpose. "I ran away because I was furious with you, Doyle Dalainn, and sore disappointed. I am still angry. But I don't—"

"You? Are disappointed in me?"

"Where is he?" Muirgheal rushed in so close to Shawna's face that she involuntarily stepped back. "Is he dead? Is that why you came back? Tell me!"

"Who?"

Doyle, too, pressed forward, and Shawna took another step back before she could tell her feet not to give way. "Your exit was so very smooth," he snarled, "it was an hour before I realized what had just happened. And now the way you said, 'Who?' Just perfect. You're excellent at pretense, which leads me to wonder how much else that I once believed is actually pretense."

Muirgheal was shrieking in that nervous falsetto of hers. "Is Connleigh dead? Answer me!"

"Connleigh? How would I know about—" And the truth hit her. Rather, the untruth. "You think I broke away and went with him. You think Connleigh and I have been together. No!" She wagged her head. "That's not true! I—"

"Get out!" Doyle's long arm and hand pointed the way out the open door. "If ever I see you in the realm of the Dalainn, if ever I see you at all, I'll kill you. Do you understand that?"

"It's not true! I haven't seen him! I've been at Ceirre's!" Shawna was shrieking too, and she didn't mean to shriek. Then she was being forced out the door. Then she was standing in the cold drizzle and the dark. She heard the oaken bar drop down across the inside of the door.

Inside she heard Muirgheal moaning and screaming about Connleigh being dead, and Doyle shouting at her. How could this happen? How could she . . .

Her muddled head let only one thought surface clearly. Doyle Dalainn did not make idle threats. If he saw her again, he would kill her.

* * *

The sky was gray-white, its usual color over Erin. A pearlescent mist obscured the low gray line on the horizon, blending gray sea, gray land, and gray sky into a soft continuum.

Land. That land. Wolf wrapped an arm around the *Swift Lynx*'s narrow neck and watched the gray land grow.

She was there somewhere. He thought he'd never return, or perhaps in the very back of his heart he always knew he would. That little point of confusion was typical of his whole state, for Ulf Arildson felt as confused as a small child at a wedding.

She was there somewhere. Over the winter he had talked with any number of young women from the village and the general area. He had grown up with most of them. In his youth most of them had ignored the kid with the gimp, the laughingstock. The rest ridiculed him. This being a hero certainly opened up one's social prospects considerably. But none of the girls he'd talked to came close to her.

She was there somewhere. He had left her, basically, without thinking, so hungry was he to get back home. It was without doubt the biggest mistake he ever made in his life. The question now was, was the mistake reversible? And the other question: Should he let well enough alone and not try to reverse it?

She was there somewhere. It would be a simple matter to jump ship and return to her. But that would put Wolf on the point of Doyle Dalainn's sword, for he was an escaped slave. Doyle's new sword. The Dalainn's old sword so masterfully wrought hung at Wolf's side this moment, and the Dalainn's favorite mare rotted in the sea. Such transgressions were not lightly forgiven, even if the Dalainn were a forgiving man.

She was there somewhere. If she hadn't married the Book Reader by now, she almost certainly would do so soon.

Ceirre would know. Of course! Ceirre would know! As they entered the Liffey, Wolf would run ashore long enough to call at Ceirre's hovel and find out about Shawna.

In fact, if he played his part well, he could get all sorts of useful intelligence from Ceirre under the guise of hungering for news of the people he knew—where Doyle was and where his military strength lay, who was aligned with the Dalainn, and who resisted those unifying gestures Skule described.

"What do you think?" Hegaard stepped in beside Wolf, and he was absolutely sneering.

Wolf looked at him. "About what?"

"About what all those people on shore are thinking. Here we are, the horrible monsters, poised off their coast ready to come ashore at any point. But whose point? Who gets the sword, and who escapes? Gives you a feeling of power, doesn't it, to decide who dies and who doesn't?"

"Life and death decisions are power, all right."

They were sailing almost with the wind. They would pass just to the east of Lambay Island. Would Wolf recognize its outline, albeit from its other side, as it were? He would ask Hegaard to bring them past Lambay close enough that he could pick out the narrow cobble beach on which his countrymen had first touched Irish soil. And if he espied the beach, he would be able to see that slope above it where Shawna's father and brothers died heroically.

Shawna's brother, Peggy's husband. *I know I'm a widow.* It seemed so long ago.

* * *

250

Two kinds of men and women served God in the many monasteries of Erin, Mahon mused, those who loved the Lord and those who wanted a little peace and quiet. Mahon would, he was certain, do anything he could for the God-lovers. He had scant use, though, for the escapists, the people who sought the protection of monasteries in order to bury themselves in study cells and libraries. They spent a minimal amount of time copying books and otherwise being useful, and spent the remainder of their time puttering about in the gardens or among the books, but puttering all the same.

And then there were the men like Doyle Dalainn, who assumed the trappings of religion with no shred whatever of the actual faith. All show. All pretense. Mahon dreaded this approaching audience with the Dalainn. He dreaded it in part because of Doyle's volatile temper. But mostly he dreaded it because it would bring shame and embarrassment to Connleigh, and Connleigh, alone among the Dalainn, was a genuine man of God. As a diversion, he turned his thoughts from the nastiness of the immediate future to the less nasty but more important options he might exercise upon his return to Armagh.

Armagh was becoming an overflowing nest of putterers. So very few there served the Lord with a whole heart. What Mahon really wanted to do was boot the putterers out and restaff the whole monastery with people of his choosing, male and female both.

Indeed, Mahon saw no real difference between the genders. Each had its self-serving putterers, and each had its true and noble scholars.

Shawna of the Behr was a scholar. If he could just convince her to come with him to Armagh, he would replace Rose with her. And Connleigh Dalainn was another person devoted in the best sense. Connleigh would make a much better prior than Archibald. Connleigh would keep first things first.

Mahon approached that oak grove where the great mastiffs had beset him. Wolves of the northern forests were no more ferocious than those dogs. And he thought again about that Northman. Talk about raw strength and courage! If only Mahon could harness the energies of about ten such Northmen, he could turn all Erin around from a land of putterers to a land of dynamic men and women of God. Pity they were pagans; the Danes were so vibrant.

He smiled at Wolf's gentle correction. Not all Danes. Danes and Norse and Swedes.

He passed the few scrubby little elders and hazels squatting on the moist, mossy ledges at this end of the grove. He walked beneath the first of the oaks.

Mahon could put Archibald in charge of the groves and orchards. What a good idea! That would keep the man busy. The "in charge of" phrase would satisfy his apparent need to be somebody. And it would keep him safely out of Mahon's hair.

Now. What ought he do about Rose? The woman considered herself better than your average Irish fishwife because she had been born in York. If coming from Northumbria bestowed such immense benefit, why were the Northumbrians falling left and right before the onslaught of the Danes? The edge of his raincloak caught briefly in a bush and let loose. The bush rattled as its branch swayed back and forth behind him. Maybe he could—

Mahon stopped in his tracks. He heard a rustling among the leaves just to the west of the track. He could not depend upon his Lord sending the Northman back to save him from the dogs again. Terrified, he clambered into the nearest oak, a venerable tree with branches bending low, a tree big enough to hold his weight for a week if necessary. He crawled up onto a heavy limb and perched, his legs drawn up (he hoped!) beyond the reach of slashing teeth.

Leaves rustled again to the west. Perhaps those horrific beasts would pass by without realizing Mahon was there. Perhaps they would not catch his scent or smell his fear. Perhaps cows fly.

The terror that sat down beside him on the sturdy oak limb quietly got up and tiptoed away. Shame stepped in and took its place. Was this the spiritually superior Mahon of Armagh casting aspersions on the putterers? Was this the man who loved God and depended utterly upon Him? Here he cowered, the great man of God, spooked by nothing more than a rustle of leaves. A squirrel, a raven, a vagrant breeze were all Satan needed to make a fool of God's servant.

Still, before he climbed down he might as well complete his prayers for the morning. He hadn't done that yet.

"Pater noster, qui es in coelis, sanctifi—"

"Mahon?" Shawna's voice, querulous, called from somewhere in the woods west of the track. "Is that you?"

"Shawna child! What are you doing so far afield this early?"

If Shawna were treed, dogs would be snarling and barking. If the dogs were about at all, these voices would have drawn them. Hastily, Mahon climbed down out of his aerie.

As his feet touched earth, the brush again rustled, and they very nearly left the ground again. But the rustling was attended by Shawna's distraught voice.

"Mahon? Oh, Mahon!"

"Here, child." If Mahon left the track they could both become lost in this tanglewood. He waited.

She came crashing amid the trees, pushing recklessly through the underbrush. She tumbled into his arms sobbing and clung. What could he do? He wrapped both arms around her in an avuncular hug and held her. She absolutely vibrated.

He waited until she had more or less pulled herself together before he spoke. "You look like you spent the night in a rabbit warren."

"I spent the night in the crotch of an oak tree. I thought I heard the Owney mastiffs, and I was afraid. You're lucky you're a man. You've no need to fear such things."

He opened his mouth to refute her statement and decided against it. That was not important. What was important was to learn what was going on here. He'd discuss his lapse of faith later, at a more convenient time. Some leisure moment.

Eventually.

He escorted her up the track a hundred yards, beneath spreading, gnarled oaks with their fresh green leaves. Oaks are among the last of trees to put on the new clothes of spring. He thought he remembered a great fallen bole somewhere around here. And there it lay, along the east edge of the track.

"Sit." He motioned to the log. When she sat down he settled in close beside her and put an arm across her shoulder. "Tell me

253

what agitates you so, that you have abandoned the hearth of the Dalainn."

It took her perhaps ten minutes to relate the whole sordid tale. Mahon's innards burned with fury. How could Doyle Dalainn even think such a thing? Did Mahon himself believe this girl? Absolutely. He knew her. He knew the purity of her walk. If she said she had not seen Connleigh Dalainn since the Dalainn did, she had not. It was that simple. If she said she had just spent a month with Ceirre fixing things, those things were fixed.

He listened to her tell about her visit to Kildare. She sounded so animated when she talked about the place. He realized with a heavy heart that he was probably about a month too late with his offer of a position at Armagh.

She expressed her concerns regarding the boys, and Mahon had to agree. Dalainn wasn't even a putterer. He was as close to God as the Northmen were, for all practical purposes.

She described her desire to raise the boys and related the abbess's offer. Mahon knew Flora. He knew how little Flora tolerated messy, unpredictable things such as children. It was a big step for Flora to make the offer, a step that had to have been orchestrated by the Holy Spirit. Nothing less would make Mother Flora desire to be a mother.

And now Shawna was sitting up straighter and turning those luminous blue eyes to him. "Mahon, it's so unfair! Doyle knows me. He knows Connleigh. How could he think that?"

"In Paul's letter to Titus he says, 'To the pure, everything is pure. To the spoiled, nothing is pure.' Doyle's accusation says much more about him than about you."

"But he said . . . and he would. What can I do?"

On hundreds of occasions Mahon was asked for his advice. Not infrequently, he provided it unsolicited. But now . . . Somehow this was different. Her situation altered his plans in that now she would almost have to be sequestered either at Kildare or Armagh for her own safety. Her story had touched him and infuriated him. And when he was so emotionally attached, he could not trust himself to provide sage advice.

He prayed for wisdom and then instructed his mind to rest

from this. He must speak from the heart and let the Holy Spirit guide. He must not depend upon his own understanding.

"What two books did you have on Lambay, Shawna?"

"Don't you remember? An Isaiah with notations, and the illuminated Psalms and Proverbs."

"Yes, I remember. Recite for me Psalm forty-six."

"I think . . ." Her voice faltered. "I can't recall."

"Deus noster refugium," he prompted, "et virtus; adjutor in tribulationibus, quae invenerunt nos nimis. From the beginning, now, in Gaelic."

She picked it up. "Our God is our refuge and strength, an immediate help in times of trouble. Therefore we need not fear, even if the earth should change, and if the mountains be shaken into the sea. Uh . . ."

With very little coaching she made it end to end, right down to "The God of Jacob is our stronghold." What a prodigious memory this girl had. And what linguistic gifts, to move so effortlessly between Latin and Erse.

"Therefore, whom do we trust?"

"But it's so hard, Mahon. Doyle is too strong, and all the other warlords are under his sway. I can't take the boys, and I can't even find refuge anywhere close. Perhaps I really should go back to Lambay. He doesn't bother to reach over there. I'd be safe."

"And the boys?"

"Hire someone to slip over to the mainland and spirit them away and bring them to me. He'd never think to look on Lambay. He probably wouldn't bother."

"Think clearly. Remember. Did you mention anything about Kildare at all in his presence? A word? A hint?"

She shook her head. "Almost instantly I was out the door. I had no time."

"Did you tell him your reason for returning?"

"No. He didn't even let them come to me."

"Good. Good. So Flora could come to his door, request the boys as his living offering to the church, and he'd have no reason to suspect you were a part of it?"

"Mahon, he'll kill me if he finds me at Kildare. His arm extends almost that far, and it's getting longer. Then where would the boys be?"

"His arm is shortening, lass, more than you know. In the month you spent at Ceirre's, out of the mainstream of news as it were, much has happened." How much should he tell her? The less she knew, the better off she was. "I have business of my own with Doyle Dalainn. If the opportunity presents itself, I shall suggest that the best way to regain some of the stature he has lost would be to assign the boys' care to a major monastery. Of course I would then recommend either Kildare or Armagh. But if I do not find that opportunity, ask Flora to come get them."

She looked dubious.

He patted her hand. "You love the Lord, lass, and He will keep you in His hand. Do not fear." He watched her face a moment. "What?"

"I don't love the Lord, Mahon."

"Splendid! Splendid! You bring your doubts right out into the open and examine them in the light. There is no healthier way to strengthen your faith!"

"Will you stop being so cheerful about ugly things? I'm not sure I can love at all. Anyone or anything. I admire God. That's not love. And Jesus? Gratitude. Obeisance. That's all."

"The Lord will make do with what He gets. Remember our Lord Jesus' admonitions to Peter at the end of John's gospel. The passage about feeding His lambs."

"I only got to read it twice. Then Connleigh took it with him."

"Ah, well. It's better in the Greek anyway. Jesus asks Peter twice if Peter will *agape* Him, the highest form of love, and Peter admits he can't handle it. Then Jesus takes a big step down, to a less demanding love. 'Peter, do you *phileo* Me?' To that question, Peter can say yes, but he says it sorrowfully, because he knows he's not meeting God's highest standard. It didn't stop Jesus from loving him back, not in the least. You respect God. Phileo Him if you can, and the agape will come with time. And trust Him. He'll make it all right."

"He didn't make Lambay right."

She had him there.

25

Owney

The Owney never did things by halves. Doyle Dalainn knew that, but the Owney rath reminded him again. As he rode up the track to visit the Owney, he noted again all the little differences he saw between this rath and his own.

The stone wall ringing their farm compound was a little bigger than you'd expect and enclosed a little more land than anyone else's. The armed retainers the Owney kept on hand were, so to speak, a bit of overkill. Those men stood about now in bier doorways and by sheds, their swords slung at their sides and battle-axes hung loosely over their shoulders. They scowled, sullen and dangerous, as Doyle and his riders entered their gate.

And the dogs. The Owney deliberately bred mastiffs for their size and ugly tempers. Losing those three dogs down in the oak grove last year didn't seem to convince Slevin Owney to keep his dogs closer home. Doyle had already passed the word to his men: If the situation deteriorates to blows, kill as many of those infernal dogs as you can manage.

A tall, gaunt man whose job apparently was to handle the dogs had called them away as the group approached. They barked and snarled now off beside a low stone building that looked as if it served as their kennel. The man was yelling orders at them and being obeyed half-heartedly or not at all.

Doyle led his troop to the front of the main house and drew the dun to a halt. The house, too, loomed a wee bit bigger than life. Carved dragon heads graced its wooden finials. They looked much like the dragon head Doyle had seen on one of the Norse ships. When you came right down to it, there wasn't that much difference between the Norse and the Erse. The Norse, the skilled seamen, followed the same patterns and lines of thought as did the Erse, the skilled farmers. Men of land and men of sea. Doyle would not be out of line in the least were he to enlist Norse into his service. They were two flints struck from the same rock.

Slevin Owney himself stepped out into the haze-filtered sun. "Doyle Dalainn. The blessings of this house fall around your shoulders."

"Slevin Owney. All the saints' best wishes descend upon you."

Slevin, frankly, looked a little bit like his dogs, if the truth be known. Heavy-jowled and snaggle-toothed, he filled the doorway of his home and then some, and none of that bulk was fat. He was broad-breasted like a mastiff and slightly bow-legged. He even wore a collar, one of the big, old-fashioned gold torques of yesteryear. Doyle assumed it had been handed down through the family since before Patrick became an Irishman.

Slevin spread his broad hands expansively. "Me wife and I were just about to sit down to a bit of bread and ale. Join us, Doyle Dalainn."

"Thank you." Doyle would let Fairleigh and his javelin take care of any dogs who broke ranks and headed for Doyle's shins. He dismounted and handed his reins off to his stablemaster. He entered the door of the main house, from filtered sun into stuffy gloom. Behind him, his troops remained mounted, ready for whatever might come to pass.

Slevin's wife was as much a throwback to the old days as was the gold torque. Three hundred years ago, when Druidism was the faith of Erin, Celtic women rode beside their men in battle, equally trained in the martial arts and equally competent. Aisling Owney would have fit right in.

Her name, Aisling, in old Celtic meant "dream" or "vision." Doyle would call her more a nightmare. He didn't like his women big and bulky, although that was apparently the current fashion. He didn't like women who could handle a broadax possibly as well as he. He didn't like women who thought. In short, he didn't like Aisling Owney.

On the positive side, she baked an excellent loaf of bread. As Doyle maneuvered his sword out of the way and seated himself at the Owney table, the aroma of her luscious bread filled his nose and his heart. His mother used to make plump honey loaves like this.

Slevin waved a hand. "You failed to arrive in time for the blessing. You can take me word it's been blessed or do it over to your own liking. Eat and enjoy. Try some of that boiled apple dressing. First apples of the season."

Doyle sliced himself a slab from the loaf and scooped a spoon into the jam pot. He slathered the rich brown apple butter across his bread. "Your sons took over that rath out near Clonmacnoise, I hear, hard by a peat bog." The bread tasted every bit as good as it smelled, and the apple dressing managed to be both sweet and tart at once. Delicious. Aisling's ale wasn't bad, either—rich and full-bodied with a pleasant after-bite.

Slevin snorted. "A rath in a peat bog. They claim, though, that they could live off the wildfowl in the lakes and marshes around there. Ducks and geese all year, and any manner of shorebirds." He spread soft cheese across his own bread. "I've heard from more than one that your eldest son has gone off a-marrying with one of the Behr." He glanced wickedly at Doyle. "I trust it was a-marrying, wasn't it?"

"No. False rumor. She's here, but he's in Rome, studying religion." And Doyle realized the error that had been vaguely nagging at him since yesterday. He should not have driven the wench off. If he still had her, he could parade her around as proof positive that she wasn't with Connleigh after all. He cursed himself for not thinking of that sooner, but her arrival had come as such a surprise—something he would never have expected—and he didn't think. A pox on himself for failing to think, the greatest failure a man can make!

Across the table from Doyle, the battle-ax spoke up. "Last new moon, I sent our herder down to the coast to trade butter for dried fish. He stopped by the hut of that old woman Ceirre of the Liffey. He says a Behr girl was there, a very personable thing. Pretty. Wouldn't be the same, would it?"

"Had to be. She's the sole survivor." So she was actually with Ceirre as she said. Interesting. So where was Connleigh? In Rome as assumed?

Slevin chewed thoughtfully, ruminating just like one of his cows. "Now, I recall that you told the Duer and the Garbhan, down by Killeshin, that the Northmen wiped out every soul on Lambay. And I was thinking to meself even as I heard that, 'Did Doyle Dalainn not adopt two sons of the Behr just this winter past? And are not the Behr of Lambay?' Now I hear of this girl as well."

"Virtually wiped out. I said virtually. Those three remain. The claim about all of them being destroyed must have been blown out of proportion before it reached you."

"Eh, the Duer and the Garbhan neither one tend to exaggerate much. One of their greatest failings."

Doyle knew perfectly well what Owney was up to, challenging his word. But he was here to build bridges, not dismantle them, and to gain important favors. He ignored the challenge completely and changed the subject. "I'm building a force to defend Erin's coasts against the Northmen."

Slevin waved toward the loaf. "Have some more. And some cheese. Goat cheese. It turned out especially well this time. Aisling makes the finest cheese in Christendom." He cut a slab of bread and offered it to Doyle. "You've been trying to do that since the Northmen first came."

Doyle reached for the cheese. "And they'll be back any time now, now that the weather's fit for sailing. I plan cavalry. Exclusively men on horse. Highly mobile, trained men who can range far and move quickly and decisively on a moment's notice. I've already set up a system of lookouts. Boys with trumpets will sound the alarm when the Northmen are sighted, and men near their landing point, wherever it may be, can be in the saddle in moments."

"That's fine for the coast, but I can't see the Northmen leaving their vessels lying on the shore while they try to penetrate this deep. I'm nearly thirty miles from the water."

"But you're not far from the river. We all must work together, Slevin, for common protection. From you I'm asking ten equipped men, mounted, and five spare horses. Not a large favor. With your retainers and freemen, you can field three times that number with no trouble. Just for the summer months."

In silence the bulky man prepared himself another slice of bread. He took a bite and chewed a moment, thoughtfully. "Me great-grandfather was named Slevin—mountaineer—and his father before him, and his father before him." More thoughtful chewing. "They lived up against the Wicklows. Real men of the mountains, back when the mountains represented all that is dark and evil."

"Which is why most ris built in the valleys."

Slevin nodded. "True. But me fathers built in the vale too. They were the ones who cleared the forests between An Nas and Kilbride. This was when Brigid's church was first built there. Me grandfather told me that his grandfather claimed that all of Erin used to be forests. All of it, hill and dale. From mountain to river, vast stands of pine and oak and birch, and the white gums." His voice dropped, wistful. "Not even the fairies and the wee folk could protect the white gums."

Doyle waited. This was surely all leading up to something.

Slevin continued. "Then came the warlords up from Cashel. They drove me family north, out of the land they had settled and made prosperous. This rath, where now you sit at table, is less than a hundred years old." Slevin looked squarely at Doyle. "Me fathers were driven out and none to save them. In turn they drove out the families who were here before them, and none to save those people either. Each man is his own strength, Doyle Dalainn. Each protects his own. Each grabs and holds, or is grabbed and held."

"Does all this mean you're not going to provide me with the men and horses?"

"You see?" Slevin addressed his wife. "A quick man is Doyle Dalainn, quick and clever to see a point instantly. I've often said that."

"Then how many men can you provide? Possibly I can put them on horseback from my own herds."

"Perhaps not so quick and clever as first I thought. Doyle, do you ken a lad named Brody? Brody of the Marshes."

"Don't know the name."

"The son of one of me retainers. He hired out with the Conroy during haying, less than a month ago."

And Doyle's heart chilled. He knew what was coming next. He had better think fast about how to handle it.

Slevin rolled on. "He brought the news. You see, Doyle, he was there when you and your force arrived at the Conroy's door. He heard your request, much like the request you've made of me just now. He fled to the alder marsh west of the rath. And from that marsh he watched you cut them down when they refused. Men and boys, women and children, slaughtered before they could mount any kind of adequate defense.

"When your men swept the area they failed to penetrate the marsh. And Brody, you see, was born and raised on the moors, quite at home in a marsh. He claims that had he not taken refuge there he would have been killed as well. He was sincere, and very frightened. I believe him."

"I see. Your Brody, Slevin, could not possibly know the whole story. The Conroy refused the conscription, yes. But there were other matters, previous matters. Matters about which Brody would know nothing. The Conroy were in open rebellion, and not just on that occasion. As ri ruirech, head of this whole province, I was perfectly within my rights to bring the rebellion to an end, one way or another."

Slevin sat erect and brushed his hands off on each other. "'Tis true, slaughter is one way. However—" he stood up "—you were demanding not horsemen but more horsemen. The Conroy had already sent you a contingent. The men best able to defend the rath against marauders—or the ri ruirech—were out on the coast, guarding against Northmen that have not appeared. No, Doyle, I'll not be sending me strength away from me own door."

Doyle felt the massive presence of this man hovering over him. He must tread carefully here. "You believe any tale told you, it appears."

"I believe a lad who arrived home here in terror, so frightened of what lay behind him that he did not fear me dogs. You are probably weighing the prospects of attacking me this moment and carrying me severed head out the door to draw me retainers over to the winning side."

Doyle smiled as he stood up. "It crossed my mind."

"I advise against it."

"You, too, are guilty of open rebellion."

"I am guilty of defending me own home. You are ri ruirech, yes, but I am a ri tuatha, responsible for me household and neighbors. You are fortunate, Doyle Dalainn, that none of the Conroy be me immediate relatives, else I would have swooped upon you in revenge by now."

He could not let this by. If Owney defied him openly, he would not only lose his tight grip on his own forces but on the other ris as well. The Conroy had balked. The Conroy had paid. It was not a question of whether to destroy the Owney, but questions of how and when.

He decided even as he praised the meal that the answers were "Here" and "Now." He rose from his bench, breathed in deeply, and again praised the food. Honestly, too.

"Very well, Slevin. Your choice is made, obviously." He turned toward the door, gauging the distances, the positions. Could his men take those retainers? Probably, and with minor loss. They were mounted. The defenders were not.

Two paces from the door he cried out, "Kill!" Even as he spoke the word he was wheeling in place, yanking his sword. Outside, his horsemen howled a battle cry.

Slevin was fast, very fast; you had to give him that. Despite the short notice, he had managed to free his sword and swing it up before him.

Doyle went not for the sword but for the arm. He sliced the arm with his edge. The sword dropped. Before the sword reached the beaten-earth floor, Doyle had arced the tip of his blade around low enough that he could drive it home just above the belt buckle.

Slevin crumpled.

Doyle pulled his sword and turned to meet the battle-ax barely in time. She was coming at him with the bread knife. She very nearly got him too. Its tip clipped his sleeve. Wild-eyed, she screamed as she came.

He swung his blade two-handed. Its edge cut into her side, stopping her charge. His sword stroke had lost nearly all its impetus, so he threw his weight into it to keep it moving. As she began her fall backward, she slid back along the blade. It eviscerated her as she went down.

Slevin was gone already, his hot blood pouring out across the floor.

Aisling lay completely relaxed except for her face. It was twisted in fury. Hoarsely she croaked, barely discernible, "God's curse be upon you, Doyle Dalainn. My bread turn to stone inside you and my honey into bees. May your bowels never move again or your soul find rest. 'Vengeance is mine,' says the Lord. 'I will require of you the blood of innocents.'"

Why did that unnerve him so? He was getting soft in his old age. This amazon was no more God's spokesperson than was his dun horse. He watched the light fade from her eyes. Her face relaxed. Outside, chaos reigned. In here, silence.

Fool! Here you stand contemplating a madwoman's idle words, while your men are fighting powerful foes! He snapped back to himself, but before he rushed to the door, he paused long enough to twist the gold torque off Slevin Owney's neck. He dropped it down inside his shirt, safe from hungry eyes.

Dogs were barking and whining, men crying out, horses' hooves clattering. Doyle's riders thundered to and fro, roaring with delight, their swords and axes bloody. The farmyard was littered with bodies of man and dog. A woman screamed, over and over, and then ceased.

Two of Doyle's horses cantered about riderless, their nostrils flared and the whites of their eyes showing. One of the two was his own dun stallion, so only one of his people had gone down under the blades of his enemies. He hoped it wasn't Fairleigh.

MacBrian of Berit Head came cantering his horse up to Doyle. His cheeks were rosy with youth and victory, his eyes bright with bloodlust as he hauled his little mare to a stop.

He grinned wide enough to fit his sword between his cheeks. "They turned tail, lord! Took their dogs and melted away! My father and three others have given chase, but they ran off into the forest."

"Sweep the area as before and assemble at the north gate. Spread the word. Catch up my horse for me first."

MacBrian wheeled his mount and took off after the dun. He cornered the half-crazed beast over by the pig sty and brought it back at a trot. He handed the reins off to Doyle and rode triumphantly out across the yard. Now there was a lad having the time of his life.

Doyle led his nervous, dancing dun out into the middle of the yard, lest he sheathe his sword to mount and a foe leap upon him from behind some wall. He swung aboard, and the horse quieted immediately under his hand. It never failed to impress him that the steadiest horse goes wild while, and only while, it is rendered riderless.

He threaded the dun among the bodies around the yard, assessing gains and losses. Four dogs down. That wasn't many, considering he saw nearly a dozen as he came in. The man he lost, the freeman from out by Slainey Beach, had been laid low not with weapons of war but with an iron hay fork. It was still in him. Doyle counted four boys and a girl, none fully grown yet, among the dead. He would assume they were not children fleeing, despite that three of them had suffered ax wounds in their backs, but children wielding weapons. The other men sprawled out here, Owney retainers all, had died by ax and sword.

Not all. One young man still moved. With a mighty effort he rolled to his side and looked up at Doyle. Doyle leaned forward in the saddle and finished him with a single sword thrust.

It took him half an hour to assemble his men. He didn't usually let them plunder, but they hadn't eaten since dawn, so he turned them loose to take what they wished. It was a minor mistake. He was another three hours getting them all in the saddle again and back on the road.

26

Wolves

There it was! Wolf pressed against the starboard gunwale, straining his eyes.

Lambay loomed in the mist, not more than a mile off their starboard quarter. They stood still, it seemed, as the island glided by in lordly dignity.

A cloud of seabirds swirled in the sky between here and the island. Shawna had mentioned that seabirds, gulls and terns primarily, nested there each summer. They flashed white and gray in the muted light, and you could just so hear their mewing if you listened.

And beyond Lambay—there was what he was really seeking. The mainland shore was almost invisible, so low did it hang beneath the sky, and so heavy was the mist. Wolf clambered up and stood on the gunwale, gaining a couple feet of height, that he might see a bit better. Jutting out beyond there must be Berit Head. Wolf could barely make it out, or maybe he was only fooling himself, but he knew where it ought to be.

He sensed movement beside him. He glanced down.

Hegaard, bemused, stood looking up at him. The Broad Back folded his arms across his chest. "So. Skule was right. You are in love."

Wolf hopped off the gunwale backward, to the deck. "Skule is right a lot oftener than most people realize."

"So I've learned. What is she like?"

"You ever meet Peggy?"

"Saw her from a distance."

"Better than that, and younger by ten years."

Hegaard grunted. "Then she's worth her weight in battle-axes. When we go ashore, shall I assign you to stay aboard and guard the vessel?"

Wolf shook his head. "She's not anywhere near where we'll be. You can depend on me."

"I know that. Never doubted you. I was thinking for your sake."

Wolf watched him a moment. "I'm grateful."

Then Arild called to Hegaard, something about a weak thong on the steering rudder, and Hegaard wandered aft.

Wolf turned his attention back to the coastline in the mist. He thought of all the times he had watched Shawna wander out to Berit Head, sit down on the bald rocks of its eastmost edge, and gaze off at Lambay. Was she doing that now? Was she espying their ships in the mist? Were they visible at all?

If so, now she would be running back to the rath to alert the others. She would be calling Doyle and his minions—Connleigh among them, no doubt—to the defense of the Dalainn.

Rest easy, Shawna. We're not going to strike your shore. We are dropping down into the Liffey, then upriver past Dublin Crossing, to wield our swords on an unsuspecting monastery well inland to the south of you. New territory for us, unspoiled by other plunderers. You are safe, you and your nephews.

But Kildare is not.

* * *

Doyle Dalainn wanted to go home. His greatest strength was his own rath and his own soil beneath his feet. He did not want to sit here in a makeshift camp in the middle of nowhere. But two men lay injured, and all that mad dashing about had worn the horses to a nubbin. Even the dun was blown out, exhausted. They could not afford to travel farther. The horses would soon start dropping.

Besides, he was not actually in the middle of nowhere. In fact, he wasn't all that far from either Dublin Crossing to the south or the oak grove to the north. It just seemed that way.

He watched as two of his men turned a mutton carcass on a spit over an open fire. The whole canty bunch here were having a rousing good time. The Conroy, and now the Owney, had proven to Doyle that so long as he provided opportunity for mayhem and a little pilferage, he could enjoy the absolute fidelity of the people

267

beneath him. Look at young MacBrian there, acting the fool and, alternately, the lord.

"Brian!" Doyle dipped his head.

Brian of Berit Head came trotting over, in as good spirits as everyone else. He hunkered down beside Doyle's knee.

"How are our wounded?"

"Milgheal bled like a stuck pig; he'll probably suffer no infection at all. Not so sure about Darren. So far, both are in good shape, and it's been hours. We changed the dressings once, and I sent Laire down to the rill to wash out the bloody ones. Might as well keep up with it while we can."

"Good. Good. New order regarding Shawna of the Behr. I've changed it. I want her, and she must be alive. I'll kill the man who kills her."

Brian looked puzzled.

Doyle would not elaborate. He need not. He had just rescinded the old directive—to bring him her head—and issued the new one. His reasons need not concern Brian or anyone else.

The old warrior nodded. "I'll make certain everyone gets the word."

"She's valuable to me. Make sure everyone understands that." He regretted his haste in threatening her. That was stupid. Now she would assiduously avoid him. She might have left the area already. After all, she had no reason to hang around, nothing to hold her here. He would keep an eye on Ceirre's place, but with his threat hanging over her head, Shawna would not likely return there.

On the other hand . . . if they did manage to dig her out of her hiding place, his error of the day before was actually no mistake at all. By letting her back into his good graces, he would render her beholden to him. She had resisted translating for him. Her indebtedness would break that resistance down.

And Connleigh. The fool lad deserted him when he needed him most. Connleigh was a lackluster fighter at best, but at least he fought. He carried the Dalainn blood. Enthusiastic or no, he did the job. Doyle could be sending Connleigh out to handle the coastal defense now.

Rome. *Hmph.*

It would be dark before long. He would remain here tonight and let his men lick their wounds—and, when they ate the sheep, their fingers. Let the horses rest well and graze this bottomland by the river. On the morrow he would return home and decide what to do next.

Things were not going at all as he had planned. He did not have the support of the southern ris that he had counted upon. The Conroy and the Owney had both tried to shake loose of his control. Who would attempt it next?

Perhaps his object lessons as he handled the rebels were clear enough, and drastic enough, that he would be plagued by no further resistance within the ranks of his own tuatha. One could only hope.

One thing was certain. He did not yet have the strength behind him to challenge the ard ri at Tara. He still was not on the path to the throne as High King.

That could change, though, if he could turn these Norse raids aside. The man who delivered Erin from the Wolves of the North could pretty well count on a seat at Tara. Much depended upon the arrival of the Northmen.

Much more than they possibly knew.

* * *

Connleigh dozed. He shifted slightly on his bed, a hard, bumpy coil of heavy anchor line. With half an ear and less than half a mind, he heard the rhythmic flap of the waves against the blunt bow of the fishing curragh. He listened to the pleasant, reassuring sounds of the wind and the sail engaging in a sotto voce discussion. The round-bottomed boat tipped slightly as vagrant sunset breezes caught the sail and nudged it this way and that.

His mind drifted. A prophet is not without honor save in his own country. If Jesus said it, it was true. No real matter. Connleigh would do without the honor. He could think of any number of fellow Gaels who either adhered to the external trappings only of the faith or didn't bother at all, paying barely enough attention to baptism and extreme unction to get them in and out of this world with a minimum of jeopardy. The shores of Erin were ripe for the ministry of a true apostle.

Connleigh would study at Armagh under Mahon part time. The rest of the time he would engage in missionary sorties all over Erin, perhaps a month or two per trip, calling all those stagnant believers to an active relationship with the living Jesus. And prophet in his own home or no, he would begin with them who needed it most of all, the Dalainn.

The boat swung sideways to the waves as the sail dumped. Connleigh forced himself nearer a state of wakefulness. They were nowhere near land yet. Why did they spill the sail?

Wynn Muir, the boat's master, was gazing off to the north, terrified. His assistants were lowering the sail far more speedily than they had raised it. Now they were pulling the pin and dropping the mast.

Connleigh sat up stiffly. He tried to wag his head free of the kink in his neck. "Why are we stopped?"

"Wolves."

Connleigh twisted to follow Wynn's gaze. He stood up to see better. His heart quailed. Veiled in mist on the horizon, three dragon ships, their sails spread broad, were aimed toward Erin.

Wynn glanced back at his crew. "They may not spot us with the mast and sail down. If we can remain undetected here until nightfall, we'll turn and sail back whence we came. Wales is safer than Erin by far."

"No, Wynn. I agree it's prudent to wait until dark, but we sail on to Erin then. We're nearly there."

"Sail into the mouths of wolves?" Wynn didn't even bother to wrinkle his nose at the thought.

And then Connleigh did a thing he almost never did. He pulled his sword—swiftly, in order to make a more telling impression—and tipped its blade up toward Wynn's gizzard. "You will put me ashore somewhere north of Wicklow Head. Then and only then may you flee the wolves."

* * *

"Ceirre, that is the most inane thing I ever heard! And I have listened to more than one three-year-old telling stories." Mahon tipped his stool back and leaned against the wall of Ceirre's hovel. "Irresponsible. I would expect better of you."

"Better? That's the best!" The crone set out a basket of nuts. "You know what Jesus said. 'I am the truth,' and, 'The truth will make you free.' Shawna must be free of this threat. Therefore, the truth. What could be simpler?"

On a stool across the table from Mahon, Shawna shook her head. "I think, Ceirre, that works only with people who value the truth. Doyle Dalainn values nothing save himself and his ambitions."

"Excellent way to put it." Mahon tipped forward again. He drew his dagger and cracked a nut with its hilt. "He utterly destroyed the Conroy, without mercy or regard. He wouldn't pause a moment to destroy Shawna. We cannot let that happen." He cracked another.

Shawna leaned forward and began picking nutmeat out of the broken shells. Mahon marveled that she could see what she was doing in the dim light of a little oil lamp. Youthful vision —something Mahon would never see again, literally.

"The fate of the Conroy proves that he's not fit to raise Peadar and Paul." Shawna looked at Mahon with her marvelous blue eyes. "I must get them away from there, Mahon, lest they think they can flout God's laws with impunity."

"Not impunity. Doyle will be punished, rest assured."

"But not in this life, perhaps. And that's what the boys will see."

Ceirre flopped down on her stool and popped a nutmeat into her mouth. "And you're sure you told him you were with me?"

"No." Shawna rubbed her face. "I'm not sure of anything. It was all a big, horrible blur. I wasn't expecting it."

Mahon nodded. "But you think you did."

"I think I did."

Ceirre looked at Mahon. "Then here is not the best place for her. It will likely be the first place he'll check if he decides to come looking."

"My thoughts exactly." Mahon could not crack nuts fast enough to serve all three appetites. He hit one off center, and it shot across the room. No one chased after it. "In theory, she can claim sanctuary in any church. But there is a strong possibility

271

Doyle would not honor sanctuary, especially in a small church. So her best safety lies in a large monastery."

"Kildare."

"Or Armagh. Armagh especially, being hard by Tara. He could hardly wrest an innocent woman out of sanctuary in the very lap of the High King."

Shawna picked at the growing pile of nutshell sherds, but she didn't seem to be eating any.

Mahon continued. "We have this comfort, also. Doyle has been trying so hard to unite the kings, and he might just succeed, but not as he hoped. He might unite them against him because of his illegality."

Shawna snorted. "He isn't breaking the law. He is the law."

"Ah, but he did break the law. Ceirre, you know Adomnan's Law. You were there when it was enacted."

She threw a nut at him. It hit him squarely in the ear. "You old badger, that was a hundred years ago!"

Shawna smiled for the first time. "What is it?"

"A law decreed by the ard ri and assented to by the ris beneath him. The Law of the Innocent, it's called. It places women and children, as well as clergy, under general protection during war. He slew innocents."

Shawna shook her head. "Who would enforce it?"

"Exactly! I learned about the Conroy when I was over by Kilbride. The Owney's sons told me. I shall confront Doyle regarding the tale, to confirm it or deny it by the words of his mouth—perhaps, if the words seem a lie, by his demeanor and actions. I will carry my findings to Tara and let them enforce it."

"Why would he admit it?"

"He probably will not. But in Matthew's gospel, our Lord instructs us to confront the person one to one. Then, if there is no satisfaction, go to others."

"Bah!" Ceirre scooped up a handful of nutshells and dropped them on her little fire. It crackled and spit sparks. "The ris have been trampling on each other for centuries. For as long as anyone can remember. It's the way kingship and power are determined. You know that. Doyle's doing no differently than ris have been doing forever. They won't move against him. Repugnant as his actions are, they understand him."

"Ceirre, Ceirre, Ceirre. You're too cynical."

"Mahon, Mahon, Mahon. I've been alive too long to be anything else. Mark me. Nothing will come of your efforts to turn Tara against him. Probably not even if you describe him as a threat to their throne."

Mahon glanced at Shawna. The poor girl looked totally dispirited. He hated to see the normally ebullient lass so disheartened. He reached forward and gripped her hand. "On the morrow we shall both go up to the Dalainn."

"Mahon—"

He cut her off. "It's on the way to Armagh anyhow. You will conceal yourself should we encounter anyone on the track. You will keep yourself hidden as I complete my business with Doyle. If the opportunity arises, I will suggest to him that I take the boys with me. If he refuses, you hasten to Kildare, explain it all to Mother Flora, and enlist her services to come up and request them.

"If he grants them to me, immediately I leave his presence I will turn them over to you, and you can sweep them down to Kildare if you wish or come with me to Armagh. Then I—or we—will continue north to deliver my observations to the High King." He spread his hands expansively. "What could be simpler?"

"A good question. Only a simpleton would enter the rath of the man who promised her death." She wagged her head. "I listened to my grandfather's tales of the past and to the stories by the Brehons who came through Lambay now and then. They talked about kings making war on other kings, of the constant skirmishing. They were just stories. They didn't mean much until it hit so close to home."

Ceirre grimaced. "That's what comes of living such a sheltered life out there on that island. No grasp of reality."

Mahon clapped his hands together. "So! On the morrow we are off and away, before first light." A sobering thought struck him. "Let's just hope the Owney mastiffs, those wolves, are somewhere else."

* * *

273

In his tent on his bed, Arild Thick Knee snored lustily. The crew of the *Swift Lynx* lay all over the ground, wrapped in their blankets and bearskins. For the twentieth time, Wolf the watchman walked the perimeter. He had seen this tiny island more than once from shore. They called it the Eye of Ireland. He never dreamed then that he'd ever camp on it with his countrymen.

He wandered down to the ships hauled up on the shore. High tide had passed and with it the danger that they might float off. He ran his fingers down the ornately carved stem of *Swift Lynx*. It was no less elaborately wrought than the Celtic sword hanging from his side. Art and blood. In either culture, Norse or Erse, they were linked in intriguing ways.

He heard a rustle behind him and turned. Skule was climbing out of his blankets. His scrawny cousin stood up, whipped his cloak around his shoulders, and came down to the shore to join Wolf.

"Nervous?" he whispered.

"Very."

"Me too. I'm trying to rehearse the way to Kildare, and I can't remember all the landmarks exactly."

"They'll come to you."

"I suppose."

Wolf looked out toward the mainland. It loomed as a black phantasm, a darker darkness in the darkness. "They probably already know we're here. They might be waiting for us on the morrow."

"Maybe not. We raised the island after dark, and our campfire looks no different from any fisherman's."

"Kind of hard to miss three dragons, given our reputation."

"True." Skule was smiling in the darkness. Wolf could just barely discern his features. "Ah, yes. Reputation. Coming back from the dead did wonders for mine. I had three different girls after me. Three! A year before, I couldn't have gotten one of them to admit I existed."

Wolf grinned. "Sounds like you should die more often." He watched the darkness, wishing he could see what was happening on the other shore. Was Hegaard erring by giving Doyle Dalainn and others time to raise a force against them?

So Skule liked the attention of the ladies. Skule always had. And Wolf could not think of any occasion where Skule was able to take advantage of it. The lad talked a fine line, but his actual luck fell woefully short.

Luck. Shawna. As luck would have it, Wolf was back. Or perhaps her God had engineered it. Who could say? Wolf must make a decision shortly. What would he do about Shawna?

Perhaps he might pray to her God. He wished now he'd been a little more diligent about picking up Latin. She claimed her God understood Erse and Norse perfectly because He created all languages—a claim Wolf found hard to accept. But Shawna then could not explain why Latin was such a big thing. If God spoke Erse, why not worship in Erse? Or Norse.

He tried to remember what Shawna had said was the basic rock-bottom prayer. *Our Father in heaven.* So far, so good. *I praise your name.* Something like that. *Let your kingdom come down and take over here.* Was that it? That would certainly bend Arild and Doyle and a few others out of shape. It would also put an end to pillaging.

Will in heaven . . . and earth . . . He skipped that part. *Give us our daily bread.* He ate well. No need to ask for that. And he could not think of the rest.

What was God's will? Shawna talked a lot about being in God's will, but how did she know what it was? Her opinion was probably not much more authoritative than Wolf's. So what was God's agenda for this whole situation? No doubt His opinions were much in line with Shawna's, or vice versa. Or were they?

And a terrible thought struck. What if Shawna was so angered and hurt by his hasty exit that she wanted nothing to do with him ever again? It could be. And she'd be justified.

She might be married too, as well as justified.

And yet, despite all the negative things he kept thinking—that an escaped slave is a marked man, that she might hate him or have married, that his father expected him to acquit himself well on this journey . . . despite all that, he had the most powerful urge, as soon as they raised the mouth of the Liffey, to jump ship.

27

Confrontation

Amazing thing, a salmon run. Shawna sat on the stream bank with her legs pulled up and her arms wrapped around them. It was chilly this morning, and bunching herself up helped her stay warm. She did not know which creek this was. Mahon would know. He knew every feature in Erin. She would ask him when he returned from prayer.

A silver fish shot straight up out of the pool to her left. Writhing, its tail flailing, it flew up the cascade before her and plopped back into the brook just beyond the rocks. It landed in water so shallow its dorsal fin stuck out. Shawna watched as, squirming, it drove itself upstream, zigzagging among the rocks. The fin sank out of sight into the next pool.

Here came two more. One landed on a flat boulder across the stream from Shawna. It flipped and flapped frantically. Three big, black rooks alighted in a tree overhead, squawking. But the fish managed to slide itself back into the water before they had gathered the courage to brave Shawna's presence and come down upon it. The rooks dispersed, seeking breakfast elsewhere.

Mahon spent an hour alone in prayer each morning, and Shawna admired that, but she wished he would come soon. She was getting quite cold. She needed to be up and moving.

Here he came. She lurched to her feet, stiff. But he sat down by the stream, so she reluctantly sat down again as well.

She watched his face a moment. "You're troubled."

"And so are you."

She certainly couldn't deny that. "I'm afraid, Mahon. I think this idea of confrontation is wrong. Dangerous. I don't think either of us can simply walk up to Doyle Dalainn and tell him he's mistaken. Not even you. And I'm beginning to doubt he'll give up the boys. I just don't know—"

276

"Specific portents? Has God spoken to you in detail?"

She shook her head. "Just a great heaviness. You?"

"Strange dreams—and a vision this morning. The dreams were of a river of flowing blood. I could tell some of it was Norse blood, but I don't know how."

"Norse! They're coming?" Her heart tickled.

"Apparently. The vision this morning as I sat in prayer was of a fair-haired young man killing a brindled bull. A yearling, it appeared. I've received nothing about what that all means."

"Fair-haired. Your assistant? That Ailan you mentioned?"

"I believe so."

"Not the Declan whom you tout so highly—the copyist."

"He's much darker. No." Mahon snapped to his feet. "Instead of traveling directly north, we will walk east awhile today. I don't know why."

She stood and fell in beside him as he moved off. She heard salmon flapping behind her. "East and then north will put us right in the middle of the Owney."

"I don't like that any better than you do, but that's the way we're supposed to go."

She knew better than to question Mahon's second sight. It was not always clear, but it was always God's will of the moment. They walked in silence. She thought about the salmon. Did salmon know their destination as they struggled so valiantly upstream? How much was sure knowledge and how much was blind obedience to an outside call?

"Smoke." She pointed toward an oak-clad hill to their right. A curl of gray emerged from the trees and melted into the gray sky.

Mahon stopped and stared. "No rath, no church, no reason for herdsmen. We shall go there."

"Brigands, perhaps. Or cattle thieves."

"Perhaps." Resolutely, Mahon took off toward the oak grove.

Easy for a monk to say. Brigands rarely troubled monks. Being a woman in the midst of outlaws was quite another matter. Mahon didn't seem to consider that. Indeed, for all his holiness, Mahon rarely looked at life from anyone's perspective save his own. With considerable trepidation, Shawna fell in behind. In fact, she stayed well behind.

Mahon pushed through the dense understory as they entered the wood. Shawna followed, shouldering through hazel and getting stuck by holly. She stumbled over the prickly ground vines. They raked her ankles. She hated woodland.

As they entered the realm of the immense and ancient oaks, the understory opened up. Few and scrawny were the small trees of the underneath. The dark oaks spread out overhead like a wondrous roof, blocking the light. Ivy clothed their knotted trunks, and small fern fronds sprouted here and there from their crotches and crevices.

Now Shawna stumbled over gnarled roots rather than berry vines, but oak roots don't leave those tiny prickles in your skin. Somewhere ahead she heard a Gaelic voice appealing to bulls.

Silent as a thought, Mahon moved toward the voice.

Shawna tried her best to make no noise. It was hard. The understory grew dense again and crackly as the wood opened into a pleasant glade. The aroma of smoke and of roasting beef drifted this way.

In the midst of the glade by the smokey fire sat a blond young man, and he had draped over his shoulders a small brindled cowhide. He hummed to himself in reverie, his eyes closed. Then in singsong he again called to the bull. He appeared to be alone, but Shawna hung back a moment anyway, making certain.

Mahon stepped soundlessly into the clearing. "Well, Ailan," he said quietly.

The young man jumped as though Mahon had just jabbed him with a lancetip. He lurched to his feet clutching at the cow skin. Then he let it slide off his shoulders into the forest duff. It looked and smelled fresh, as though just taken. "Mahon. Peace be with you."

"And also with you. I've come for my ax. I see it lying there beyond the fire."

"Of course. Your gift from the Abbot of Kells." As if prodded with a bull pike, Ailan leaped from stunned stillness into frantic motion, grabbed the ax, and brought it to Mahon handle first.

"Thank you." Mahon accepted the weapon and slid its handle into his belt behind his back.

"Do you—uh—have another assistant?"

"As a matter of fact, God has provided me an able young man, eager in the Scriptures, a lover of the Word. I've sent him ahead to Armagh with a letter of introduction. He is to begin working there on the minor prophets." Mahon then folded his arms and simply looked at the slim young man. He didn't stare. He didn't glare. His face motionless, he looked.

Should Shawna step out into the glade? She decided to wait and watch.

The young man shuffled about and fidgeted until the silence became too heavy to stand. "The old ways." He waved a hand toward his fire and the meat roasting on a spit. "There's much to be said for some of the old ways." He watched, expectantly, for an answer.

"I agree."

Silence.

Ailan exploded into motion again. He wheeled and marched off across the glade. He wheeled again to face Mahon from that safer distance. "Christianity is ruining Erin, Mahon! It separates us from nature, from the real world. It tames our men too much and doesn't give our women enough credit. It dulls our senses so we can't hear the voices of the wildwood and the land. The old gods are tired of being shunted aside. That's why the land is plagued with war and death."

Silence.

Ailan took a few steps in closer to Mahon. "Erin deserves better than a religion that fails to honor the land or the old ways." He held Mahon's eye for a moment or two. He burst out, "Speak to me!"

"What would I say? You've turned your back on the living Christ. It doesn't sound like I can sway your convictions, however wrong they may be."

"But I'm not wrong. You've read the books, the Brehon law. Deep down, you know I'm right. The power of the land is in the old ways."

"And the power of a bull?" Mahon nodded toward the discarded skin.

"And the power of the bull. Yes. I'm tapping into that power, Mahon." Ailan waited, glaring defiantly. He seemed to straighten as the moments passed, to stand taller. "Aren't you going to defend the faith? Or do you find defense impossible in the face of reality?"

Mahon watched him a few moments more. Then, "Tell me about John Baptist."

"What?" Ailan studied the wrinkled face and apparently saw nothing there. "He was the precursor to Christ. You know all about him."

"So do you. And you know he said, 'He' —meaning Jesus— 'must increase and I must decrease.' He prepared the way. I submit to you that Druidism did much the same thing. Druidism was Patrick's John Baptist."

Ailan glared suspiciously.

Mahon's voice rumbled gently, smoothly, unruffled and unhurried. "You've apparently studied Druidism in greater detail recently. So you know the druids teach that the soul lives on eternally. I could give you another half dozen major parallels, all of which tell the druid, 'Jesus Christ is the culmination of all you've learned.' In Druidism, the Irish were being prepared for the Christ child just as the Hebrews were five hundred years before."

"No!" The blond young man looked confused, even desperate. "That's not what I thought you would say—I mean, if we met like this. I didn't think we would meet again. You don't understand. The church refutes the sacred nature of the land. It—I don't—no!" His head wagged.

"You've seen monks from France. Their tonsure—their hair— is a circlet round their head, shaved on top and trimmed around the sides. Where do you think our Gaelic tonsure comes from?" Mahon ran his hand across the shaved front of his head. "Druidry, Ailan. You knew that once, I'm sure, but you've forgotten. Ailan, my dear son—" Mahon sounded so sad that Shawna's eyes grew hot "—sing with me a hymn of Patrick."

"I don't think I—"

But Mahon had already begun the hymn Shawna knew so well. She yearned deeply to join in, but she kept silence and watched.

His voice rang strong in the glade.

"I arise today through the strength of heaven;
   Light of sun, radiance of moon;
   Splendor of fire, speed of lightning, swiftness of wind—

"Sing with me, Ailan. A song of joy and praise as the worshiper revels in the world God created."

"Sung inside a church with ought but wooden walls around."

"How often, lad, have you worshiped at my side beneath the open sky at the foot of a high cross? Churches are nice in inclement winter, and oratories are nice in which to get apart. They protect when protection is needed. They hardly separate us from our world."

Ailan shook his head. "You don't understand! Through my own efforts—"

"I understand far more than you realize. You are trying to plumb depths by paddling on the surface. Your efforts are surface efforts, Ailan. You can no more grasp the power and glory of God by these motions than you can stir porridge by skimming a spoon across the surface."

"The methods work! They're recorded by men of God—by monks."

"True. But you don't even have the surface gestures right. The use of a bull in Druidism, such as you are attempting, is only to predict the identity of a future king. To determine the ri to come, not general prophecy. Not only are you abandoning Christianity, you are maligning druidic precepts. My son, I implore you to—"

"Jealousy! That's it! You're afraid of my power!"

The old man sighed heavily.

"Power!" Ailan pulled his dirk from its sheath. "I killed a bull to usurp his power. I could kill you right now and usurp your power. I have the power! Mahon, you are a false prophet."

Soundlessly, Shawna moved forward out into the glade, placing her bare feet carefully to avoid any noise whatever. She moved in behind the frantic young man.

Mahon stood relaxed. "You do not begin to understand power."

"Don't I? What is to stop me from killing you now?"

281

Casually, defiantly, Mahon crossed his arms.

Shawna dived forward and with the heel of her hand flung a flying chop against the backs of Ailan's knees. She used to do it to her brothers, just to hear them roar.

Ailan tumbled backwards, sat roughly upon Shawna, and continued down. His head whumped against the ground.

Shawna was not frightened, or annoyed, or bemused. She was livid! This high-minded young oaf would dare raise a hand against the Abbot of Armagh? She leaped to her feet and stomped upon Ailan's wrist. His hand opened, and the knife fell away. She kicked it off into the brush.

He stared at her wide-eyed, open-mouthed. She stood arms akimbo and glowered.

He squirmed to his feet and, gripping his wrist, ran off into the forest.

Shawna listened to his passage as he crashed through the brush.

This twisted young man had once been Mahon's protégé. How her heart ached for the old man.

28

Declan

Ghosts and monsters watched from behind trees, waiting, both possessed of powers beyond ken. Dogs and swine ranged free, prowling, both possessed of long, sharp teeth. Brigands and free-booters roamed the remote tracks of Erin, robbing, all possessed of no scruples whatsoever.

Declan scurried along the track alone, not knowing where he was, not even certain he was on the right road, for in this gloomy overcast he could not tell north from south. Constantly did his thoughts remind him of the looming dangers of solitary travel. How he abhorred this!

If he was travelling north, he could assume he was safely beyond reach of Doyle Dalainn by now. If his sense of direction was behaving in its usual confused manner, though, he could be walking through the heart of Dalainn territory. He got this horrid sense of direction from his mother, and she admitted it. Why could he not also have received her beautiful spiritual gifts?

He thought about how safe he had felt in Mahon's company. The old man might not be physically powerful, but his wisdom and his spiritual power served them far better than mere strength of arm.

And he thought about Mahon's surmises regarding Lambay Island. Independently, both Declan and Mahon carried Mahon's suspicions to Armagh and Tara. What would come of them?

Tara. The hill of might and legend. His whole life, Declan heard about Tara and the heroes of yore who ruled there. The real power now resided in Armagh and Kells, within the church. Yet, Tara loomed just as bright in memory as it had in fact. Whoever ruled Erin ruled from Tara, no matter where he might reside.

The track wound up a slope through a dense birchwood and out into an opening at the crest of the hill. From this craggy overlook, Declan could see for miles all around. He paused on a rock outcrop, laid his heavy carrying sack aside, settled into a chair-shaped boulder, and rested. Dark green forests clothed the low hills undulating off to the horizon. The vales between the rises were all cleared into bright green pastureland. The clearings extended partway up the slopes, ragged-edged. Rings of sod or wood, the barrier walls around raths, and hedges snaked across the pasturelands in all directions. A few of the low hills, too, were cleared, with ringed walls perched atop them. Peace. It looked much like home, though Declan missed his wild south coast with its seabirds.

Not that these birchwoods lacked birds. Afar off to the south, where Declan had passed a pond, a flight of birds lifted above the trees—ducks and a few white swans. A minute later, a cloud of jackdaws burst up out of the forest. He sat erect, frowning. What monsters, swine, dogs, or men would startle two different flocks?

Moments later a pair of pink jays came squawking up out of the birches, closer. Someone was moving rapidly this way along the track. Snatching up his burden bag, Declan leaped to his feet. Fear—nay, call it panic—welled up inside him. A farmer or trades-man would not move so swiftly. The weight of his bundle threw his balance off as Declan worked his way along the rocky outcrop. The dizzying drop lay to his left and the track, untrodden, to his right. The outcrop curved around and melted into the steep hill-side. Declan heard a waterfall in the distance where this hill met with the next in a deep, narrow crease.

He stumbled awkwardly, straight down the hill, making far too much noise. When the cliff became too steep to negotiate, he angled right, toward the waterfall's roar. He ought drop his wool-wrapped burden, but he could not. Besides, should they find it, it would tell them loud and clear that Declan had passed this way.

A cascading creek tumbled down the narrow gorge between the hills and dropped off into a waterfall ten feet high at least. The crystalline water crashed against rocks down into a broad, glassy pool. That short rest sufficient, apparently, the water chattered on down the defile, swirling amongst the dark boulders of the creekbed. Everywhere around the watercourse grew moss and ferns and a hundred different gangling plants with dark shiny leaves.

Slipping on the moss and wet rocks, Declan worked his way back to the waterfall. He paused, gauging the safety of the rocks at its base. With a deep breath he clutched his burden against his breast and stepped forward, through the crash of water, into the narrow, misty cave behind it. Soaked with icy water, he crouched against cold, wet rocks and wrapped his arms around his legs. The cavity behind the fall was not quite as deep as he was broad; his right elbow was poured upon no matter how tightly he scrunched up against the wall. And his bag—he must keep that as dry as possible.

He could not see well through the curtain of water, and he could hear nothing at all save its incessant roar. For hours—for weeks—he sat there, stiff with cold and fear. Too few minutes later he heard men's voices shouting. They sounded distant, perhaps in the next kingdom, but they were definitely men's. Dogs barked.

Men were tracking him with hunting dogs!

He could hear his heart thumping, and he was certain they would hear it too over the howl of wildwater. Through the distorted blur of his curtain Declan could see movement on the hillside. The dogs were following him to this very spot. Then, confused, the dog forms seemed to spread out along the creekbed.

Declan could make out men now, with their colorful tunics, as they worked their way down the steep hill. The blurry blobs of color seemed as confused as the dogs.

Perhaps the falling water was carrying his scent downstream, or at least enough of it to throw the dogs into disarray. Perhaps he was saved after all.

Only one dog form in the blur approached the fall. The dog placed itself where Declan had entered the water and began barking directly at him.

Above the pounding roar, a man's voice shouted, "Gwynna!" in a scolding tone.

Gwynna. During the time he and Mahon were visiting the Dalainn rath, Declan had made good friends with a miserable cur named Gwynna Fat Feet. She had been declared too old and stupid to hunt effectively, and many were the tales of her bungling. If that was Gwynna, these men and their dogs were of the Dalainn, and therefore after Declan's life itself.

Pater noster . . . Domine . . . salvame . . . If only Mahon were here! Mahon would know what to do. Mahon's faith was strong, a saving strength, and Declan's faith so very, very weak. Too young to die, both physically and spiritually, Declan had so much growing to do yet. *Domine Jesu, salvame!*

More shouting. They were milling about now, men and dogs together, just downstream of the pool. Any moment, a javelin would come slicing through the curtain into Declan. He knew it. He just knew it.

He curled his body over his bundle and rested his forehead on his drawn-up knees. He closed his eyes. The cold, the wet, the crashing water still intruded, but they, being natural, spoke gently to him.

A part here and a part there, Declan had read through the whole Bible, both testaments. Already he had copied perhaps a third of it all told. He thought about the many streams of water he had read about. Over and over, God likened the Holy Spirit to life-giving water in the wilderness.

He cowered behind it at this moment, protected.

Whup! The bundle in his lap jolted. He recoiled, startled, and stared at the arrow protruding from it as the men's voices picked up beyond the curtain.

The curtain darkened as a huge fellow came wading over to the waterfall. A burly arm and hand reached in blindly, seized Declan's arm, and yanked. Declan shot out through the icy curtain just as swiftly as had that arrow. He tumbled into the boulders. As his head clunked, a spray of lights flashed. Stunned, he felt himself being jerked and dragged about.

By the time his head cleared enough to think and see, the burly fellow was hauling him to his feet on the stream bank by the little pool. He felt a warm trickle running down his cheek just in front of his ear. He resisted the impulse to reach up and touch it. Besides, the side of his head ached more and more with every passing moment.

If he displayed the fear that gnawed on him now, he would shame Jesus and Mahon and his mother and all mankind. He stood straight, his fingers laced together loosely in front, and looked from face to face. "You are of the Dalainn, but I don't recognize any of you."

"Now how would you know that?"

"Am I wrong?"

The burly fellow snickered. He was a massive man, all the more massive for a thick, unruly bush of a brown beard. His eyebrows met together in the middle, making his face all the darker. "You are right." He waved a hand at a lad Declan's size and age. "Retrieve my arrow."

The boy bolted forward and clambered down across the rocks to the waterfall. Declan heard him slipping and splashing behind him. As soaked as Declan, the lad sloshed ashore and handed the bundle to his master.

The burly fellow clawed the coarse-spun woolen bag open. "Books. Aught but two books."

Gwynna Fat Feet pushed up against Declan's legs and shoved her head into his hand. Absently he scratched her behind the ears. "What were you expecting?"

The man pulled the bag free of the books. The arrow was still buried in the text of Psalms, Proverbs, and Song. He thrust the books at Declan so roughly they slammed into his belly and knocked his wind out. "Show me where it is written about the Dalainn."

"Which do you mean?" Declan had trouble getting enough air flow to speak. "Something specific about Doyle, or what God's Word says about kings in general?"

"At Mahon's behest you wrote down something about the Dalainn to deliver to Armagh. Show me." From between the two books, Declan's parchment letter fluttered to the ground. "Ah. There we are. Read it."

Declan picked it up and began at the beginning. "'My beloved brothers. This is—"

"Point to the words as you go. I want to see the words."

Declan began again, pointing. "'My beloved brothers. This is to introduce Declan of Ardmore, a ready lad who loves the Word. Receive him as you receive me. I have asked him to prepare study texts from those uncials we have stored on the upper shelf of the

287

annex. He does splendidly with study texts and will soon be ready to take his place among our skilled scribes. Greetings to all from Flora.'"

"That's it?"

If Declan feigned ignorance, this fellow would not believe him, and his lying would reflect poorly on his Jesus. His mind a-spinning, he decided, for better or worse (probably worse!) to be fully honest. His doom was sealed anyway. The man had already once tried to kill him, with the arrow.

He handed the letter to the man. "That's it. We did not commit to writing Mahon's belief that the Dalainn, not the Norse, destroyed every man, woman, and child on Lambay. And then there is the matter of the Conroy."

Gwynna, dissatisfied with Declan's inattention, pestered him for more patting.

The burly fellow stared at him the longest time. Suddenly he bobbed his head. "In the books. You wrote it in a book."

"The Dalainn are indeed discussed in this book right here." Declan thumped the little study text of psalms and proverbs, the one with the arrow in it.

The fellow nodded gravely. Declan opened it slowly. In his mind, he ran down through the first lines of the Psalms, trying to decide which to quote. He would not have much time. The second and fourth would do. "The Word of the Lord. Here, for example. This is in Latin. *'Astiterunt reges terrae, et principes convenerunt in unum adversus Dominum et adversus Christum ejus.'* Translated, it says, 'The rulers convene together to take counsel against God and His Christ, saying—"

"I understand Latin as it is spoken." The man seemed uncomfortable. His lips pressed together grimly.

Declan hastened on, not translating every word and phrase but hitting the high spots. "'He who sits in the heavens laughs at them. You,' meaning God, 'shall break them with an iron rod and smash them like a clay pot.' Now over here a couple psalms later, David says of God, 'You hate all evildoers. The Lord abhors bloodthirsty and deceitful men. Make them bear their guilt, O God! Let them fall by their own counsels because they've rebelled against you.' Remember this is the Word of the Lord through David, a warrior king who slew hundreds by his own hand and led men into battle to die. Now over in this other, the one beginning with *Domine Deus meus, in te speravi,'* it says—"

"That's enough!"

Declan closed the little volume, the arrow still buried in the back half, skewering, probably, the whole book of Proverbs. "The word of God is very clear in the matter. Unless he repents and repents mightily, Doyle Dalainn is doomed, as are all who enter into evil with him." Declan shrugged helplessly. "I'm sorry. It's not my opinion. It's God's."

The others in this group, six armed men altogether, had gathered close around. The javelin or battleax that ended Declan's life could come from any direction. They stood silently, watching their stocky leader, listening.

The burly man waved the parchment letter. "You are traveling to Armagh."

"Yes."

"But you are on the road to Tara."

"I must take your word for that. I'm not at all certain where I am."

"You were traveling that rapidly in a direction you know not?"

"You may truthfully assume I have no idea within a hundred miles where I am right now. I would have guessed, since you are of the Dalainn, that I had inadvertently wandered back south. Look at the sky. The overcast is thick enough I cannot discern directions."

The fellow grunted. "Why did you run from us?"

Declan waved an arm randomly at the forest of weapons. "My good fellow, figure it out. You cannot imagine the fear in my heart this moment."

A chorus of voices laughed. From behind Declan a man's rumbling tenor spoke. "The Dalainn knows what the Scriptures say. He knows God's opinion if anyone does. He's ri ruirech. It's his monastery down by the alderwood."

"What are you saying, Michael?" The burly man glared past Declan's shoulder at his fellow brigand.

"I'm saying the Dalainn knew before he sent us what God thinks of his political ambitions. I'm saying we've been sent on a merry chase that can do us nothing but harm."

"You help the Dalainn put down rebellion and thereafter share in the spoils. No harm there."

"And I burn in hell forever so that the Dalainn can firm up his political grip. Not I. This man speaks the Word of God. I'll not touch him."

The burly fellow looked from face to face. "You others?"

There seemed to be a general consensus.

The burly man seemed unconvinced. "So we let him go his way, and he brings the wrath of Tara down upon the Dalainn. Where does that leave us?"

"Better the wrath of Tara than the wrath of God."

Again a mumbling consensus.

Gwynna rubbed her hard hound head against Declan's pants leg. He was so cold with his soaked clothing that he was beginning to tremble.

The burly fellow stabbed at the book with a finger the size of a hazel stump. "You were skipping around. Read it clear through."

"Gladly." Declan opened to the second psalm and gave it all he had, Latin and Erse. He continued on, knowing well that the full text was far more damning, more penetrating than his excerpts could be. His arms ached from the cold and the weight of the book. His chilled legs turned stiff standing there. And his head ached terribly. It robbed him of his ability to think just when he needed it most.

His audience sat down on the rocks and grass round about, listening. He could not allow himself that luxury. Mahon commanded respect simply by entering a room, with his gray hair and monk's tonsure. Mahon could assume the authority of God lying supine. Declan could not. He was young and boyish looking. He must command a maximum presence, an authority, and that was best done standing. He represented the Christ now.

The man named Michael seemed not much older than Declan. His was the softest, silkiest blond beard Declan had ever seen, well cared for and well trimmed. The throat of his tunic gapped open. The hair on his chest was the same soft yellow as his beard.

"Rory," Michael said as Declan closed his book again, "I see Doyle Dalainn paying a heavy price. If there is a choice between receiving and paying, I want to be on the receiving side. I do not care to help him pay his debts."

The burly fellow had sprawled out across a patch of bald rock, apparently unmindful that his bed of rest was—well, rock hard. "What do you suggest?"

"That we take the side of God and travel with this man to Tara and Armagh."

"And abandon the most powerful ri in the region?"

"What better time to do it than before the power shifts?"

Rory smirked. "If we let this man live, and let him carry his tale to Tara, the Dalainn is destroyed. We will have acted treacherously. Not that he is innocent."

Innocent. Where was that passage? Declan leafed through pages rapidly. Here. Halfway down this psalm. "It's talking here about the wicked, whom God is about to destroy. *'Sedet in insidiis cum divitibus in occultis, ut interficiat innocentem.'* 'He cowers in ambush in the villages. In his hiding place he murders innocents.'"

Rory grimaced. "Yep. That's Doyle. What shall we, lads? Slit this fellow's throat before he speaks another word, or betray the ri-ruirech?"

Declan's heart flittered at the mention of throat-cutting. It was one thing to anticipate that it might happen. It was quite another to hear it openly discussed. Already they had drawn blood. It was drying on his cheek and neck.

Gwynna flopped down to lying on his foot and slurpily began licking her paws.

One fellow in a stained brown tunic rubbed his hands together. "All my life I've heard of Tara and Armagh, but I've never seen either. Good a time as any, I'd say, to correct that oversight."

Michael warned, "You can't go home again if we turn against the ri. What about that little hedgeflower in the Sord dell? She'll wilt without you."

The fellow's cheeks turned pink as his companions roared. "Mayhap I'll slip back some night and lure her away." His face sobered. "I find myself at night thinking, *What if she had been of the Conroy?* There is no human soul safe in the region of the Dalainn—not any ri tuatha nor the innocents in his care."

Rory bobbed his massive head and addressed Declan. "My little man, your ready tongue has saved your throat and won us to your side."

"My Lord's side," Declan corrected. "Not mine."

Gwynna lurched to her feet and licked Declan's wrist.

Rory shrugged. "As you wish." He flung his huge body to its feet and stretched. "Let us be on our way, lads. We can be nearly there by nightfall."

With some difficulty, Declan wiggled and pulled until that arrow, the arrow meant for him, worked free. He handed it back to Rory and picked up the damp woolen sack. As he slipped the books back inside it, he thought of Mahon. He had watched Mayhon's gnarled hands do this same thing. Where was the old saint now? They talked of carrying the news, and the suspicions, north independently, to double the chances of the word's getting through. Mayhon expected trouble, clearly. And just as clearly, God's guidance and protection was keeping Declan safe. He prayed the same for Mahon.

Michael led off, clambering up the steep slope toward the track. Declan shouldered his burden and did his best to keep up. Gwynna leaped and lurched her way upslope, so close to Declan she kept tripping him.

Declan gasped, thoroughly winded, as they reached the ridge and the track. Gwynna gave his hand a sticky lick and fell in hard beside him.

Rory seemed not the least discomfited. He clapped Declan on the back. "Anything you wish, little man of God?"

Declan snorted and followed behind Michael as the young warrior strode smartly off down the track. "Because I am a man of God, though not yet in orders, I cannot do what I devoutly wish. I will maintain the decorum of the Lord's servant."

"And that devout wish is . . ?"

"To kick this infernal dog off the face of the hill."

29

Peacemakers

He was poking his slumbering troops with a toe, kicking this fellow and that, when he heard the horn toot. Doyle stood tall and tipped his head high. They were blowing the trumpet in the far, far distance.

"Up!" he cried. "Up! This is it! The trumpet!"

The trumpet sounded again, just barely audible.

His men scrambled for their gear. They ran around, yelling, accomplishing far too little far too slowly. They rushed to the outer perimeter of their camp to relieve themselves after their night's rest.

It occurred to Doyle at this absolutely inane moment that his bowels had not moved this morning. He was extremely regular, normally. And the twisted face of Aisling Owney came back to him. He brushed the coincidence aside. Hardly! God did not work that way, even if He did listen to Aisling, and Doyle doubted He would stoop to entertaining that old battle-ax.

Fairleigh had his stable boys whipped to a lather as they saddled mounts and pressed bits into horses' mouths. Doyle shouted at them to hurry, but his admonition wasn't going to do much good. The dolts were already moving about as fast as they were able. He swung aboard his dun stud the moment the bridle was slipped on.

The trumpets had been told to sound the alarm the instant they spotted Norse ships in the open sea. Doyle's blood ran cold as a vivid fear struck him. What if the watchman merely saw passing ships? What if the dragons were continuing to the south, perhaps off the south coast of Erin beyond Doyle's reach, or over to Wales? Perhaps even beyond, into Frankish territory?

He would press east with his troops and hope the marauders raised land somewhere within striking distance, preferably this side of the Liffey.

Here came his sons. Fairleigh himself was saddling up. Of Doyle's eleven cavalrymen here, nine were ready to go. The other two could catch up.

"Leave the sleeping gear! Brian, don't bother with the pots now. Weapons only. Strip for battle!" He pulled his sword and pointed it at God. "Our golden moment, for our families and for all of Erin. We know the fiends are here. They can't surprise us. We have reinforcements in the saddle even now, hastening in from the other raths to join us. Here is where we turn the monsters around!" With a mighty war cry he wheeled his stallion aside and rode east. His men's war cries made the welkin ring.

The Conroy and the Owney were rehearsals.

This was the real thing.

* * *

He was winded, weary, spent. And it only just dawn. What did that promise for the rest of the day? Connleigh paused. He was still several miles from Ceirre's place. Or was he? He could not remember the sequence of landmarks along this shore, for he had come this way but once. He knew he was very close to the mouth of the Liffey. Walking all night certainly takes the juice out of a fellow. He rested a few minutes and continued, still incredibly weary.

The trail left the brushy glen and wound down to the water's edge. He walked out onto the shore. Several miles offshore in the mist, the dragon ships cruised. The breeze was too unsettled to permit them a fast run down the sea. Unless they decided to drop their sails and row ashore, Connleigh had a few hours. But if they were planning to raid ashore in Erin, why were they so far out in the open water?

And if they did come ashore, whatever would he do, specifically? He wasn't sure. He certainly wasn't going to take on three loads of Northmen single-handed. He would follow at a distance. If other fighting men engaged these Northmen in battle, Connleigh would plunge in and do his part. If the Northmen struck unopposed, as they usually did, Connleigh would have no recourse but to lie low, then give aid and succor to the survivors afterwards.

He praised God that Shawna was miles away, safe with his mother and sisters. He thanked God that the Northmen were venturing nowhere near the rath of the Dalainn. Shawna had suffered enough already. And he didn't want his mother to suffer at all.

The ships rounded the head and reset their sails for a fresh run westward, up the bay toward the mouth of the Liffey. So that was where they were headed. That was logical. A number of prosperous raths clustered on the floodplain, many of them with attendant small monasteries. They were rich pickings, but not easy ones. Most of the ri tuatha hired retainers for purposes of defense. You had a lot of armed men in a small area there, and some of them on horseback. Did the Northmen know that? Probably not. How could they? They were raiding blind, so to speak, with no prior knowledge of their targets.

With renewed vigor, Connleigh hastened up the track toward Dublin Crossing.

* * *

Fifteen minutes down the track, Doyle smugly congratulated himself on his decision to use horse soldiers exclusively. When they paraded the Northman around, they traveled only as fast as the slowest man on foot—which was the Northman, usually. Today, they had gone the distance from their camp very nearly to Dublin Crossing, and in the time a force on foot would take to get to Mindeaugh Cross.

They entered an alder grove within a mile of the river. The dun stud was snorting and blowing, his neck and flanks white with lather. The stallion cantered forward bravely.

Fairleigh came clattering up alongside. "We'd best stop a few minutes, lord."

Reluctantly, Doyle drew his dun to a walk. "Why?"

"We're moving too fast. Some of the horses are in extremity back there, and the two men behind us haven't been able to catch up yet. I'm not worried about your horse or mine keeping the pace, but some of those horses are pretty small, with heavy loads."

Doyle ducked a limb that the men on smaller horses didn't have to worry about. "What th—" He yanked his dun to a halt.

As if Doyle had all day, Mahon of Armagh stood in the middle of the road where it passed through an alder thicket, effectively blocking the way.

A civil tongue would probably work a lot better in this situation than a short one. Doyle forced a smile onto the front of his face. "Peace be with you, Mahon of Armagh."

The appropriate response was "And also with you." Mahon did not make an appropriate response. "Word has reached me of an atrocity, Doyle Dalainn. The Conroy. What say you?"

Doyle ceased bothering with the smile. "What shall I say?"

"Dependable witnesses identify you as the murderer."

"Later, Mahon. We're on our way to save Erin. The Northmen are back. Move aside."

"I've just crossed the ford. I know of no Northmen. I do know of dead women and children. The Law of the Innocent, Doyle. When you assumed your title at Tara, you swore to enforce it. Do you confirm or deny your involvement?"

"Move aside, old man!"

"Confirm or deny?"

Doyle knew what the old goat was really saying. "What message do I bear the High King?" This meddler, this self-styled conscience of the king, would bring his case before the ard ri. Doyle knew it. Mahon knew Doyle knew it. All sorts of unpleasant repercussions would result. And if things looked bad now, just wait until Mahon got wind of the Owney.

Doyle did not believe in losing opportunities by thinking too long, and two challenges hung pregnant here—the danger the Northmen posed and the danger this old man posed—and therefore two opportunities to overcome them. Not only that, Doyle must not appear before these men around him, who were all eagerly listening, to harbor any weakness or gentleness. They would follow a hero blindly. They would pay no loyalty to a thinker.

He thought no longer. "Confirm."

He expected the old goat to glow in triumph, his darkest suspicions delightfully confirmed. People are like that, always looking for the worst. But instead, an expression of profound sadness flooded the old man's face.

Too late, old man, to feel sad and sympathetic, though heaven knows why you would. Doyle didn't need his sword for this. He pulled the dirk from his belt even as he spurred the dun. He had only to lean out and forward—his horse did the work. The dirk caught the old man in the throat just below his chin. Warm blood sprayed across Doyle's arm, his hand, his trousers leg.

One challenge met, one to go.

From among the trees, a woman's voice cried out in anguish as the old man dropped. Doyle recognized that voice.

"Shawna of the Behr!" He waved the bloody dirk toward the woods in the direction of the cry. "A prize to the man who brings her to me alive!"

As one, his horsemen charged off through the grove. From the sound of their progress, Doyle discerned that at least one horse tangled in the understory and went down. Through the trees he saw a low branch lift that young firebrand MacBrian off his horse. Men shouted and cursed. The lass must be leading them quite a merry chase.

He, the warrior king, might just possibly end up as a peacemaker, if he could manipulate the girl well enough. Peacemakers are always blessed by God. Mahon himself would be the first to say that. In fact, that might be another lever to use on the girl. "Do you want peace, or don't you?"

This was splendid! This couldn't be better! He needed her desperately. With the Northmen here, he must have some means of reaching them, of talking to them. And now he did.

God certainly does help those who help themselves.

* * *

Ailan stood, leaning his back against an ancient, knobby oak. The forest wavered in lazy undulations. He closed his eyes and swallowed. He would lose his stomach soon; he felt it coming. He inhaled deeply, again and again.

The nausea subsided, and reality began to nudge out the dreamlike quality of what he had just seen.

Mahon. Butchered like a boar. Mahon, protected from Ailan by angels one moment and delivered into the hands of a ruthless ri the next. The angel and Mahon had walked together for miles. Suddenly the angel had disappeared. And then this.

This was all beyond his comprehension. He lurched erect and stumbled out to the road. Was it God in heaven, the Father of Jesus, who directed him to follow Mahon from afar? Or was it the new spirits of the land that he now served? And where ought he go next?

Mahon.

His heart in turmoil, he began walking mindlessly toward Dublin Crossing.

* * *

Swift Lynx dropped out of her glide and wallowed in the riffled waters of the bay. Hegaard barked some orders around, just to show that he remembered how it's done, but they weren't needed. His men could strike and stow a sail in minutes with no help from their ship's master, thank you.

Wolf watched two men on ropes align the sail yard fore-and-aft, high at the top of the mast. The yard jerked its way down from the realm of flying birds to the realm of mortal men as the sail crew let out halyard line. The linen sail dropped in folds to the deck. Four crewmen, Wolf included, gathered the sail up against the yard and tied it in place with the short gasket ropes. He reveled in this feeling of teamwork, of group effort and group efficiency. In moments they had stowed yard and sail together on the supports along the ship's center line.

The heavy mast took a bit longer. It required more men on the ropes.

Wolf took his place at an oar. They would row up into the Liffey, for the winds were not dependable enough to try sailing in the narrow river course.

Hegaard paused beside him and jabbed his shoulder. "Ship your oar and come."

Puzzled, Wolf pulled his oar inboard far enough that it would not foul the oars of the men before and behind. He followed Hegaard up to the stem.

Arild, Halvor, Hegaard, and Skule were all crowded around the dragon's neck. Wolf moved in against the starboard gunwale.

"Hold!" Halvor raised an arm. As one, all thirty oars dipped into the water and froze. The water out there whished against the blades. *Swift Lynx* dropped instantly out of her glide and bobbed to a stop.

Skule's knowledge was respected here, and he was clearly and obviously basking in that. He pointed out raths dotted here and there. "Quite a retinue in that one—eight or ten retainers. He's a local king, just a minor ri tuatha, but he acts important. And over there . . ."

Wolf scanned the shoreline for armed men. He saw none, which did not mean they were not there.

Skule went on and on and on.

Arild turned suddenly to old Halvor. "What do you think?"

The ancient one nodded slowly. "You'll have constant skirmishes, as they try to oust you."

"I know that."

"And you ought to consider that area there, first." He pointed to a headland extending across the north of the bay. "Too, that peninsula is easily defensible with a few good men. Also, I'm looking at the stone. Stone for building. You don't want to have to sledge it in from all over, as you would if you built by the river. See? No stone around the river mouth. Besides, you've no idea what it's like during spring freshet."

"Still fordable." Skule knew the answer to that one.

Halvor shook his head. "You know only one year. You must know what the river does through twenty years."

Wolf stared at Halvor. He gaped at Arild. And it all dawned on him. He raised hand and arm to point to Arild. "That's why you wanted to come along! That's why you brought Halvor. You're not just interested in raiding. You're thinking of colonizing, and he's an expert. He led colonists to the Shetlands."

Skule shook his head. "You don't want to live among these people. Trust me. They're all mad. They think the highest goal in life is to steal your best friend's cows. They measure all worth in cows. Even slaves are valued in cows. None of your livestock would be safe. They're terrible neighbors. They do nasty things to each other. Not to mention that they love to kill Northmen."

Hegaard pointed. "Natural harbor, as good as any in the North. A few days' sailing to any port in the Franks' lands or the Saxons' or Northumbria. Two weeks gets you home, three to Hedeby for trading. Perfect central location for trade with anyone in the world. The whole world. Where does the river go?"

Skule pointed. "Around those Wicklow Mountains there and down toward the south. We'll follow it south a few miles before striking off west to the monastery."

Hegaard nodded triumphantly, his point made. "And a gateway into the interior for raid or trade, whatever's your fancy."

Arild turned to Wolf. "You're the key here. Skule says you speak the language better than he does. You are our link between us and them."

"You want me to negotiate for you. So you can build a beachhead here, and a colony."

"You can do it."

"What of all these men you brought down to win pelf? Don't you think they might be disappointed? And the syndicate who financed the expedition. They want something back besides a trading port."

"And a-raiding we'll go! Elsewhere."

"The people here don't know that. They'll attack first, and when they learn you want to establish a colony, they'll attack harder."

"You can talk to them."

Wolf's memories were nagging at him. "Yes." He grimaced. "I can always talk to them." He backed off, uncertain.

Halvor was pointing out the relative advantages of this location and that. He was listing supplies needed for this place as opposed to supplies for that one. He described how to unload horses and cattle.

Wolf turned away and watched the headland to their north. What was tickling at his mind? Was it Shawna's meddling God again? Whether His divine arm reached the Northland was beside the point. Here Wolf stood in His heartland.

Peacemakers. That was it. Peacemakers, her Jesus claimed, are blessed, in God's opinion. Jesus, murdered by soldiers, valued peacemakers. Jesus the Lamb of God loved peace. Shawna loved Jesus. Shawna of all people—except, perhaps, Peggy—ought to be ready for peace.

And Saint Ulf of the Coastlands could contribute to that peace. Whether Shawna ever spoke to him again, whether or not she was married now, he could make a contribution to peace in her beloved Erin.

He had at first resisted the idea of a Norse colony in this alien land. The more he thought about it, the more he embraced it.

And he could be a colonist.

30

Hunted

Her very life depended upon her not breathing. And her very soul screamed that she must sob and weep. Mahon. *Dear God in Heaven! Mahon! Libera me!*

She lay face down behind a fallen log, stretched out thin, and jammed herself under the round bole as far as she could get. She was insane to cry out when Mahon fell, but the noise escaped before she could stop it. And now that one small mistake would cost her her life.

Doyle told his retainers to bring her back to him alive. Obviously he wanted to murder her personally, as he had Mahon, and no doubt as he had the Conroy.

A horse approached at a gallop. Closer. Closer. From the other side it leaped over her log and came down inches away. She watched it run on through the woods. It had no rider. Moments later a man's feet came racing through the dry duff of the forest floor. He, too, leaped over her log and continued on, running after his lost horse. Young MacBrian of Berit Head.

A hundred yards off, one yelled, "Here she is!" Horsemen converged on the spot. A startled stag came plunging through the woods from that direction. The men shouted epithets and curses, blaming each other. The stag spotted Shawna at the last moment and turned aside. He bounded away.

Now was her chance, while the searchers prowled elsewhere. She skinned out of her hiding place and hurried, bent low, into the nearest thicket. It wasn't nearly dense enough to cover her. She continued on, trying to make no sound in the duff and sticks. She worked her way from tree to tree until she popped out onto the track. She broke into a run, flying south in the direction from which she and Mahon had just come.

Mahon.

For a few fleeting moments she doubted God's providence—

302

doubted His very existence. No, that wasn't true. She did not doubt His existence. It would appear He was alive and well and deliberately orchestrating horrible things to happen. Who would guess they would find Doyle Dalainn on this road? Why was the man down in this area at all, if not by the hand of God?

Who could possibly imagine that Doyle would be so bold and so heartless and so stupid that he would murder Mahon and think he could get away with it? But then, if Shawna did not escape, not only would he have no clear witness to his crime, he would have another murder to his credit. Hers.

She thought of the peace in that garden at Kildare and regretted that she had squandered it fixing the gate in the wicker fence.

She rounded a curve and skidded to a stop in the damp dirt. Her heart thumped. A dozen armed men, strangers all, blocked her way. They stared at her.

For a long, long moment, until she could gather her wits back together, she stared at them. "Please, sirs, I must get by! And if you've any heart at all, you'll tell no one you saw me pass."

Too late.

She didn't have to turn around to know whose horses were clattering up behind her.

Doyle's voice crowed, "I rather figured when you were giving my people the slip that you'd work your way back to the road."

One of the strangers grinned and waved a hand. "Friend of yours? We didn't interrupt something pleasant, I trust."

"She was a friend once. Lord willing, she will be again."

She turned to stare at him. He had just murdered one of the best friends he could ever have, a friend with a clean heart and a clear conscience. What infernal pretense was he setting up for these strangers with his friendship nonsense?

Doyle wiggled a finger. "You'll ride with me, Shawna, and ahead of my saddle. I don't trust you behind me."

She took a deep breath. Her response surprised even her. "I would rather die." And she realized she meant it.

She could go to her death sniveling, or she could go with dignity, like any other martyr. She crossed herself, folded her hands, and stood in the middle of the road with her eyes closed.

"Deus noster refugium, et virtus; adjutor in tribulationibus, quae invenerunt nos nimis. Propterea non timebimus dum turbabitur terra; et transferentur montes in cor maris." Mahon's warm voice seemed to whisper along with hers until the two were blended, hers and his, beyond reality. And God was a part of it too, in some way, though she did not hear Him.

He came to her then, God did. A marvelous peace wrapped her in soft wool, buffered her in a gentle cloud. She only wished she could describe this wonderful peace to Wolf, that he might believe in Christ Jesus. But even if he stood before her this minute, she would not be able to find words adequate in either language.

The strangers were laughing and good-naturedly ridiculing Doyle's rare way with women.

"Enough!" He seized her arm and literally dragged her up onto the horse before him. "We don't have time. The trumpets sounded half an hour ago, so they're surely on shore by now, or near it. Who else is coming?" He spurred his dun forward.

The strangers named three raths as they turned their mounts around. They all clattered off southward, toward Dublin Crossing.

Shawna could fight and try to slide off, or she could do nothing. She opted to do nothing. Actually, by doing nothing she just might fall off. They were jogging their horses, and the jarring gait jolted her all around.

Doyle's voice rumbled behind her. "So you were traveling under Mahon's aegis."

Mahon. She began to weep. Finally, the sorrow could come pouring out. She covered her face with her hands and sobbed in rhythm to the jogging horse.

After five minutes they slowed to a walk, albeit a rapid one. She heard more horses joining them before and behind. She was in the midst of an army. Was this, she wondered abstractly, what it was like amid the angelic host, as they rode forth on their horses of brilliant color? The sobbing abated, though the sorrow did not. She wiped her nose on her sleeve for the hundredth time.

"I apologize," said Doyle Dalainn, and she never thought she would ever hear that from him. "I was preoccupied with other matters and wasn't thinking. If you say you were with Ceirre and did not see Connleigh, I believe you."

"When I arrived at your door, everyone was home. I rather wondered why. Then Mahon told me about the Conroy. You were all gathered there for safety, weren't you? Expecting an act of vengeance by relatives of the Conroy."

"The Conroy incident is vastly overblown. It wasn't like that at all. The ri and I argued. That's all. Mahon received false information."

"I heard you, Doyle. 'Confirm.' And that, I assume, seals my doom."

He was silent a few moments. "That depends. You will recall I asked you once to act as interpreter for me with the Northmen. You refused. You have changed your mind, Shawna. Now you will serve as I requested."

"Never."

"Then the blood of scores of Erse and Norse together will be on your hands. It is a peacemaking mission. You can prevent killing, if you will."

"Prevent it now to foment it later. I will not be a part of your joining Northmen to your cause against other Erse. No." She twisted to look at him. "What gall you have, Doyle Dalainn! You accuse me of being responsible for death even as you dish it out right and left —to innocents! And yes, Mahon was innocent. Pure. I pity you."

"Your pity is misplaced."

She straightened around to face front, for she was getting sore where she met the horse, and twisting made it worse. "Not this time."

* * *

Wolf jabbed his father's arm and pointed. Down off a gentle copse near Dublin Crossing an army of mounted warriors appeared. Arild muttered under his breath. They rode directly down to the river and lined out along the far northwest shore.

"How many do you count?" Arild's lips moved rapidly.

"Fifty-five or sixty. Don't let overconfidence get you. Sixty of them are probably pretty close to a match for ninety of us. They practice on each other."

"We practice too."

"Not for keeps."

305

Proudly, undaunted by the enemy before them, the three ships slid gracefully up into the river.

Skule pointed to the near shore. "Dublin Crossing. You see the track going down into the water there. It's about three feet deep. Less."

Hegaard nodded. "Good. Then we can pass easily. We don't draught anywhere near three feet."

"But they can wade out and attack at that point."

Hegaard cackled cheerfully. "How effective are horses going to be in three feet of water? Like a cow in deep mud. Let 'em come!"

Wolf added, "Also, they like to open the action with arrows. So keep your shields ready to hold high."

Hegaard passed the word back to the other two vessels and slowed the pace. Wolf wondered about that at first. He thought about it and smiled. In no hurry, three shiploads of dangerous men were cruising in casual nonchalance past their foes. Strutting, if you would. Beautiful. The younger Dalainn sons, though not Connleigh, frequently employed a gesture with a very crude meaning. Wolf was sorely tempted to use it on that defensive force ashore.

They would soon reach the ford. He crossed to the larboard gunwale and looked up the track toward Ceirre's. The mounted force effectively killed any thought of going ashore. On land he'd be vulnerable to any defender who could reach the other side. And any of them could by riding upstream half a mile and swimming their horses across. Out here on the water he was safe. Ashore on either bank he would not be.

Skule joined him. "Good old Ceirre."

"Who is Ceirre?" Now Halvor stood beside them.

Wolf looked at Skule. "Halvor, my friend, in Ceirre of the Liffey you would meet your match. She's—what, Skule?—ten feet tall at least?"

"Sees over the tops of trees." Skule nodded. "Ah, Ceirre. A hundred years old or more, and all the vigor of her youth yet. She doesn't dress game with a knife. She rips it apart, bones and all. I wish I had half her strength."

"And a temper . . . virago is such a polite word to use regarding her."

Skule's mouth dropped open. "Ceirre!" He pointed wildly.

Wolf gaped. "And the boys!"

She and the two boys had just walked down out of the trees toward the river. They stopped. They stared at the ships. Wolf could see them waving their arms around excitedly and even from this distance heard children's voices. He could easily imagine the flow of words gushing from the boys just now.

Wolf forgot about vulnerability. Here was the woman he needed, within a quarter mile. "Stop!" He called to Hegaard. He leaped into the water off the bow, just ahead of the lead oar. The oarsman barely avoided hitting him. He was short of the ford by a hundred yards, so he began swimming. His sword nearly pulled him under.

Ceirre and the boys turned and disappeared into the trees.

Wolf's foot touched bottom. He struggled up out of the water and began running. It surprised him that, after swimming so hard, he could barely run at first. For a hundred strides his body would not adjust itself into the swift smooth gait he normally enjoyed.

He was running well, though, by the time he reached a familiar glade. He saw Ceirre with Peadar under one arm and a battle-ax on the other, hurrying into the woods at its far side. If ever he needed Gaelic, now was the time.

"Peadar! Paul! Ceirre! Don't run! It is I, Wolf!"

They disappeared into the forest.

"Please stop and talk to me! I won't harm you! It's I, Wolf!"

He entered the trees beyond the glade and skidded to a halt. Ceirre stood alone in the track, gripping her battle-ax in both hands. He saw no sign of the boys and didn't look for them. He moved within fifteen feet of her and stopped again.

He spread his hands wide. "I give you my word. I won't try to harm you or seize you. Or the boys either. Will you talk to me?"

Silence.

"Tell me of Shawna. Has she married? Is she still with the Dalainn?" He waited. "Please speak."

Her lips quivered. She shook her head. "It's all . . . Doyle banished her under threat of death. I'm taking the boys to Kildare, to sanctuary. They ran away from the Dalainn, and I'll not take them back there."

Wolf had trouble digesting all this. Everything was upside down. "Banished . . . But why?"

Men were running in the glade. Wolf wheeled and pulled his sword. Three Northmen from the *Swift Lynx* slowed and stopped. Friend, not foe. They looked at Wolf, at Ceirre.

Ceirre's voice stayed firm despite that she must be terrified. "You gave your word."

"And it's good." He switched momentarily to Norse. "An old friend, here, gentlemen, literally and figuratively. Ceirre of the Liffey. Rosh, you were at the lead oar. You heard Skule and me describe her to Halvor."

Rosh roared with laughter. "Sees over the tops of trees! She does indeed!"

"And she'll tear you limb from limb if you get near. So hold your distance, for your own safety."

"We tremble with fear." Rosh and his oarmates were grinning broadly.

"As well you ought." Wolf turned back to Ceirre and switched to Erse. "It's safe. We won't harm you. In fact, if you're taking the boys to Kildare, you'll want protection."

Ceirre's face softened. "We could well use some." She studied him for long, long moments. He held her eye casually. It suddenly occurred to him that this woman served her God as devotedly as Shawna did. So without speaking aloud, he appealed to her God to ease her mind and convince her to trust him. He even crossed himself after his mental prayer, since Rosh and his mates had no idea what the gesture meant.

Ceirre's face changed from suspicious to relieved. "Boys!" She waddled hastily forward, and to Wolf's astonishment wrapped her arms around him in a monstrous hug, her ear pressed against his breast. For lack of knowing what to do he put his arms around her. Sure and he could not be all that good a candidate for a hug, for he was still sopping wet from swimming in the river. She didn't seem to notice. She was trembling and felt cold.

"Shall we draw our weapons and protect you?" Rosh heckled.

"No. She's so tough you'd break your swords."

The boys appeared from nowhere, from hiding places in the woods. They ran to Wolf and clung to him. Wolf noticed, though, that he did not have their undivided attention. They were peeking around him at his companions.

Paul babbled rapidly. "We ran away from the Dalainn. Doyle was getting dark. He was even darker than you. And Muirgheal screamed at us all the time, and said we were terrible, and kept saying terrible things about Aunt Shawna all the time, and Peadar and I decided it's better to live with Ceirre. We won't be able to eat any more beef or lamb, but we decided chicken is better than getting yelled at."

Terrible things about Shawna? About Shawna?

Ceirre's hug loosened. Her eyes were wet.

Wolf held her eye. "I'm a hunted man here. Those horsemen across the river surely saw me come ashore, and they will surely work their way around to this side. I must get back to the safety of my ship. Will you come with me? I promise. I promise! You are not captives. You and the boys can come and go as you wish. Of course, you will keep your weapon with you. I must know what has happened."

"Yes. Yes, we'll come."

Wolf put an arm tenderly around those hunched and bony shoulders. Ceirre seemed to have aged since last he saw her. He pried Peadar loose from his leg, and they started back.

What a crazy world this was. An old Erse grandmum and two boys now traveled under the protection of four powerful Northmen with axes and swords.

He heard on the hasty walk to the ship about the atrocity against the Conroy and about Connleigh and Shawna and the part Kildare played in all this. His fury mounted and burned so bright that he translated summaries for Rosh. Rosh made true and appropriate comments about the barbarity of the Celts.

Wolf must somehow protect Kildare. He must turn his countrymen away from the place. It must remain a sanctuary for Shawna and Ceirre, for the boys, for all who crossed the path of that madman.

He had no idea yet how he could go about that.

But he would.

31

Ambition

Wolf felt a heady pride. They sat in the bow of the *Swift Lynx*, he and Ceirre, Halvor, Arild, Reidar, and Hegaard. Skule was off showing the boys the ship and introducing them to a crew of hulking warriors who could not possibly understand a word they said.

All three vessels had thrown out an anchor. They lay just far enough offshore to be safe, with the Liffey's gentle current to keep them bow-headed-upstream. All three had shipped their oars, which may have given the horsemen a false sense that they were helpless. Hardly. They could have their blades in the water in moments, to maneuver, to attack, to literally turn around in place.

The pride came from Wolf's ready skill with the languages. He was translating Ceirre's tale for Arild and Hegaard very nearly as quickly as the words left her mouth. His speech overlapped hers, and not more than a sentence behind her.

He nodded. "So you couldn't let the boys stay with you. Doyle would come seeking Shawna and find them instead."

She seemed more relaxed now than when she first came aboard. "That's right, and so I was taking them to Kildare when you showed up. When next I see Shawna I'll tell her where they are, if she doesn't know already. She may well return there when she learns the boys are not with the Dalainn."

Hegaard listened to the translation and rumbled, "I suppose this means the raid on Kildare is off?"

Wolf stared at him. He couldn't tell if Hegaard was serious or not. He looked at his father, at his father's face, and a burden as big as a horse lifted off his heart.

Yes. The raid was off.

For this expedition, at least.

He explained, "These poor Erse need someplace to hide from the madmen Dalainn and others. One of the most powerful laws here, a law all observe, is that churches and monasteries are sanctuaries. Once you're inside, no one is allowed to enter and drag you away."

He nodded off toward Skule. "Skule and I, we'll find you another ripe plum to pluck." He turned to Ceirre and shifted back to Erse. "Who are the horsemen, do you know?"

She shook her head. "Didn't get close enough to see faces or recognize mounts. Doyle Dalainn, I presume, and anyone he could scrounge up for his defense force."

"So if we get you past them, you're safe." Wolf grimaced. "If we get us past them, we're safe."

Skule flopped down beside Wolf. "Hegaard, you might take note here of Ceirre and her battle-ax. When the fighting breaks out, she can show you how they're used."

Halvor burst into a fit of giggles.

Skule translated, mostly for the boys' sake as they settled in beside him. Paul launched into a vivid, even say epic, description of how Ceirre killed a fox just last month with her ax and then had a terrible time sewing the pelt back together.

From his place at the rail, Reidar leaned down and jabbed at Wolf. "What's this?"

Wolf lurched to his feet and joined Reidar at the gunwale. Reidar pointed to the horsemen.

One of the men had dismounted. He stood on the bank of the river alone, apart from the horsemen, with one arm raised. At his left he gripped a woman by her wrist.

"Doyle Dalainn himself." Wolf's heart leaped. "And Shawna of the Behr."

Such a flurry of feelings rushed into Wolf's heart that he couldn't sort them out. Shawna. Not safely tucked away. Here in the midst of it all. Shawna.

Everyone crowded around Wolf, but he could only see those two on the shore.

"What is she doing with him? He swore to kill her!" Ceirre sounded ready to charge forth and do the fellow in.

Hegaard clapped Wolf on the back. "I can see from here you've good taste in women. Just like your father."

Arild grunted. "So that's the ri ruirech himself, eh? King of the whole region, you say? I want to talk to him."

Wolf pushed away from the rail. "Then let us talk."

They had anchored in the ford itself when Ceirre came aboard. Wolf pointed out the shallowest passage in the water beneath them, and Arild went over the side with his shield on his arm, his ax on his shoulder, and his sword diplomatically sheathed. Wolf kept his sword sheathed as well, an act of extreme diplomacy, since the weapon had once been Doyle's. He borrowed Rosh's shield, lacking one of his own. He jumped down behind his father and waded ashore onto Erse soil behind Arild Thick Knee, a very strange experience.

This whole business was exceeding strange.

Two dozen crack Norse archers lined up along the starboard gunwale, their arrows nocked and pointed at the Liffey, their bows relaxed, so far. That, too, could change in the blink of an eye.

Shawna stood transfixed, her hand clapped over her mouth, and watched them come.

Wolf could understand why she would feel dumbstruck. But how did she feel about him? That's what he most desperately wanted to know, and he could not ask it here.

Arild waded up out of the water and stood loosely, boldly, as if he already owned this land. Wolf moved in beside him.

Doyle stepped forward. He wore a sword every bit as ornate as the one at Wolf's side now. He had hooked a battle-ax casually over his shoulder. "So. I don't need my translator after all. You owe me a horse and a sword, lad."

"Don't ask for the sword, Doyle. You might get it. This is my father, Arild, leader of this expedition, jarl of jarls, ri ruirech of his domain in the north." Wolf decided not to use the Thick Knee. It didn't translate well in Erse, and it might detract from his father's dignity.

Shawna's face was wet with tears. She burst out suddenly, loudly in Erse, "Ulf, he murdered Mahon!"

Murdered! Not "accidentally killed." Not "struck down in self defense," as if the kindly old mystic would set himself to harm someone. Drying blood was sprayed across Doyle's left sleeve and pants leg. Was the murder that recent?

Wolf wheeled to see if Ceirre had heard. She had. She covered her face with her hands, and Wolf could hear her moan from here. She crossed herself.

Wolf switched to Norse. "The boys are aboard our vessel. We'll give them safe passage to Brigid's monastery."

"Praise God! Oh, thank God!" She lapsed into Latin. Doyle eyed her suspiciously.

Doyle smirked. "I find myself at a disadvantage. You two can discourse freely. I'm not certain I can trust anything you tell me, for I sense she's more on your side than mine."

"I can see why. Mahon, Doyle! A man of God."

"What would you know about men of God, pagan?"

More than you could possibly imagine, Celt. But Wolf didn't say it aloud.

Doyle continued, "I seek an audience with your father, to cut a covenant."

Shawna spoke in Norse. "He's not getting the strength he needs among the Erse. He wants to engage Norse mercenaries to advance his own fortunes."

Wolf studied the face of this ri ruirech. The man was hissing at Shawna to keep silence and at the same moment trying to appear friendly. Wolf translated Doyle's words for his father just as he received them.

Arild turned to him and frowned. "What the girl said. Is it true? Hire us against his neighbors? That's despicable."

"He's a despicable man. But ambitious."

"Ambition. Now that I can understand." Arild stared, smiling, at the ri ruirech. "Explain to him my desire to establish a trading colony at the mouth of this river. Point out that my military presence here would fit in well with his own plans."

Wolf did so. From now on he would not filter anything. He would simply translate whatever came, just as it came, sentence by sentence, as he did with Ceirre aboard the *Swift Lynx.* If he did nothing else with his life, in these next few moments he could perhaps spare Erin. Well, maybe not all Erin, but this part at least.

Doyle crossed his arms. He locked one knee and cocked the other, apparently settling in for some heavy thought. "Where?"

Arild pointed toward the bluffs to the north. "At the base there or on this south shore."

More concentration. Doyle nodded. "Land for a trading colony, with pastures and fields to support it, in exchange for the services of a militia for three months of the year. Minimum of a hundred swords and thirty bows."

Arild listened to the translation. His face didn't move much, and Doyle would read nothing there. But Wolf knew the man. The Thick Knee wasn't much impressed. Arild turned to Doyle and stretched his back to full height. "I will carry your offer to my seconds in command, for their opinion. I have excellent advisers. It profits me to use them."

Doyle smiled. "I await your reply." He backed up, dragging Shawna with him. Then, in a magnificent gesture of trust, he turned away from Arild and Wolf and strode back toward his lines and his horse.

Shawna twisted, looking over her shoulder, and Wolf's heart tangled itself up into painful knots inside him.

She called out suddenly in Norse, "I love you!"

I love you! I love you I love you I love you! The knots, though no less painful, untangled. This was what he had most yearned to know! Praise God!

And he caught himself short. As he waded out to the ship behind his father, he pondered what had just filled his mind. He had just praised Shawna's God. He never meant to do that, and yet it came. Apparently he was fully in the grip of this God who would sacrifice His own Son.

He thought about Mahon's discussion of prayer, on that very first occasion when he met the amusing old fellow. God reaches down first, and prayer is our response to His reaching. Well, God reached down just now, and Wolf had responded without thinking. Were all Wolf's sins and wrongdoings truly forgiven?

Why would God let Mahon see harm? Never mind. Shawna had once explained all that to him too. It simply had never struck this close to home before.

Then what about Doyle's sins? To murder Mahon, the man of God?

Despicable!

*   *   *

Shawna sat cross-legged in front of the little fire and stared at the embers without seeing them. Back on Lambay, when the Northmen first struck, she had felt overwhelmed by the enormity of all the things happening at once. That feeling had returned. Mahon. The loss hit her nearly as hard as the loss of her father had. Mahon. The man most undeserving of death in the whole world. And such a senseless death, by the hand of a ri.

And Ulf Arildson. Here. When she called out her love to Wolf, he did not reply. He just stood there, with that stupid look on his face.

Did his failure to respond mean he did not love her in return? Of course it did. He ran off and left her, didn't he? On the other hand, here he was, back on Erse soil. And the look on his face as he came out of the water beside his father was that of a man who cared. Perhaps he could not speak of love with his father listening. They had never mentioned customs of that sort in conversation, but there might be some taboo.

The one thing she wanted most to know—what were Wolf's true feelings for her?—she had not dared to ask.

And Wolf's father, the ri ruirech of the North. Wolf was right about the similarities between Doyle and Arild. They were two pups of the same litter.

And all these horsemen, and the wolves from the North, and Ceirre out there on that ship trusting the wolves more than she trusted Doyle Dalainn . . . and for better cause.

Two men were roasting slices of lamb over the fire, holding them on skewers hard by the embers. It smelled good. Shawna almost wished she were hungry.

Across the fire from her sat Doyle Dalainn, eating the first of the lamb to come off the coals. He balanced a chunk of barley-cake on one knee. He watched her as a cat watches a bird. "You're not eating."

"And I see you're not eating with your usual gusto. Don't you feel well?"

He grimaced. "A bit of dyspepsia. A touch of constipation. It will pass. It interests me, though, that you inquire about my health. It shows me you're softening up a little."

"Not at all." She looked him in the eye and repeated from the litany for the ordination of a king. She remembered nearly the whole litany because her father used to say it every year at first harvest. "The justness of the king is the peace of the people, the protection of the land, the invulnerability and protection of the people, care for the weak, the joy of the people, mildness of the air and calmness of the sea, fertility of the soil, consolation for the poor, the heritage of the sons, its hope for future salvation, the abundance of grain, and the fruitfulness of the trees."

He raised his eyebrows, bemused.

"Justness. You, Doyle Dalainn, are unfit to serve as a ri in any capacity. The blessing of God through the church is essential to a kingship, and you have sacrificed that."

"I've always been impressed with your gift for words."

The leader of the horsemen who intercepted Shawna, a ri tuatha named Ronan of the Dark Moor, came shuffling up. He hunkered down beside Doyle and pointed to a slice of lamb on the embers. The cook instantly gave it to him. He pulled a chunk of wheat bread out of his shirt. "You may want to look at your dun stallion then. He's off his feed. Not grazing."

"I shall." Doyle licked his fingers. "What are our numbers now?"

"We're up to seventy since the Owney joined us."

Doyle's head snapped up. He looked strangely grim. "We don't need them."

Ronan scowled. "What do you mean? Even counting them, we still lack twenty men of evening up the sides. Of course we need them!"

Shawna watched Doyle's dark face carefully. What was it about mention of the Owney that hit him like that? Was he that terrified of their mastiffs? He tossed his barleycake and lamb aside and sprang to his feet. He strode away, out toward the horses.

Shawna looked at Ronan. Ronan looked at her. He shrugged and bit off a chunk of meat. "You speak Norse, huh?"

"And Ulf Arildson, the young man with the Norse ri, speaks Gaelic well."

316

He nodded and swallowed. "That's good. It helps us that they can't say anything we can't understand, and of course it also helps them."

"So true." And a plan, an evil plan, was beginning to take shape in Shawna's mind. "And attitudes. For instance, when I told that ri, Arild, what Doyle has in mind, he called Doyle despicable. Which he is, of course. And since I could understand what he said, we now know Arild's opinion of Doyle. That could be helpful to someone in negotiation, I suppose."

Ronan was frowning. "That pagan is a satanic fiend, wholly outside the will of God, and he thinks Doyle Dalainn is despicable?"

"Says something about Doyle, doesn't it?"

Ronan and half a dozen other men nearby seemed suddenly all ears. Ronan asked, "Exactly what does Doyle have in mind? What did you tell the Northman?"

Shawna dipped her head and kept her voice light, as if she did not care. "The truth. That Doyle wants to join forces with the Northmen—a military venture. Hire them as mercenaries. I don't know what for. I think Mahon knew. That could be why Doyle killed him this morning. Just a mile or so up the road there."

"Mahon of Armagh?" Ronan was staring at her intently. "Not so!"

Shawna pointed to a slice of lamb, and the cook gave it to her. She could not feel less like eating, but she must maintain an air of casualness. She pulled off a bite. "Too bad the human eye cannot discern between blood of pigs and blood of people. You could see that it was not a pig he butchered this day. I heard him tell you it was."

The men had moved in close. She could feel the tension in them.

Ronan asked, "What did the Northman reply?"

"He wants to set up a trading colony here on the river. Bring in lots of Northmen and put them on lots of land. So Doyle suggested swapping fighting men for land. Mercenaries. I don't understand the details."

I'm just a guileless girl, who obviously does not know what

317

she's saying. She looked so intently at Ronan's bread that he gave her a piece.

His voice pierced, so intent was he. "Why is his horse so spent if he came directly down from his rath? It's not that far. Do you know?"

She shook her head. "I haven't been there. I was down with Ceirre of the Liffey all month."

Ronan scowled. "And why did he instantly get so nervous when I mentioned the Owney? Like a cat on a hot griddle."

She tore herself off a bite of bread. "Maybe he doesn't like dogs, you think? I certainly don't like them. I'm terrified of them, every time I pass the oak grove and the great lea."

Ronan glared at Shawna. "The reputation of the Behr for honesty is unspotted. If you're lying in these matters, I'll kill you myself." He looked up at a man by Shawna's shoulder. "Go north up the track a couple miles. Investigate. See what you find."

The man and a companion slipped soundlessly away.

Shawna rehearsed all she had just said. There was no untruth in it. What really bothered her was that Doyle had simply left her sitting here. What would seize his thoughts and distract him so completely that he would forget about her? It must be something dark and deep. Why, she could simply get up and walk away from here.

So she did.

32

War

Reidar in his childhood had been a snitch, no two ways about it. Almost always it was Wolf he snitched upon. So as much as he loved to bear tales and tattle on anyone, he made the perfect watchman to keep an eye on the horsemen. Every now and then he would report on their movements, even though nothing at all remarkable seemed to be happening over there.

Wolf lounged against the railing beside Reidar, his back to the water. Arild sat leaning against the ship's stem, much relaxed. Skule and the boys were off somewhere trying to teach cat's cradle to Rosh. Halvor, a couple of other minor jarls, and the masters of the other two vessels completed the group. It seemed so casual, this war council, but it would shape events for years to come.

Hegaard summed up the feeling of just about everyone there. "A hundred and thirty men? That's twice what he can field now. We would be his army. I say forget him and continue on our way. When we decide to plant a colony, come do it."

Arild rumbled, "Why should I buy with men what I can take for nothing? He has gall. You have to hand him that. And he's pompous and then some." His mouth twisted within the beard. "So she loves you, eh?"

Wolf felt his cheeks turn hot. "And if I can get her away from those people, I'll take her home with me."

Reidar snapped crossly, "You important personages had better quit talking about love and make some decisions, and you'd better do it fast. They're gaining strength over there. They just picked up five more."

Wolf rotated in place. He squinted. "I see them. At the extreme southwest, where the horses are grazing. They're the Owney."

Reidar glared at him. "You can't see that well."

"I can see their dogs. Big as brown bears, and twice as fierce. See them? Tan colored dogs, and grays, and brindles. Only the Owney breed those giant mastiffs."

Arild drew a grain-basketful of air in through his nose. "My decision's made. And I trust it's all of ours. Now all we have left to do is tell them." He grinned like a fool. "Oh, yes. And one other chore. Rescue Wolf's sweet Erse flower."

* * *

Doyle Dalainn's belly felt like it was full of mud. He had a headache. His nerves were on edge. He didn't need this on top of it all. The Owney. How could they show up here? He would do well to face this head on and with his ax on his shoulder. Ronan had approached the fire from the southwest, so Doyle started off toward the southwest.

On the edge of camp, over where the horses were grazing, he saw a cluster of Owney mastiffs on leashes. Surrounding them stood five armed men, and Doyle recognized at least three of them as paid Owney retainers. He stopped before them and looked from man to man.

"Who speaks for you?"

"I speak." A tall, gangling fellow, lean as a gate rail and meaner looking than the dogs, sagged against a small hazel tree. He looked utterly bored.

"Why are you here?"

"Why should we not be here? The man who paid us is gone, as no one knows better than yourself. We've no reason left to be there." And his eyes, dark as freshly forged iron, pierced to the quick. "Possibly we'll find a new household here and hire on."

Doyle nodded. "You're in my service. Same rate of sustenance and pay. You'll have to build quarters by my wall, particularly if you have families. I don't have housing for you."

The gaunt man nodded solemnly.

With a quick glance at the dogs, Doyle walked off to the pasture. All the horses save one were grazing on the rich grass of the bottomland, their bridles tied across their saddles and their girths loosened. One, Doyle's dun stallion, stood dejectedly off to the side, its nose low, its ears flaccid.

320

Doyle went over the big horse inch by inch, practically. Eyes? Fairly clear. Temperature? About normal. He rubbed the horse's cheeks. The dun didn't toss its head, so its teeth probably weren't bothering it. Its belly gurgled normally. Beneath the tail he saw no splattering or other signs of diarrhea, no suggestion of digestive problems.

Doyle chalked it off to exhaustion, although the horse had never given out on the track before. He detested guesses and unknowns. He much preferred clear symptoms and definite diseases to—

Shawna! He had left her alone. He headed back to the fire at a jog. She was gone, of course, and he cursed himself. What stupidity! With Wolf here, he didn't need her for translation, but she knew who stabbed Mahon of Armagh. Except for her, he could simply accept the news that Mahon had been murdered with a shocked "How terrible!" But, unlike his retainers, whose hands dripped as red as his own, she could not be trusted to keep silence. Indeed, she had already blurted it out once, down on the shore.

And what was it that she turned around and shouted in Norse as they were leaving the Northmen?

Ronan of the Dark Moor and his companions stood about the remains of the fire. No one spoke. Their demeanor felt hostile and eerie, as the Owney men's had.

"The girl. Where did she go?"

"Up into the woods." Ronan's voice didn't lilt, the way it did before they ate. "Probably female business, I'd suppose."

"I want her." Doyle's initial instincts when first she appeared on his doorsill had been good. He should have killed her when he found her, as he had threatened. But how was he to know the slave would return and that therefore he didn't need her?

Why weren't they going off to find her for him?

"I said, 'I want her.'"

Ronan smirked and pretended it was a smile. "At least you're honest about your lusts. We're here to defend our families against the Northmen, not seek out your ladies."

More rebellion. But six men stood here, to Doyle's one. He'd

321

have to go get Brian before he could do anything about Shawna or the rebellion either one.

Down by the riverbank, Brian was bellowing, "Saddle up!"

Good. It provided a legitimate exit. Doyle didn't have to look like he was accepting Ronan's insolence. "Let's go." He turned on his heel and headed for the horses.

No. Arild and Wolf and two other men were jumping down out of their ship, splashing into the river, wading Dublin Crossing in this direction. Let Fairleigh bring the dun. Doyle veered aside and strode down to the riverbank to greet the party.

He heard the grass rustle behind him. He turned. Ronan and two others from the Dark Moor had followed him down. They stood, silent and unsmiling, behind him.

"I'll handle this." In other words, *Get out of here.*

They did not speak. They did not move. Doyle's nerves prickled.

He could not chide them or order them away because the Northmen had arrived. Wolf understood everything that was said. He'd pick up the dissension instantly, and his father would capitalize upon it. The man might be a blusterer and a pagan, but he was canny.

Wolf introduced the two newcomers as his brother, Reidar (the callow one with the sullen scowl; Doyle could get along with that young man), and Hegaard somebody. Arild was big enough, but this Hegaard was broader still, a great, wide bull of a man. Why did Arild bring them?

Wolf stood beside his father. "We have a counter offer for you. You provide us land for a trading colony, and pastures to support it, and enough hay to see our animals comfortably through the winter. In return we'll abstain from attacking targets within your realm."

Ronan took a few steps closer. "What was his original offer, Northman?"

"That's not important," Doyle cut in. "What is important is that I'm refusing this latest. You'll have to come up with something better if you want to trade out of the Liffey."

Ronan's voice cut cold. "Answer me, Northman."

Wolf jabbered in that alien tongue. His father and the broad stranger answered, and he jabbered some more. He switched to Erse. "Why not answer? There's nothing hidden here. Doyle wants a—"

Doyle interrupted him. "Enough. The business at hand . . ."

But Wolf rolled on undeterred. ". . . hundred swordsmen and thirty bowmen in return for land for a town here on the Liffey. A town is a cluster of homes and other places, places where you buy goods and sell or trade things you've made. A town is a great company of raths in a small space."

"A Norse town in our very midst."

"Of course."

"Now just a minute!" But Doyle was too late.

Ronan roared, "You were selling us out! Dealing with our enemies!"

Doyle heard Ronan's sword whisper as it left its sheath. The four Northmen were going for their weapons. Instantly they wielded swords or axes behind those great wooden shields. Doyle discerned how the Behr, the toughest warriors in Erin, could be cut down so quickly. But at the moment, the pagans were not his enemy.

He wheeled to face Ronan, and just in time. With a howling cry the man came at him.

Doyle met Ronan sword to sword. The momentum of the man's charge threw them both spinning into the Northmen. A roar went up from the ships, answered instantly by war cries from ashore.

With difficulty—he was moving so sluggishly, it seemed—Doyle broke away from the mass of struggling bodies and turned to meet his enemy. He slashed out with his sword blindly. Wolf's voice shouted. Doyle had to quit flailing. He must focus on his target and take it out permanently. What was wrong with him that he would neglect so basic a rule of battle?

His sword flew from his hand and his knuckles spurted blood. He snatched his ax off his shoulder and swiped it at Ronan. The fellow fell backwards.

An ax was coming at him, and Doyle's arm was at the wrong end of the swing to counter it. He flung up his shield; the axe struck, slammed the shield against his face, and knocked him straight back. He lit on one shoulder. He couldn't breathe.

The horsemen, now mounted, were charging forward toward the river. The sky filled with arrows in both directions. The Northmen's first boat had beached on the riverbank already, and fighting men were pouring down out of it. The second was rowing ashore swiftly. How did they get their oars out and operating synchronously so quickly? Doyle didn't even see the third ship, but he well knew it was coming.

They were all coming. The Ronan were against him. Did they turn the others against him too, or was their rebellion a small aberration in a large battle? Where did the Owney retainers really stand? The terrifying part: with Ronan and possibly the Owney against him, he didn't know whom to trust.

He waited another minute or two as the battle surged around and past him. There lay his sword. He snatched it as he leaped up. Then, sword and shield in hand, he ran down the riverbank into the water, directly between the two ships.

A fellow from the third ship took a few sloshing steps in pursuit and turned away.

He must reach his horse. Aboard his horse he could fight or run with equal speed and vigor. He could command from horseback. Afoot he had no voice. He dropped into water too deep to walk. Flailing, struggling, he made his way around the stern of the longship. He was no swimmer.

His feet touched the ford, and he lurched forward. The battle had commenced so quickly, Fairleigh may not have had time to bring Doyle's horse into the fight. He would make his way to the meadow where last his horse had been. if the dun was not there he would take any horse available.

He floundered out onto the bank and stopped cold.

The gaunt man from the Owney blocked his path. Behind him, the other four Owney retainers stood, swords in hand.

Doyle straightened. "I hired you. Remember?"

"Bought us off. We remember."

"One of you bring me my horse."

The tall, gaunt fellow stepped forward, his shield raised. Doyle perceived no one here was going to bring him a horse.

"Doyle Dalainn, you murdered good people, the Owney. And as you rode about the yard afterward, the lad you may have noticed by the chicken shed, with his throat cut—" his voice almost broke "—my son. A half-grown lad who never did harm to anyone."

"Slevin Owney and his wife attacked me. I fought in self-defense. And you cannot lay the excesses of my men at my door. They had no orders to kill innocents."

"Too bad you will never be able to tell that to the Conroy or the Owney, or to my son. They all stand before Jesus in heaven. You will never see the divine face. Sure and you will burn in hell forever, though, Doyle Dalainn, and starting right now."

All five moved forward toward Doyle, but obviously the tall spokesman was going to be allowed the first stroke. Doyle heard sloshing behind him. Curse his sluggishness! When he emerged from the ford he did not bother to glance behind, and now he must defend front and back both. He may well go down now, but he would bring down some of these self-righteous commoners with him.

The attention of the five was divided now, for they were watching intently the sloshing fellow behind Doyle. It couldn't be a friend, someone from Doyle's retinue. They were all before him, on the north rivershore.

Even as the gaunt man struck, Doyle heard the wild and welcome war cry of the man behind him.

Connleigh!

Doyle managed to parry the man's initial sword blow and turn the fellow aside. He struck a sideswipe with his ax and engaged the fellow's shield. He lashed out with a foot and caught the back of the man's knee. The gaunt man's knee folded, and he toppled.

Doyle yanked his ax free and swung its blade at the man beside him. The burly fellow deflected it with his shield and thrust his sword solidly. Its tip caught a rib and shoved Doyle off balance. Before the man could recover from his swordstroke, Doyle sliced at him with the ax. He caught the fellow's sword arm and nearly severed it. The man fell backwards with a scream.

The gaunt man was on his knees, halfway to his feet. Doyle kicked his shield and knocked him back down, not a hard thing to do with the man off balance already. He stomped on the gaunt man's shield, flattening it down against the him and pinning his sword hand to the ground. With his ax he struck the man's head.

He wheeled to help Connleigh, and just in time. Connleigh had laid one of them low and now stood in three feet of water fending off the other two with might and main. The front of him was bloodied, but Doyle could not tell—nor did he care—whether it was Connleigh's blood or some other's.

From behind, Doyle drove his sword through the fellow whose attentions were solely upon engaging Connleigh. Two to two now; no problem. It took several minutes of heavy swordwork to lay the one man down. He was a tough bird, and wily, and Doyle doubted for a fleeting moment that he could best him.

Beside him Connleigh dropped his man.

Then Connleigh's arms sagged to his side. His sword slipped from his hand. "Father . . ." He was not smiling. In fact, his face did nothing but gaze blankly upon Doyle. "Turn to Jesus, Father. Please." His knees buckled, and he collapsed into the Liffey.

Doyle plunged forward and seized Connleigh's shoulders before his head went under. He dragged the boy ashore. Connleigh seemed taller and heavier by far than when Doyle had last seen him, and that was ridiculous. It had been less than two months. He hauled his son up the bank beyond the rising tide.

The blood had not been someone else's. Doyle spoke to him. Nothing. He shook the lad's shoulders. He called his name.

The eyes opened and gazed at heaven. In a dragging whisper barely audible, his lips moved. "Tell Shawna I . . ." The lips closed. The eyes did not close.

33

Peace

What manner of religious observance does one make in the heat of battle? If one is *not* directly engaged in that battle?

Ailan had not even the ax anymore. His knife could not be considered a weapon at all in a battle of this intensity, pitting scores of trained warriors against each other. He cowered behind the trees above the lea where the battle raged, and listened to mayhem and chaos. What to do? What to do?

Mahon had the power. And yet he did not. Had he true power he would have known the hour of his death and avoided it.

The old chronicles of the kings of Israel talked about a deceiving spirit. Ailan recalled an occasion when a major king of Israel called up a Wiccan at Endor. Wicca, in some arcane ways, was related to Druidism. Wicca and druids observed the same calendar but with different ceremonies. They pursued different ends, but both considered the land sacred.

Perhaps Ailan held the power after all, and Mahon was nothing more than a deceiving spirit—a deceiving spirit struck down by the gods because he dared confront Ailan.

Yes! That had to be it. It all fit together so logically, so neatly. Ailan peeked out from his hiding place to check the progress of battle. To his utter amazement he saw Fiona, standing in the close-cropped grass of the meadow and raising her arms in a beckoning gesture.

Boldly, at her behest, he stepped forward away from the safety of the trees. No one paid him any mind. He took three steps toward her. She did not move her legs, and yet she remained as distant as when he first saw her.

He walked another ten yards toward her. Not an inch closer than ever, she continued her beckoning gesture. She was a phantasm, obviously, a spirit who moved as he moved. He stopped. She hung in place.

Spirit or no, she was right. Following her, he was immune. A Celt came running up the hill toward him, desperate to escape the Norse brigand directly behind him. With a howl the Dane threw his ax. The Celt fell. Neither the unfortunate Celt nor the berserk Dane took notice of Ailan. It was as if he were not there.

The vision of Fiona was leading him to safety through the very heart of battle by rendering him invisible! He smiled. He grinned. He laughed, at once both incredulous and completely believing.

He marched straightway down to the water's edge and out into the ford. Cold water boiled all around, for the tide was surging in against the river current, causing eddies and mushrooming piles of water. He disliked fast water, but the vision had led him safe thus far. She hung suspended, up to her knees in water, and yet her skirts did not move in the least.

Come, she called. He came.

And then the bottom dropped out from beneath his feet. Curse the luck! She had led him aslant of the ford into the deep pool downstream of it. Totally drenched in cold, swirling, muddy water, he took a stroke with one arm. Then an undercurrent caught his legs and pulled him under. Choking and gasping, he pulled himself to the surface. A mushroom humped up beneath him. The pile of water shoved him upwards and then dropped him in a trough. Another swirl caught his body and drilled him under.

He made the error of taking a breath before his head came up. He could not breathe. The cold contracted his throat as the water stabbed his lungs with pain. His face reached the surface, but he could not inhale or cry out. The last thing he saw was the silent vision of Fiona, smiling sweetly and beckoning.

* * *

Everyone knows that the child who is terrified stops growing. Ceirre knew it. These little boys had been terrified a score of times in the last year. It wouldn't do to expose them to another horrible incident, a living, breathing battle, but here they were, cowering in the Northmen's boat.

The Northmen's yet!

The Northmen went tumbling out with war cries that would curdle a mother's milk. Beyond the gunwales, war cries and screams and the squeal of horses told her this would not be a simple skirmish. This was pitched battle.

What should she do? Whatever could she do?

"I know!" Ceirre gathered the boys in close against her. "I will push this boat out into the water. We'll let the current carry us safely downstream. When the ship grounds, we will go ashore and make our way to Kildare. Out and around the Northmen and the Dalainn both."

She stood up. "You boys stay here. I'll shove us free."

"Auntie Ceirre. You can't do that. It's too big."

"It draughts shallow, and the tide is coming in. I will. It will practically float off by itself."

She hurried to the gunwale. Here was the first problem. She did not have half a dozen strong hands to lift her back into the boat once she left it, and no way out save to jump over the side. Perhaps she ought wait until the boat floated free of itself.

In Erse a familiar voice cried, "Ceirre! Help us!"

Wolf and that Broad Back came sloshing out into the water, and they supported Arild between them. The Thick Knee's thick knees no longer functioned. His legs dragged in the water, limp. What a sad end for a proud man! Ceirre's heart ached for him.

A third Northman, the one called Reidar, crawled up over the gunwale and reached down. Ceirre reached down too and grabbed a clammy wrist. She could not draw Arild up, but she could hold him firmly until Wolf scrambled aboard.

Arild, the tough old man, managed to help pull himself inboard with his brawny arms. He thunked onto the deck and rolled to his back. His whole lower half was no more than dead weight.

He seized Wolf's sleeve and shouted in an imploring tone.

Ceirre frowned. "What did he say?"

"He's asking us to kill him."

Arild grabbed Reidar's pant leg and clung desperately. He began begging the young man in plaintive tones.

Wolf translated Reidar's reply. "I dare not, Father. You didn't die in battle. Who can presume to kill a warrior whose time has not yet come? No. I'm sorry."

Reidar wrenched free and swiftly jumped over the side.

Arild turned to Ceirre. His voice was strident now.

Wolf shook his head. "He says, 'I implore you, old woman. It's not difficult. You slay foxes. You can end my misery.'" Wolf held her eye. "I beg you, Ceirre, not to do it."

"Much as I pity him, I will not."

The jarl looked at the boys, his eyes hollow. Paul cringed against Ceirre. Peadar hid in her skirts.

Wolf laid a hand on Ceirre's shoulder, a gesture of affection, and leaped over the side.

Enough of this. The boys needed no more horror. Ceirre herded them to the rail.

"Come, boys. We're going over the side. We'll cross to the south shore and follow the river track as best we can without being seen."

Arild's voice had turned husky. His hand trembled as he raised it. He was asking something else. The words sounded different. He struck one hand against the other.

"He wants his fire flint," Paul said. "I know where it is."

"Wait! Why would he want that?" But Ceirre's words were too late. The lad ran off. He came back moments later with a cunningly carved box. He handed it to the tortured man.

Arild nodded. He spoke something gentle.

"Come!" Ceirre snatched up Peadar by both wrists and lowered him over the side. Peadar dropped into water above his armpits. He screamed in terror. Paul leaped over by himself.

Ceirre glanced back at Arild Thick Knee. The jarl was fumbling at the box, opening it. She picked up her battle-ax, gathered her skirts, climbed onto the gunwale, and more or less tumbled off. She landed off-kilter and went under completely. With the dignity of a drowning cat, she pulled herself to standing. She sputtered and coughed.

With the tide in, the ford was probably too deep to get the boys across. She should have thought of that before. Now she would have to carry one across, come back, and carry the other over.

No. She couldn't leave either one alone. Horror or no, they would just have to follow this north bank along the river. The fighting seemed to be about over. If the boys didn't look at the fallen bodies—mostly Celts, it appeared—and just ran, they'd get through this yet. They sloshed out onto the north shore.

Paul cried out, "Connleigh! Auntie Ceirre . . . Oh, no!" He dropped to his knees beside a fallen warrior. He was sobbing as Ceirre pulled him off the body.

So Connleigh had returned.

Her heart wept.

* * *

The unknown Celt came at Wolf, screaming. The fellow charged with his shield artfully positioned. There was no way Wolf could reach him with a sword thrust. Wolf held his own shield high—just as artfully.

And then he employed a trick Halvor had shown him. He leaned forward, signaling to the Celt that he would attempt to break the charge by throwing his weight forward. Instead, still leaning, he took two quick steps back just as the Celt's shield hit his own. Gaping surprise seized the Celt's face as he fell forward, losing his stride and balance.

With his own shield, Wolf brushed the fellow's shield aside and drove the ornate sword home. It was probably not a fatal thrust, but it was a disabling thrust. The Celt cried out in anguish as he dropped.

Twenty feet beyond, Halvor was engaged in a hot face-to-face skirmish with not one but two Celts. Two Celtic warriors in their prime were one too many for an old man in his dotage. Wolf bolted forward to Halvor's aid.

Halvor, apparently, did not need aid. Before Wolf could render any effective help, the old man dropped one of his foes by slicing across the front of the fellow's legs. In the same swift motion, he brought his shield around and swung his sword toward the second. His sword whanged against the fellow's shield and bent neatly in half.

Wolf was there, then, driving the Celt backwards by the sheer force of his charge. He tried to take the fellow's head off but caught him above the ear instead. The warrior went reeling.

Immediately Wolf wheeled a full turn in place. The first rule of battle: Never neglect behind you. Beside him, Halvor was deftly stomping on his sword, straightening it. All around them rode Celtic cavalrymen. Wolf and Halvor stood in the midst of a cavalry charge.

Without thinking Wolf swung around back to back with the old man. Halvor ought to be terrified—they were facing their end. But he roared the lusty, eager, joyous battle cry of a twenty-year-old.

He was right! An old man and an untried novice faced six seasoned warriors on horseback—what a glorious end, if end must come. Exuberantly, Wolf echoed the old man's cry.

And Wolf had an added reason to press the cause. He was fighting now not for Arild Thick Knee, or for himself, or even for Halvor, but for love. *I love you.* If he survived this he would find Shawna. She was probably still somewhere on this horrific field with Dalainn. He prayed her God's hand of safety upon her. Most likely his mates would not deliberately kill her, but she could die so many other ways.

Then Wolf put thinking aside. He would trust his arm's instincts first and let the head take second place.

Three horses were upon them, the riders' lances slashing forward. A horseman on a bay erred by slowing his mount nearly to a halt, the better to aim his blade. With his shield Wolf deflected the lance thrust of the second horseman as he grabbed the bay's bridle and hooked his leg behind its knee. He wrenched the horse's head.

Squealing, it crashed heavily on its side.

Halvor had somehow yanked the third fellow off his horse and lost his sword in the process. With shield and dagger he parried a lance thrust. As Wolf wheeled to join the second rider in hand-to-hand combat he saw Halvor drop his shield and dive to the ground. The wily old man snatched up an abandoned battle-ax and swung it mightily as he rolled to his back. His foe crumpled, legless from the knees down.

Barely in time Wolf averted the lance thrust of the man still mounted. The horse stepped on his foot even as its shoulder tipped him off balance. One foot pinned to the ground, Wolf could not twist to catch himself. *Keep your shield up!* He fell flat on his back, and the fall knocked his wind out. The horse was on top of him now, literally running over him. The lance blade chunked into his shield, glanced off it into the ground beside his ear, and broke on a rock. Eight hundred pounds of horse loomed above him.

Screaming men and horses, snarling dogs, clattering hooves and shields, legs and arms and weapons, the stench of hot blood and disembowelments assailed Wolf. He felt he was losing his wits at the time above all times when he must not.

The horse above him lunged, squealed, thudded to the ground beside him. A sword had been thrust to the hilt in its breast where the throat meets the brisket. As it flailed in its death throes its feet battered Wolf's leg and hip.

He rolled away and practically impaled himself upon a fallen lance. He snatched it up as he lurched to his feet.

Halvor had just dispatched the rider with his battle-ax and was wheeling to meet still another mounted lancer.

Wolf beat him to it. As the fellow came broadside, intent upon skewering Halvor, Wolf slid his own lance in behind the shield. It found home just below the fellow's ribs and ripped out of Wolf's hand as the man tumbled backward off his horse.

Wolf was about to swing around back to back again with Halvor, but the battle was departing from them. With gleeful war cries, the Norse were surging up the slope, the Celts falling away. If Wolf and Halvor stood still now they would find themselves behind their own lines.

Halvor's face bright, he grabbed Wolf's arm. "You were splendid, lad! You saved my life!"

"You saved *my* life!" Wolf could feel Halvor's exuberance, then he realized it was his own. They were winning! They were surviving! Amid all this carnage they would live to fight—and love—again. Nothing could match this heady joy.

Wolf's foot hurt, but it still supported him all right. He glanced down. A dark, shiny scuff raked across the top of his boot where the horse had stepped on him. Had it not been for Shawna's stuffed pad, his foot would have been crushed.

* * *

If Shawna felt overwhelmed before, she felt utterly crushed now. She was surrounded by enemies, and she didn't even know which ones they were. Would the Northmen kill her as they killed her mother? Doyle certainly would, given half a chance. And Ronan didn't look happy.

What had reduced those peace talks, as Doyle called them, to a battle frenzy?

Hunched up and hidden among the trees, she could not see a thing. She could hear just fine, however. And her ears told her the battle was coming this way. Even as her head was telling her feet to run, her heart was praising God. The fight was moving away from Ceirre and the boys! They were getting safer by the moment. Her feet paid no attention to her head.

With much trepidation, she uncurled herself from her hiding place behind an oak stump and moved to where she could see beyond the trees. She looked out upon a horrific sight. With screams and crashing noise, a hundred men—nay, far more than a hundred—were joined in hand-to-hand combat.

The Celts on their horses were beating down upon the Northmen, and the Northmen were holding their round wooden shields high. One would think the horses gave the Celts advantage, but the Northmen were canceling that advantage by hamstringing the horses.

Shawna covered her face. She begged God's mercy on the poor horses. And the widows and orphans created this day. She could not fight effectively, but she could pray. She dropped to her knees and began fervent prayer to God to end this chaos quickly with a minimum of loss. She begged God to forgive the foolishness of these men and mitigate its toll. And in the midst of it all she realized she was speaking to Him in Erse, imploring Him in the language she knew best.

But on her knees was no place to be as the Celts broke and ran this way. Their line was crumbling rapidly. She scrambled to her feet to search for another hiding place. And quickly! Only a slim alder separated her from the frenzied war out there.

A hundred feet away, one of Ronan's men rode this way at a canter. Hard behind him, a burly and handsome young Northman made a wide, swinging swipe with his ax. A few scant yards from

Shawna's tree, the horse squealed as its hind legs gave way. Even as it flopped down onto its side, its rider leaped off.

Shawna should have screamed, "Keep your shield up!" at the Northman, for the insane young man was lumbering along with his shield at his side. Even Shawna knew better than that.

The Celt drove his sword into the callow warrior, yanked it out, and continued running. Panting heavily, he plunged past Shawna and kept going. She heard his bootsteps crashing up the hill through the weeds.

The young Northman cried out, "Father! Help me!"

Father? Was that young man a Christian, calling on God? He couldn't be. And yet . . . Shawna charged forward without thinking, and caution had to step lively to get out of her way. Others came riding by or running, turning tail before the onslaught of the Northmen. It was a rout, plain and simple.

She dropped down beside the young man and spoke in Norse. "Are you a Christian?" She knew a part of the rite of extreme unction. She was certainly not ordained, but in an emergency of this sort legalism took the hindmost.

As for tending his injury and perhaps saving his life, she saw no fond hope. He might linger a day or two, but he wasn't bleeding enough to avoid infection. Besides, intestinal dirt was oozing out of the wound. A man gutted invariably died.

His eyes went wide. "Tell my father to come get me. Please."

"Oh. You're not a Christian. Who is your father?"

"Arild." He took a deep breath and curled up onto his side. His arms wrapped around his middle. "Thick Knee."

No. Oh, God, no!

"You are Reidar."

He looked at her.

"Your brother talked about you." *And not in affectionate terms, particularly, but I'm sure he would now speak with utmost affection, were he by your side this moment.*

"Hegaard's right." He was rapidly losing his ability to speak. His face, formerly drained white, now turned a deathly shade of blue. "Wolf has good taste. In women."

What could she do? She recited rapidly what she remembered of extreme unction anyway, just in case it might do some

335

good. His hand reached out and opened. It waved aimlessly. For lack of knowing what else to do, she took it in hers.

"Hold me." He squeezed her hand, but not strongly. By degrees his hold relaxed. Suddenly he gripped tightly and jerked so violently she almost let go. He was gone.

A horse fell beside her. Its flaying hoof knocked her flat and kicked the breath out of her. Panicked, she leaped up and began to run.

* * *

Ceirre dragged the boys out into the big meadow where the Erse had been grazing their horses. She was having a terrible time driving the boys along and hanging onto her ax. She really ought to drop the axe. But she couldn't.

The battle seemed over, with Celts fleeing into the pastures and woods to the north. To Ceirre's right a man was calling out— Doyle Dalainn, rallying his troops! He waved his sword high and galloped this way!

He was injured—blood soaked his left side and spattered his arm and leg. The fresh blood mingled with other bloodstains on his sleeve and pant leg, and those stains looked dry. The battle had been raging but a few minutes. How could blood dry so fast?

Ceirre and the boys would not be able to outrun him. And they certainly could not trust him. Ceirre yanked Peadar around to her back. "Stay behind me!" Paul ducked behind. Both boys were keening now. She gripped her ax two-handed. That murderer might decide to kill the boys, but he'd have to get past her.

On the other hand, he seemed to pay no attention at all to her. He would pass close by, and he certainly knew her, but he gave her no notice. That just goes to prove how men pay scant attention to old women.

A tall, gaunt man, staggering from a grievous wound in his head, made his way slowly across the meadow. As he lurched toward Ceirre, he shouted, "Cu! Cu!"

From up near the copse beyond the lea, two of the Owney mastiffs came running.

"Sic! Sic!" He was turning the dogs against her!

336

No, he wasn't. The dogs fell upon Doyle's horse, just ahead of her. What a crazy thing to do! That big stallion could stomp them flat in a moment.

But the horse did not. It struggled, uncertain, as a huge brindle snapped at its hocks. Its backside collapsed in mid-stride. Hamstrung, the horse fell heavily. Instantly, the tan mastiff plunged at its throat.

Doyle flew sprawling practically at Ceirre's feet. With instincts for survival intact, apparently, he hauled himself to his knees and freed up his sword.

She saw his face then clearly, and her blood ran cold. His eyes burned bright. She could see no sign in his face that he was rational, let alone that he recognized her or anyone else. He raised his sword against his nearest enemy. Ceirre.

And suddenly Ceirre didn't care what the boys saw or did not see. White fury seized her. She did not care whether they escaped. All she could think of was that this minion of Satan destroyed as he wished, without regard to God or man. As Herod had murdered John Baptist, the man of God, so did this monster murder Mahon, the man of God.

Jesus said of Herod, "Go, and tell that fox. . . ."

Ceirre swung her ax and killed another fox.

* * *

Wolf stood numbly, surrounded by carnage, his sword arm limp at his side. For the first time in his life, he had taken part in a true battle. He had imagined in his youth that a battle such as this would be glorious, with ample derring-do and ample reasons for all who partook to enter into Valhalla.

Valhalla had lost its glamour.

Probably two score men lay dead, all told. By far the most were Celts. The Norse had not lost many.

Well over a score of lathered horses squirmed and whinnied on the ground, most of them sitting, so to speak. Their front legs hauled them up, but their hind legs, the tendons cut through, would never support them again.

Slain dogs were scattered here and there. There must have

been a dozen of them. The few left whole were falling upon the crippled horses.

The human wounded—another score of men, at least—moaned and called for help. Their din rose, all over the field.

The flies had found the blood already. They gathered everywhere in growing clouds. Their whining and buzzing grew louder by the minute.

And the stench. . .

The Norse who had run off in pursuit of the fleeing enemy came back in groups and clusters. They laughed and boasted and joked with each other. They fell to stripping the slain and picking up the weapons lying around the field. Norse smiths would never have to forge another weapon again.

"Wolf! Over here!" Hegaard was calling from the far end of the field, down by the meadow.

Wolf could not feel less like going there. He stumbled a bit and picked up the pace, walking through grass made slippery with blood.

Hegaard joined him at midfield. "Look. I took it off Doyle Dalainn himself. He had it secreted in his shirt." He held up a brilliantly wrought torque, a heavy golden collar such as Wolf had never seen before.

So the man was dead.

Wolf pointed. "I see you have his sword as well."

Hegaard patted the hilt in his belt. "Whoever delivered the death blow knew what he was doing. Clean hit, split his skull. Two of those big dogs were worrying his horse. I killed one and the other ran off. Monstrous beasts. It's not like me, but I took pity on the horse. The dogs had dragged it down, so I put it out of its misery. Well. Guess I better go start counting casualties. Are you going to see to your father?"

Wolf nodded. "I don't have much hope for him. The ax blow got him in the back, down low. Slow death."

"Wolf?" Skule moved in beside them. He glanced guiltily at Hegaard. "I—uh—I found this." He handed Wolf a sword.

Wolf stared at Skule a moment as the enormity sank in. The lump in his throat was growing rapidly. "Reidar's."

Skule nodded. "I'm sorry." He turned away suddenly and examined various parts of the sky. He had never been able to express his feelings, and obviously he never would.

Hegaard, nonplussed, shifted from foot to foot. "So, Ulf Arildson, you are now the jarl of jarls." He brightened. "Unless, of course, your father surprises us both by surviving. He might sit between his house posts yet." He shrugged. "You don't know."

Wolf stared at the sword in his hand.

"Yes, you do know. Look!" Skule was pointing toward the river.

The lump in Wolf's throat became his heart. His eyes turned hot as the tears welled up and over to flow freely down his cheeks.

Aboard the *Swift Lynx*, flames leaped high amidships. Already they had caught the sail and sailyard. Now they were racing down the length of the yard, and dancing. Burning linen dropped to the deck in fiery wads as black smoke boiled up into the sky.

High tide had lifted the *Swift Lynx* off the riverbank. She floated out in the current, riding gracefully toward the misty sea.

* * *

Shawna stood by the little alder that had been her shelter and surveyed the battlefield. The Northmen were gone. They left so very quickly, taking their dead with them. She knew, because Reidar was not there anymore.

Perhaps she should not have run away, should not have gone back to the place of Mahon's death. But she was glad she did. She arrived there not long after Ronan's two men found him. Minions of Doyle Dalainn had dragged the old man off into the bushes, but the thickening pool of blood in the road told the whole world where he had died.

She was able to say good-bye to the gentle man, after a fashion, before they wrapped him in his own cloak and draped him over a saddle. She was glad she got to do that.

Now she was back, drawn like a moth to the flame to the stench of blood and death.

Why did women always find themselves cleaning up the messes men made? Before her were women wrapping the dead, keening and moaning. They would be the ones to suffer. They always were.

Just beyond a gentle rise, about where the Liffey met the sea, a column of black smoke rose. She couldn't bear to watch it. It looked too much like the smoke that had come up off Lambay that day.

So. Reidar was dead.

She had no idea what happened to Arild, or to Wolf. He was probably dead, or dying. Surely, if he were alive, if he cared at all, he would have at least made a feeble attempt to seek her out. He knew the area, and he knew she was here.

She thought about the shock, and the thrill in her breast, as he leaped over the side of that dragon ship and came wading ashore. The tears began anew.

Would the dragon ships abort their expedition and return home to their Northland? Hardly. Why let a little thing like eight or nine deaths stop a summer of grand fun?

She should start down the road to Kildare, but her desire had seeped away. She didn't want to be there anymore. She didn't want to study and read or see the boys. She hated herself when she felt this way, so flaccid of spirit.

The women down on the shore were laying out a second body beside that of Doyle Dalainn. Apparently they were grouping retainers together with the households they served. But then, none of the other bodies were being grouped that way. How would the women know which retainers accompanied which ri?

For the longest time she stared at the quiet, empty riverbank where those dragon ships had beached.

She stepped out into the sunlight, away from her sheltering tree. She stopped. She really ought to go help the women. She didn't want to do that any more than she wanted to go to Kildare.

"Shawna."

She wheeled, and her heart stopped beating.

Wolf stood in the track to Dublin Crossing, a hundred feet away, and he was watching her. Dirt and sweat—a lot of sweat—and blood made him grimy, like a man who had just been through a battle.

340

His voice shook a little. "I couldn't find you. I ran down the road toward Kildare and found Ceirre and the boys on their way there. Then I ran up part way toward the Dalainn, but you didn't go that way. No footprints in the track. So I hoped you must have come back here."

"You just ran ten miles." She stammered. "You're not with your people. You survived." She was babbling like a fool. Her thoughts refused to order themselves. They tumbled out her mouth all at once, disorganized.

"I am jarl of jarls now. But I won't go back there if you don't want to go there."

"Are you saying . . ?" Now her thoughts would not even leave her mouth at all.

He shrugged helplessly. He seemed as much at sea at she. "We could perhaps take the boys up to their mother. Peggy would—"

"Peggy!"

"—like that. I guess I didn't get a chance to tell you she's there. Junken would like it too. He didn't have any children by his first marriage."

"Marriage. Peggy . . ."

"I'm sorry. I can't think right." He flapped his arms helplessly and spoke plaintively, uncertainly, like a small boy. "So much happened today. I've lost a great deal today. So much. And I gained some. And . . . and I was afraid I lost you. I was afraid . . ." He flapped his arms again.

He walked to her then and closed his grimy hands around her cheeks. "Whatever you want, that's what we'll do. Please . . ." He sighed heavily and wagged his head. "I'm sorry. I can't say what I want."

She smiled and wrapped her hands around his back. His shirt felt very warm and damp, and very manly. Her poor put-upon heart finally started beating again. He was right. Losses and gains. So many of both. "You've said it beautifully."

Postscript

More than forty years after that first raid on Lambay, the Vikings, as they came to be called, established a town site at Dubhlinn Ford (Dublin Crossing) for trading purposes. Viking towns, the first true towns in Ireland, followed at Waterford, Wexford, and Limerick. They did much to alter the old Erse ways.

The Erse fought to defend their territory, their farms, and farmlands. But the Vikings were not greatly interested in territory. They wanted booty and trading ports and just enough land to support themselves. They consistently defeated the Erse, but they did not diligently follow up their victories with inland conquest.

By destroying the Irish leadership while providing none of their own, they threw into chaos the Celtic feudal system that had functioned for eight hundred years. This disruption paved the way for the conquests and incursions by the English and others that cause Ireland grief to this very day.